The *Nanny* AND THE
BEEFCAKE

BOOK THREE

USA TODAY BESTSELLING AUTHOR
KRISTA SANDOR

CANDY CASTLE BOOKS

For Carrie

ONE

LIBBY

TODAY WAS NOT the day for Libby Lamb to lose her mind.

Too bad her brain hadn't gotten the memo.

She exhaled a slow breath, then focused on her reflection in the ladies' room mirror. Her heart hammered in her chest as a bead of perspiration trailed between her breasts.

"Stay calm and breathe. Maintaining a sense of tranquility is literally a yoga teacher's job," she said, trying to calm the tittering, raven-haired nutjob looking back at her.

Unfortunately, her words couldn't permeate the aura of chaos that had engulfed her for the last seventy-five days.

Seventy-five days.

It was insane that it had been that long. And she could still recall the exact moment when her sacred inner equilibrium had been blown to psychic smithereens. But she absolutely, positively could not allow her mind to go there.

No way!

She had to keep that cosmically cataclysmic event out of her head.

Embrace positive energy.

Do not think about stupidly sexy rippling torsos or beautifully beefy biceps.

"Distract your mind and put your intention elsewhere."

Picture a time when you were truly happy. Hold that feeling inside your chest, close to your heart.

This guided meditation usually worked like a charm, but she was too keyed up to concentrate.

Try something else!

"What do you see?" she whispered, then shifted her attention to her clothing.

Looking yoga fabulous, she'd chosen a sparkly gold sports bra and paired it with white yoga capri pants and a ruby-red, long-sleeved wrap that accentuated her long, jet-black hair. She capped off the outfit with a bracelet.

And it wasn't just any bracelet.

She'd chosen to wear her beaded green jade bracelet with a Buddha charm—a gift from her brothers. Granted, with that color scheme, she was rocking a quasi-Christmas vibe in mid-June, but she hadn't chosen these pieces willy-nilly. Today was too important for just any yoga ensemble, and she required every drop of positive juju the universe could supply.

She adjusted her sports bra, smoothing the twisted strap, and straightened her shoulders. Gold held a crazy amount of psychic energy. Representing luck and power, she zeroed in on her heaving breasts encased in the shimmering color as her chest rose and fell with each ragged inhale and every shaky exhale. She caught the glint of green jade at her wrist, and the tense muscles at the base of her neck relaxed a fraction.

Like gold, green offered luck. She not only needed loads of that, but she also required the color's power to regulate physical and mental energy.

Her breathing evened out as she dropped her gaze to her legs. The white yoga capris caressed her curves and drew on the healing and protective properties of the color that also signified a deep desire to serve others. And that's exactly what she wanted to do more than anything—to serve others and assist adults and children in achieving and maintaining a healthy sense of balance.

Moment of truth—she sure as hell could use some of that balance. But she couldn't dwell on the sorry state of her inner tranquility—or lack of it.

She brushed her bangs to the side and concentrated on her bold, red wrap.

This color was her secret weapon.

Red emanated passion, strength, and courage. And she needed to project these qualities in spades.

In terms of psychic energy, was red a slightly aggressive hue?

Yes.

Was it the shade most closely related to flying off the handle in a fiery rage?

Roger, that!

But she had to risk it. Red was her ticket to achieving success. She required an injection of confidence. A booster of boldness! Standing in the restroom of a downtown Denver skyscraper with barely fifteen minutes to go before the biggest meeting of her life, she had to let go of her fears and welcome red's properties of kicking ass and taking names—metaphysically speaking, of course. She, in no way, condoned violence.

Dressed in colors to psychically slay, she had a date with destiny. Even her horoscope was in agreement. As a Libra, Friday was her day—the day of the week Venus ruled, and Libras should, hypothetically, win.

And sweet Buddha's belly, she needed a win.

It was a stroke of luck she'd even come upon this opportunity a few weeks ago.

She rarely perused the internet.

It wasn't that she was opposed to technology—the length of her text strings with her best friends, Penny Fennimore, Harper Presley, and Charlotte Ames, could circle the entire planet at least once, if not twice. She loved connecting with her girls at the drop of a yoga mat. But when it came to her career as a yoga instructor, she sought connection through movement and meditation. That's why it was so miraculous she'd learned about this opportunity on social media. But once she saw it, the post rattled around in her mind until she couldn't help but fill out the attached application and hit send.

She could see it now.

Denver-based venture capitalist group, Tri-Derrick International, is looking to promote the next female wellness and fitness sensation, age 21 to 26.

Prize: twenty thousand dollars plus seed money of one hundred thousand dollars to invest in the winner's business plan.

This money could change everything.

She'd dreamed of working with children and adults in her own yoga and meditation center—and now it was within her grasp. She'd drafted a stellar business plan and had finalized her pitch last night. She'd also dressed the part, and as long as she could keep her wobbly chi in check, she truly believed sweet victory would be hers.

But there was more. This prospect would make all the difference for her brothers as well.

She unzipped her yoga bag and reached between her rolled-up mat and portable gong and found her cell phone. Scrolling through her text messages, she landed on a line of text and a picture that reminded her of why she was here today. And why she had no other option than to go big and turn this interview into an offer—an offer that included a bonus of cold hard cash.

She studied the image on her phone, and a lightness came over her. Four years her junior, her twenty-one-year-old twin brothers, Anders and Alec, stood together grinning with a group of children and a half-built structure in the background. Then she read the message accompanying the jovial photo.

We were accepted into the study abroad program in Quito. Pre-med, here we come.

Her brothers had spent the last few months building a medical facility in a remote village outside of the Ecuadorian capital as a part of their university's study abroad program that partnered with a local nonprofit. They'd been accepted into their college's accelerated medical track to study medicine abroad in Quito.

Seemed like a dream come true, right? Young men wanting to become physicians to give back and help those who needed it most.

Here's the kicker.

The whole *here-we-come* part only worked if she could pony-up sixteen thousand dollars in sixty days. Eight thousand each for the twin's room and board. And while her brothers had received grants and loans to pay for most of their education, not everything was covered. And it wasn't like they could depend on their father for help.

She was it. She was all they had. And she'd made a promise to watch out for them, to be the big sister. And if one thing were true in this life, it was that Libby Lamb didn't break promises.

That was her father's department.

So far, thanks to her yoga teaching gigs, she'd been able to help support her brothers in their studies—an accomplishment she truly treasured. Did it mean renting a tiny apartment under dubious ownership and zipping from class to class in a hunk of a rusty, aging Buick? Yep, it did. And she got it. The gas guzzler was the height of earth unfriendly, but her brothers came first. She'd pretty much raised them since she was twelve, and they were raven-haired, knobby-kneed, eight-year-olds. This opportunity in Ecuador was everything she'd wanted for them. And come hell or high water, she'd make it happen. And maybe, if she convinced the venture capitalist group to invest in her idea, she could pay for her brothers' schooling and follow her dreams in the process.

Two birds. One stone.

But that was a lot easier said than done—especially with the off-kilter energy she'd been grappling with for the last wretched seventy-five days, which could be broken down into one thousand eight hundred hours. Or one hundred eight thousand minutes. Or six million four hundred eighty thousand seconds.

Not that she was counting.

Fine! She'd been counting since that monumentally awful day when a beefcake had jacked up her life force, screwed up her guiding energy, and had caused her steady vibe to go hysterically haywire.

Goodbye, balance and serenity.

And hello, raging yoga bitch.

Seventy-*six* days ago, she wouldn't have believed raging, yoga, and bitch could coexist in one sentence, let alone inside a human being. But they could. Oh, they could because it wasn't just her balanced chi that had high-tailed it out of town.

She'd lost her O.

Yes, that O.

The *oh, yes, don't stop* erotically cathartic climactically superb orgasm. Once her chi had gone off the rails, her O had skipped town like a thief in the night. One day, it was there. The next, adios apex of desire. Sayonara, glorious gratification. And bye-bye, blazing bolt of heady bliss.

Had she tried to recover her lost O?

Hell yes!

Over the last seventy-five days, she'd amassed quite a stash of vibrators and clitoral stimulators. Big or small. Buzzy or pulsing. No matter how hard she tried—and she tried and tried and tried—there was no sign of her O. Not a glimpse. Not a quick catch of breath. Not a dreamy sigh to be had. She'd gone full-on Sahara downtown. Dry and deserted, if she didn't figure out her no-go O, she wouldn't be surprised if buzzards started circling.

And she hadn't only relied on sex toys. She'd racked up more than a few one-night stands over the last six billion four hundred eighty million milliseconds.

Libby Lamb was a free spirit. She followed her intuition. She read her aura. She was a woman in charge of her body and her sexuality. And most of all, she enjoyed consensual sex.

She wasn't looking for Mr. Right.

Heck no!

Her energy migrated toward Mr. Right Now.

She didn't want a boyfriend, period, end of story.

She had her brothers, her best friends, and her yoga. Maintaining a steady guy in her life wasn't in the cards. And if life had taught her one thing, it was that she knew better than to trust a man with her heart.

But never in her wildest dreams did she think one roaring, inconsiderate beefcake of a man could get under her skin so thoroughly and so incessantly that it would shred her chi and drive her O out to pasture. Not to mention, get her fired from a few yoga studios. Okay, not a few. Eight out of the nine studios she taught at had sent her on her merry way with a namaste followed by the slam of a door.

She couldn't blame them. Everything set her off these days.

If she caught yoga participants whispering, she'd remove her mini gong from her bag and bang it like she was auditioning for the part of a fire alarm.

If she noticed someone glancing at their phone during class, she banged the gong.

It was safe to say she was having gong issues.

Yep, that was a thing.

She'd turned the meditative healing tool into a menace to society.

She'd become the yoga version of the glowering Miss Trunchbull character.

In the past seventy-five days, she'd had a little trouble—no, a lot of trouble—keeping her cool which was why everything was riding on today.

She dropped her phone into her yoga bag and spied the golden mini gong tucked next to her mat.

She could almost hear it whispering to her.

Grab the mallet and strike like there's no tomorrow, sister.

You know you want to do it.

Maybe if you bang me hard enough, you'll be able to bang that British beefcake out of your head.

She blinked and looked away from the bag as the tightness returned to the base of her neck with a vengeance.

If any gal on the planet needed an earth-shattering orgasm to loosen her up and set her chakras right, it was Libby Lamb.

And it wasn't for lack of trying.

Along with amassing an army of vibrators, she'd had a decent amount of sex.

She'd had big cocks and little cocks. Guys who went to town downtown and men who could thrust and buck like world champion bull riders. And still, her ability to meet sweet release was nowhere to be found, thanks to the muscled creep. Like a patient flatlined on the table, her love button was DOA.

Dead on arrival.

She fanned herself. It was getting warm in there—and not in the liberating, hold a plank with sweat dripping onto the mat hot yoga sort of way.

"It'll come back. It has to. Your O is simply on a hiatus. A journey. A retreat."

But every time she pictured her absent O, the beefcake's image flashed through her mind. Cocky and arrogant, the taker of Os couldn't have cared less about who he bothered or whose restorative process he'd crushed.

The worst part? She had to keep his identity to herself. That's why she hadn't revealed the orgasm thief's name to her friends. It was bad enough that the guy had annihilated her chi and stripped her of her ability to reach carnal nirvana. She'd wanted to tell her friends—to spill the beans and explain precisely why she'd become a raging yoga bitch. But as much as she loved her besties, the last thing she wanted was her girls weighing in on the situation because...

They knew him.

All she could do was ride out the cosmic catastrophe and pray that her O would come home, and her chi would stabilize.

She rolled her head from side to side, then checked her watch.

Eight minutes until her appointment.

Plenty of time to see if her O had decided to return.

If it did, it was a sign.

Exhaling an uneven breath, she glanced at the door. The coast was clear. She slipped her hand past the waistband of her yoga capris and headed south. "Are you there, clitoris? It's me, Libby Lamb," she whispered, channeling the brilliance of Judy Blume because it was quite literally the last thing she hadn't tried to jump-start her libido when the door to the restroom swung open in a rush of giggles and floral perfume.

"Tell me everything, Cleo. What happened when you and Eli left the bar?" an attractive brunette asked a tall blonde as the young women filed into the restroom and sidled up to the counter.

Libby froze like a petrified rabbit. Had she been busted for attempted public masturbation? Her cheeks bloomed scarlet as adrenaline set off in rapid-fire pulses through her veins. She swallowed hard, then shifted her gaze to the women. Luckily, the pair hadn't seemed to notice that she'd jammed her hand down her pants like some creeper.

She had to get ahold of herself.

Breathing a sigh of relief that the women hadn't shrieked and notified the authorities about the restroom masturbator, Libby adjusted her yoga capris as the bubbly blonde and giddy brunette continued their conversation.

"There was kissing, Laney. So much kissing. Then we went back to his place," the blonde replied with a dirty twinkle in her eye. And sweet karma pie, something in Libby's belly, or possibly lower, twinged. But it wasn't a rev-your-sexy-engine twinge. It was more of a sad, lethargic putter. Not to mention, it had been weeks, *weeks*, since she'd sported a dirty glimmer in her eyes.

What she wouldn't give for a slightly untidy flicker of lust.

"And? Don't hold back, Cleo," the brunette, Laney, coaxed.

The blonde, Cleo, pulled a tube of lip gloss from her purse. "We did it on the kitchen table, in his bathroom, and on the living room floor," she answered, counting off the sex spots on her fingers with the tiny tube.

Libby swallowed hard as her heart thrust into jackhammer mode.

"Cleo, you are a naughty, naughty girl. What about his bed?" the brunette probed as she smoothed one of her brown curls.

No, no, no!

Libby steadied herself. She needed cold, cold water, Arctic water to tamp down her cockeyed libido.

Here's the thing.

Her body remembered the bliss of ramping up—emotions swirling and sensual energy churning. The gasps, the caresses, the grind. But like a stranger in a strange land, she'd lost the way to Orgasm Town. That precarious position had left her in a sexual purgatory without any relief in sight. The last thing she needed was to walk into the meeting of a lifetime with the lady equivalent of blue balls. She fumbled with the faucet and splashed a bit of cool water on her cheeks, focusing on the sound of the spray.

"We made it to the bed at some point," the blonde continued, applying the gloss, "because we broke the headboard banging it against the wall over and over again. By that time, I'd lost track of how many orgasms I'd had."

"And did you let him use the prototype on you?" Laney pressed.

Cleo fanned herself. "Oh yeah, the vibration on that sucker had me screaming in minutes."

Wild-eyed, Libby didn't know what type of prototype they were talking about, but sweet Buddha, she required a ticket to O Central—and she needed it pronto. She assaulted the soap dispenser, and the creamy white substance splattered across her hand. She stared at the thick material that resembled—

Stop. Do not go there.

"Cleo, you truly look like a woman who's been ravished within an inch of her life. You're luminous. Wouldn't you agree?"

Libby froze as the brunette turned from the blonde and pegged her with her gaze. "Isn't my friend shimmering with post-orgasmic bliss?" the brunette continued.

Libby vibrated—and not in the sexy, luminously orgasmic way. In terms of vibration, she was rocking more of a weed whacker meets chainsaw cadence.

Get it together!

She plastered on a grin, then took in the blonde. "Yes, you do have a glow to your skin."

"A glow?" the brunette crowed. "She's a sexed-up beacon of screw-your-brains-out light."

"Oh, stop, Laney," the blonde woman cooed.

And yes, for the love of unbalanced psychic energy, Laney, please stop!

"I'm not the only one here who spent the night clawing their fingernails down the back of a ripped, handsome man," Cleo tossed back. "I saw you and Grant together. You couldn't keep your hands off each other."

Laney slipped a compact from her bag, then applied a fresh dusting of powder to the apples of her cheeks. "That's what happens when you knock out a quickie in the car. It leaves you wanting more."

Quickies in the car?

Nails clawing muscled backs in bouts of reckless abandon?

This was too much. Her off-kilter chi couldn't handle another blow.

"Um...miss?" the blonde said, concern marring, but not erasing, her glimmering sex eyes.

"Yes?" Libby eked out.

"The sink."

"The sink?" Libby looked down as a cascade of water gushed over the edge of the counter. When had she pulled that plunger thing in the sink that kept it from draining? Her addled mind had no idea. She gasped, reaching for the lever to turn off the water, but in her discombobulated state, she grazed her hand across the sink and sent a cold spray of liquid straight to her exposed abdomen. The water hit with a shock, then dripped down her yoga pants, soaking the white material. She banged the plunger with her fist to drain the sink, shut off the tap, then caught a glimpse of herself in the mirror. She looked like a sparkly gold woman in desperate need of an adult diaper. And holy Buddha balls, she had to get out of there. She checked her watch. She only had five minutes before her appointment with destiny.

"Here you go," the brunette said, handing her a paper towel. "Sorry we bombarded you with our girl talk. But you know what it's like when you start seeing someone. The butterflies. The tingles. And all the new relationship orgasms."

"So many orgasms," the blonde added, leaning against the wall, her voice sounding far-off as if she'd fallen back in time to the night of a thousand climaxes.

Libby did her best to sop up the water, but the flimsy paper napkin was no match for soaked, sustainably-sourced stretchy pants. She gave Laney a weak grin and thanked her for the paper towel. Once upon a time, she would have welcomed a conversation like this. The version of Libby Lamb with her chi and O intact would have adored this exchange. These women had great energy. And who didn't like a bit of spicy talk in the girls' bathroom? From their days in Ms. Miliken's kindergarten class, back in elementary school, to the present day, she, Harper, Charlotte, and Penny were the queens of ladies' room countertop gab sessions.

And she didn't limit her girl-talk gatherings to her besties.

Over the years, she'd found herself chatting up total strangers on the street, on the bus, in the market. Wherever life had taken her, she'd connected. She vibed with her surroundings. Her blissful chi had flirted and mingled among the masses like a butterfly bobbing and weaving through a lush garden. And this little butterfly, whether she was with a man or cuddled up in bed with her battery-powered boyfriend, used to be able to knock out a cosmic climax like nobody's business. Before the sexual Sahara set in, she could knock out an O faster than you could say...

Beefcake.

The minute she laid eyes on the juiced-up jock, she'd whispered the word like an ominous incantation. Unable to stop herself, the two stupid syllables had unleashed some straight-up Voldemort black magic, chi stomping, O crushing energy.

Beefcake.

And that was it. After one exchange, where he'd flashed a smirk and zapped her with his cocky, arrogant vibe, she was a changed woman. Not only had he screwed with her chi, but his beefcake energy had also jacked with her sacral chakra—the spiritual core of her sexuality. And in that cosmic event rivaling the big bang, the shelf of her sexual stability had collapsed in a beefcake-laden blowout. He'd jolted her once unwavering chi and sent her O packing. He'd left her percolating with the pops and pings of grating irritability while teetering precariously on the edge of spiritual volatility.

It didn't take a genius to deduce this wasn't the best mindset for a yoga instructor—or honestly, anybody with a pulse.

Cleo picked up her yoga bag. "You don't want this to get wet," the woman said, handing over the tote but not before glancing inside. "Is that the kind of gong you use in a yoga class?"

Libby hooked the strap over her shoulder. "It is. I'm actually here today because of yoga."

"Are you here to meet with the Tri-Derricks for the fitness thing?" Laney asked.

Libby brightened. This could be the break she needed. How had she not connected the dots? These lovely sexed-up ladies must work on this floor. Perhaps they could offer up some info on the venture capital group. And it would be a godsend since she hadn't been able to find anything about Tri-Derrick International online.

A comforting kernel of hope bloomed in her chest. "I am. Did my outfit and yoga bag give it away?"

"Yeah," brunette Laney answered, then shared an uneasy look with Cleo, whose blond, bubbly countenance vanished.

Yikes!

The warm, glowing kernel of light in Libby's chest petered out.

"Do you know much about the Tri-Derrick venture capitalists?" she continued. Her appointment was mere minutes away. This was her last chance to ask. Laney and Cleo could have pertinent information to give her the jump on her competition. But there was more. Despite her current karma conundrum, she didn't believe in coincidences. Everything happened for a reason. And like dominoes, perhaps this is why the universe had facilitated a chance meeting in the bathroom.

Cleo pressed her lips into a hard line. "The Tri-Derricks have been renting the conference room on our floor this week. We've seen a few women dressed like you come and go," she answered as the ladies shared another unsettling eyeball exchange.

Libby's pulse kicked up as her gaze bounced between the pair. The energy had shifted. The sunny yellow auras Laney and Cleo had sashayed in with had morphed into a dishwater gray. She parted her lips, prepared to ask the women to elaborate, when her phone rang. She pulled her cell from the tote, and that little kernel of light brightened.

It was Anders and Alec.

"I'm sorry," she said, holding up her phone. "My brothers are calling. They're in Ecuador, and I hardly get to talk to them. I should answer this."

"Sure, good luck with your appointment," Laney replied with a manufactured grin before sharing yet another look with her companion.

"Yeah, I'm sure you'll be...fine," Cleo added with a plastic expression.

What weren't these two saying?

Libby tried *not* to take the women's aura sea change to heart. Perhaps they ran a rival venture capital group. That had to be it. Tri-Derrick must be their competition. She nodded to the ladies as they exited the restroom, then picked up the call.

"How are my two favorite college students?" she crooned, pushing aside Cleo and Laney's foreboding energy.

"Hey, big sis. We're doing great. We called to see how your meeting went. Are you the world's next yoga sensation?" Anders asked.

She retrieved another paper towel and patted her damp yoga pants. "I don't know anything yet. My meeting starts in a few minutes."

"I told you, Anders," Alec chided playfully. "We're a two hour sahead."

"Then it's a good thing we got you before you went in," Anders continued, unfazed by his brother's teasing rebuke. "We can wish you luck. There's no better yoga instructor than Libby Lamb. You've got this, sis."

She leaned against the wall, picturing the twins with their broad shoulders, dark hair, and amber eyes, like hers. While her brothers were identical twins, she could always tell them apart from their voices and their energy. Easy-going Anders's tone rose and fell like the calm waters of a lake at dawn, while driven Alec's voice hit each syllable with a crisp, precise cadence. Despite their bickering, the twins balanced each other and were the distraction she needed after the strange end to her conversation with Cleo and Laney.

"I'll text you later and let you know how it goes. Thanks for calling, boys."

Boys.

Despite being a good foot taller than she was, in her heart, Alec and Anders would always be gap-toothed, gangly eight-year-olds. The same little boys she'd made peanut butter and jelly sandwiches for and read to each night before bed.

"One last thing, Libbs," Anders said, and she could hear the rare uptick of unease in his voice.

"Sure, what is it?"

"The university doesn't need us to pay the balance now. That's due in sixty days, but they did want us to sign the letter officially accepting the spots in the program. I wasn't sure if—"

"Do it. Tell them you both accept your spots," she blurted, cutting him off.

"Are you sure?" Anders asked, trepidation still lingering in his tone.

She stared at the gong in her bag. "Don't you worry. I've got it covered. I've got everything under control."

Okay, having lost the majority of her teaching gigs over the last seventy-five days might not be the definition of having it under control. Still, despite the hit to her chi and her absent O, she knew today, a door would open—a door that would lead to prosperity. And that prosperity would ensure that she could help support her brothers.

"Thanks, Libbs, you're the best. We owe you everything," Alec replied as a calming relief coated his words.

"We love you, yoga master sister," Anders chimed.

A warmth spread through her as she ended the call. She sighed, then peered at the spot where Cleo and Laney had stood—their floral scents still lingering in the air. She couldn't let the women's cosmic karma one-eighty cloud her perception of the Tri-Derrick group. There could be several reasons why the women had soured when she asked for their opinion on the company. Perhaps they needed the meeting room, and the venture capitalists had reserved it first. That could be it. It could be as simple as a scheduling snafu.

She closed her eyes and released a slow breath. "Your path will lead you to your intended destination," she whispered, her words mingling with the faint floral wisps of scent. She checked herself in the mirror and lifted her chin, taking in the hues of green, red, white, and gold. She was cloaked in the colors that would usher in success. She opened the door to the restroom, searched the hallway for the meeting room, then spied a piece of torn notebook paper taped to the wall.

Tri-Derrick Venture Capitalist International this way was scribbled in black ink with an arrow pointing to the left.

She started down the hall and inhaled the floral scent. Laney and Cleo must work down this corridor, too. She turned the corner, then startled as a young woman barreled down the hallway, sniffling and wiping tears from her cheeks as she charged toward the bank of elevators on the other side of the building. The blubbering gal disappeared in a bluster of muffled whimpering when a harsh voice called out.

"Are you Libby Lamb?"

She turned toward the sound and saw a man standing at the entrance of a glassed-in conference room. "Yes, that's me. I'm here for the interview with the Tri-Derrick Group."

The man looked her up and down once, then twice, then a third time. A sickening sensation washed over her, and she closed her wrap, concealing her exposed midsection as she did her own once-over on the guy.

She didn't know any venture capitalists, but she certainly hadn't expected one to dress like this. Sporting track pants and a faded T-shirt with Greek letters printed across the front, he looked more like someone heading to a kegger than a business meeting.

Maybe this man was an assistant.

She glanced past the guy in leisure-frat attire. Two other men sat at a long conference table in giant overstuffed chairs. A few sheets of paper were strewn haphazardly across the table where one man sat snapping selfies and another focused on his phone. Both men were clad in outfits mirroring the guy at the door. Across from the imposing table, a lone chair sat in the center of the room like an island divorced from the mainland.

"Are you coming in or not?" the guy asked.

Libby touched the jade beads at her wrist for luck. "Yes, I'm coming in. I'm prepared to present to your group," she replied, all business.

The guy shrugged, then plopped onto a third overstuffed chair as she scrambled in behind him. The door caught halfway, and she tried to pull it closed but to no avail. And she sure didn't want her first impression to be one of breaking their office space. That was no way to make an entrance.

"Don't worry about the door. I told my dad about it," the man who'd met her outside the conference room offered.

"You told your dad?" she stammered, scanning the room before heading toward the chair that had to be a good twenty feet from the conference table. Something had been off with her energy for weeks, but even her discombobulated chi was aware of the psychic alarm bells going off left and right. Neither of the men at the table even registered her presence. No matter. She was there to wow and impress. Pulling the little gong from her bag, she set it on the chair and rested the mallet beside it.

"My dad owns this building," the guy answered, then pulled his phone out and joined the other men in obsessing over the internet.

She took in the not-so-corporate lay of the land. These guys were probably rich, but they'd have to be. That was the whole point of venture capitalism, right? She mustered a grin. Did her frazzled chi make her want to march up to them and rip their cells right out of their hands?

Yeah, it did.

The explosive anger that had been simmering in her belly the last seventy-five days was even okay with her taking the tiny mallet and smashing the hell out of their devices. But she couldn't allow her unsteady energy to screw this up.

Don't make snap judgments based on appearances.

Since she'd become a yoga instructor, she'd taught at senior living facilities, community rec centers, and pricy, high-end studios. And for the most part, it didn't matter if she was leading a class of millionaires or folks popping in for a free stretch. Those who practiced yoga were good, kind people. She was teaching a restorative yoga class at an exclusive studio in the Crystal Creek neighborhood tonight.

The breath caught in her throat. This was the only studio where she still held a steady teaching gig. The simmering anger in her belly morphed into a slow boil at the thought of tonight's class. The beefcake creep who'd wrecked her chi trained at an exclusive private boxing gym next door. Would he be there this evening to thwart her meditative practice, again, banging and crashing and hollering like he was the King of the Jungle?

"Libby?" the guy who'd led her into the conference room called, his voice snapping her back to this monumentally huge moment that she wasn't about to let some beefcake ruin.

She straightened and clasped her hands in front of her.

Resonate peace and tranquility.

"I'm grateful for the opportunity to share my vision and my business plan with you," she began, projecting poise and serenity. "Where would you like me to start?"

So far, so good.

The young man lounging in the center overstuffed chair looked up from his phone, then raked his beady eyes over her body like she was a piece of meat. He leaned forward. "Well, Libby Lamb," he began in a syrupy tone as a smarmy grin twisted his lips, "we'd like you to start by bending over."

TWO

LIBBY

HAD this T-shirt-clad bro asked her to present her ass for the group to assess?

This had to be a joke.

"You want me to bend over?" Libby repeated, doing everything in her power to keep from unleashing a verbal tirade.

"Yeah," the guy answered smugly before leaning back in his chair.

She pursed her lips, then peered down at the conference room's faded black and gray checkerboard carpet.

Should she do it?

She studied a black square. As far as colors go, black was a tricky shade. It could promote deep meditation, but it could also signify an impasse—a mysterious, dark obstacle hindering one's quest for balance. And then it hit her. This had to be a test. Yes, the venture capitalists must want to observe how she'd handle a professional hiccup.

If she remained calm, she'd be fine.

She picked up the mallet and struck the gong gently. She'd lost her cool with the poor instrument more than a few times over the last seventy-five days.

Stupid lopsided chi.

It freaked people out to see a yogi serene one minute, then wild-eyed and working the gong like a game of Whack-a-Mole the next.

But as hard as she'd tried, she couldn't help it.

Anytime the beefcake invaded her mind, or an inconsiderate, beefcake-like guy wandered into her orbit, it dashed her communion with calmness. And the harder she'd tried to get the beefcake out of her head, the more frequently he'd pop up. The release of striking the metal wasn't a substitute for the earth-shaking orgasm she so desperately needed. Still, it acted as a pressure valve, dispelling a portion of her grating agitation. And at this very moment, the unsettling energy inside her wanted to bang the hell out of that mini gong like she was one of those wind-up monkeys holding a pair of cymbals, but blessedly, she held back.

"What's that for?" the guy who'd opened the door barked.

She breathed a sigh of relief.

At least she'd changed the topic from bending over.

It was go big or go home time—and she had to knock this out of the park. This presentation required a full-court positive karma press. And the gong, when she wasn't banging it within an inch of its life, was the perfect place to start.

She surveyed the men who couldn't be much older than she was. Three white guys with blond hair coiffed in the same GQ long, but not too long, stylish cut. They looked like they hit the gym—a good sign. Still, they might not be familiar with the benefits of yoga, but their interest in fitness had to be why they'd invited her here today. Somewhere beneath the faded Greek letters, they harbored the desire to learn. Experiencing a renewed sense of purpose, she went into instructor mode.

"I rang the gong to clear our minds and align our chakras," she announced, exuding tranquility.

Ha! She could maintain her calm like a true professional and educate these guys on the benefits of yoga in the process.

The men stared at her, wide-eyed, before the guy at the far-right end of the table huffed, then went back to scrolling on his phone.

The gong could only do so much. She needed to change tack.

"Which one of you is Derrick?" she asked, hoping to build rapport—again, like a true professional.

The door guy leaned back, rocking in the office chair like a toddler. "We're all Derricks. I'm Derrick Doyle. That's Derrick Dawson, and Derrick Dirks is the dude at the end," the man answered as he gestured down the line.

This was a start—and not a bad one.

She took a step toward them as an idea sparked. "The power of three!" she exclaimed.

The Derrick on the left cocked his head to the side. "Is that an indie all-girl rock group?"

Oh, boy!

"I'm not sure," Libby began. "But it's an important number in the practice of yoga and meditation. The number three holds great spiritual energy. Think of an equilateral triangle or picture the sun, the moon, and the earth. In addition, three signifies harmony, wisdom, and understanding."

The Derrick in the center frowned. "What?"

She looked down the line of Derricks, then cleared her throat. "There are three of you. Three Derricks."

"Which one of us is the moon?" the Derrick on the left asked as confusion marred his expression. But before she could respond, the center Derrick perked up.

"I dated a chick named Harmony once. Does that count?" the guy asked.

"Well…" Libby started, but the Derrick to her left clapped his hands.

"I remember Harmony. She was hot. What happened to her?"

The center Derrick shrugged. "She wanted a commitment, so I dumped her ass."

"Commitments blow, dude!" the Derrick on the left replied, spinning around in the leather chair before sharing a bro-tastic fist bump with the center Derrick. Then the Derrick on the left gasped like he'd solved the climate crisis. "Would you mind if I banged her?"

"Go for it, man. She's an animal in the sack," the center Derrick added.

The muscles at the base of Libby's neck tightened, and the agitation she'd endured for the past seventy-five days grated and clawed, setting her on edge.

She needed a quick fix to release some tension.

Picture a time when you were truly happy. Hold the feeling inside your chest, close to your heart.

She employed this meditation technique in her classes but grimaced when the stupid beefcake's face popped into her mind.

Blast her crazy chi!

She returned her attention to the Derricks, who were arguing over Harmony's bra size when a glint of gold caught her attention.

The gong.

Sweet Buddha, send her strength.

Oh, how her off-kilter chi itched to grip the mallet and strike that golden gong so loudly and so forcefully that it pounded the misogynistic talk right out of the glassed-in room.

No, she couldn't do that.

Breathe. Breathe. Breathe.

She released a shaky breath and regained her bearings. If this were a test, she couldn't afford to fail. She shifted her weight from foot to foot. "Have you invested in any other fitness ventures?" She needed to get these guys back on track, and she needed to gauge the room. This wasn't something new for her. She did this often as an instructor.

Is anyone new to yoga?

Is this your first time in class?

The more she understood about her students, the better the practice. And she needed to understand the Derricks.

The Derrick on the left shared a curious look with the Derrick in the center, then the center Derrick cleared his throat. "This is our first...venture."

They were new at this. That explained the unorthodox interview.

"How did you decide to team up?" she continued, throwing a glance at the Derrick on the right, who still had his eyes glued to his cell.

No matter.

The center and left Derricks were talking, and the more information she had, the better she could tailor her pitch.

"We were in the same frat," the Derrick on the left answered.

"And we've got killer trust funds, so we can do whatever the hell we want," the Derrick in the center crooned with an egotistical smirk.

The grating irritation in her chest intensified. Her beefcake had flashed a similar expression. Libby peered at the gong mallet, then pasted a grin to her face.

Reframe this situation and breathe. And under no circumstance can you lose your ever-lovin' mind.

These guys might be a little rough around the edges, but she'd taught yoga to three-year-olds in a toddler move and groove class. Nothing could be more challenging than that, right?

"Any particular reason you chose to invest in fitness?" she probed, taking another peek at the gong, then mentally chided herself.

No crazy gong antics.

"Can you stop talking and take off your sweater thing?" the Derrick in the center called, then held up his phone.

Was he recording her?

She glanced at her sparkly gold sports bra peeking out from beneath the ruby-red fabric and suddenly wished she'd come clad in snow pants and a woolly winter coat. "My wrap?" she echoed.

"We need to confirm that you've got the physique we're looking for," the center Derrick continued.

"Physique?" she squeaked.

"And turn around, and do one of those dog poses for us, and try not to burst out into tears like the last chick," the Derrick on the left directed.

That poor girl! And crap, they were back to the bending over business.

"You want me to take off my wrap and demonstrate the downward-facing dog position?"

The two Derricks shared a smarmy exchange before the center Derrick raked his gaze over her body. "Yeah, that's exactly what we want you to do. We're asking every applicant to demonstrate this...position."

Heat crackled and popped in her chest, raw and unyielding. She leaned—but did not bend over—and plucked a folded sheet of paper from her bag. "Before I demonstrate the pose you requested, I'd like to share my strategic business plan."

The Derrick on the far right, who hadn't made a peep,

looked up from his phone and wagged his finger. "Hold on, baby."

"Baby?" she snapped.

Oh no.

The irritation in her chest hissed and snarled, but this Derrick didn't respond. He hadn't even registered that she'd spoken.

He rolled his chair toward the Derrick in the center. "Dudes, they announced it. The London Lion is fighting the Snake on Pay-Per-View in sixty days. This is huge—the boxing event for the ages. I'm putting my money on the Snake. He holds the heavyweight title, and the guy bobs and weaves like a viper."

The Derrick in the center swiped his phone from the table, sending a few sheets of paper floating to the ground. "I got an email notification, too!" he exclaimed, gawking at his cell. "I didn't think the Lion had it in him. Sure, the dude is a power-house, but he's lost his swagger. He didn't even show up to his last fight. The British Beast bombed hard. To be fair, the Snake may be the current champ, but he'll need to beat the Lion if he wants street cred."

"Whatever the outcome, they'll make a shit ton of money fighting on Pay-Per-View. I'd love a cut of that," the Derrick on the left squealed—actually squealed. "And rumor has it that the Lion is training in Denver."

"No way," the center Derrick shot back.

"Yeah, I googled it. Somebody posted that his old trainer is here," the Derrick on the right answered.

The Derrick on the left twirled in the chair. "If he is here, he must be keeping a low profile."

"Wouldn't you after totally humiliating yourself?" the Derrick on the right replied with an arrogant lilt to his words.

Libby watched their exchange, dumbfounded, as the last drop of patience drained from her body.

"Excuse me, we're in the middle of an important interview," she announced, holding up the copy of her business plan—the plan she'd spent hours researching and crafting.

"Give us a second. We're talking about boxing, baby. Nothing to worry your pretty little head about," the Derrick on the right tossed out without giving her the basic courtesy of even making eye contact.

"Baby," she muttered. She was done being referred to as *baby* by this insensitive, rude man, and she didn't have a second to give. Not to mention, she understood the plight of the Incredible Hulk and Dr. Jekyll and Mr. Hyde. In the center of that glassed-in conference room, she stood at the precipice, her toes dangling off the cliff of a savvy businesswoman as she stared across the void into raving-mad yoga bitch land.

"This is bullshit, isn't it?" she called, raising her voice enough to quiet the Tri-Derricks' boxing match blathering.

The Derrick on the left held out his phone. "No, it's the real deal. The Lion and the Snake will go toe to toe in sixty days. I ordered it on Pay-Per-View. We can watch it up at my parents' place in Aspen...unless we can get tickets. I can't believe we get a heavyweight championship fight here."

"Dude, we should get tickets. Front-row. I'll text my dad," the Derrick on the right cried with a clap of his hands.

Indignation permeated every cell in Libby's body.

She knew what was coming, and it wouldn't be pretty. She attempted to quell her beast within with a cleansing breath, but not even deep breathing could save her now.

"I'm not saying that the fight is bullshit," she began, ice coating her words. "And for that matter, what kind of human being enjoys watching two people beat the crap out of each other?"

The Derricks sported shocked expressions. "Like a billion people. It went live two minutes ago, and over one hundred thousand people forked over a ton of cash to watch it," the Derrick on the left answered.

"Forget the fight," she continued, lowering her voice to a rumbly growl. "The bullshit I was referring to is the investment in a fitness venture. Are you interested in hearing my plan or not?"

"Oh, yeah, that," the Derrick on the left replied with a sheepish expression.

The Derrick in the center searched the conference table, then pulled one of the errant sheets of paper toward him. He straightened in his chair, then studiously focused on the page. "You're one of our top three choices." He tapped the page with his meaty index finger. "It says it right here."

Her chi may be scrambled, but it didn't take a Zen master to deduce this guy was lying. And hello, raging yoga bitch! She dropped her business plan, grabbed the mini gong in one hand and the mallet in the other. Then, with the strength of a thousand yogis, she gave the instrument two swift strikes. The sound waffled through the room, harsh and clanging, and had rendered the Derricks mute.

"Show me what's on that piece of paper," she demanded, eyeing the center Derrick.

"Show you what?" he asked, squirming in his chair.

She banged the gong, sending another wave of frenzied vibration through the air as the sound ricocheted off the glass walls. "The paper," she commanded.

Startled, he flipped the sheet around, revealing...nothing.

A sea of white.

A blank page.

She glared down the line of Derricks, then went to town, striking the metal.

Clang, clang, clang!

One bang for each douchebag of a Derrick.

With each echoing pang of sound, the men's complexions grew paler and paler.

"You're going to tell me what's going on. Is this a real opportunity to partner with a venture capitalist company?" she questioned, when out of the corner of her eye, she sensed movement.

Thanks to the crash of the gong, people from the surrounding offices had stepped into the hall to check out the commotion. She heard a low murmur through the half-opened door, then inhaled a floral scent. Cleo and Laney must be among the crowd. But she didn't have time for girl talk. She glared at the Derricks as the trio exchanged pained glances, neither saying a word.

It was time to pull out some seriously spiritual shit.

One by one, she pointed the mallet at the men. "By the power of three, you are going to tell me everything," she proclaimed, then banged the hell out of the gong.

"What are you—some kind of hot yoga witch?" the Derrick on the right spewed, but as soon as she zeroed in on him, he sank into the chair.

Hold on to your hats!

"Oh, I'll show you what kind of witch I am." She struck the gong, then stared up at the fluorescent lights. "By the power of three, I call on the universe to—"

"Stop! Don't curse us," the center Derrick pleaded. "I put a huge bet on the Snake. I can't have your crazy karma magic costing me twenty grand."

Libby froze.

She wasn't exactly sure what she was about to call on the universe to do to these jackasses. She was pretty much making it up as she went, but the mere threat of psychic vengeance seemed to be enough to scare the swagger out of these bros. She lowered the mallet. "You bet twenty thousand dollars on a fight?"

"Yeah," the guy eked out.

That money would change everything for her and her brothers. And here was this spoiled Derrick, casually placing a bet on something as senseless as boxing.

Her heart sank. "Why are you here? Why did you advertise an opportunity to invest in a fitness business?"

The Derrick on the left stared at the table. "We did it to meet hot chicks."

"You lured women here under false pretenses just to meet them?" She had to be sure she'd heard him correctly.

"We were pretty drunk when we made the post. We didn't think anyone would apply. But shit, there's a bunch of hot fitness chicks looking for a break," he replied as a blush ripened on his cheeks.

"Twenty thousand dollars plus a substantial investment is a big deal to a lot of people," she answered, hoping she'd knocked or gonged some sense into these men.

But she'd given them more credit than they deserved.

A stupid, self-righteous smirk bloomed on the center Derrick's lips. "If you think about it, we didn't trick anyone. There is a prize."

She cocked her head to the side. "And what would that be if it's not the investment and the prize money?"

"Forget that stuff," Derrick continued. "We're the real prize."

"You're the prize? The three of you?" she barked.

The nerve of this guy!

"Yeah, what chick wouldn't want to date one of us?" he tossed back, looking mighty proud of himself.

She sized up the center Derrick. "You could be sued for this. This is fraud and false advertising."

"Are you going to sue us, yoga witch? Do you think you could go up against our parents' attorneys?" He sank into the oversized chair and rocked a few times like an overindulged schoolboy. "I bet you twenty K you don't have an attorney on retainer like we do," the center Derrick snarled.

The guy wasn't wrong. She didn't have any recourse, and this prick knew it. But that didn't mean she had to walk out of this room with her tail between her legs. The former, orgasm-laden, balanced Libby wouldn't contemplate revenge. But in this conference room, vibrating with an unstable fury, that Zen master was nowhere to be found.

Still, she had to be careful when it came to karma. Blasting a bolt of negativity at this creep could clear and enhance his aura and blowback negatively on her. However, with her whacked-out chi and all hope of funding her brothers' education shredded, there wasn't much more the universe could throw at her.

She concentrated on the center Derrick, whipping up a tornado of energy. "It might not happen today or tomorrow, but your luck will run out. Mark my words, Derrick..."

"Dawson," the center Derrick supplied with a syrupy twist to his lips.

She grabbed her bag, swung the strap over her head, jammed the gong and mallet inside, then turned to the man. "Derrick Dawson, I predict that a shitstorm of spiritual energy will knock you on your ass," she snarled through gritted teeth.

Oh, how she wanted to punch his lights out. Her hands balled into fists as her vision grew glassy and that tornado of rage threatened to tear her apart. Tears welled in her eyes, but she blinked away the emotion.

She would not cry—not in front of these jerks.

Turning on her heel, she bolted from the room, passing a bevy of bystanders as she swung open the door to the stairwell. Taking the steps two at a time, she cursed her unstable chi—that gnawing off-balanced energy, gurgling and sloshing around inside of her like a bucket of brown, putrid mop water. She should have known better than to peg not only her hopes and dreams but the hopes and dreams of her brothers on this wild goose chase.

A searing truth cut through her frantic aura and flashed through her mind like a bolt of lightning.

If it weren't for the beefcake, none of this would have happened.

He'd knocked her off her spiritual foundation. He'd mixed up her metaphysical mindset.

She wouldn't have lost most of her teaching gigs and, in turn, the majority of her revenue if it weren't for him. Had she not been running on spiritual empty, she would have directed her energy toward a legit means of funding her brothers' education. With balanced energy and a clear mind, she would have seen through the Derricks' post.

Twenty thousand in prize money and one hundred thousand invested into a start-up?

It was too good to be true.

She hit the first floor, tore through the lobby, then booked it to her Buick. She sat in the driver's seat and banged her fists on the steering wheel. She'd thrown some majorly bad spiritual juju at that Derrick Dawson—and it was probably a waste. With her luck, the douchebag had lawyers for fighting bad energy, too. Now she had to prepare for the karma calamity heading her way. Whatever one puts out into this world, good, bad, or tremendously irresponsible, it will come back to them.

But she couldn't ruminate on her divine destiny or when fate would send another one-two punch her way. She had to get home, make a new plan, then hightail it to teach at her last remaining yoga gig. She reached into her bag, found her keys, and thanked Buddha as the old Buick groaned to life. She merged into traffic, driving the familiar Denver roads, and willed herself to calm down.

Picture a time when you were truly happy. Hold the feeling inside your chest, close to your heart.

She exhaled a sigh of relief as an image of her friends fluttered in her mind, recalling how they would cruise around Denver in Penny's old Jeep. Her shining stars in a sea of jacked-up chi. She imagined Penny's blond hair framing her face, Charlotte's rose aura emitting kindness, and Harper's uniquely wry vibe making them howl with laughter.

She had to keep the good vibes.

Focus on what you can control.

Unfortunately, besides her besties, there didn't seem to be a heck of a lot she could depend on.

"What will I say to Anders and Alec?" she whispered. "I could use a little help, universe," she finished as she turned onto her street and noticed a truck parked in front of her apartment building.

And there were men.

And these men had her stuff in their hands.

Hitting the brakes, her car screeched and heaved. She cut the engine, grabbed her bag, then sprang from the Buick. "What are you doing with my stuff?" she shrieked, then gasped and snatched her sacred Buddha statue from one of the men.

"Talk to your landlord, lady. He says you have to move out. This stuff is going into a storage unit," the mover finished, then handed her a card with an image of a storage locker emblazoned on the front. "The code to open the locker is on the back."

"Wait here. This has to be a misunderstanding," she stammered, then booked it up to her second-floor apartment.

She couldn't fathom moving out. She loved her place. It was compact and had come partially furnished. She'd made it her own, decorating with plants and healing crystals. Facing east, she woke welcoming the sun each morning in her little slice of solitude. As much as she loved her brothers, living with two men, and her father when he decided to grace them with his presence wasn't her idea of paradise. She'd been over the moon when the boys went off to college, and she found this unit.

And it had come at a steal.

Rent in Denver was sky-high, but this place fit easily into her tight budget. That might have something to do with her landlord. The guy went by Hash Pants, a moniker he'd told her he'd acquired for dabbling in the herbal arts. Thanks to partaking in loads of his product, he was as easygoing as one gets —until he decided to throw her out, that is.

She scanned the hallway and found her apartment door wide open. She sprinted inside, then came to a jarring halt before nearly stepping on a body.

"Why are you on the ground, Hash Pants?"

With his long hair flowing and the scent of bud reeking, the guy stretched across the hardwood floor, looking as peaceful as a long summer day.

Libby stood over the man. "What's going on, Hash Pants? Why are there movers in my apartment?"

"Because that's what movers do. They move things," he murmured as he folded his hands on his belly.

This could not be happening. Her baked landlord could not be kicking her out.

Not today of all days!

She surveyed the space as the moving guys returned with a lava lamp and a wrought iron birdcage.

"I texted you a few weeks ago," he said, remaining on the floor with his eyes closed.

"You texted that change was in the air. I figured you were high. You didn't say anything about moving out today," she replied, her heart hammering in her chest.

"This is what I meant when I said change. You were a cater-pillar, Libby, but now you're a butterfly. It's time to spread your wings and leave the cocoon."

As much as she loved a good butterfly analogy, this didn't make any sense.

"Why do you need me out so soon?" she pressed.

"My great aunt Ida is alive," the man replied.

Note to self: in your next apartment, make sure the landlord isn't stoned out of his mind twenty-four seven.

"That's great, Hash Pants. I'm happy she's okay," Libby replied, not sure there was an eloquent way to respond to the man's declaration. "But why does your aunt's life force have anything to do with me?"

"This is her place. I was supposed to check in on it while she was away, but I've been subletting it to finance my herbal endeavors. Great Aunt Ida's been at a yoga retreat in Tibet for the last ten years. My family wasn't even sure if she was still alive," the still prostrate man explained.

"Wow," Libby uttered. "That must be quite a relief."

"Yeah, I'm sure Great Aunt Ida feels the same way, too. That's the reason for the movers. I have to put her stuff back and remove yours. You know, restore the balance," the man mused.

What she wouldn't give to know the peace of a restored sense of balance!

She watched as the men set a rainbow-colored rocking chair next to the sofa, then looked around the space as karma dealt her another blow. She ran her hands down her face. "Can I have a few days to get my stuff together?"

The guy cracked open a bloodshot eye and checked his watch. "Sorry, Libby, Aunt Ida landed at the airport. She should be here any minute."

"Any minute!" she shrieked.

"Yep, that construct of time is a tricky dude," Hash Pants replied. "And there's one more thing."

"What's that?" she asked, hardly able to believe that this was it.

No new fitness venture, no money for her brothers, and now, she was minutes away from being homeless.

"The moving guys got most of your stuff, but they didn't want to touch your...devices."

She glanced in the tiny kitchen. They must have already gotten her toaster and blender. "Which devices?"

Hash Pants propped himself up onto his elbow. "The devices on your bed. And by the way, that's one hell of a collection. You must go through batteries like a maniac."

Her stomach dropped as heat rose to her cheeks.

Just when she thought this day couldn't get any worse, she remembered what she'd left on her bed.

She swished past a mover lumbering by with a coatrack, then skidded to a stop at the entrance to her bedroom.

If a human being could melt into a pool of complete and utter humiliation, she would have done it.

There, in their vibrating glory, were sixteen, that's right, sixteen vibrators spread across her bed.

Before she'd left for the meeting with the Tri-Derricks, in a fit of frantic energy, she'd tried them out, only to confirm that yes, her O was still on hiatus. Then, for reasons she could only blame on having an acute case of lady blue balls, she organized the vibrators from largest to smallest.

Laid out in every color of the rainbow, the presentation reminded her of the glass cases in the Museum of Nature and Science, with species of beetles and butterflies pinned side by side to compare the insect's traits and varying characteristics.

What traits did these sex toys share?

In the last seventy-five days, not one had gotten close to getting her off.

She scrambled to her bed, opened her yoga bag, and chucked the vibrators into her tote.

"It's an impressive collection, lady."

She looked over her shoulder as one of the movers nodded in appreciation, and humiliation tore through her body. But there was no time to waste. She grabbed a suitcase from under the bed and threw in her laptop, her passport, and important papers before sprinkling in her crystals and as much clothing as she could manage, along with her toothbrush and a few other toiletries.

"Libby, you've got to go! Be the donkey and get your ass across the pass."

"What are you talking about?"

This guy really needed to lay off his product.

"Now, leave now! My aunt Ida texted. Her cab is five minutes away," Hash Pants shrieked, entering the paranoia phase of his altered state.

She nodded, dragging the near-bursting bag through the apartment as her phone's alarm chimed. She nearly forgot. She had a restorative yoga class to teach.

With her bag of vibrators and her suitcase stuffed to the gills, she dragged the lopsided luggage down the stairs.

Clunk, clunk, clunk.

As she worked her way to the first floor, each thump and thud elicited a jolting pang of anger laced with regret straight through her heart. Her brothers. Her dreams. It had gotten flushed down the toilet. She shouldn't have thrown psychic shade on the Tri-Derrick bro. And karma sure didn't wait around to deliver the colossal cosmic blowback.

She tossed her bag into the Buick's trunk as the moving truck pulled out and grumbled down the street. She rested her head against the side of the car as a pair of headlights illuminated the road.

"Just make it to your class. You'll figure something out for the twins," she whispered as the headlights nearly blinded her. She shielded her eyes as a flowing form came toward her. Was it an angel, a spirit? Was it the karma police coming to drop another catastrophe in her lap?

"You need to do something about that," came a woman's purring voice.

Libby released a heavy sigh. "I'll move my car," she said, feeling the weight of the world on her shoulders.

"No, not the car," the woman answered, her bracelets clinking as she gestured. "That rage. By Buddha, your aura is positively crimson."

Libby stared at the woman. With a slim build, flowing white hair, and several giant crystals hanging from her neck, it was as if she'd bumped into a mystic. And then a tingle traveled down her spine, followed by an urge—a strange call to action. "Who are you?" she asked as a door slammed in the distance.

"Aunt Ida, it's so great that you're not dead. Your apartment is just like you left it, and there's no way any yoga chick's been living there," Hash Pants called from the entrance of the building.

The woman nodded to her nephew, then Aunt Ida gave her one more curious look. "That rage in your aura will eat you alive. Take this," she said, plucking a stone from her pocket. "It's an aquamarine. Rub it with your thumb. It promotes emotional wellness and can assist in releasing rage. And, honey, you've got enough of that emotion to power the city for days. Whatever you need to do to rid yourself of that negativity, you better do it. I've never seen chakras more out of alignment."

"Um...thank you," Libby uttered, quite surprised as she accepted the smooth object. But the woman wasn't wrong about aquamarine's healing properties. Often called the breath stone, aquamarine fostered transformation, rebirth, and trust.

Trust.

"Now, go restore the balance and overcome the barriers in your life. Namaste," the woman answered with a bow, then clinked and jingled as she glided toward Hash Pants.

Libby blinked. Ida was back, and she was out.

How's that for balance!

She gazed at the stone. She was usually the one dispensing spiritual advice. It was odd to have someone off the street read her aura. But the woman's words hit home.

That rage will eat you alive.

That was the understatement of the century.

She slid the cool aquamarine stone into the pocket of her wrap as a storm of emotion welled in her chest. She inhaled a breath and focused on one word.

Rage.

Twilight had engulfed the city, and she stared up at the darkening sky as a jet-black crow swooped in the air above her, and for a brief second, her spirits lifted.

Crows were thought to have psychic abilities and were gifted creatures that some believed could see the past, the present, and the future. From the time she was a little girl, thanks to her jet-black hair, she'd always identified with the bird.

"It must be a sign. Soon, this rage will disappear, and I'll regain my chi and soar," she whispered. But as the words left her lips, the crow squawked loudly and swooped through the air. She turned away as the bird buzzed by her, the tip of its wing stroking her cheek, then gasped as something hit her shoulder. She looked down to find a patch of milky white bird crap dripping down her sleeve.

There's some karma.

Fuming, Libby got into the Buick, slammed the door, and started her up.

Karma was a real bitch, and thanks to a certain beefcake, she'd suffered its epic wrath.

She let out a high-pitched cry of frustration. Raw and animalistic, the sound vibrated through her as an idea took hold —well, more of a call to action. She had one opportunity left to restore her balance and purge herself of the rage she'd carried these last seventy-five days. It was a desperate move—a spiritually risky alternative. She'd only read about the practice, but after what she'd endured, she was out of options.

Libby Lamb was a desperate woman. Her karma was in the crapper, and she had nothing left to lose.

Revenge was a dish best served cold, or in her case, after a sixty-minute rejuvenating yoga flow.

Tonight, she was leading a yoga class in the studio where it started—where the beefcake in the boxing gym next door had clanged and roared, disturbing her class and wrecking her chi.

All she'd done was slip out of class to ask the man to keep it down.

He could have nodded or acted like a human being and apologized.

But he didn't.

He donned a cocky smirk and had looked right through her.

Like she was nothing.

Like she was less than nothing.

His stupid beefcake vibe rippled through her and had ignited a psychic firestorm.

He'd be there tonight, roaring away, making a raucous.

She could feel it in her bones.

It was time to turn the spiritual tables.

"It's beefcake or bust," she growled, then hit the gas.

THREE

ERASMUS

"LION, Erasmus, look this way! Let's get a picture of the British Beast growling. Show us the face you're going to make when you go toe to toe with Silas Scott, the Irish Snake," called one of the journalists in the room, jockeying for the best shot among the photographers and cameramen.

The Lion, Erasmus "Raz" Cress, former four-time Boxing Heavyweight Champion of the World, also nicknamed the British Beast, thanks to his ripped physique and six-foot-five frame, bounced from foot to foot in front of a ruby-red punching bag hanging from the gym's ceiling inside a boxing ring. The PR people had set up lights that cast him in a social-media-ready glow.

In nothing but ruby red boxing trunks, gloves, and shoes, the stage was set.

Every muscle was on display—every move calculated. This was it. In sixty days, he'd either reclaim the title of heavyweight champion or prove the naysayers right. At thirty-two years old, after disappearing from the boxing scene for the last three years, this would either be his comeback or the final nail in the coffin of his spectacular downfall. He turned toward a bevy of cameramen and flashed a cocksure grin. "I growl when I want to growl," he snarled in his grittiest East London accent, and the press ate it up.

"Follow the rules, please. No calling out. Give the Beast space to move," Briggs Keaton, his posh sports agent and business manager, instructed in an accent, mimicking the Queen's English. Raz glanced at the little man clad in a three-piece suit, salivating over the coverage with dollar signs in his eyes as he stood near the media brood sent to cover the impromptu exhibition.

Win or lose, this well-dressed bloke would make a fortune. He could be a right prat, but he wasn't a bad guy. He'd flown in from London to wrangle the press. Then again, money could do that. Thanks to Pay-Per-View and the bloodlust of millions across the globe, this match-up would bring in hundreds of millions, if not billions, in revenue. Raz nodded to his agent, and the guy gifted him with a syrupy smile.

Wanker.

Erasmus Cress had been a professional athlete long enough to know the difference between who was there for the flash and the cash and who'd be there, win or lose, after the last punch had been thrown. A knot twisted in his gut, but he couldn't reveal a sliver of trepidation or an ounce of apprehension. This would be his first fight with one less person cheering him on—the compassionate woman who had meant everything to him. He looked over his shoulder at the corner of the boxing ring where one stool sat and recalled the time when there had been two. He gritted his teeth and exploded into a series of swift, clean jabs.

Bam, bam, bam, bam.

The pop of his gloves hitting the bag matched the click of the cameras.

You know what they want. Be the bloody champion.

He had to maintain the persona of the Lion, the cocky British beast who paraded around the ring like he owned it. He had to become the arrogant, dominating force that hit hard, moved fast, and radiated alpha energy. It wasn't that difficult when he was the center of a media storm. He could play the part. He knew how to please—knew how to allow them to live vicariously through him.

Men wanted to be him, and women wanted to do him.

He could pick up a woman and screw her brains out in a sweaty bout of meaningless sex any night of the week and twice on Fridays. He didn't remember their names, and their faces had become an inconsequential blur. Sex served as a release. A hollow act. A vehicle to let off a little steam.

Was he proud of that?

Honestly, he didn't give it much thought.

He chanced another glance at the corner's lone stool. He wasn't in the market to fill a second one. At least, that's what he'd been telling himself until seventy-five days ago when a pair of amber-colored eyes nearly brought him to his knees.

He thought he knew what it was to live with the hole in his heart—a hole that had left him a gutted and unsteady sod these last three years. He'd donned a conceited mask to hide the pain, and for the most part, it worked. It dulled the ache. It concealed the hurt.

Then she opened the door and peered inside the gym.

Who obliterated his defenses with one look?

The raven-haired, ruby-lipped Libby Lamb.

That was her name.

Of course, he'd recognized her when she'd popped in to ask him to keep it down, but he sure as hell didn't let her know. He'd been a right prick when she appeared out of nowhere, standing in the doorway, barefoot and wearing a tiny sports bra that showcased her breasts and toned abdomen and a pair of yoga pants that accentuated her curves.

Jesus, that woman had an arse that wouldn't quit. Like a perfect plum, it was ripe, round, and begging to be bitten. But it wasn't her delectable petite build and shiny, jet-black hair that had thrown him for a loop. It was her eyes—those amber eyes. With one glance, she saw everything. He'd had no time to put up his defenses, and for a split second, she'd peered into his very soul.

Once upon a time, another woman had done that to him. And he thought he'd found the one, his match, his perfect equal.

But the universe had other plans.

Bloody universe.

Like him, the universe had proven time and time again that it could be a colossal prick.

Libby Lamb had entered his orbit not long after he'd arrived in Denver, a little over four months ago. An acquaintance of sorts, he knew her through his nanny match men's group.

Nanny Match Men's Group.

Stupid name. They should come up with something better.

And why was he in something as ridiculous sounding as a men's nanny match group?

Finola Arcadia Cress.

Age: eighty.

Occupation: Colossal ball-breaker and the maker of the best biscuits in the UK.

Otherwise known as Granny Fin.

After he'd won his first heavyweight title and became a bona fide multi-millionaire, he'd moved his granny and sisters into a posh flat in London's Chelsea neighborhood—a posh flat that happened to be near the nanny matchmaker extraordinaire, Madelyn Malone's place in London.

Madelyn Malone specialized in connecting prominent

single men of wealth and status with high-end nanny services. But that wasn't everything she seemed to do. He'd decided Madelyn was part witch, part bitch, and a hell of a lot of mystery. Not many people intimidated him. But this senior citizen with her tumbling dark hair highlighted with a lone silver streak, rich vibrato voice, and thick Eastern European accent had a headmistress vibe that prompted him to watch his language and dust off his manners. The woman had a way about her, and he could see how his granny Fin and the nanny match-maker formed a friendship. A pair of no-nonsense women, neither took any shit—especially not from him.

Despite being slightly afraid of the matchmaker, he'd be lying if he said he didn't need some help in the nanny depart-ment. In two days, Granny Fin and his six-year-old son Sebas-tian would leave the buzz and grind of London and arrive in the Mile-High City.

Granny Fin had insisted on coming to the states to be with him after Sebastian finished school. But with an arthritic hip that had slowed her down in the past few months, she couldn't keep up with the energetic Sebastian anymore. His younger sisters, Calliope and Callista, had helped out as much as possi-ble, but the twins were twenty-one now and had headed to South Korea to teach English abroad. He was bloody proud of them, but it had put him in the precarious position of needing assistance. And that's why Madelyn was in his life. Someone needed to be tasked with caring for Sebastian.

Sebastian.

Regret panged in his chest when he pictured the boy, because, when it came to his son, one thing was undeniably true.

The kid deserved a better dad.

Sure, he could send the lad to the best schools and buy him the latest electronics and toys any kid could want. Thanks to his boxing windfalls and past lucrative endorsements, he was worth over five hundred million dollars. He hadn't known wealth growing up in Granny Fin's place, tightly packed into one of East London's terraced houses that lined the winding road like books on a shelf. But it didn't matter how much money he had. It didn't give him the ability to connect with his boy. Emotional stuff was never his strong suit. No, that gift belonged to—

Shut it down. Don't go there.

Not today.

A muscle ticked in his jaw as he zeroed in on the ruby-red bag and knocked out another series of punches, then caught a glimpse of his longtime cornerman and trainer, Augie Bimston, leaning against the wall.

With a toothpick sticking out of his mouth, the old man crossed his arms, resting them on his protruding belly as the old codger's scowl deepened. Augie's bald head glinted under the light as he sauntered over from the other side of the gym where he'd been rolling his eyes at the media hubbub. But that was just a front. For his curmudgeonly ways, the man had welcomed him into the old East London boxing gym when he was nothing but a mouthy fourteen-year-old in need of an arse-kicking. The man was like a father to him. And he recognized the look on his trainer's face.

Augie entered the ring, playing the part of the watchful coach, then stopped a foot or so away from him, positioning his body so the bag would hide him from the photographers and cameramen. He removed the toothpick from his mouth and slipped it into his breast pocket. "For the bloody life of me, Erasmus, I still cannot believe you agreed to this. And tighten up, boyo. You're wobblier than a thirteen-year-old who snuck his first pint."

Boyo.

That word was Aug's tell. The sign that the wry quarter-

Welsh part of his trainer had broken through and wasn't bloody amused with the British Beast's performance.

Narrowing his gaze, Raz gave a slight nod, acknowledging the man's cheeky comment. Blowing out a hard breath, he executed four powerful jabs as camera flashes erupted into bursts of light.

Good old Aug—crusty as ever, the man never let money or fame change him.

Well, maybe it had a bit.

Augie was why he'd come to Denver to train—which was no small thing. The last place he pictured the bloke was here, running a fancy boxing gym in Denver. It was a far cry from the dank boxing spot he'd owned back in East London. But life had moved on, and Augie with it.

Here's the thing.

He'd lost touch with most everyone in his life, Augie included.

No, saying he'd *lost touch* with the man wasn't exactly what happened.

During the three years he'd spent wallowing in regret, shirking his responsibilities as a father, and screwing anything with a nice arse and a pulse, he'd stopped taking the man's calls. Despite everything he'd owed his trainer, he'd shut Aug out with the rest of the world.

Yeah, he'd been a real knob, a true prick.

But when he finally picked up the phone to ask Aug to train him again, he couldn't believe where life had taken the man.

During those three years where his life had come to a grinding halt, Augie, who he thought would remain a lifelong bachelor, had fallen in love with a woman he'd met online—a geologist named Luanne. The old man had picked up, left his gym in the UK, and moved to the states. He'd opened this place shortly after he arrived. It was a very un-Augie-like thing to do.

The man clearly had a secret side and was a testament to the *old dog, new trick* saying.

Which begged him to ask the question.

Could he do a one-eighty with his life like Aug had? Was happiness even possible for him?

Could lightning strike twice?

An unsettling shiver ran down his spine.

That was his answer.

His path was set in stone.

Fight. Win. Repeat.

Love wasn't part of the equation.

He glanced at his trainer, knowing the cameras were following his every move. He couldn't show it, but he asked himself the same question Aug had posed—a question he'd asked himself every day since he'd arrived in Denver.

What the bloody hell was he doing?

Actually, he knew the answer. It wasn't rocket science to decipher.

He was here because of his ego. If he wasn't a winner, then what the bloody hell was he? Only a winner was worthy of her —the woman he'd loved and lost.

But he wasn't performing like a champion.

Thanks to the cards that life had dealt him, Augie was right. He was a wobbly git who could barely tell up from down and left from right. Like a ship adrift, he'd lost his moorings. Unsteady and unstable, his true north was nowhere to be found.

Six months ago, he'd been back in England in his second Chelsea flat—his bachelor pad. But that night, he didn't have a carnal itch to scratch. Fighting another bout of insomnia, he'd made the mistake of scrolling through social media. To his agent's disappointment, he didn't do much online. His private life was private, and he wasn't one of those idiots who posted every time they took a shite. But that night, he'd seen a post—no, not just a post, a challenge.

A challenge from the current heavyweight champ, Silas Scott.

The Irish Snake, Silas Scott, is the true King of the Ring. The fossil of a fighter, Erasmus Cress, wouldn't dare face me in the square.

He'd read the post, then, as if his hands had a mind of their own, he'd hammered out a reply.

Name the time and the place, wanker. I'll be there.

He'd hit enter, and with one tap of his finger, he'd ignited a sports-media frenzy.

Turns out, Silas Scott has a couple million followers—followers that included prominent promoters. The internet exploded, and before you could say Bob's your uncle, he'd agreed to fight.

The Snake versus the Lion.

The matchup of the century.

This fair-haired, Irish-born Silas Scott was five years younger than him, two inches shorter, and slippery like his moniker, but he wasn't unbeatable. He had weaknesses. While the Snake could bob and weave and duck a punch, he couldn't handle a pummeling. A smart, well-timed combination could lay the bloke out flat.

The question was, was Erasmus Cress the fighter who could execute that punishing takedown? Oh, he was still as strong as an ox. Strength wasn't his problem, but they were back to Aug's words again.

Tighten up, boyo. You're wobblier than a thirteen-year-old who snuck his first pint.

Aug saying that he was wobbly was being generous.

Thanks to the bloody soundtrack in his head, he couldn't tap into his inner control—that focused balance he'd come to innately before the world crashed in on him.

One thing was for sure. He wouldn't beat Silas Scott without it.

The camera flashes continued as he danced around the bag, throwing a right hook, then a left, and giving the media what they wanted. This promo blitz was a taste of what was to come —a little piece of the dog and pony show that was modern professional boxing. He continued with a round of uppercuts when his phone buzzed an incoming text from over on a shelf that housed a row of towels. He looked from his mobile to Aug, and the man gave him a slight nod.

Unless it was an emergency, there was a good chance it wasn't his granny Fin calling. Seven hours ahead, it was barely three thirty in the morning in the UK, but it could be Madelyn Malone. Like it or not, he'd been on pins and needles since she'd mentioned she'd found his nanny match.

Augie planted himself in front of the bag and eyed the press. "I think we've worked the British Beast long enough tonight. Any questions for me, boyos?" the trainer called, taking the spotlight.

"Are you training the Lion as hard as you used to?" came the first question.

Augie huffed. "What do you think I've been doing with the Lion for the last five months? Playing patty cake and whipping up a little Yorkshire pudding?"

A low chuckle floated through the room.

For a crotchety old geezer, Augie knew his way around the press. With his arms still folded and a drip of mustard on his wrinkled white button-up shirt and the sleeves rolled to his elbows, he came off as that cantankerous uncle everybody secretly loved, and the media wasn't immune.

Raz stepped out of the ring and removed his gloves. Using his teeth to unwind the tape from his fists, he checked his phone. There was a text, but it wasn't from Madelyn or Granny Fin. He surveyed the room as another chuckle escaped from the men gathered around his trainer. He could take a few moments. Aug had the press eating out of his hands. He had a second to breathe and deal with the gits texting him—gits who were as chatty as a bloody sewing circle. He plucked his hoodie from a hook on the wall, zipped it over his bare torso, then opened what he liked to call the bloody prick group chat.

Bloody Music Prick Landon Paige: Have you talked to Madelyn? Did she introduce you to the nanny yet? It has to happen soon. Your son's coming in a couple of days, right?

Two days, to be exact.

Bloody Nerd Prick Rowen Gale: Let me know if you want to sign your son up for any summer camps. We've got Phoebe signed up for a few in Denver and a couple in Aspen.

Raz's pulse kicked up as a thread of anxiety wove its way around his heart.

He didn't know if his son would even be interested in a summer camp. He loved his son. Of course, he did. The boy was as smart as a whip. He could do anything he wanted—be a doctor or a scientist. But over the last several months, the lad had fixated on boxing, and the last thing he wanted was for the boy to follow in his footsteps.

That was never the plan.

Boxing was a brutal sport, but it was all he knew.

On the other hand, Sebastian had options that didn't include bruised ribs and bloody noses.

But the older Sebastian got, the more the boy wanted to be like him.

And he couldn't have that.

He didn't know what else to do besides put distance between them.

He hadn't seen his son since he'd left five months ago to train with Augie. Yes, he could tell himself that Sebastian was in school and that he didn't want to disrupt the boy's schedule. But now the lad was off for the summer, and with Granny Fin insisting they come to the states, he'd run out of excuses. The clock had run out on his reclusive respite.

Change was on the horizon, and he'd need to adjust to life with not only his granny and his son again but a nanny under his roof. He swallowed hard.

He'd have to remember one rule with whomever Madelyn matched him with.

Under no circumstances could he shag the nanny.

It shouldn't be hard to follow.

But the stats told another story.

Out of the nanny match men's group, two of the men, Rowen Gale, a nerdy tech wanker, and Mitch Elliott, a famous chef wanker, had already been matched with nannies.

But there was more.

Rowen and Mitch were currently engaged to those nannies. Yeah, Rowen and Penny Fennimore and Mitch and Charlotte Ames were nauseatingly happy.

Cheers to them. Truth be told, Penny and Charlotte were terrific women. But he wasn't looking for that type of match.

No bloody way was he falling for a nanny.

When Madelyn had messaged him about finding a suitable candidate, he knew one thing for sure. He wouldn't be proposing marriage to this woman. No way! He'd had his one perfect love, and despite his strength and with every resource at his disposal, he'd still lost her.

He'd lost his Meredith.

Christ, he missed her every day.

She would have known what he should do to bond with his son. She would have understood how to guide him in the right direction. Meredith was intelligent, artistic, and valued volunteering and community service. Those qualities were part of Sebastian's DNA. The boy would have to see the better path was to be less like his father and more like his mother.

His beautiful, vivacious mother.

Raz banished the thoughts, tucking away the memories of her not quite blue and not quite green eyes and her dark flowing hair.

She was gone.

As far as he was concerned, women were for fucking and forgetting now. That's the way it had to be. And it had been that way right up until a pair of amber eyes lassoed his pitiful soul.

Stop.

He stared hard at his mobile, trying to get Libby Lamb out of his head when dots appeared on the screen.

Bloody Nerd Prick Rowen Gale: Regarding your pending nanny situation. I could hack into Madelyn's phone and see what I could learn. Once I have the nanny's name, I can hack into her accounts. It would take less than five minutes.

Raz shook his head as more dots appeared, and another text from Rowen flashed on the screen.

Bloody Nerd Prick Rowen Gale: Sorry, Raz. Penny tells me I can't do that—the hacking part.

But we can help you out with the kid camp information.

How did that man survive before he had Penny?

Bloody Music Prick Landon Paige: If we had her name, we could see if she's in one of my fan clubs. There are over 3.4 million Landon Paige fans worldwide. Just saying...

Bloody Nerd Prick Rowen Gale: Sorry, Landon, Penny again says there will be no hacking into fan clubs. She also says you only have 3.2 million followers.

Bloody Music Prick Landon Paige: I lost followers?!?!

Bloody Chef Prick Mitch Elliott: I'm in the middle of a damned dinner rush, and you guys are texting me about hacking and fan clubs?

Bloody Chef Prick Mitch Elliott: Raz, want me to have a couple of grilled cheese sandwiches sent over to the gym for you and Augie?

Raz emitted a low growl. These bloody American knobs.

Erasmus Cress: It's a cheese toastie, you culinary wanker.

Bloody Chef Prick Mitch Elliott: My sandwich. My name. What's the nanny situation?

In any other world, would Erasmus Cress be chatting it up on his mobile like a preteen with a nerd, a chef, and a heartthrob?

No.

Did he like these blokes?

No.

All right, maybe he liked them a bit. There's something to

be said about seeing the change in the men who'd been matched. Did it warrant an Augie-sized eye roll? Yeah, but he understood it—and understood he couldn't have it. He checked on Aug. The press was still laughing at something the codger had said.

He stared at the screen. He wasn't about to tell them he was nearly coming out of his skin with anticipation.

Erasmus Cress: No word yet on the nanny.

Dots instantly appeared.

Bloody Chef Prick Mitch Elliott: Be prepared, man. Madelyn sent me on a wild goose chase to find Charlotte, but looking back, I wouldn't change a thing. She's made me a better man. You never know—your match could be the match that changes everything.

It was nearly impossible to tell that, a few months ago, Mitch was one of the angriest, hotheaded chaps he'd ever met.

Erasmus Cress: Giving up cooking to write commercials for dating apps, are you, Chef? It must be all that cheese you use on your cheese toasties going to your head.

He'd played it off, but emotion clogged his throat. This nanny would be a nanny. Nothing more and nothing less. There was too much at stake. If he didn't want to be written off as a loser in the annals of boxing history, he had to regain his focus and find the equilibrium he'd lost. He started to type, telling the men there would be no falling for the help when Aug called to him from across the room.

"Raz, want to stop gawking at titties on your bloody mobile?" Augie gave him a look that said, get your arse in gear, lad. We're working.

"We have a few minutes left before we need the Lion to get

back to his training," Briggs announced when a reporter raised his hand.

"What about a few questions for the British Beast?" the man called.

This was part of the game. They billed this as a spur-of-the-moment photo-op only event, but just like concert-goers understood that the artist would reemerge for an encore, the sports press knew the star athlete would take a few questions at the end.

Raz pocketed his phone, then sauntered over, playing the part of the aloof champion. "Yeah, I'll bite."

"You're training here with Augie. Do you plan on staying in Denver?" a man called.

Raz cleared his throat. "Not sure. I'm playing it by ear."

"There are reports you've visited a few private elementary schools in the area. Is your son coming to live with you?" a man with slicked-back hair tossed out.

The muscles in Raz's neck tightened.

Bloody press.

"Let's stay on topic. We're here because of the epic matchup between the Lion and the Snake. Stick to the fight, chaps," Briggs chided, but Raz had a different approach.

"My son is none of your bloody business, you nosy twat," he growled, pinning the weasel of a reporter with his gaze.

"What about your wife? This will be your first fight since she died, right? That is, unless you skip out on this one like you did the last one. Any comment on that, Lion?" the absolute sod of a human being continued. He had to be from one of the UK tabloids that lived to tell half-truths and rip people's lives apart for sport.

"Oh, I have something to say about that, you greasy-haired sod," he roared, his blood running hot.

"Erasmus," Augie cautioned under his breath, but Raz couldn't let the sleazeball off so easily.

He took a hulking step forward, towering over the reporter when a rhythmic ringing cut through the tension in the room.

"What is that?" a voice mused.

"A pair of symbols?" another threw out.

A cameraman addressed the group. "No, it's some fit chick with a gong."

Raz's jaw dropped as his heart swelled in his chest. "Bloody hell, it's her," he murmured, disbelief coating the words.

FOUR

ERASMUS

LIBBY LAMB, what in the bloody hell are you up to?

Raz shifted his focus from the wanker reporter to the woman with jet-black hair. But his fascination with her quickly turned to concern.

She taught at the yoga studio next door, that much he knew. And she did ring that blasted thing. That's how he'd know when she was there. The sound would ripple through the wall. It drove him mad. Instantly, he'd be off his game—well, more off than usual. Sloppy and distracted, the thought of those amber eyes searching his soul was enough to send him reeling.

Barefoot, she stood on the sidewalk outside the boxing gym, clanging away with a large tote slumped over next to her on the pavement. In the glow of the outdoor lighting, he caught the shimmer of a gold sports bra peeking through a red, draped top and white leggings with her jet-black hair piled on top of her head. Raven tendrils danced across the apples of her cheeks as she massacred that bloody instrument.

"Is that lady okay?" a photographer asked, snapping a shot.

"Somebody should call the police. She must have escaped from a psychiatric facility," came another musing.

Raz shook his head, agitation prickling through his veins. "Hell's bloody bells," he mumbled, weaving his large frame through the sea of journalists, cameramen, and photographers. He had to send her on her way. She didn't need the media capturing this yoga tantrum on film.

He opened the door, prepared to tell her to take her crazy elsewhere, when she stopped banging the gong and pointed the mallet at him.

What did she want—a gong duel? Mallets at sunrise?

In the hazy halo of light, her amber eyes flashed penetrating rage. He could feel the intensity coming off her in angry waves.

"Don't say a word. Not a word, beefcake. I need to demonstrate a technique to my class, and you are the inspiration," she bit out.

Beefcake?

That's what she called him when she'd popped in, and he'd given her the cold shoulder.

He scanned the posh yoga studio and found a group of men and women holding yoga mats with their heads cocked to the side, looking as confused as he was.

"Class, this is an example of rage yoga," Libby continued, her voice rising a tenuous octave.

Rage yoga? Was that even a thing?

He studied her closely and noticed a white substance caked on her shoulder.

What the hell was that?

Bird shit?

Was she mad at a bird? Did she contract a bird virus that caused her brain to malfunction?

But before another thought could cross his mind, Libby raised her arms as if she were challenging the moon to a brawl, then let loose with a scream that would have put a horror movie howler to shame. Primal and undeniably visceral, the screech of a sound blanketed the area. He wouldn't have been surprised if his granny Fin heard her from across the pond.

"I am reclaiming my chi! I desperately need to revive my O!" she shouted, then dropped to her knees dramatically as another bloodcurdling shriek cut through the air.

This tiny thing had quite a set of lungs.

He didn't know what the bloody hell this chi and O business was, but before he could stop himself, he sprinted to her, gripped her arms, then lifted her to her feet. Wild-eyed, she stared up at him. Those amber eyes burned with such fury, if he'd slapped a pair of boxing gloves on her, then tossed her in the ring, he'd bet everything he had that her opponent would be out for the count before the bell rang.

Unfortunately, he seemed to be the opponent she'd set her sights on.

He couldn't look away.

He couldn't move an inch.

Despite the very real possibility that this woman was on the verge of knocking his lights out, he tightened his hold. He'd never touched her before. He'd only seen her a handful of times, but he hadn't expected the pulse of energy to pass between them like two live wires popping and hissing as they went head-to-head.

The need to gather her into his arms and press his lips to hers tore through him. Her breasts heaved as she inhaled shallow gulps of air as if she couldn't quite put together how she'd gotten here. He stroked her arm with the pad of his thumb as they froze, gazes locked, neither seeming to want to sever this strange, almost cosmic connection.

He wasn't a fan of spiritual mumbo jumbo. But in that moment, where time stood still, she felt it, too. He could see it written on her face as it rendered her mute. He drank in the comfort of her nearness as the rise and fall of her chest slowed. Their breaths mingled in the space between them, and they found a rhythm, a synchronicity. It was as if they'd left their bodies and were fused together in some alternate reality. The storm in her eyes calmed, and just like that, she peered into his soul. He felt her presence with every fiber of his being. A man could disappear into the pools of heavenly amber and lose himself in the depths of this woman's bewitching glow and her healing light.

Could Libby be his light?

He blinked as the myriad of flashes illuminated her face in pops of light, breaking the spell.

Bloody hell. They had a shit ton of journalists watching from a few paces away, gobbling up this moment.

He caught his breath and regained a fraction of stability. "What's this wham, bam, thank you, Libby Lamb business? Libby, have you fallen completely off your rocker, babe?"

Babe?

He'd only called Meredith by that name. But he didn't have a second to work out the slip. The fury in Libby's eyes returned as she wriggled free of his hold and took a step back.

She feigned surprise. "You do know who I am, you O-stealing, chi-rattling, muscle-flexing beefcake!"

What was her deal with chi and the letter O? Had she entered some yoga state of complete insanity?

Best to play it cool.

He cleared his throat. "Yeah, I know who you are."

He hoped that declaration would take some of the crazy out of her sails.

It didn't.

She stared up at the moon. "Seventy-five days ago, this beefcake chose to bang and clang and roar like a beast while I tried to teach a yoga class next door."

She'd stirred up a well of emotions within him. The pull had almost been too much to resist.

But he couldn't bloody say that.

He glanced over his shoulder at the press and the disturbed yoga patrons, then lowered his voice. "Babe, who are you talking to?"

Blooming idiot! There he was with the babe again.

She banged her gong. "I'm communing with the universe."

She'd be communing with a padded cell if he couldn't calm her down.

He took in the scene.

Cameras flashing and tape rolling, the sports media was lapping up this catastrophe while some of the yoga crew held out their phones, documenting the melee.

She poked him with the mallet. "And don't you dare call me babe, baby, or babykins."

"Babykins? What the bloody hell is that?" he shot back.

Confusion marred her features. "I don't know. But I ban you from calling me those names. And sugar plum. It's off the list, too," she added with a huff.

The list?

On second thought, maybe a padded cell was exactly what Libby Lamb needed.

"I can't call you sugar plum either?" he pressed. "Isn't that a fairy? Yeah, there's a sugar plum fairy. It's from the Nutcracker. Do you have a thing against fairies, or are you just nuts? You're dressed like you fancy Christmas, though. You'd have to take away the bird shit on your shoulder, of course, unless getting crapped on by birds is something you're into."

She gasped. "I have nothing against fairies, nuts, or Christmas. Nor do I have any weird bird fetishes. I chose this outfit strategically to harness the spiritual power of color, and nuts are an excellent source of fiber, fat, and protein. And everyone loves fairies. It's a given fact."

"Can't argue with that," he said under his breath, hardly able to believe they'd shifted the conversation to winter holiday nut fairies covered in bird shit. Still, it was better than having her bang that gong and scream at the moon.

She shook her head as if she were trying to rid her brain of the crazy her mouth was spewing. "Forget the fairy nuts. You don't get to call me anything."

He reared back. "Fairy nuts?" Now there was something nobody wanted to picture in their heads.

"You know what I mean," she hissed.

He crossed his arms. "That's not exactly fair, though, is it?"

"What do you mean?" she barked, not backing down.

"You're telling me I can't give you a pet name while you've called me beefcake more than a few times?"

Beefcake.

It was a ludicrous word, a slight for sure, but something was amusing about her lobbing the two syllables at him. Something that got his heart pumping and his cock...

Dammit! Did it turn him on?

She lifted her chin. "You deserve to be called a beefcake after what you took from me."

He threw up his hands, frustration mixing with the completely inappropriate arousal coursing through his body. "I barely know you, Libby. What could I take from you?"

"My O," she seethed.

They were back to the alphabet. "You've got to stop acting mental, plum," he replied, trying to think of anything that would calm her down.

"You think this is mental?" she threw back, giving him a grin that rivaled the criminally insane.

"Yeah," he answered with an arrogant smirk. "You're waving

your hands around and yelling letters at the moon in front of a crowd. You're the bloody definition of acting mental. How about this, plum? Why don't you put on some trainers like a normal human being, take a walk, and cool off?" he offered, but he should have known better than to go full-on cocky boxing bastard beefcake.

Like an out-of-her-mind nut fairy glittering in a gold bra, Libby cackled like a bloody witch, grabbed her bag, then reached inside. "Oh, I'll show you mental. This is what happens when a beefcake rocks a person's chi, then rips the O right out of her. You end up with sixteen of these. Sixteen of these, and none of them can get the job done!" she shouted, and God help him, she whipped a giant vibrator out of the bag and held it above her head like she was the dirty version of the Statue of Liberty—Libby, the Statue of Trying to Get Off.

"Jesus, have you lost the plot completely?" he cried, taking a step back.

"No, you stupidly sexy heap of beefcake. I've made this abundantly clear. It's your fault that I've lost my O." Libby wound up, then chucked the vibrator at him. It cartwheeled through the air, headed straight between his eyes. He ducked as another, then another vibrating sex toy zoomed past his shoulder.

How was he supposed to stop this X-rated version of Mary Poppins with her carpetbag full of dildos? The woman was relentless. He barely had time to react as a rainbow-colored hunk of vibrating plastic rocketed right for his crotch.

"Not my dangly bits, plum," he called, turning away as the vibrator got him right in the hip. "Ouch!" he cried like a lad bawling in the street.

"Oh, your dangly bits will pay," she growled, chucking another.

He fended off the sex toy as it joined the others, littered

about the sidewalk. "How many of those are you going to throw at me?"

Like a crazed beast, she pawed through her bag, then looked up, and pinned him with her wild eyes. "Sixteen! And I plan on throwing every single one of them at you, beefcake. You've ruined everything! My teaching gigs, my apartment, my sanity! Thanks to you, my karma is crap, and I've lost it all," she exclaimed, hurling another vibrator.

The woman might be half out of her mind, but she had one hell of an arm.

One after another after another, she launched vibrator after vibrator into the air. The hum of the vibration added a mechanical twist to the scuffle as if she were propelling cock-sized bombs at him, left and right.

"What's she throwing at the Lion?" came a voice.

Bollocks!

He couldn't let the press photograph him dodging flying vibrators.

He sprinted back and forth, collecting the pulsating tubes from the ground, cradling them in his arms. It was a damned strenuous workout, bobbing and weaving and sprinting and dashing to scoop them up as Libby maintained her rapid-fire pace. Something small came at him. A rock? He juggled the vibrators in his arms, snatched the stone out of the air, and shoved it in his pocket.

"Plum, you've got to stop," he panted, glancing up at Libby as the golden glow from the streetlights gave way to a red and blue flashing hue. He blinked, and before he knew it, the screech of tires and the smell of burnt rubber hijacked his senses.

"Drop the weapons. Step away from the bag," a stern voice commanded.

He glanced to his left and had to do a double take.

This vibrator tossing frenzy had escalated to the next level: police involvement.

He stared at the vehicle as two officers exited the squad car, guns drawn.

Bloody guns.

He could not get shot dead with his arms filled to the gills with sixteen sex toys.

"You, the big guy in the hoodie. Drop your weapons. Hands in the air," the taller of the two male officers called, shining a torch in his face. Blasted light! He couldn't shield his eyes. That would mean dropping the bloody vibrators.

"They're not weapons, officer," he called.

"We've got a bag. This is a possible bomb situation," the shorter officer cried, pointing his torch at Libby's yoga tote.

"Bomb!" Libby screeched as the onlookers inhaled an audible, collective gasp.

"Are you confirming the existence of an explosive device, miss?" the cop barked, turning the torch on Libby.

"A what?" she stammered, looking around. Shock and utter confusion were written on her face as if aliens had returned her to her body and thrown her into a dire situation.

Honestly, he probably had the same expression. Things bloody well had become dire.

He needed to defuse the situation. "There are no bombs or weapons, officers. This is a misunderstanding," he said, keeping Libby in his sights.

Wide-eyed, with her hand pressed to her chest, she nodded.

"Plum, tell the nice officers that you aren't carrying any weapons and that you wish no one any harm."

She continued to nod, her head wobbling rapidly like one of those bobblehead dolls. "Erasmus is correct. There are no—"

"Wait a second," the taller officer called, lowering his weapon. "I recognize one of those. We don't have a bomb threat on our hands, Joey. Not if the big guy is holding what I think he is." The officer holstered his weapon. "I'm going to approach you, sir."

"Approach away. Like I said, I haven't got any weapons on me," he replied, and never in his life had he been so happy to have an armful of sexual stimulation devices.

The officer advanced slowly, then studied the cadre of vibrators pulsing and convulsing like a den of rabid dildos. "That's the Rainbow Screamer," the cop said, his tone losing the whole I'm-about-to-shoot-you quality.

Raz glanced at the buffet of plastic cocks cradled against his abdomen. "The, what?"

The officer pointed to the colorful vibrator. "The rainbow one. My girlfriend has this." The cop leaned in like they'd become best mates. "She loves it. We both do. She takes it everywhere—even on vacation."

Raz gave the officer a weak grin. "Cheers, mate. Here's to good times on holiday."

The shorter officer checked Libby's bag. "All clear, George. We've got a yoga mat, a little Buddha statue, a tiny gong, and a pair of sneakers."

"Bring the bag here, Joey," the cop directed.

Raz breathed a sigh of relief as the shorter cop handed Libby's yoga tote to the taller one.

"Dump the items inside, sir," the officer directed.

Happy to comply, he followed the officer's command and breathed a sigh of relief. Yes, this looked insane, but no one was any worse for wear. The best-case scenario? They bid goodbye to the men in blue and pretended like this never happened.

"Miss, would you join us?" the shorter officer called to Libby. "Stand right next to the big guy and tell us your name."

She hurried over and saddled in by his side. "I'm Libby Lamb."

"Lamb? Are you related to a Connolly Lamb?" the officer asked, eyeing her.

Libby swallowed hard. "I don't know who that is."

"And you?" the cop asked, turning to him.

"Erasmus Cress."

"The Lion? The British Beast?" the taller cop asked, cocking his head to the side, as the shorter one repeated their names into the walkie-talkie strapped to his vest.

"Yeah, that's me," he answered, but he was far more concerned with making sure Libby was all right than meeting a fan. He touched her shoulder—the one that wasn't covered in bird shit. "You okay, plum? Got that crap karma sorted?"

Trembling from the onslaught of adrenaline, she leaned into him. And God help him, he couldn't keep from wrapping his arm around her.

"That was quite a convergence of energy—truly an astral projection. My conscious emptied out of me and flowed into the cosmos," she replied, making no bloody sense, but she wasn't assaulting anyone with plastic dicks or howling at the moon. So, all in all, it was an improvement.

"Much ado about nothing, right officers?" he remarked, pulling the policemen's flummoxed gazes from the yoga nutter curled into his side.

"Not exactly. We still have to take you in," the taller cop answered.

Double bollocks.

"You do?" Libby shrieked, gripping the edge of his hoodie and balling the fabric in her hand as she anchored herself to him.

"What are the charges?" he asked.

"For one thing, the two of you are disturbing the peace, and we also observed you engaged in lewd conduct," the shorter cop announced.

"Lewd conduct? What makes you think we were engaged in lewd conduct?" Libby stammered.

A good question.

"We observed a sexually charged act intent on stimulating another in front of a person or persons," the taller cop rattled off like he was giving his usual order at a coffee shop. Bloody hell! Did people throw sex toys at each other so often in this city that the cops had the ordinance memorized?

Bugger. This was bad.

"That's not what was happening. I can assure you of that," Libby pleaded.

"We saw what we saw, Miss Lamb. Getting off on throwing sex toys at your boyfriend in front of a group of bystanders is considered lewd behavior," the taller cop explained while the shorter one mumbled into his radio.

"But I'm not his girlfriend," Libby stammered.

The tall officer's demeanor sharpened. "You throw vibrators at random people for fun? Be careful how you answer, miss. That's a crime, too."

This had gone tits up in a hot second.

"Libby, I've watched enough American crime dramas to know we need to stop talking and play nice," he cautioned.

"We're being arrested?" Libby blurted.

"You are," the shorter cop answered, then started reading them their bloody rights.

"Just give me a second. I need to let my friends know what's happening," Libby blathered, the words spilling out in a frantic tumble as she removed her mobile from her pocket and hammered out a quick text.

He watched as the light from her cell lit her face and pulled his mobile from his pocket. It wasn't a bad idea to reach out to friends. Rowen could hack into the police database and erase this, or Mitch could cook for the cops and charm them with his delicious food. Maybe Landon could sing or play guitar or piano—whatever the hell he did. Jesus, his thoughts were reeling as he banged out a message to the bloody prick chat group.

Erasmus Cress: How's your Friday night going, chaps? I'm getting arrested.

Brief, polite, and to the point. Quite British of him, if he should say so.

He pocketed his mobile, then glanced at the boxing gym. Augie stood there with his mouth ajar and a toothpick hanging from his lip.

"Hold tight, Raz. I'm working the phones to see what I can do," Briggs called, pacing across the pavement with two mobiles, one pressed to his ear as the agent stared at the other.

"Bloody hell, plum," he huffed. "What have you gotten us into?"

Libby released his hoodie and scoffed. "Do not blame me. This is a result of your cocky, beef-tastic karma. You put this energy out, and now we both have to pay for it."

The nerve of this woman.

"I can't believe you're blaming me for this. And by the way, girls don't seem to mind my cocky, beef-tastic ways," he snarled.

She barked a little laugh, brimming with skepticism. "Maybe that's true. But I'm no girl. I'm a woman. A woman who finds your arrogant act ridiculous and a danger to others' auras and sense of chi."

"There you go again, talking crazy! It's no wonder we're getting arrested," he chided as the officer gestured for them to put their hands behind their backs.

"Handcuffs!" he eked out.

"This is as much for your protection as it is for ours," the shorter cop replied, eyeing Libby warily. And the cop was right. The shaken, wounded bird version of the yoga babe had vanished, and in her place, this plum nutter looked ready to scratch his eyes out.

The click of the cuffs added to the snap and flash of a dozen photographers capturing this salacious moment.

What a bloody catastrophe!

Side by side with their arms pinned behind their back like shameful purveyors of lewd acts, the cops grabbed Libby's bag, marched them to the squad car, then helped them inside. George and Joey, their arresting officers for the evening, slid into the front seat. And just like that, they were off.

"How will I balance my chi after something like this?" she lamented, glaring up at him.

"I don't know," he replied. "How about chucking nipple clamps at random people on the street or spice it up with a cock ring. So many random options to consider when balancing chi."

Was he losing it, too? He didn't know a damn thing about balancing chi other than, when attempting to do it with sex toys, one could find themselves in handcuffs.

She stared into his eyes, her gaze softening. "This wasn't random," she said, the anger draining from her voice. "This was supposed to set everything right. The rage yoga should have dispelled the energy. I thought that's what Ida wanted me to do."

He couldn't look away. In the back of the squad car headed to the clink, he couldn't ignore her pain and frustration. Sure, she was bonkers, and who the hell was Ida? He sure didn't know. Ida could have been what she named her vibrators, or it could have been the name of the bird that shat on her shoulder. Nonetheless, her words tore into him. She was hurting, and more than that, she believed he was the cause of the pain. He needed to sort through her mystical gobbledygook and figure out what was going on.

"Why the vibrators, plum? Were those part of the dispelling

plan?" he pressed, leaning in. He could feel her warm breath and sensed her frenzied energy mingling with his. Then everything shifted, and the off-kilter vibe between them evened out like the sea calming after a storm. He'd never experienced peacefulness like this. Serenity thrummed through his body in gentle beats like pearls of rain.

"The vibrator thing happened in the heat of the moment," she answered, her voice barely a whisper.

The air transformed between them. As if he'd been entranced, he would have sworn that he could see the energy—a vibrant blue-violet hue engulfing them, cocooning them in their own private world. He focused on her face. She was doing it again, looking at him as if she saw every broken part. Like she could see what was beneath his cocky veneer. And those ripe lips of hers taunted him, called to him. Christ, the drive to kiss the bloody chi right out of her was impossible to ignore.

"Do you go everywhere with sixteen vibrators?" he asked, lowering his voice as he fell under her spell.

"Not usually," she replied, her eyelids fluttering closed.

The light came and went, illuminating her face, then casting her in darkness as the squad car wove its way through the city streets. One second, he could only make out the curve of her neck and the apples of her cheeks. The next, he saw everything. The brush of dark hair across her forehead, the plump set of her lips, the slight upturn on her button nose. She was a bloody stunner, even if she was the craziest woman he'd ever met. "Libby Lamb," he whispered, not knowing why, at that very instant, he wanted, no, needed to speak her name.

And then he got his answer.

The beginning of a smile tipped the edges of her lips, and bloody hell, watching her reaction to him simply saying her name sent the same jolt of victory through his veins as flattening an opponent in the ring. The ghost of a grin pulled at the corners of his mouth as his lips dusted hers—touching but not quite meeting. It had been ages since he'd savored the seconds before he kissed someone. But he could live here, in this blue violet-hued sacred space, anticipation tingling from the crown of his head to the tips of his toes.

Libby inhaled a slow, steady breath, melting into the moment with him. Could an almost-kiss border on erotic? The thought barely had a chance to bloom when one of the police officers cleared his throat—loudly. In the blink of an eye, the calming glow that had engulfed them evaporated as they pulled apart, their legs squeaking as they slid across the slick faux-leather seat—each to their own side.

"How about you cool it down and refrain from engaging in another lewd act in the back of a squad car," the tall cop barked over his shoulder.

Good bloody advice. What the hell did he think he was doing?

They rode the rest of the way in silence. He stared ahead, and reality set in. How many cameras had caught their vibrator-laden brawl? Twenty, thirty, forty? It could be streaming to a billion mobiles at this very moment. He could see the headlines.

British Beast Enjoys American Kink.

The Lion Wanted Victory, Got Vibrators.

The police station came into view. In one of the cones of light cast by the lampposts illuminating the front walk, he would have sworn he saw a flash of red entering the precinct. He shook his head. Red, blue, violet. What was next? Would a conga line of dancing rainbow vibrators shimmy across the street?

Get your head on straight, man.

The officers exited the car when another cop walked up to them. The three men chatted, glancing back at them, still safely restrained in the police cruiser.

"What do you think happens next?" Libby asked with a shake to her voice.

He sighed and stared at the roof of the car. "I don't know, plum. We wait."

"I messaged my friends," she offered.

"Penny, Charlotte, and Harper, right?"

She nodded. "Hopefully, they'll know what to do."

"What about your parents, plum? Will this throw them for a loop? Their perfect little yoga daughter getting pinched?"

She looked away, then swallowed hard. "I don't—" she began when the back doors of the vehicle swung open.

"Let's go," the shorter cop said, waving them out. The man had Libby's bag in his hands.

Ah, evidence.

"Are we getting booked?" he asked, maneuvering his large frame out of the car.

"I don't know what's going on with the two of you. It's bizarre," the man answered. "I've never had anything like this happen before."

"What does that mean?" Libby asked from the other side of the car as the taller officer unlocked her cuffs. She rubbed her wrist. "Can we go home?"

"No, the chief wants to see you," the shorter officer answered.

"The police chief wants to see us? Why would he want to do that?" Raz pressed as the cop uncuffed him. He couldn't make heads or tails about what was happening. Had Briggs come through? Had Rowen preemptively searched the police database for their arrest and overturned it?

"The chief is a *she*. And why do people feel the need to hurl sex toys at each other in front of an audience? Your guess is as good as mine, buddy," the taller cop answered, then gestured for them to enter the precinct.

They walked into the bustling station, and the shorter cop gestured to a bench, then handed Libby her bag. "Have a seat. You can put on your shoes while you wait."

That's right. She'd been barefoot this entire time.

She unzipped her bag, then removed her trainers. He leaned back and ran his hands down his face when that flash of red returned.

But this wasn't a magical hue. No, it was bloody Madelyn Malone. She tossed the scarlet scarf over her shoulder as amusement glittered in her eyes.

What was there to be amused about?

The matchmaker glanced between himself and Libby, busy tying her shoes.

"Erasmus Cress," Madelyn said, her rich Eastern European accent massaging each syllable of his name. "You've beaten me to the punch."

Libby looked up from tying her laces. "Madelyn?" she uttered, bewilderment woven into the word.

"What do you mean, I've beaten you to the punch?"

"I had planned on introducing you to your nanny candidate tomorrow morning," she replied smoothly.

Did she track him down to a police station to discuss nanny business?

No, there was more to it. There always was with this woman.

"And?" he pressed as electricity thrummed in his veins.

A slow smirk bloomed on Madelyn's lips. "She's seated right next to you."

FIVE

ERASMUS

"LIBBY LAMB IS THE NANNY CANDIDATE?" he shrieked like a schoolgirl.

No way. No bloody way.

He turned to Libby and watched the color drain from her cheeks.

"I don't know anything about this, Raz. I never agreed to nanny for you." She flicked her gaze to the nanny matchmaker. "This is the first I'm hearing about it. You never even spoke to me, Madelyn."

Unbothered, Madelyn smoothed the lone lock of silver that cut through the maze of her dark tumbling curls. "But I did. I emailed you both a few hours ago and proposed the nanny match."

"You sent us an email? That's it?" he asked, his tone taking on an accusatory bend.

"You sent Penny to Gale Gaming, not knowing anything about the guy," Libby chimed.

He nodded. "And with Mitch, you had him searching for a golden key that led to Charlotte thinking that he'd kidnapped her."

"Very true," Madelyn agreed, looking bloody pleased with herself.

"You're saying all you did for us was bang out an email?" He had to check. After what Rowen and Mitch went through, he'd expected his nanny introduction would be a little more involved than a simple correspondence.

"Look for yourself," Madelyn suggested.

He removed his mobile from his pocket as Libby did the same. And there it was. Sent two hours ago, before Libby threw a screaming wobbly outside the gym, an email from Madelyn Malone sat unopened in his inbox, sandwiched between emails from his sisters and Granny Fin.

"Dear Ms. Lamb," Libby read, "as you probably know, thanks to your friendship with Charlotte Ames and Penny Fennimore, I'm tasked with finding a nanny match for Erasmus Cress. I believe you'd be an excellent candidate to assist him in caring for his six-year-old son, Sebastian." Libby rested the mobile in her lap and turned to him. "Your son's name is Sebastian?"

"It is." He stared into the depths of her amber eyes. They welled with such kindness it nearly cracked his cocksure mask.

"Is he like you?" she pressed.

He wasn't expecting her to ask him that. And how was he supposed to answer? He swallowed past the lump in his throat. "Not if I can help it."

It hurt like hell to admit, but he couldn't lie to her.

The kindness in her eyes morphed into a curious glint.

"Does that make the job more or less attractive?" he asked.

Was he considering this? Did he want this yoga nutter to become part of his life?

The uptick in his pulse and the semi he had going on in his boxing trunks answered for him. He shifted his weight on the bench, then forced himself to imagine what Granny Fin would say if she learned he'd been hauled into an American police station for lewd behavior. Now there's the way to wreck one's libido.

His cock *should* be the last thing on his mind. Unfortunately, when it came to Libby Lamb, his cock had quite an appreciation for her perfect arse and that bloody cute as hell button nose.

He zeroed in on Madelyn, resolving to push any lewd thoughts of the yoga beauty out of his mind. "I figured there would be more drama in the whole nanny selection process," he said, schooling his features.

Madelyn surveyed the hallway as two cops wrangling a large unruly man lumbered past them. "I think you'll both agree that you've added enough drama for one night. You are, of course, on the brink of incarceration."

Bollocks!

Between Libby's amber eyes, the semi between his legs, and Madelyn Malone ambushing them in the bloody police station, he'd nearly forgotten that he was on the cusp of being charged with disturbing the peace and lewd behavior.

"Despite your rocky start, I have some good news. I've arranged a remedy for your precarious situation," the woman added.

"A remedy?" Libby echoed when an officer walked up to them.

"This is for you, Ms. Malone," the policewoman said, then handed the nanny matchmaker a note. Madelyn scanned the slip of paper, then nodded as her lips twisted into a knowing smirk. "And the chief will see you and your clients now," the officer finished before heading down the hall.

"Excellent," Madelyn remarked, dropping the paper into her purse. "Let's have a chat with Letty."

"Letty?" he asked as he and Libby came to their feet.

"Letty Ramirez, Denver's Chief of Police," Madelyn answered casually.

He shared a look with Libby. "You're friends with the chief of police?"

"I have many, many friends," the woman answered with a nonchalant flick of her wrist before heading down the hallway.

"Raz, what's happening?" Libby asked, grabbing her bag of sex toys as they hurried to keep up with the well-connected senior citizen.

He ran his hands through his hair. "I don't know."

"You didn't know about the match—about me?"

He was still reeling from that revelation. Sure, Madelyn had sent the email, but he only checked his inbox a few times a day. And what would have happened if he'd seen the match-maker's note? Would he have hired Libby to be his son's nanny? Then again, Libby hadn't agreed to anything yet, either. Nothing was set in stone. What did he want? He didn't know. In the last hour, his entire world had been turned upside down.

"Raz?" she whispered, and God help him. He liked hearing her say his name.

Bugger! Get it together.

"Madelyn mentioned she'd found a candidate a few weeks ago. She didn't say anything about the nanny's identity. Rowen offered to hack into Madelyn's mobile to learn more, but Penny wouldn't let him."

Libby released a nervous little laugh, then stilled. "It sounds like them."

"It does," he replied, studying her face. He forgot what it was like to have this with a woman. Back in school, he and Mere had quite a social circle. Pints at the pub, laughing as they traded stories and gave each other shit. Back in the day, when he didn't worry about the press or sponsors or titles—back when there was joy, real make-you-smile-the-moment-you-woke-up joy.

Do not go there.

He released a shaky breath. This couldn't work—not with Libby Lamb. How the hell was he supposed to concentrate with her buzzing around his orbit, wearing form-fitting yoga clothes and those little sports bras. This gold number she had on was already doing a number on him. A bloody twenty-four-seven hard-on would zap his energy before he'd even donned his boxing gloves.

"We don't want to keep the chief waiting. Not when your freedom hangs in the balance," Madelyn called, gesturing for them to hurry up.

How did he keep forgetting that good old Mr. Short Cop and Mr. Tall Cop didn't look keen on letting them bugger off scot-free?

Madelyn knocked on a mahogany door with *Chief Letitia Ramirez* stenciled in bold white letters. "I'm back, Letty."

Back? What had Madelyn and the chief discussed?

Madelyn opened the door for them to enter. "Go on."

"Have a seat. I'm Chief Ramirez. I presume you're Libby Lamb, and you're Erasmus Cress," the chief said, pointing to a set of chairs in front of her imposing desk. Letitia Ramirez crossed her arms. With her dark hair pulled into a tight bun, the woman's sharp, stone-faced demeanor gave nothing away. "You're fortunate that Madelyn speaks so highly of the two of you. I respect her opinion." The woman leaned forward. "How about we cut to the chase?"

"Okay," he answered, anticipation nearly tearing him apart as he shared a look with Libby.

"There is a way to chalk up tonight's charges as a misunderstanding," the chief explained, and bloody hell, that was a relief.

"That's exactly what it was, Chief Ramirez, a misunderstanding," he answered as Libby nodded. And bugger all, they were in the clear. He'd have to thank his granny Fin for introducing him to Madelyn. The woman and her vast collection of connections were worth her weight in bloody gold.

"And we're happy to do whatever you ask of us," Libby added.

"Are you up for volunteering to help the city?" the chief pressed, sharing a look with Madelyn, who stood a few feet away from them, observing closely.

At the mention of volunteering, he couldn't help but think of Mere.

What would she say if she could see him now?

"Absolutely, we'd be happy to volunteer," Libby answered, pulling him from his thoughts. He needed to be grateful they were getting off with a bit of community service. He could manage that. Hell, Briggs would probably find a way to publicize it.

"But understand this," the chief continued, "if you choose to decline the offer, you will be charged and booked."

"We understand, Chief Ramirez," he answered.

"Good, then I can give you these." The chief swiveled in her chair and removed two folded items from the shelf behind her. "You're officially Denver's *Asinines*."

"Ass in what?" he exclaimed.

What kind of bloody volunteering did this woman want them to do?

"Asinine, like something stupid or foolish?" Libby stammered as Chief Ramirez came from behind her desk and presented them with T-shirts printed with a donkey on the front.

"No, it's *Ass-in-Nine*," the woman clarified, without clarifying anything. She spoke slowly as if she were addressing a pair of asinine idiots, which, honestly, she may be doing exactly that because he still had no bloody idea what she was talking about.

"It's a nine-mile race that takes place in a small mountain town not far from Aspen called Rickety Rock," Madelyn added.

"You'll be representing Denver's first responders in the race. You do support the men and women who protect and serve this city, I presume?" the chief asked, her expression hardening, and there was only one acceptable answer.

He straightened in the chair like a schoolboy. "With all our hearts and twice on Thursdays."

Had he gone bonkers?

Possibly, but all things considered, this race had to be the best possible punishment compared to being labeled a sexual deviant.

"Just to be clear," he asked cautiously. "If we compete in a nine-mile race in the mountains, the charges against us will be dropped?"

Chief Ramirez nodded. "That's correct. The race is in about seven weeks. That'll give you plenty of time to train."

He sat back in the chair and crossed his legs. The anxiety that had built up in his chest gave way to relief that welcomed back the slightly smug, self-assured part of him. "No training needed, Chief. I could run nine miles in my sleep. I'm not sure if you recognize me, but I'm quite a big deal in the boxing world. I'm in excellent physical condition."

There it was. His trademark swagger was back.

Hello, British Beast! Good to see you, Lion!

"You're required to run the race together," the chief continued.

"That's not a problem. I can run nine miles, too," Libby answered.

He sized her up, slipping further into his boxing persona. Sure, Libby was fit as hell but stretching, banging gongs, and throwing sex toys didn't count as conditioning in his book. "You think you could run nine miles and keep up with me?"

She sharpened her gaze, those amber eyes boring into him like lasers. "If I can teach three ninety-minute power yoga classes in a row, then I'm in perfect shape to run nine *measly* miles."

The competitive part of him couldn't hold back. "You may be exaggerating there, plum. No need to fear, though. I can get you into shape." He turned to the chief. "If she had to walk, would that be a problem?" But before the chief could answer, Libby tugged on the sleeve of his hoodie.

"Hey, beefcake, I'm stronger than I look. I don't need a man to train me to do anything," she shot back, then bolted to her feet. "Do you mind if I make a little room? I'd like to demonstrate something," she asked, already pushing her chair against the wall.

What button did he push on the yoga nutter now?

The chief and Madelyn shared another knowing look. "Knock yourself out," Chief Ramirez answered, leaning against the side of her desk.

Libby moved a few more chairs out of the way, kicked off her shoes, then faced the group with her hands pressed together like she was auditioning to be a monk. She shot him an icy glare, peeled off her bird-shit-encrusted little red wrap, then tossed it to him. Inhaling a breath, her demeanor shifted as the anger in her eyes changed to a look of focused determination.

"*Eka hasta vrksasana.* One-handed tree pose," she announced.

This was not the time to teach a yoga class.

He shook his head. "It's called standing, and it won't help you run nine miles."

She ignored him, then as gracefully as a bloody swan, his yoga nutter folded forward and lifted her legs into the air.

"You can do a handstand. Congratulations," he muttered.

Who did she think she was going to impress with that move?

But Libby clearly wasn't bothered by his skeptical narration. Although she was upside down, he observed the sly grin that slid across her lips. As if it took no effort, she parted her legs into a V, then lifted one of her bloody hands off the ground. Defying gravity, she remained in the pose. Her limber legs and ballerina arm projecting from her body looked as if she were doing a set of jumping jacks at the exact moment the world flipped over—and her with it.

He rose to his feet. "Bloody hell, plum! How long can you balance on one hand?"

"Longer than you," she tossed back, still upside down, with one hand pressed to the ground. She didn't shake or tremble. There wasn't a wobble to be seen—just fluid motion and the strength of an elephant packed into one tiny, completely off-her-rocker woman.

"There's another catch with the race," the police chief added.

He caught Libby's eye. "Are you coming back up?"

With practiced ease, Libby pressed her free hand to the ground, then gently lowered her legs and came to her feet.

"What's the catch?" he asked, ignoring the yoga nutter showoff.

"You run the nine-mile race with a donkey. That's why it's called *Ass-in-Nine.*"

He cocked his head to the side and stared at the police chief. The woman's expression remained muted, but she had to be kidding. "A nine-mile running race with a donkey. That's an actual thing here?" He turned to Libby, who looked just as perplexed as he was.

"It celebrates Colorado's mining roots," Madelyn supplied.

He stared at the stylish woman. Now, she was an expert on donkey racing, too?

"I remember learning something about this when I was in elementary school," Libby added. "It's called pack burro racing, right? The donkey carries mining equipment."

"You remember correctly. It's our state's heritage sport," the chief answered.

Heritage or not, this race sounded absolutely insane.

"Why don't they make you run with a bar of gold or silver or whatever miners mine in this place?" he blathered.

The chief peered at him. "That's not how the race is structured, Mr. Cress."

"So, you want me to run a race with a donkey and an ass?" Libby clarified.

He turned to her. "No, plum, it's you and me and a—"

Bugger! This was not the time to come off a thick prat.

"Very funny," he said under his breath.

But he had real questions. Did donkeys even run? When he pictured a donkey, which he didn't often do, he thought of them as slow, meandering animals. How do you get one of them to sprint on command?

"It's quite a challenging endeavor. You'll need several weeks to prepare. But you both appear to be in tiptop condition. Excellent candidates, Madelyn," the chief answered when someone knocked. The chief pointed at the closed door. "Is that the second part?" she asked the matchmaker.

"There's a second part to this? And I'm not sure I can commit to weeks of donkey training. I've got a fight coming up," he rattled off.

"That's right, you're a big deal in the boxing world," Libby crooned.

"Yeah," he answered, feeling like the bloody opposite of a big deal.

"There's no reason to fret about your upcoming fight," Madelyn began. "We've considered everything and found a lovely home for you to rent in Rickety Rock that can accommodate the equipment you need to train. My people are preparing your lodgings as we speak."

She had to be kidding!

This fight was his make-or-break moment to prove he was still the best. He didn't have a second to waste, and he certainly didn't have time to run around the mountains with a donkey in tow.

His mobile chimed an incoming text, and it dawned on him that he had another problem. "What about the media? The little misunderstanding between myself and Libby must be streaming on social media by now."

"We can address that. Come in, gentlemen," Madelyn called.

The door opened, and bloody Briggs and Augie sauntered in.

"Aug?" he said, staring at the man.

"Who are these people?" Libby asked.

"Augie Bimston and Briggs Keaton. They work for me," he answered as the men nodded to Libby.

"This is Libby Lamb," he said. "She's..."

Where the hell did he even start?

"Oh, we know, lad," Augie answered as he shook Libby's hand.

"I hope you don't mind, Erasmus. I contacted your trainer and your agent," Madelyn said, then addressed the new arrivals. "Erasmus is concerned about his championship fight and how tonight's turn of events may impact his image and standing in the boxing world. Maybe you could shed some light on how we can address his concerns."

Briggs puffed up. "The video of you and Miss Lamb is

everywhere. The whole boxing world has seen it. Honestly, anyone with a mobile has probably seen it. But don't you worry, mate. I took care of the media for you."

Bloody hell.

"And how did you do that, *mate?*" Raz pressed, his voice a low rumble.

Briggs smoothed his sports coat. "I explained to the press that what they witnessed was simply part of your training."

"My training? Did your mum drop you on your head when you were a baby? We got handcuffed and arrested," he shot back.

"Look," Briggs continued, holding out his phone.

Raz glared at the screen.

In the dim glow of the streetlamp, he sprinted and turned on a dime, snatching up vibrators as Libby launched them haphazardly at him.

"We're calling Libby your spiritual advisor," the agent gushed with a dumb grin plastered on his face.

"His what?" Libby exclaimed.

Raz shook his head. "You've got to be kidding."

"Not at all. I made it up on the spot," the sports agent answered, looking pleased as punch.

"Aug, this is for real?" Raz asked, searching his trainer's face.

Aug sighed. "Briggsy here did most of the talking. But yes, we told the press what they'd witnessed was a facet of your training, and the arrest was an exercise in handling stress."

"A yoga teacher hurling sex toys at me is a *facet* of a professional boxer's training?" he replied, incredulity coating the words.

He couldn't believe what he was hearing.

"Listen, mate," Aug said, pointing at him with his toothpick. "You'd be smart to put on a smile and be right chuffed about this. It was that or take the chance that the press would peg you and Miss Lamb as bloody perverts."

Shit! Was Aug right? Had he and Libby been backed into a corner?

"Fortunately, the audio on every recording of the event we've seen is garbled. It's hard to make out much besides Ms. Lamb demonstrating rage yoga with that bloodcurdling scream and the words *chi, plum,* and *beefcake.* That bit of luck allowed me to inform the media that what they'd witnessed was a new, cutting edge, unorthodox training method, carefully crafted to make you ready for anything at any time, any place." Briggs paused dramatically, then lowered his voice. "As vigilant as he is powerful, the Lion is always ready to pounce. An agile power-house, the British Beast doesn't win. He dominates. He obliterates."

Everyone stared at Briggs, who now assumed the role of the room's chief lunatic.

Raz scrubbed his hands down his face. "That's what you said?"

"Yeah, and it's everywhere," Briggs answered, his eyes glittering. "Word is, Silas Scott's people are getting nervous. That's what we want, champ."

Did people actually believe this?

"Aug, you're on board with this?" he pressed.

"Briggs threw that bucket of bullshit at the media, and they gobbled it up. I nodded along, but there might be something to it, lad."

"To training me with plastic cocks?"

"To keep your reputation intact and to bidding bloody farewell to the wobbly git who's got a fight in sixty days. Watch the video, Raz. I timed it. You cut two seconds off your sprints chasing those plastic cocks," his trainer replied, tapping Briggs's mobile as he spoke.

"And that's where you come in, Libby. We need you to agree to this," Briggs added.

Libby scoffed. "You're serious? You want me to be his spiritual advisor and his son's nanny?"

"We do," the agent agreed. "There's no wiggle room. You either agree to the terms, or you'll be seen as an unhinged sex maniac obsessed with Erasmus Cress. That's the contingency plan we're prepared to go with if you decline the offer. As the agency representing Mr. Cress, I hope you can appreciate the position we're in. We need you onboard, Libby."

Briggsy, you little wanker!

He didn't give two shits about what Briggs and the agency needed. The drive to protect his plum yoga nutter superseded his concern over his career. He gripped the collar of his agent's pricy button-up and got in the man's face. "You're not messing with her life like that. I will not allow it."

"Her reputation is on the line, too, Raz," Briggs squeaked. "And the agency doesn't want to ruin her life. We want to improve it."

"How?" he growled when something warm touched his arm. He looked away from Briggs, the sod, and stared into a pair of amber eyes that took his breath away.

"I have a few questions I'd like to ask your agent. Don't pummel him yet," Libby said gently.

And like magic, the anger tearing through him dissolved with her touch. He released the man and took a step back.

"Save that energy for the fight, yeah, mate?" Briggs blathered through a nervous laugh as he adjusted his jacket.

Libby pinned the agent with her amber gaze. "How do you know I'm qualified to be a spiritual trainer? How do you know anything about me at all?" she challenged.

Briggs shot him a glance, probably making sure he wasn't going to throw a right hook in his direction, then returned his focus to Libby. "Excellent question! We've done a full background check."

Her posture stiffened. "When?"

Briggs cleared his throat. "Somewhere between you throwing the third or fourth vibrator at Raz, I asked the yoga people who you were. The owner gave me your name, and my team went to work. Oh, and I almost forgot. The owner of the yoga studio asked me to relay a message."

"Which is?" Libby barked.

Briggs shot another glance his way.

"You can tell me, Briggs. I won't let Raz pummel you...yet," Libby said, her tone growing firm.

She might be a yoga instructor, but she could turn on the fight when she wanted.

"Yeah, I'm a bit frightened," Briggs admitted. "I'm not sure who scares me more—you or the Beast. You've got an arm on you, Miss Lamb."

"Briggs," Libby snapped. "What's the message?"

The agent glanced away. "You're fired from teaching at that studio."

Libby sighed, then stared at the ceiling. "I figured that might have happened," she lamented before zeroing back in on his agent. "Now, what do you know about me?"

Briggs tapped his mobile's screen. "Ah, here we are. I've got the report. You're Libby Caroline Lamb. Age twenty-five. Graduated uni with honors. Double major with bachelor's degrees in kinesiology and physical education with an emphasis on elementary education. You're a yoga instructor with several fancy accreditations. Your mother, Aurora, is deceased. Your father, Connolly, is alive, but he's got a patchy job history."

Connolly?

His ears perked up at the mention of Libby's dad's name.

Hadn't the cop asked her if she was related to a Connolly Lamb? She'd said no. Had she lied to the police?

"Your younger brothers," Briggs continued, "both twenty-one years old, Anders and Alec Lamb, are attending uni in Ecuador in a study abroad program that incorporates a volunteer component. They've been accepted into a program there to study medicine. Their admissions status is pending, awaiting a final tuition payment, and your landlord says he had to kick you out tonight. It's been quite a day for you, Miss Lamb."

Libby sighed. "It has. I'm a cosmic karma catastrophe."

"Does that sound about right?" Briggs pressed.

Her shoulders slumped a fraction. "Yes."

Raz stared at her. They had more in common than he thought. "Your younger brothers are twins?"

Libby nodded as the ghost of a grin cut through her forlorn expression. "They want to practice medicine in impacted communities. They're good men."

"And that's how my company wants to help you, Libby," Briggs slipped in, back to looking like a puffed-up peacock.

Libby shook her head. "I don't understand."

"To sweeten the deal," Briggs continued, "my sports management firm would be happy to cover the costs of the lads' schooling in exchange for your spiritual advisor services."

"You'll pay the balance?" she stammered.

Briggs stared at his mobile's screen. "A little over sixteen thousand dollars?"

"Yes," she replied, her voice a scratch of a whisper.

Raz couldn't take it. He couldn't stand there and watch his agent manipulate her.

"You can't threaten her like that, Briggs," he said, closing in on the man again. "What you're doing is blackmail."

The agent raised his hands defensively. "It's not a threat, champ. It's an offer."

"Aug?" Raz bit out, turning to his trainer. "What do you have to say about this?"

The toothpick pressed between Augie's lips swiveled as he pondered the question. "I'd say after tonight's episode, you and Miss Lamb are inextricably connected. The best option for both of you is to work together. That's the only way you come out of it without looking like bleeding deviants." Aug studied Libby, then gave her a nod. "What's the harm in letting her be your spiritual advisor? She may teach you a thing or two. She's already improved your sprints, mate. And you need someone to watch over Sebastian."

The gravity of the situation hit like a swift jab to the gut.

"What about my training, Aug? Am I supposed to commute to the city each day between donkey practice runs?"

"Lad, I have a place near Aspen," the trainer replied.

Raz's jaw dropped. "You have a mountain home?"

"Yeah, most rich people around here do," Aug replied with a shrug.

"I never thought of you as a rich person."

"Think of the quid you've got piled up," the trainer tossed back.

"Yeah?"

"I have twenty percent of that. I'm bloody rich by any standard," Augie exclaimed, quite animated for the usually stone-faced bloke.

Raz shifted his weight. "Why didn't you mention you had a mountain house?"

"Never came up. Luanne likes it. She can wander around, finding interesting rocks and gemstone and take in the scenery. And I've come to appreciate hiking."

"Hiking?" Raz exclaimed.

Bonkers! The world had gone blooming bonkers.

If the crusty Augie Bimston could enjoy lollygagging and

bloody hiking around where the rich and famous congregated, any damn thing was possible.

"This is a win-win situation," Madelyn offered smoothly, sliding into the conversation. "Erasmus, you'll be able to train in the mountains. I have a feeling the preparations for the Ass-in-Nine race will coincide nicely with your boxing regiment."

"I believe it will," Augie agreed. "I already have Raz running five to ten miles three days a week. I don't bloody care if he does it with a donkey, a goat, or a mythical unicorn with a flowing white mane. He needs to get in the miles for endurance."

"And Libby," Madelyn continued as his head was about to explode, "don't forget, the nanny position pays very well. With the sports agency prepared to make the final tuition payment for your brothers, the income you generate as a nanny is yours to do with as you wish."

Raz surveyed the room, working to get his bearings.

All these damned rules!

He wanted to whisk Libby off her feet, throw her over his shoulder like a caveman, and bust out of this room.

"Libby, Erasmus, here's what it boils down to," Augie began. "Best-case scenario. You run the race. You train together and present a united front. Otherwise, you know what happens, Raz. You become fodder for the tabloids. It's not a lot of time to commit. The fight will be here before you know it. It's in—"

"Sixty days," Madelyn interjected. "The same amount of time as the nanny match trial period. You know how it works, don't you, Libby?"

Libby nodded. "At the end of the trial period, the agreement can be voided by either party. No questions asked."

"That is correct," Madelyn purred.

"Then, Lion, you regain your title of heavyweight champion

and return to the UK, a beloved national treasure," Briggs added, finding his voice.

Could it be that easy?

"You're not staying in Colorado, Raz?" Libby asked, watching him closely.

He shoved his hands into his pockets. "I don't know, plum."

"I saw you visiting Mitch and Rowen's kids' school a few months ago. I thought..."

He glanced away. "I was just taking a look."

"I see," she answered.

He returned his attention to her face, to those eyes that saw everything. "Is that a problem?"

Did he want it to be a problem? Did he want her to want him to stay? A bloody ludicrous notion. They barely knew each other.

She twisted the bracelet around her wrist. "No, it's not a problem."

"The race is in seven weeks. The fight is a little over a week after that. There's one choice that makes sense—one path forward for you both," Augie offered.

"One path where you aren't charged with lewd behavior," the chief added.

He almost forgot about the bloody vibrator incident.

"Libby," he began, but she waved him off.

"Briggs, did you mean what you said about your company covering my brothers' tuition?"

"Every word. I've got the contract right here. We'll pay half now and the other half just before the fight," Briggs answered, holding up his mobile.

This was insanity!

He paced the length of the office. Off-kilter and damn near ready to fall arse over elbow, he tried to regain his balance. One minute, Libby's lobbing cocks at him. The next, she's his spiritual advisor.

It was too much.

He needed to give her some time to process this.

He needed time to process himself.

Standing in the Denver police chief's office, staring at a donkey T-shirt and his bloody agent, it was safe to say time wasn't on their side. His son would be here in two days. He had to keep training. Still, he hated to see Libby cornered like this.

"Plum," he began, but she cut him off.

"Your trainer's right, Raz. This is the way forward—the only way forward." She swallowed hard and released a shaky breath, then turned to Madelyn and Briggs. "You want my answer? You've got it. I'll do it. I'm in."

SIX

LIBBY

LIBBY WATCHED the traffic light change from red to green, then glanced at the hulk of a man sitting next to her in the driver's seat.

Your path will lead you to your intended destination.

Oh, sweet Buddha, you have one utterly jacked-up sense of humor.

She hadn't expected her path to lead her here, sitting in Erasmus Cress's gargantuan Hummer. As of a half-hour ago, she'd become not only his kid's nanny but his spiritual advisor as well.

She didn't even like boxing—or know anything about it. And what was there to spiritually advise about when it came to two men bashing each other's faces in?

How had it come to this?

How had she allowed herself to spiral out of control?

Sure, her chi was trashed, and her O had skipped town, but like a maniac, the unadulterated, fierce energy that had coursed through her as she chucked vibrators at the beefcake had completely taken over. And then, in the blink of an eye, or in her case, the whir of a police siren, the pendulum had swung. As she'd stared into the beefcake's eyes in the back seat of the squad car, a beautiful stillness had engulfed them. Shrouded in a hue that flowed from blue to violet, their auras met, mingled, and caressed each other.

Yes, met, mingled, and caressed. It was like an out-of-body experience. She'd never felt anything like it.

She'd read others' auras and interpreted their energy, but her aura had never called out to another's like this.

Was Raz's chi as screwed up as hers?

But there was more.

With his lips hovering a breath away, the maddeningly lopsided set adrift life force she'd been grappling with for seventy-five days evaporated. In that hazy slice of time, everything about the man had centered her. With his muscled body and earthy, physical scent, his beefcake pheromones infected her brain, rendering her a woozy heap of well-balanced swoon. But it wasn't just her mind that had buzzed with a frenzied intensity. Her chakras had taken notice.

In particular, the sacral chakra.

The spiritual home of her sexuality had twitched. Like in the movies, when doctors think that a patient has flatlined, then suddenly, there's a blip, a beep, the monitor flashes.

She's alive! She's alive!

For an intoxicatingly fleeting moment, her libido had been resurrected. She could almost hear her O calling out, *I'm here. Come and get me.*

Had Raz's beefcake chi jumpstarted her like an old Honda?

No, she could not go there—and she couldn't start calling her O an old Honda either. What O would want to return home to that sort of welcome?

But the facts were the facts. The man had wrecked her with his arrogant energy.

She couldn't allow herself to fall for him. The whole

centering bit had to be due to stress—the stress of getting hauled into the police station for chucking sex toys at a boxer in public.

And the complete cosmic catastrophe was available to view on the internet for all to see.

She wrapped her arms around her body, holding herself together when her fingertips brushed against something crusty. "Oh, gross!" She gasped, then wiped her hand on her knee.

"What is it?" Raz asked, worry creasing his brow. "Do you need me to pull over?"

The breath caught in her throat at the sound of his voice. Lit by the glow of the car's dash, she studied his profile as he flicked his gaze back to the road. Briggs had driven Raz's car to the station, and Madelyn had insisted on having her people transport her Buick to Raz's home. That meant her first act as a spiritual advisor was to take a car ride with her client.

Her client.

That's how she had to frame it. She had to forget the almost-kiss in the back of the police cruiser.

She was an employee.

His employee.

They'd barely spoken since they'd left the station with their donkey T-shirts and, thank you, universe, without a summons to appear in court for lewd behavior. She pressed her thighs together, attempting to calm her sexytimes chakra from firing up, but his voice, that sexy, rolling British accent that she should not find appealing, sent a delicious tingle down her spine.

She checked her hand for bird crap. "It's my wrap. I forgot about the bird poop on the shoulder," she replied, then cringed. Here she was, casually mentioning bird crap with her nemesis new boss.

"We can throw it in the wash when we get home," he said, eyes trained forward.

Home.

His home was about to become her home—well, his Denver home, and then they'd head to Rickety Rock for the summer. In a darkly humorous way, it made sense that her energy would attract someplace rickety.

Her phone pinged in her bag, and she slid her focus from Raz's profile to the tote.

"Do you need to get that?" he asked.

She fidgeted with her bracelet. "It's my friends. I should text them back, but I'm not sure how to explain what happened tonight."

He sighed a heavy breath. "That makes two of us, plum."

Plum.

Was that a British thing or some strange term of endearment he employed with women, akin to babe?

She'd been explicitly clear when she'd ordered him not to apply the term to her, but there was something oddly sweet about being called plum. She was about to ask him about it when a robotic voice rang out over the car's speakers.

Call from Calliope.

She tensed. Holy Buddha's belly, who was Calliope? Was this Raz's girlfriend calling? A booty call? It was Friday night. Her pulse hammered in her throat as a thorny sensation prickled through her.

Jealousy.

Jealousy was a sensation she rarely experienced, especially when it came to men.

No, she wasn't jealous.

No way! No how!

Erasmus Cress could bang half of Denver, and she wouldn't care, right? Nevertheless, a hot streak tore through her. Blast her cockamamie chi. "Do you need to get that?" she asked, unable to stifle the huffy trill in her tone as she borrowed his words.

Raz huffed. "It's my little sisters. Do you mind if I pick up? They've already left five messages tonight."

Sisters?

It was hard enough picturing the arrogant ass as a father. And then it hit her. Sebastian had to have a mother. Did Raz have an ex-wife or ex-girlfriend out there? The thought of this man being connected to other humans was both incredibly foreign and weirdly comforting.

A strange sense of relief flooded her system. "Go ahead. Take the call."

He tapped a button on the steering wheel. "Hey, Calliope," he said wearily.

"Finally, Erasmus! Bloody nice of you to pick up," came a woman's teasing British accent.

He released a frustrated breath. "I've been busy."

"Yeah, brother, we, along with the rest of the world, got to see exactly what you were busy with tonight. What a cock-up," a slightly higher voice chimed.

"Hello, Callista," Raz grumped with a distinctly resigned air to the words.

Libby listened intently. She thought back to Alec and Anders driving her bonkers with their video games and piles of dirty clothes haphazardly littering the floor next to the empty laundry hamper.

"We've got a question for you, Raz," Callista continued.

"And what would that be?"

"Where do we sign up for the Libby Lamb fan club?" Calliope answered, and Libby's jaw dropped.

"Why would you ask that?" he shot back.

"Because the woman is brilliant. We haven't seen you jump like that in ages," Callista replied. "We even came up with a snappy tagline: the Lamb schools the Lion. What do you think?"

Raz released a lion of a sigh. "I think you're both are off your rocker. And shouldn't you be teaching English? I didn't send you to South Korea on holiday. You're supposed to be taking classes, contributing to society, and getting cultured and educated. You know, the things your big brother missed out on."

Libby watched Raz closely. It warmed her heart to see him play the role of beleaguered big brother.

"We're on a break. Now, who is this woman? We need to know everything," Callista answered.

"She's a crackin' stunner, Raz, that's for sure. And she's got spirit. We think Meredith would have adored her," Calliope added, but Raz didn't serve up a cheeky response. Instead, the air inside the cab of the giant car grew thick with tension as the rush of bitter sadness rolled off the man in mighty waves.

Meredith—that had to be Sebastian's mother. But what was she to Raz?

"Girls, Libby's right here. We're in the Hummer," he replied as his grip on the steering wheel tightened.

"Bugger all, Raz!" Callista's high trill chided. "Why are you driving a giant hunk of metal?"

"It's like screaming to the world that you've got a tiny cock and need to prove your masculinity with that ridiculous car," Calliope added.

Raz reared back. Even in the dim light, she could tell his eyes were about to pop out of their sockets.

"I will not be discussing my manhood with either of you. And like I said, Libby can hear this. She's in the bloody car."

Libby couldn't hold back as a tumble of giggles slipped past her lips. Raz stopped at another light, hung his head, and shook it—again exemplifying the plight of the pestered older brother. "Libby, meet my twin sisters, Calliope and Callista Cress. They are, as you can probably tell, a right pain in the arse."

"Twins," she repeated, surprise coating the word.

Raz nodded. "Yeah, they're the same age as your twin brothers."

Libby stared at the man. An hour ago, she would have sworn they had nothing in common.

"What's that? Libby's got twin brothers?" Callista prompted.

"I do," she answered.

"And I doubt they call her to scream about cocks," Raz grumped.

Libby released a nervous laugh. "Thankfully, we've never breached that subject."

"Libby Lamb, let us be the first to congratulate you," Calliope crooned.

"On what?" she asked as Raz hit the gas, turning onto the road that led to the uber-exclusive Crystal Hills and Crystal Acres neighborhoods.

"On doing what most women on the planet want to do at some point in their life," Callista finished.

"And what would that be? Make a fool of themselves for the world to see?" Libby answered, feeling her cheeks heat.

How many people had watched her pelt Erasmus with over a dozen vibrators?

"No, you harnessed your power and let a bloke have it. Well done! Womankind thanks you," Callista cheered.

"It was hard to hear anything on the recording," Calliope added, "but were you calling our brother a *beefcake*?"

That word.

"I might have used that term," Libby answered as a fresh wave of mortification hit.

"And you aren't trollied?" Callista chimed.

"Trollied?" Libby repeated.

"It means drunk, plum," Raz answered with a tinge of amusement in his tone.

She gasped. "No, I wasn't trollied! That was a bit of rage yoga gone awry."

"And by the way," Calliope added, "that rainbow vibrator is phenomenal. In like ten seconds, my eyeballs are rolling back in my head."

The car came to a screeching halt at the entrance to the ritzy Crystal Hills neighborhood. In the heart of the city close to the Crystal Creek shopping district, its multimillion-dollar homes belonged to Denver's rich and famous crowd. Penny and Rowen's mansion was here, and Charlotte and Mitch were close by in Crystal Acres.

"Stop!" Raz cried. "I don't want to hear another word about sex toys."

"Such a prude," Callista teased.

Libby sat back and took in the show.

"All kidding aside, are you and Libby okay, Raz-a-ma-taz?" Calliope pressed, concern laced into the question.

Raz sighed and eased onto the gas as they continued into the neighborhood. "Don't call me that, Calliope."

"You didn't mind when we were little," she shot back.

"Well, you're not little. And Libby and I are fine."

"Back to Libby," Callista chimed.

Libby braced herself.

OMG, these girls didn't slow down!

"Was that vibrator episode planned because you looked ready to tear my brother apart? Are you really his spiritual advisor and Sebastian's nanny like that prat Briggs says?"

Libby's mouth opened and closed like a confused flounder. What was she supposed to say? She couldn't tell them their brother had wrecked her life, banished her orgasm, and set in motion the events that changed everything.

"It's a long story, but yes, I was hired to do both jobs," she answered, settling for vague yet polite.

For a second, then two, neither twin spoke.

Were they in the clear? She caught Raz's eye, knowing he was wondering the same thing.

"Another quick question," Callista mused.

"Yes?" Libby answered.

"Are you doing each other?" Callista continued with a cheeky lilt to the question. "Because if you're not, maybe you should. Calliope and I could feel the heat between you two coming right off the computer screen. What a bloody scorcher!"

"Callista!" Raz exclaimed. "I'm ending this call. Be good, girls. I love you both."

"Before you go, Raz-a-ma-taz, Granny Fin is—" Calliope began, but Raz wasn't having it.

"Goodbye," he growled like an exhausted bear, then pushed the button to end the call.

"Raz-a-ma-taz?" Libby repeated.

"It's what they liked to call me when they were little. I'm eleven years older than they are. I helped raise them with my granny. I can tell you this. It was easier when they were toddlers and could barely talk."

He didn't mention his parents. What had happened to them? But she wasn't about to ask—not now. Then again, she'd rather eat broken glass than discuss her father.

She pushed the thought aside. "Your sisters seem great, Raz. The teasing means they love you."

He nodded. "They're studying to be schoolteachers and spending the summer in South Korea helping kids learn English," he said, and in the glow of the dash, she caught the hint of a grin—and not the cocky, shit-eating grin he was so good at deploying. No, this expression radiated pride.

She understood the reaction.

A grin matching Raz's pulled at the corners of her lips. "My brothers are abroad for school, too. They want to be—"

"Doctors," Raz supplied. "Remember, Briggs knows—"

"Everything about me," she finished as a chill ran through her.

Did he know about her father? Surely, a background check would have revealed more than his name and employment status.

"Libby, plum, I'm..." Raz began, then leaned toward the windshield and slowed down. "Bollocks," he whispered.

"You're, *bollocks?*" she asked, confusion marring her features before she caught sight of several vans parked outside a gated drive.

"Bloody press," he mumbled as they pulled up to the gate. He looked her over. "Just smile and act...spiritual." The proud big brother had disappeared as the vapid athlete took over.

Did he really think yoga and spirituality were an act?

Before she could protest, he rolled down the driver's side window as beams of light lit him in a harsh blast of yellow.

"Lion, is it true? Does your training involve a guru?"

"Are you afraid you can't beat the Snake without going to extremes?"

The questions came at Raz in sharp pops of sound. She ignored the jittery men calling out and focused on the boxer in the seat next to her. A muscle twitched on his cheek before he donned a cocksure grin.

Was this his mask, or was this the real Raz? Who was he at his core?

"You know better than to think that the British Beast is afraid of anything," he boasted. "I crush whoever's across from me in the ring. You saw me tonight, lads. Your girlfriends wish you were half as fit and jacked as I am."

A few of the men chuckled, but Libby recoiled.

What a smug asshat!

"Are you planning on showing up for the fight? It's a fair question, knowing your history," called another reporter.

Raz clenched his jaw as angry energy tinged with bitter remorse built around him in invisible plumes of fury. Her chi may be off, but she couldn't mistake his vibe. For the last seventy-five days, she'd lived it.

"Oh, I'll be there," Raz growled. "This is the fight of the century, mates. And you're looking at the winner."

Was she utterly disgusted with this egotistical version of the man?

That would be a Buddha-licious yes.

This creep wrecked her inner balance.

But she had questions.

What had happened to him? Why had he skipped out on his last fight? He didn't seem like the type to back down from anything. And then she remembered the Derricks. This must be the fight they'd been talking about.

"Hey, look, it's Libby Lamb! She's with him," a reporter yelled, cutting into her thoughts. She pulled her wrap around her body as the media migrated to her side of the car like a swarm of hornets.

Raz rolled up his window. "Don't worry. They can't see you. The windows are tinted." He pressed a button on the dash. The creak of the gate opening sent the reporters dashing away from the car like a bunch of cockroaches. With a smug expression pasted to his face, he maneuvered the Hummer through the sea of flashing lights.

"Get used to it. It's part of the show," he muttered.

Libby seethed as they headed up a hill toward an enormous hulking mansion. It made sense that he'd live in a monstrosity of a home in Denver's priciest neighborhood. He drove a monstrosity of a car and behaved like a monstrosity of a jerk. "Just when I was starting to think you were a real human being, you revert into that chi-crashing, O obliterator," she hissed under her breath.

"What does that mean?" he shot back, irritation infused into the question.

"Why do you do that, Raz?" she asked, shaking her head in disgust.

"Do what?" he barked as he slammed the car into park in the center of the circle drive, then turned in his seat and gave her that look.

Inside his stupidly tricked-out, giant testosterone mobile with his giant mansion looming, and that smug smirk slapped to his face, he'd done it again. He'd given her that look. The same look he'd given her seventy-five days ago. His gray gaze cut through her as if she didn't exist.

On the brink of a karma cataclysm, she unbuckled her seat belt, grabbed the drawstrings on his hoodie, yanked his stupidly sexy body her way, then sized him up as the vibrator chucking part of her took over. "Why do you act like an arrogant, self-absorbed jerk?"

He unbuckled his seat belt and leaned in. The tip of his nose brushed past hers. Time slowed to a crawl as the air sparked with an impassioned intensity. "It's my job. I'm a fighter. It's what the boxing world wants," he countered in an infuriatingly sexy rumble.

He might think this beastly lion business scared everyone into submission. But it didn't work on her. Her pulse raced. Her chest heaved. The peace and love version of herself made way for a woman scorned. And this woman didn't back down. "I don't care what the media wants. What do you want?"

The air crackled between them on the verge of igniting as breathless anticipation sent a furious charge through her body.

"What do I want to do right this very minute?" he asked. The heat of his breath tickled her lips. He gripped her shoulders. The raw strength of his hands holding her in place sent a ripple of warmth between her thighs. Hot, wet, and ready to spring across the console and mount this man like he was a wild stallion; she was on the brink of losing total control. And look who'd decided to say hello. Nice to see you again, sacral chakra. And it wasn't only the seat of her sexuality taking notice. The seven energy centers in her body lit up like a Christmas tree.

This was bad. This was very bad.

She should let go of the drawstrings. She should sit back in her seat, smooth her bird-shit-covered wrap, and forget about his scent and his touch and the way nothing and everything made sense when their lips were mere millimeters apart.

Did she dare press him to answer, or did she know deep in her heart what this hulk of a beefcake really wanted?

Her body took over, and she parted her lips. "Tell me what you want," she whispered, when her phone chimed an incoming call.

As if they'd been doused with a bucket of icy water, she gasped. Raz released his grip, and she scrambled to get herself together. Glancing into her bag, Anders and Alec's picture flashed on her phone. "It's my brothers," she stammered, heat rising to her cheeks as another helping of mortification washed over her.

What was she doing? Erasmus Cress was her boss.

"You should answer. We know why they're calling. You should let them know you're okay," he said with a nervous shake to his voice before sinking into his seat, then running his hands down his face.

"I'll be quick." Adrenaline coursed through her veins as she nearly dropped her phone, attempting to answer the call.

"Hey, boys," she said, trying to sound as if she *wasn't* on the verge of screwing the brains out of an annoyingly sexy professional boxer.

"Hey, Libbs, we're so happy for you," Alec sang out.

"We didn't think things would move so quickly," Anders chimed.

Libby stared at Raz, looking for answers, but the man simply shrugged.

"It's been quite a day. I'm not sure I know what you're talking about. I need you to be a little more specific," she replied, damn proud of herself for putting together a cohesive thought that didn't include her lips attached to Erasmus Cress.

"We saw the video of you *training* the British Beast, Erasmus Cress," Anders answered.

"You did?" she squeaked. Welp, if the video had made it to remote parts of Ecuador, it had made it about everywhere.

"It freaked us out when we first saw it, and we almost booked flights home, but then Briggs Keaton called and explained the situation," Alec clarified.

Okay, this couldn't be that bad. That Briggs guy was all about damage control. Hopefully, he'd employed the same tactic with her brothers.

"At first, we were surprised when he described what you were doing. We know how you feel about competitive sports," Anders added gently.

Libby squeezed her eyes shut for a second, then released a slow breath. She could feel Raz watching her, but she couldn't worry about him—not with her brothers listening in. "And what did Briggs say?" she asked, keeping her tone even.

"He said that you've been brought on to act as Erasmus Cress's spiritual advisor and that you'll also be his son's nanny," Anders answered.

So far, so good.

"We told Briggs you'd make an awesome nanny, Libbs. You pretty much raised us single-handedly after Mom died, and when Dad—"

"And did he mention your tuition payment?" she blurted,

cutting off her brother. She could sense Raz's intensity dialing up.

Block out the beefcake.

"Yeah, he said that part of your compensation package was to cover our tuition," Alec answered.

"Thanks, Libby. Seriously, you're the best sister in the entire universe," Anders added.

She blinked back tears. "I promised I'd take care of it. And you know I don't break promises."

She couldn't get emotional.

Not now.

Not with Raz watching her every move.

"He said the company would pay half now and half on the day of the fight," Alec supplied.

Libby swallowed hard. "And that's okay with the university?"

"It's no problem. The final payment is due the day of the fight. Some guys down here just signed up to get the Pay-Per-View package. Are you going to be on TV with the Lion?"

"I don't know. I don't think so," she stammered, not daring to look at Raz.

"Did you know that the venture capitalist company was tied in with a sports management agency? You didn't mention that when we talked this morning," Anders asked.

They thought she'd gotten the Tri-Derrick deal. And sweet Buddha's belly! Had it only been hours since they talked? It felt like a million years had passed since she'd last heard their voices.

"They're actually two different things. The opportunity to work with the sports management agency presented itself after I met with the venture capitalists."

She could feel Raz's concentration sharpen.

"How did that meeting go?" Alec asked.

Libby chewed her lip and glanced at Raz. Yep, he was watching her like a hawk.

"It didn't go very well, possibly a disaster. There might have been some karma cursing involved, but nothing to worry yourselves over. The cosmos has spoken. I'm a bona fide spiritual advisor slash nanny, at least for the next sixty days," she blathered, cringing at that word salad of a reply.

"Is there something you're not telling us, sis?" Alec pressed.

Oh no! She couldn't worry them. She had to alter the trajectory of this conversation.

She met Raz's gaze. "Do you want to say hello to Erasmus Cress? He's right here."

"He's with you now?" Anders exclaimed.

"Hey, Anders, hello, Alec, it's nice to meet you. Libby says you two are at uni studying to be doctors," Raz said, swooping in as he dropped the smug athlete vibe.

"Thanks to our sister," Alec answered. "And holy shit! This is so cool. We're on the phone with the British Beast."

"Alec, language," Libby chided.

"We're lucky to have your sister onboard," Raz answered with a chuckle. The man sounded almost like he meant it. Then again, he was skilled at playing the part of the super athlete. She'd seen him turn up the wattage for the press.

"We can't wait to watch the fight. The Snake seems like a real asshole," Anders offered.

Unable to stop herself, she went into strict big sister mode. "Hey, what did I say? Watch the language."

"Sorry, Libbs," Anders replied just like he used to back when the twins were wily preteens, experimenting with colorful words. She sighed. They were men—men who were on track to become physicians. They didn't need her censoring their language anymore. "Sorry, guys, sometimes I forget you're not twelve anymore."

"It's what Mom would say if she were still here," Alec said softly.

Libby swallowed past the lump in her throat. "It's been a long day. I should get going, and I'm sure you need your rest. You're still building the clinic, right?"

"We'll be back at it, volunteering bright and early," Alec answered, his tone lightening.

Libby tapped the darkened screen on her cell and smiled at the picture of her brothers. "I'm proud of you both."

"We love you, Libbs," her brothers called out in unison.

"And it was so great to meet you, Mr. Cress," Anders added.

"You can call me Raz."

"We get to call the British Beast, Raz," Alec gushed, and Libby shook her head.

"Bye, boys! We'll talk soon," she said, then ended the call. She stared at the screen and studied the boys' smiling faces until it switched back to power-saving mode and went dark.

"They sound like good lads," Raz said, his voice floating in the darkened cab of the SUV.

"They are."

The shift from despising this man, to finding him endearing, to hating him, to swinging back to sort of liking him was giving her emotional whiplash. And that didn't even count the number of times she'd wanted to climb him like a tree and kiss the arrogant smirk right off his face. And don't even ask about what her chakras wanted—especially the one that manifested sexual energy. That sacral chakra had quite a dirty little mind.

"Kind of funny how we each have twins for siblings," Raz offered, glancing away, which gave her a second to pull herself together.

Was he trying to connect? One minute, he was a colossal jerk. The next, simply a guy who was an older brother.

Libby dropped her phone into her bag, then something

caught her eye. She studied the darkened house. Had something moved in there?

"Should we go inside?" she asked, ignoring the shadows.

Raz stared ahead, avoiding eye contact. "Can I ask you something first?"

She fidgeted with her jade bracelet. "Sure."

"What were your brothers talking about? Did you have a job interview today?"

"The other opportunity?" she answered, recalling the first gong episode in her gong-a-licious day.

"Yeah," he said, leaning into the seat.

She closed her eyes and released a slow breath. Something was calming about sitting in the darkness that made her want to tell Raz everything. Or perhaps it wasn't only the darkness.

"I had an interview with who I thought were venture capitalists looking to fund a fitness venture. I put together a business plan for a yoga center, but the whole thing turned out to be a sham."

"A sham?" he repeated.

"Three rich douchebags named Derrick put an ad on social media pretending to be venture capitalists. They weren't looking to invest in anything. They did it as a joke to meet women."

"That's awful," he growled.

"Don't worry. I let them have it."

He chuckled. "I bet you did. If it was anything like what happened tonight, I'm sure they're shaking in their douchebag boots."

Was this man sympathizing with her?

She chanced a look at him and didn't find him smirking or sneering. "They actually mentioned you, Raz."

He sat up. "Me?"

"Well, the fight. The worst Derrick, Derrick Dawson, said he was going to bet twenty thousand dollars on the Snake."

"What a wanker! Now, I really despise these prats. You point out this Derrick, and I'll give him a good jab in the solar plexus," Raz teased, and it was oddly sweet.

"I need you to know that I'm not usually a vindictive person. My chi—my energy—has been off since..." she trailed off.

"Since that day at the gym," he supplied.

"Yes."

He nodded as if he were turning something over in his head. "Can I ask you another question?"

"Shoot."

"What's this O you keep going on about?"

She shifted in the seat. "It's the big O."

He cocked his head to the side.

Why was this so hard to say? She was a grown woman, entirely in charge of her sexuality. She cleared her throat. "Orgasm!" she exclaimed, her voice echoing through the car like she'd called out into the depths of the freaking Grand Canyon.

Orgasm, orgasm, orgasm, orgasm!

Raz's jaw hung open. "That O? You haven't had one of those in seventy-five days?"

She crossed, then uncrossed her legs. "That's right."

"That explains the vibrators," he said under his breath.

She threw up her hands. "It's not for lack of trying, but they've been useless. Even the Rainbow Screamer. That one used to work like a dream, but it won't get me there anymore. You know, the one your sister likes."

He waved her off. "Let's not mention my sister and sex toys in the same sentence. But..."

"What?" she pressed.

"One of the cops mentioned his girlfriend had one. He said she loves it," Raz added.

"And I loved mine, too," Libby gushed. "I loved every one of them until you broke me."

Take it down a notch, you unbalanced chi-monster.

"You're sure it was me who did this to you?"

"I know it was. I felt the shift in my chi. It was like somebody threw it in the clothes dryer's tumble cycle. And then there's my long-lost O. I've tried to get it back. I've used dildos, vibrators, my fingers, and my toes."

"Your toes?" he exclaimed.

"Yeah, I'm super flexible," she replied, then lifted her leg and tucked it behind her neck. "See."

"Bloody hell! You are." He pulled at the collar of his hoodie. "Have you tried anything besides sex toys?"

"You mean actual sex?" she answered, lowering her leg.

He cleared his throat. "Yeah."

She deflated into the seat. "I've had tons of sex over the last seventy-five days."

His eyebrows rocketed to his hairline. "You've had tons of sex?"

She shot back up and exhaled an irritated breath. "You're not one of those, are you?"

"One of what?"

"A judgmental hypocrite. A guy who believes it's totally fine for a man to sow his wild oats and enjoy pleasure. But if a woman engages in the same behavior, you look down your smug nose at her."

"My nose isn't smug, and I'm all for women owning their sexuality," he answered, gripping the steering wheel like he was ready to rip it clear off the console.

She looked him over. "Then why are you making that face?"

"I'm not making a face, plum," he snarled.

There he was, calling her plum again.

"You are," she corrected. "You look like you either want to punch someone in the nose or desperately need to get to a toilet to take care of a terrible case of raging diarrhea."

"I do not bloody look like a man with raging diarrhea," he grunted as a vein pulsed on his forehead.

She shrugged. "Now, you sound like one, too."

"Plum, you might kill me," he muttered. A slice of silence wove its way through the darkened vehicle before Raz cut through the quiet. "But none of the blokes you were with could—"

"Get me off?" she supplied. There was no reason to beat around the bush. Yes, Raz was a Brit, but this wasn't Victorian England. "Nope, none of them could get the job done."

The hint of that cocky boxer returned with a coy twist of his lips. "Maybe you're picking the wrong guys."

He was fishing—trying to figure her out.

She tucked an errant lock of her hair behind her ear. "It doesn't work like that for me. It doesn't matter who I sleep with."

"What do you mean?" he asked, leaning in.

"There's no right guy for me. Don't get me wrong. I'm not sleeping with ax murderers. But if I meet someone and we enjoy each other's company, I don't think there's anything wrong with sleeping together. I love sex—or loved it before I lost my ability to have an orgasm. But you see, for me, sex is a release. I don't want monogamy. Sex is sex. I'm not looking for anything more."

"Ever?" Raz threw back, curiosity woven into the word. "You don't want a boyfriend or a husband someday?"

She shifted in her seat. It wasn't usually difficult to answer this question. She thought she'd made her peace with the answer. "No," she rasped, grateful she was able to produce the syllable. The word seemed stuck—like it didn't want to come out.

"You weren't kidding tonight when you said you didn't need a man to teach you anything," he said, letting go of the steering wheel and resting his hands in his lap. "You're a rare find, Libby Lamb."

But she wasn't. She was simply cautious—or broken. She wasn't quite sure which one she actually was. She'd seen first-hand what one reckless man can do to a fragile heart. She had to play it safe, and that meant keeping her guard up.

"In my experience," she began, "when it comes to the big stuff, the heavy stuff, the stuff that isn't easy, most men are remarkably unreliable. When the chips are down, I have my friends and myself. I'll never rely on a man."

She left out a pertinent word.

Again.

She'd never rely on a man ever again.

"What about your brothers? Would you say they're unreliable?"

"That's different. They're good men."

"Couldn't there be other good men out there?" he challenged.

"Perhaps, but they're not meant for me."

"Just sex, no love?" Raz continued.

"That's right, just sex," she repeated, working to keep her tone even.

Why was that so difficult?

She and Raz stared at each other as another gulf of silence encapsulated the car. Her eyes had adjusted to the dim light, and she watched him study her. What was going on in his mind? Had she shocked him? Did he assume every woman dreamed of falling in love?

Had he been in love? Was he still in love with someone?

She'd never even entertained the thought that this stupidly sexy, arrogant beefcake of a man was even capable of the emotion.

"Libby," he said, his voice taking on a gravelly quality that had her libido taking notice.

"Yes?" she breathed as a flash of light lit his features.

"I agree with," he began, then reared back. "Bloody hell!"

"What?" she asked, searching his face as the light faded to black.

"There's someone in my house. The lights just flickered," he replied, looking past her.

"Should we call the police?" she asked, turning to survey the massive home.

"No, they already think we're crazy. Stay in the car. I'll handle this," he said, opening his door.

If Erasmus Cress thought she was a stay-in-the-car damsel in distress, he had a lot to learn.

"You're not going in there alone," she called, grabbing her yoga tote and meeting him on the walkway that led to the front door.

He looked her over. "What will you do? Throw vibrators at the burglars?"

She checked the bag. "I don't know. There's a mini gong in there, too."

"Brilliant, we can gong the thief. Great plan!"

"At least it's a plan," she threw back.

"Let me take care of it, Libby. They don't call me the Lion for nothing."

"If that's because you're big and dumb, then I can see where you got the name," she hissed. She was not the type of person who hissed, but this man, when he wasn't making her head swim with dirty thoughts, made her blood boil.

He lifted a lid near the door handle, revealing a keypad, then entered a code. The bolt clicked.

"If you insist on coming with me, we're going in on three," he whispered.

She nodded.

"One, two—" Raz counted when the mansion's grand front door swung open in a whoosh of air.

She shrieked as two tiny forms loomed in the darkened doorway.

"We thought you'd never get out of that giant car," came a girl's huff of a voice.

Then the other pint-sized person shrouded in darkness lunged toward them. "Say, beefcake!"

SEVEN

LIBBY

BEEFCAKE?

"Smile for the camera!" came a boy's familiar voice.

Light blasted from below, followed by a sharp, mechanical hum.

She screamed bloody murder, then jumped into Raz's arms.

As if he were expecting her to hurl her body at him, he caught her and held her close. Instinctively, or maybe it was the adrenaline surging through her veins, she nuzzled into him. Their bodies melded together in a predominantly chaotic yet slightly erotic motion. Her hammering heartbeat evened out as she inhaled Raz's virile, earthy scent. It made her want to press her lips to the hollow of his neck and lick a trail down to his rock-hard torso.

This man was built like a brick house—and clearly, she was a-okay with that.

Sweet Buddha's belly, she could not allow her mind to go there.

She only had a second to get her bearings before the smack of plastic meeting a hard surface erupted in a cascade of cracks, rattles, and an echoing buzz.

The vibrators.

A jarring clang—her gong—accompanied the cluster of sex toys that proceeded to vibrate on the polished floor as the sound echoed through the cavernous, darkened room.

She'd barely caught her breath when the lights came on, and an ornate chandelier illuminated the grand foyer. She shielded her eyes from its glow. Blinking as her pupils responded to the onslaught of the glare, she squinted and took in not an intruder or a thief but six pairs of eyes attached to six of her favorite people. Six people who stood stock-still, staring at her slack-jawed.

What in the world were they doing inside Raz's house?

Libby surveyed the stunned group. Penny cocked her head to the side then shared a curious look with Charlotte as Mitch and Rowen stood there, dumbfounded. She focused on the little bodies that had met them at the darkened doorway and spied none other than her favorite six-year-olds, Phoebe Gale and Oscar Elliott.

For what felt like half a century, no one moved.

Libby forced herself to employ her yoga and meditation training.

Breathe and be mindful.

She took stock of her body—a body that clung to another body. And this other body, Raz's body, cradled her in his arms like this was some deranged version of whooshing a bride across the threshold. Except this bride didn't come in throwing bouquets of roses and lilies. Nope, this modern woman chucked vibrators at the guests.

The mechanical hum that greeted—or scared the ever-living crap out of her—cut through the stunned silence as Oscar snapped another shot with his Polaroid instant camera.

"Here," Oscar said, pushing up on his tiptoes to hand her a

photo. "This is the first picture I took. It sure looks like I surprised you."

Libby stared at the blurred image. Looking positively terrified, the flash lit them in a harsh burst of yellowy-orange as they clung to each other, wide-eyed. They looked like they'd emerged from one of those jarring so-called fun houses with mirrors that distorted bodies and uneven flooring that could make the most balanced human feel off-kilter enough to lose their lunch, which wasn't too far off from what she'd experienced tonight.

"Thanks, Oscar," she said, accepting the image, then showed the shot to Raz.

Shell-shocked, the man nodded. "Brilliant work, lad."

"It sure caught the emotion of the moment," she said to the boy, then realized her feet were dangling. And, oh no! She was in Erasmus Cress's arms in front of everyone.

She leaned in as all eyes remained locked on them. "You can put me down," she whispered.

"Yeah, good idea," he replied, gently lowering her to the ground.

She was about to ask her friends what in Buddha's name they were doing inside Raz's home when Phoebe pointed to the floor.

"Those are from the video!" the child exclaimed, delight written on her face.

Libby felt the blood drain from her cheeks.

Phoebe Gale had seen the video?

And then she remembered the words that preceded the burst of light.

Say, beefcake.

Oscar had seen the video, too.

She didn't have a second to get a word out before Phoebe started speaking again.

"Are those tiny torpedoes, Libby? Is that why you were throwing them? Can we put them in the pool? Can we race them? And, boy oh boy, now that I can see them up close, they look like big plastic hot dogs with little motors, and you've got a ton of them. There's a pretty rainbow one. I call dibs, Oscar. That one is mine," the little girl finished.

Libby inhaled a tight breath. She didn't think adding another layer of humiliation to this evening was possible.

She was wrong.

"Do not touch anything, Phoebe," Rowen called.

"Same goes for you, Oscar. Hands where we can see them," Mitch exclaimed as Penny and Charlotte slapped their hands over their mouths to restrain what looked like a serious bout of giggles.

Oscar crouched down and took a picture of the Rainbow Screamer, then handed the still-developing Polaroid to Phoebe. "Here you go. I don't know why we can't touch the hot dog torpedoes, but you can put this picture in your room."

The little girl twirled and pressed the photo to her chest. "I'll tape it to my door, so we can see it every time we walk down the hall." The child paused, then squealed. "I have a better idea."

"What is it?" Oscar chimed.

"I'll use my magnet and put the rainbow hotdog torpedo on the refrigerator. Then we can look at it while we eat dinner. What do you think, Penny and Uncle Row? It's a pretty awesome idea."

Rowen adjusted his glasses, but even the thick lenses couldn't hide the complete look of mortification on the man's face. He parted his lips, but nothing came out.

"Phoebe," Penny said, stifling a grin. "We can talk about that when we get home."

Phoebe shared a look with Oscar and groaned. "That means

no in adult-talk," the little girl whisper-shouted to her buddy, then beamed at Raz.

"Hi, Erasmus Cress! We like your house," she tossed out, not missing a beat.

"Thanks?" the man stammered. He blinked a few times like he still wasn't sure what was going on.

That made two of them.

"Libby, guess what?" Phoebe continued, undeterred by the bevy of vibrators scattered across the floor.

"What?" Libby replied, attempting to appear as normal as possible after dispersing sex toys in front of minors. She could feel her cheeks heat, but Phoebe, and Oscar for that matter, were quite unbothered by the strange set of events.

"Oscar and I were having a sleepover at my house. We were playing Go Fish in the living room when we saw you and Erasmus on the TV."

"You're good at throwing things, Libby," Oscar added.

"And then Uncle Row turned off the TV real fast, and Penny ran into the room and said we were going on a special trip to Erasmus's house. But there were a bunch of vans parked outside your gate, so we came in through the back. And we had to be quiet like cheetahs about to pounce on a gazelle because we didn't want the people outside to know we were here."

"Yeah, we got down real low so nobody would see us," Oscar added, acting out the covert movements.

"But then we got bored waiting for you guys to come inside. And you don't have any cookies or hot dogs here," Phoebe continued, giving Raz the stink eye.

"I don't eat cookies and hot dogs when I'm training," Raz replied, sounding like a man who wasn't sure if he was asleep or awake when Rowen found his voice.

"Is there a safe place for children to play in this house without any access to social media or televisions?"

Mitch shifted his stance as he took in the sixteen vibrators. "A place without—"

"Mechanical hot dog torpedoes," Oscar supplied.

"Yeah, those," Mitch agreed, his eyes still about to pop out of his skull.

"There's a room with vintage arcade games and pinball machines down the hall," Raz answered, gesturing to the right.

Libby took a second to survey the gilded foyer that could rival any high-end hotel. The entry boasted not one but two chandeliers and an enormous staircase. It was like she'd walked into an updated version of Downton Abbey.

"Are you sure you don't have any hot dog torpedoes in the game room? We could have mini sword fights with them, too," Oscar exclaimed.

"No, lad, there aren't any mechanical hot dog torpedoes in the house," Raz answered, and the words sounded even more ridiculous in a rolling British accent.

"Why don't you two find the pinball machines. We'll come to get you when we're ready to leave," Charlotte said, patting the kids on their backs.

"Are you sure you don't have any cookies in this place, Raz, like under your bed, or behind the aquarium, or in the garage in a box marked *not cookies*?" Phoebe asked, eyeing the man.

"Phoebe? Do you have cookies hidden in those places at our house?" Penny asked.

The little girl grabbed Oscar's hand. "Let's play pinball," she cried, grinning from ear to ear as the pair sprinted from the foyer and disappeared down one of the sprawling hallways.

"I was wondering what was in that box," Rowen murmured, shaking his head.

With the children out of earshot, Libby looked from Penny to Charlotte. "What are you doing here?"

Charlotte crossed her arms. One didn't need to be a psychic to see that her girls were about to break into mother hen mode.

"Oscar already answered that," Char replied.

Libby frowned. "I don't understand."

"Beefcake," Penny tossed out, then raised an eyebrow.

Libby braced herself. Here it comes.

"Why didn't you tell us that Raz was the beefcake you've been going on and on about?" Charlotte pressed.

"You've been going on and on about me?" Raz asked, curiosity lacing the question.

The mortification meter kept on ticking.

Libby cringed. Out of every word that had gotten jumbled in the recording of her confronting Raz, it was just her luck that *beefcake* would ring out with acoustic precision.

She ignored Raz's question. "So, you've seen the entire viral video?" she asked, surveying the couples.

Rowen laughed. "Oh, Libby, of course, we have. The sports shows and websites picked up on it first. But now it's made it to the nerds and the hackers. There are already tens of millions of views." Rowen slipped his phone from his pocket. "Wow, almost one hundred million now. Pretty soon, nearly the entire planet will have watched it. And I almost forgot. Even people off-planet know about it."

"Off-planet?" Raz repeated with a crinkle to his brow.

Libby swallowed back a wave of nausea. It was one thing to have a decent percentage of the population of the planet revel in her embarrassing moment. Who in the world off-planet could have seen the video?

Rowen held out his phone. "They showed it to the astronauts on the International Space Station."

"They're floating and laughing," Libby lamented.

"Tell them the good part, Row," Penny said, beaming at her nerd.

"The astronauts are rooting for Raz to win in the upcoming fight. So at least you've got that," Rowen added as he grinned at Penny.

"It's pretty great," Mitch added, pulling out his phone. "They reenacted the vibrator throwing in space using extra PVC tubes. People love it."

"Is screaming and throwing things a yoga technique?" Charlotte asked.

Speechless, Libby shared a look with Raz. In his eyes, she saw the same question she had.

How had this blown up so quickly?

"We get it," Raz began. "You've seen the video. People floating in space have seen it. But why are you at my house? I don't mean to be rude, but how the bloody hell did you get in?"

"Obviously, we broke in," Rowen supplied smoothly. "Scratch that. I hacked in and bypassed the alarm."

"Now, Raz," Penny interjected. "I usually stop Rowen before he does anything like this, but we had no other choice. Neither of you would answer your texts."

"Penny's right," Mitch continued. "First, Libby texted her friends, saying that she was getting arrested, and then you texted us and said the same thing. What were we supposed to do?"

Raz scoffed. "Oh, I don't know—not break into my house."

Her beefcake had a point. This was going to the extreme. Then again, she would have probably freaked out if Penny, Harper, or Charlotte texted a going-to-jail message, too.

"We went to Libby's place first, but some lady named Ida lives there now. When did that happen?" Charlotte questioned, then narrowed her gaze. "And what's that on your shoulder, Libbs?"

Libby stared at the sea of vibrators scattered across the floor before taking in her crusty shoulder. "It's crow poop."

"Crow poop?" Rowen, Penny, Charlotte, and Mitch exclaimed.

Libby sighed. "It happened after I got kicked out of my apartment."

"And what about your meeting for your yoga center?" Charlotte asked, coming to her side.

"That turned out to be a sham. They weren't looking to invest. It was a joke to meet women."

Just saying that out loud made her want to throttle the stupid Derricks.

Penny joined Charlotte as the women huddled. "No wonder you went a little crazy, Libbs."

"And shame on you, Erasmus," Charlotte said, turning her wrath on the boxer.

"Shame on me? What do you mean?" the man exclaimed.

"Her chi, Raz," Penny chided, getting in on the Raz bashing.

"And don't forget about her O," Charlotte added.

Mitch sucked in a tight breath. "That's a tough one, Libby."

"Yeah, the worst," Rowen agreed.

And the humiliation hits kept coming.

The mortification meter had blown clear off the charts.

"Listen," Raz explained. "I don't know how it happened. I never meant to *de-chi* or *de-O* your friend. But now, we have to make the best of this peculiar situation."

Peculiar was one way to describe it. Totally freaking insane was another.

"So, it's true? Libby is going to be your son's nanny and your spiritual advisor?" Mitch asked.

"Yes, and you can add burro racing partner to that list," Raz said.

"Burro racing and mechanical hot dog torpedoes?" Mitch observed the vibrator-laden floor, then shook his head. "This night keeps getting weirder and weirder."

The vibrators!

She'd almost forgotten about them, and she sure couldn't leave the sex toys on the foyer floor.

Libby grabbed her bag and tossed a few inside when a crash erupted from inside the house.

"That can't be the kids. The sound came from the other side of the house. How many people are breaking into my place tonight?" Raz growled.

"Jesus Christ, Landon! Sneak into mansions much?"

"Um...no, like most normal people, I usually use the front door," an exasperated man's voice shot back.

Libby craned her neck to look past Raz as two people rounded the corner.

"Harper?" she exclaimed.

"Landon?" Raz cried.

Welp, the whole gang had made it.

"I got the texts about meeting up here and to enter through the back," Harper said in a tumble of words. "Now," the woman continued, taking in the scene, "what the hell happened outside that boxing gym? And also, Libby Caroline Lamb, why didn't you tell us Erasmus Cress was the beefcake?"

"We've already yelled at Libbs for that," Penny said gently.

Harper's chestnut brown ponytail swished as the woman zeroed in on Raz. "And you!"

"We took care of that, too," Charlotte interrupted.

Harper threw up her hands. "Then why am I here? Who am I supposed to yell at?"

"We're here because we love Libby and care about Erasmus, and we needed to make sure that they were okay," Penny supplied.

"Gotcha," Harper answered, but the fire in her eyes hadn't diminished. "Libbs, that video is crazy town. Where are your crystals and your Buddha stuff? Should we chant or burn some sage?" She turned to Raz. "Do you have any sage on hand?"

The man was back to looking befuddled. "No."

Harper tapped her chin. "There's yoga. It's your thing, Libbs. We could get into tree pose or donkey pose."

"Donkey pose!" Mitch exclaimed.

Harper met Charlotte's gaze. "Is your food truck fiancé okay, Char?"

"I'm fine, I'm fine," Mitch replied. "You said donkey, and that made me think of Raz."

Harper studied Mitch, then eyed the four men. "You guys have a strange dynamic going on."

"It's nothing creepy," Mitch clarified. "Before you got here, Raz mentioned that, in addition to Libby getting hired on as his nanny and spiritual advisor, she was also his burro racing partner."

"Okay, the smarmy British guy on TV went on and on about The Lion bringing on a spiritual advisor to take him to the next level, whatever the hell that means. But he didn't mention anything about a donkey race," Harper snapped.

Libby waved her hands to get the group's attention. "Just listen. Here's the rundown. You saw me throw the vibrators at Raz and then watched as we got arrested, right?"

Everyone nodded.

"After that, Madelyn met us at the police station. We didn't know what she was doing there, but it turned out to be a godsend. Before the arresting officers could book us, Madelyn intervened. She dropped the whole nanny match revelation, then, since she's a close friend of the chief of police, she worked out a deal to get the charges put on hold."

"That woman knows everyone," Penny supplied, shaking her head.

"But how does donkey racing fit in?" Mitch asked.

Libby rubbed her temples. The whirlwind of a night had her brain ready to explode.

Raz tapped her shoulder. "I've got this, plum," he said, then addressed the group. "The police chief gave us an ultimatum. Libby and I had to agree to train and compete in something called the Ass-in-Nine Burro Race to represent Denver's first responders. If we don't do it, they'll charge us with lewd behavior."

Mitch ran his hands down his face. "I did not see that coming."

"The race is held in Rickety Rock. A town near—" Libby began when Rowen snapped his fingers.

"It's near Aspen," the nerd announced.

"Yes, Raz and I agreed to live there for the summer and train for the race," she answered.

"And after that, I've got my fight," Raz finished, shifting his stance nervously.

Maybe the beefcake wasn't the conceited, cocksure fighter who'd oozed buckets of confidence in front of the press.

Penny shook her head. "I'm the writer here, but even I couldn't have cooked up something like that."

"It's pretty insane," Libby answered.

"And what about Sebastian?" Mitch asked. "He should be arriving soon, right?"

At the mention of his son, Raz's throat constricted as he swallowed. "He arrives with my grandmother in a couple of days, and then we'll figure out when we can head to Rickety Rock."

"This is encouraging news!" Rowen exclaimed—looking downright upbeat.

"There are plenty of words that could describe tonight. I'm not sure encouraging is one of them, mate," Raz answered.

"I was remarking on the proximity. We'll be in Aspen for much of the summer," Rowen continued.

"Each of us has a place up there," Mitch explained, gesturing to Rowen and Landon.

"And we've got Phoebe and Oscar signed up for a bunch of Bergen Adventure Camps in the area. Sebastian might enjoy it, too," Charlotte added.

"Is he into outdoor activities?" Mitch asked.

Raz parted his lips and...nothing. Not a word escaped. But after a few seconds, which felt more like a few millennia, the man rebounded. "Sure, I think he'd enjoy that."

Harper raised her hand. "Yeah, not everyone can escape to million-dollar mountain homes. Some people stay in town and wake up early to teach piano lessons to booger-eating elementary school children. Just saying."

Penny wrapped her arm around H's shoulders. "You're always welcome to stay with us when you have time. And on that note, now that we know Erasmus and Libby are okay, it's time we let them get settled in. Not to mention, it's way past Phoebe and Oscar's bedtime."

"Come on, guys. Can you show us the way to the game room, Raz?" Rowen asked.

"Libby?" came a voice—Raz's voice. Something was off. She couldn't read him. Was that sadness in his gray eyes—or trepidation?

"Yes."

"I'll be right back."

"And I'll clean up the rest of the *torpedoes* while you're gone," she answered, hating this awkward energy simmering between them. Then again, their lives had been turned upside down and inside out in a matter of hours.

Raz nodded, then filed out of the foyer with the men, giving her a much-needed moment alone with her girls.

Penny surveyed the floor. "It's not every day you see a home in the fancy-pants Crystal Hills neighborhood decorated with vibrators."

"Quite a daring choice of décor," Char chimed.

"The sheer number is utterly breathtaking," H added.

Libby smiled. Her friends were trying to lighten the mood.

Harper held up the multi-colored vibrator, then dropped it into the bag. "Ah, the Rainbow Screamer! The perfect complement to our Libby, the yoga screamer," she remarked, but her signature smirk melted into a look of genuine concern. "Libbs, are you all right with being the beefcake's nanny and spiritual advisor? He hurt you, honey. We've seen what you've been going through these last couple of months. You've been a wreck."

Libby dropped an armful of vibrators into the bag as Char added the gong and mallet, and Penny zipped the tote.

"Yeah, Libbs, that video was intense, but then there was this moment. Did you guys catch it?" Penny said, eyeing Char and Harper.

"The hoodie grab?" Charlotte asked.

"Yeah, I saw it," H added.

Libby's gaze bounced between her friends. "What are you talking about?"

Penny pulled her phone from her pocket. "I'll show you."

"I don't want to see it, Penn," Libby said, waving away the phone. "I'm not sure how much more mortification I can take today."

"I won't make you watch the video, but look at this screenshot," Penny nudged as she tapped her phone, then held it out for them to see.

Libby stared at an image of her and Raz. The man had his arm wrapped around her protectively as she clutched the fabric of his hoodie in her fist. A shiver passed through her. No, it wasn't a shiver. That tingling response was her body aching for the beefcake's touch. She ignored the sensation. "I was pretty freaked out at that point. It was like I'd left my body while I was screaming, then returned to it to find flashing lights and policemen calling out commands."

"What made you think yelling outside his gym was a good idea, Libbs?" Char asked gently.

Libby sighed. "Ida."

Char raised an eyebrow. "The lady in your apartment?"

"It's her apartment. Hash Pants sublet it without her knowledge while she was away at a meditation retreat." Libby pictured the woman with her flowing hair and jangly jewelry—a woman she'd sworn she'd seen or possibly met somewhere. But that couldn't be. Hash Pants said his aunt had been gone nearly a decade. "I briefly interacted with her when I was getting kicked out of my apartment. Ida stopped me before I got into my car. She gave me a stone, then told me I needed to release my rage. I've tried everything else to balance my chi and get my O back. I figured, why not go big and see what would happen if I opened a can of anger yoga on Raz. And now the world and everyone on the International Space Station know what happened next."

"Can you handle it, Libbs? Can you be around this guy twenty-four seven?" Charlotte asked.

Libby shrugged. "I don't have much choice. I've been fired from every studio, and Raz's sports agent arranged to pay for Anders and Alec's schooling in exchange for my services as a spiritual advisor. The guy made it up on the fly, and now between that and the threat of being charged as a sexual deviant, I'm stuck seeing it through."

"You can rest assured that you'll be a terrific nanny. You practically raised your brothers. I'm sure Sebastian will adore you," Penny offered.

Sebastian.

Just like the first time she'd heard Raz's son's name, a warmth filled her chest.

"And what about the whole boxing thing?" Char questioned. "That can't be easy for you."

Libby's pulse kicked up. With the excitement, she'd almost forgotten she'd be spending night and day with a world heavyweight champion boxer. An icy chill ushered out the warmth, and she released a shaky breath. If there were ever a time a gal could use a dose of balanced energy, it was now. Too bad her chi was more out of whack than ever.

"It must make you think of your dad," H added.

"When was the last time you heard from him?" Char asked.

Libby swallowed past the lump in her throat. "He texted a few months ago."

"You didn't mention that to us," H remarked.

Libby stared at one of the ornate empty vases placed in the corner of the great space. "There wasn't much to mention. It's always the same thing. There's some business venture or some sure-thing he has the inside track on, and if he could borrow two or three grand, he could get in on the deal or make the bet that would pay out ten times what he put in," she finished, the words tasting of searing disappointment.

"Connolly Lamb is one piece of work," Harper lamented.

That was an understatement.

But talk of her deadbeat dad ended when Phoebe rounded the corner and called out to them. "Libby, Harper, Penny, Charlotte, the game room is awesome! It was so big Oscar and I played hide-and-seek in there. This whole house is like twenty houses in one," she exclaimed before belting out one behemoth of a yawn.

"It sounds like you've had quite an adventure," Penny replied, smoothing a lock of Phoebe's hair.

The guys returned with Mitch carrying a sleeping Oscar.

"Where'd you find Oscar?" Phoebe asked with another yawn.

"Under the pool table, asleep," Mitch answered, shifting the boy in his arms as Charlotte removed the Polaroid camera from the child's grip.

"That explains why he didn't come out when I called to him. He can't party like we can, right girls?" Phoebe mumbled, rubbing her eyes.

Libby chuckled. A little dose of this hilarious girl helped ease the pain that came along with the thoughts of her father. She and her friends bit back grins as Rowen scooped the pint-sized party animal into his arms. Phoebe let out a dreamy sigh, then relaxed into her uncle's embrace.

"Thanks for checking on us. I'm not sure you needed to break into the bloody house. But I," Raz turned to her, "I mean, Libby and I, *we* appreciate your concern."

Libby nodded as that rush of tingles returned.

We.

"Yes, thanks," she stammered.

She had to get herself under control, especially when it came to Erasmus Cress.

"Would you like to leave out the front? The press is probably gone," Raz added.

Rowen gestured with his chin toward the back of the house. "We'll go the way we came. We're parked on the street behind your place."

"And we'll go ahead and sign Sebastian up for the camps and activities Phoebe and Oscar are doing in Aspen," Charlotte added.

"Yeah, thanks," Raz answered with that hint of trepidation in his tone that seemed to accompany any talk of his son.

Libby twisted her jade bracelet as the sound of her friends' footsteps faded, and then it was just the two of them.

The two of them and a bag of vibrators.

She glanced around the ornate foyer. Decorated with opulent, Victorian-style carved cabinets, antiques, painted vases, and two high-back chairs angled toward each other that screamed, *do not sit on me! I'm for looks only.*

"You have a beautiful home. This entryway is...lovely—so spacious."

Buddha, help her! After everything they'd been through over the last handful of hours, that's what she had to say to the man?

Raz scanned the vast entryway. "The house came like this. It's a rental."

"Well, it's a nice rental. Lots of...character," she replied, sounding like a deranged real estate agent. Still, how was she supposed to navigate this strange new life? One minute, she's ready to kiss the guy into oblivion, and the next, they're staring at each other like two awkward preteens at a middle school mixer.

"Are you hungry?" he asked, then gestured toward another hallway. "The kitchen's that way."

She shook her head. "No."

"Would you like to see the laundry room?" he continued.

She stared at the man. "The laundry room?"

"For your jumper." He gestured toward her shoulder—her shit-covered shoulder.

"You mean my yoga wrap?" she corrected.

"Whatever you're wearing that's covered in bird shit. Would you like to wash it, or do you prefer your clothing covered in animal crap?"

"I prefer *un-crapped* clothing," she answered as the awkward meter skyrocketed.

"The laundry is upstairs on the same floor as the bedrooms." He shook his head. "I don't know why I said that. There are also closets and bathrooms on the second floor. And doors, plenty of those," he finished, looking more discombobulated by the second.

"Yeah, that happens in many houses on the second floor, here, in America. We have doors and closets and bathrooms," she answered, then shook her head as her cheeks burned and another dose of mortification hit her bloodstream.

She had to pull herself together.

She lifted her chin to project an air of purpose and a determination to rid herself of shit-covered clothing. She cleared her throat. "Maybe we should go upstairs and do it."

Dear universe, please render Libby Lamb mute ASAP.

"You want to do it?" he bit out, his jaw nearly hitting the floor.

Libby pasted a plastic grin to her face, hoping to disguise the feeling of complete and utter embarrassment that tore through her like a runaway freight train.

Could a person combust from mortification?

She was about to find out.

"The laundry. Do the laundry, not each other," she clarified, not doing a hell of a lot to dig herself out of the humiliation hole that kept getting deeper and deeper.

"Let's just..." Raz said, then pointed to the grand staircase.

She nodded, then, without a word, fell into step with the man.

Opting for nonverbal communication was a good call.

Raz was right about the doors. This place was enormous. They passed a ton of them before he opened the one at the end of the hall. He flicked on the lights to reveal a room larger than her last apartment. With shiny appliances, cabinetry lining the walls, and a quaint seating area, this was the type of laundry room celebrities must have in their homes—or at least, that's what she figured. It almost made ironing and sorting socks sound enticing.

"Washer, dryer, detergent," the man grunted as he pointed out the items.

Okay, she could do this. It was laundry. She removed her wrap, then tossed it into the washer.

"Could you throw this in, too?" Raz asked.

She peered over her shoulder, and hello, abs for miles! Raz had unzipped his hoodie, and he didn't have anything on underneath it. She stared at the rock-hard wall of muscle. "*Beefcake*," she whispered, her mouth moving of its own volition.

"Do you mind washing my hoodie with your wrap?" the man tried again, snapping her out of an abs-induced stupor.

"I'd be *abby* to. I mean, *happy* to," she yipped, accepting the item while trying not to lean forward and lick the man's torso. She cleared her throat, then fell back on a habit from when she used to do the twins' laundry. She reached into the hoodie's pocket, feeling for pens or loose change when her fingertips brushed against something cool and smooth. Immediately, she knew what it was. "My aquamarine gemstone," she said, removing it from Raz's pocket before tossing his garment into the washer. She kept the stone in her hand, added detergent, then started the machine. With the hum of the washer beginning its first cycle, she studied the stone. She hadn't really looked at it yet. An oval-shaped piece of polished aquamarine, a little larger than a quarter, with a greenish-blue tinge. It honestly wasn't that extraordinary. Aquamarine was Colorado's state gemstone. Any rock shop or new-age boutique in the area carried them. But like the woman who'd gifted her with the stone, there was a familiarity about it.

"I forgot I had that. You threw that rock at me after you ran out of vibrators," Raz commented as a rosy blush dusted his cheeks.

She sighed, feeling a strange sense of calm as she rubbed her thumb over the stone's smooth surface. "I bet that's something you never thought you'd say."

"You seem to bring out another side of me," Raz remarked.

She smiled. "It's safe to say you've done the same to me."

"I didn't mean to mess up your chi. It wasn't intentional. I didn't expect..." he trailed off.

"What didn't you expect?" she asked, her voice barely a whisper.

"That's not important. But I want you to know, if there was something, anything I could do to fix it, I would. But I should warn you. I'm a boxer. I'm better at breaking things than I am at putting them back together, plum."

Had more heartbreaking words ever been spoken?

A wave of compassion washed over her, and the only thing she wanted to do was to shield this man from whatever demons put that thought into his head.

"Why do you keep calling me plum?" she asked, shifting gears.

He glanced at the ceiling. "I don't know. You said I couldn't call you *sugar plum*. Maybe I call you plum to piss you off? I am quite good at that," he added with a stupidly sexy boyish grin. And Buddha, give her strength. That smile, coupled with the man's Adonis of a body, was almost too hard to resist. "And of course," he continued, "plums are purple, and I saw the violet and blue around us in the cop car."

Her heart nearly stopped. "You saw those colors when we were in the police car?"

"Yeah, I did, but it could have been the light from a neon sign or something."

But it wasn't. She knew it wasn't that.

"You're sure it was both colors?" she pressed, hardly able to believe a man who clucked and paraded around like the King of the Beefcakes could perceive auras.

"Yeah, bluish-violet. But what does that matter?" he asked.

"I noticed it, too. It's called an aura. It's curious we both saw it and that our observations are so much alike." She paused as an idea sparked. "So much alike—like treats like," she whispered.

He took a step toward her. "Are you okay, plum? Do you see colors again, or fairies, or whatever yoga people see?"

She shook her head. "No, I don't see any fairies, but something came to me—like the universe whispered into my ear."

"And what did the universe have to say?" There was a decent amount of skepticism in his voice, but she ignored it.

"It told me there might be a way to get my O back," she answered, her heart in her throat. The idea was absolutely insane, but it was her last hope. She looked her half-naked beefcake up and down, then locked onto his gray, piercing gaze. "And Erasmus Cress, you're the only one who can help me do it."

EIGHT

LIBBY

LIBBY STARED at her beefcake as the remedy to her situation ricocheted around in her mind.

Like cures like.

So simple, yet so complex, it was worth a shot.

This might be the karmically craziest thing that had ever crossed her mind.

"What did the universe tell you to do?" Raz asked, concern marring his features, which wasn't that surprising. There was an excellent chance she resembled a mad scientist ranting in a eureka moment. She paced the length of the laundry room, then stopped in front of a still befuddled-looking Erasmus Cress.

Here goes everything.

"The universe reminded me of a homeopathic concept called like cures like."

He frowned. "I've never heard of it."

Her apprehension gave way to a bubbling euphoria that thrummed through her veins. This had to be the solution. What else could foster steady chi and the return of her O better than a metaphysically balanced approach?

"There are lots of examples of like curing like or like

treating like. They mean the same thing. Onions, for example," she tossed out, excitement lacing her reply.

"Onions?" Raz repeated, looking quite the opposite of convinced.

She had to slow down and harness her excitement bordering on mania, or she'd lose him for sure.

"Onions can make you cry," she began.

Raz sniffed, then glanced away. "I don't cry, but I see what you're getting at."

"Onions," she continued, leaning against the washer, "are the main ingredient in a homeopathic remedy that treats watery, irritated eyes. Like if you've got hay fever or caught a cold."

Raz moved forward and rested his hands on the vibrating washing machine, one beefy paw on either side of her, as he caged her in. "I still don't understand what that means for us? You're not suggesting we only eat onions for the next several weeks, are you?" he asked, his voice doing things to her that it absolutely should not do.

The breath caught in her throat as she stared up at him. The zing of anticipation invaded every cell in her body. The intensity coming off the man in near-tangible waves combined with the motion of the washer had her reeling. She willed herself to ignore his all-encompassing vitality, then formulated her reply. "Since you're the cause of my condition, you could also be the cure."

He sharpened his gaze. "How would that work?"

The energy flowing between them sent her chakras into a berserk kinetic overload—or perhaps it was the washing machine. Still, whatever gave her this idea, she knew she'd stumbled onto something big.

She ignored the desire to trace every carved muscle on this man's chiseled body. "There are two issues to address," she continued. "Balancing my chi is the first condition. But balance is a pretty broad concept, and it would be most advantageous to treat the second more acute ailment."

"Which is?" Raz pressed.

Her heart was about to beat itself clean out of her chest.

Just say it.

"My inability to have an orgasm."

Holy Buddha's belly! She blurted it out like she was ordering a vegan burrito.

"You want me to get you off? You're proposing we shag?" he asked, his eyes widening.

She winced, then looked away. "I'm sorry. It must sound outrageous. Not to mention, I don't even know if you have a girlfriend."

"I don't," he interrupted, urgency lacing his hasty reply. He gently cupped her face in his hands. "I don't do relationships. Like it is for you, sex is just sex for me. No feelings. No love. No commitment. Only release."

He was lying. She didn't know how she knew, she just did.

"There's no Miss Right out there for you?" she asked, attempting humor, but the intensity in Raz's expression didn't let up.

"No," he bit back through gritted teeth.

He was lying again. She felt it in her very being—or was that her discombobulated chi throwing mixed signals again?

It didn't matter.

She knew where she stood when it came to men, love, and sex. And as crazy as it sounded, the like curing like method might be her last hope to work this beefcake out of her system, welcome back her long-lost O, and balance her chi.

"Since we're on the same page when it comes to how we approach sex," she went on, treading carefully. "We could treat my condition with an academic approach and employ a curriculum with benchmarks. That's how I teach my yoga classes. My background in physical education and kinesiology pull from science and clinical observation, while my yoga training harnesses the unseen piece, the current of energy that flows through us."

"So, a little science and a little yoga mumbo jumbo?" Raz replied.

"Something like that. When I teach, I pick a skill, then work toward attaining it with my students. The skill in our case would be my O. We could measure progress by testing methods to attain an O together and then test if I can complete the goal by myself. After that, I'd move on to achieving completion with an outside partner. This experiment combines the best of qualitative and quantitative analysis, which I believe will support a productive outcome."

There! That was a mouthful, but surely, her kinesiology professors back in college would have given her high marks for such a well-thought-out physiological goal. And the yogis who taught her along the way would have to agree that using like forces to overcome an energy blockage was a sound technique.

Raz frowned. "Can you say that in English, please?"

She focused on his gray, piercing eyes. "If I can get off with you, the *curriculum* would be considered a success if I were able to masturbate to completion. That's the first benchmark. And then, the final test would be to see if I could climax with another partner. That's the second benchmark."

Well, that was weird. Had she ever actually said the word climax aloud?

"Climax with another partner?" the man growled.

Had she struck a nerve?

"Yes, then we'd know that the skill had been mastered and that it was able to be reproduced in different domains," she answered, sticking with the science.

"Reproduced in different domains?" the man repeated, no, growled, again.

Now she got why people called him the Lion.

This shouldn't upset him. It was just sex, right? Or maybe she simply sounded like a maniac. She honestly couldn't tell. With Erasmus Cress cradling her face in his strong, warm hands, it was hard to focus on anything. Using the pad of his thumb, he caressed her jawline, and the contact sent a delicious buzz through her body that settled between her thighs.

"I didn't understand half of what you said, plum. But here's what I know. Something is going on between us. I felt it when you came into the gym all those days ago and asked me to keep it down."

"That was the shift. That's when my chi went crazy," she whispered.

"And all of a sudden, the air thrummed with electricity—all blue and violet, like what happened tonight," Raz answered.

He might be a big, beefy jock. Still, when Erasmus Cress dropped the arrogant act and referenced auras, he was utterly irresistible.

"Okay, we'll follow the curriculum. And don't worry," she continued, "I can promise that this experiment won't interfere with my ability to be your son's nanny or your spiritual advisor. I take my responsibilities seriously. And when I commit to something, when I make a promise, I see it through." Her voice quivered as flashes of her past tried to invade her mind, but she regained control. "We're talking about purely physical acts. No emotions involved."

She remained stock-still as she waited for the man to reply. With the washing machine humming in the background and the air around them on the brink of igniting, neither said a word as he devoured her with his gaze. The intensity of this man could power the city for days. And as much as she disliked boxing,

Raz's ability to fiercely focus must serve him well in the ring. It certainly had her spellbound.

He brushed his thumb across her bottom lip, then turned her head to the side. Leaning in, his lips skimmed the shell of her ear. "I'm going to take a step back, plum, and then, right here, right now, you're going to strip for me."

Strip...for Erasmus Cress...in a fancy laundry room?

And he wanted to get down to business now?

This man didn't mess around.

Raz made good on his word and moved away from her. And then, as if she were caught in a dream, she kicked off her sneakers, peeled her white yoga capris from her body, then slipped the shimmering sports bra over her head and let it fall to the floor. She had no issues with nudity. The human body held the spirit. It was a vessel to be revered. But when she glanced down at her nude-colored underwear, which, *oh no*, bordered on granny panties, she felt her cheeks heat. Of all the days to go beige, this wasn't one of them. In her defense, when she woke up this morning, doing a striptease for Raz in his apartment-sized laundry room was the last place she'd expected to end her day.

She shifted her stance. "Pretty boring in the underwear department, but there aren't many options with white yoga pants," she added with an insanely awkward flick of her wrist.

That's the first thing she says after the man commands her to disrobe?

What was she doing—schooling him on the art of wearing white?

But the glimmer in Raz's eyes didn't channel disappointment or the desire to discuss panty lines. Not breaking eye contact, he ran his tongue across his top lip. "I'd imagined what was under that red jumper. But this...you...you're bloody perfect. Nothing on that body could be considered boring."

He'd thought about her naked.

She shouldn't like that—not at all. But her body couldn't lie. Her nipples tightened into pink pearls as she allowed her hungry gaze to rove over him.

"Your turn," she directed, then gestured to his boxing shorts.

A dirty smirk pinched his lips. "You want me naked, plum?"

"It's for purely academic reasons."

"Is that so?" he queried.

"It could assist in inducing arousal," she answered with another ridiculous wrist flick. She'd come down with carpal tunnel if she kept this up.

Raz's cocky smirk, which was, surprisingly, starting to grow on her, stretched into a dirty grin as he took off his shoes, then removed his shorts and his boxer briefs. The man stood, towering over her, and her jaw dropped. Erasmus Cress possessed what could only be described as one magnificent cock. Rock-hard, the man was glorious—a buck-naked gladiator with great hair to boot.

She'd had a decent amount of sex in her life. But no man had ever exuded this kind of magnetic masculinity before. If she knew anything about sculpting, she'd spend her last penny on clay and recreate this man's appendage for humanity to appreciate. However, there was no way she would admit this to him.

Play it cool! This is an academic exercise. Science, think about science.

"From my vantage point, you appear to possess adequate equipment for our experiment," she observed, like an idiot, gawking at his manhood.

Thirsty much, Libby Lamb?

"And what about you?" he asked in a low, sexy rumble. "Don't I get to assess your equipment?"

"Here I am," she replied, raising her arm in a ta-da position.

"Your knickers, plum," he remarked, zeroing in on the most boring shade of beige known to mankind.

She stared at her panties. "You want me to take them off?"

"For purely academic reasons," he answered, stealing her words.

And burning Buddha's balls, it had gotten hot!

She slid the beige fabric down her legs, then kicked her underwear onto the pile of clothing. Naked and completely exposed, she released her hair from its bun and shook it out. The long, black waves passed her shoulders as the locks teased her taut nipples.

"Libby Lamb, look at me," Raz said, no, *commanded*.

She flicked her gaze from the pile of clothing, then observed as the man's expression grew positively carnal.

"You're an absolute stunner, but it's your eyes, plum," he remarked, moving toward her like a predator, closing in on its prey.

"What about them?" she whispered.

He brushed her hair over to one shoulder. "It's like they can see everything," he rasped, the raw honesty of his statement striking like an arrow to her heart.

"That's not what this is about," she replied, working to maintain the conviction in her voice.

"No, it's not. This is just sex," he agreed—or did he? He'd spoken the words, but that little voice inside her head wasn't so sure he'd meant it.

He dropped a kiss to her shoulder, and every ounce of rational thought drained from her brain. She released an audible sigh, then gripped the washing machine as Raz pinned her between himself and the vibrating device.

"I'm going to kiss you," he said, making good on his announcement as his lips trailed along her skin. "Then I'll touch you," he added, skimming his hands down her torso. "And after that, I plan on thrusting my cock inside of you and making you come so hard, your O will get down on its little O knees and beg for more. Does that work with your curriculum, plum?"

Oh, yes! That worked!

He cupped his hand between her thighs, applying just the right amount of pressure. She inhaled a tight breath as he rocked his palm against her tight bundle of nerves.

Was she in over her head?

The man was built like a Greek god, and he possessed dirty talk skills!

But there was no turning back now.

Libby closed her eyes, giving in to the sensations engulfing her body. "Your plan is in line with the curriculum. You can certainly try to test that approach," she bit out, finding it harder and harder to form actual words.

He stilled, his eyes blazing with fierce determination. Here was the fighter, but instead of this quality turning her off, his drive turned her on. "I don't try, plum," he breathed. "I succeed. I win. I triumph. I'm a bloody champion."

Wow!

There was a lot to unpack with that string of arrogant proclamations. But sweet karma pie, she wanted him to be right —no, she needed him to be right.

In reply to that verbal brag-fest, she rolled her hips, riding his hand as the man returned to peppering her jawline with kisses. Each point of contact sizzled beneath his heated breath. He dipped his index finger past her delicate folds and teased her entrance. All she could do was brace herself against the vibrating machine as his lips dusted kisses across her cheek. A lightness took over as if a weight were being lifted. She moaned, crying out, powerless to hold back the lusty sound—a motion her beefcake didn't let go to waste. Raz took full advantage of her parted lips and captured her mouth in a passionate kiss.

Their first kiss.

But this was no ordinary first kiss.

Their tongues met in a sensual dance. And despite his searing intensity, the man was in no rush. He kissed her deeply, employing a tenderness she hadn't expected. He explored her mouth as if he were silently recording every lick, every hum, and every point of contact. Luckily, this man was not only a good kisser. He was a multitasker. He never stopped working her with his hand. Strumming her most sensitive place, he slipped his other hand into her hair, twisting the locks around his fingers, then tugged.

He pulled hair like a master tugger!

The sweet bite of pain combined with the pressure building between her thighs had her panting. Her eyelids fluttered open. "I didn't expect for you to be so attentive," she got out between kisses.

"I told you, I'm the best."

She couldn't challenge that assertion.

"There's a lot you don't know about me, plum," he added, his voice growing hoarse.

She stared into his penetrating gray eyes, gasping for breath, peering into the windows to his soul. There was anguish hidden behind the cocky layers of the fighter, but that wasn't all she saw. The man carried an abundance of love in his spirit. Untapped or possibly overlooked, it was there, dormant beneath the mask.

He slipped another finger inside her wet heat, and she tightened around him.

"Bloody hell, plum, you could lift a piano with your core muscles."

"Yoga...really...works," she said between gasps, then raised her hand. "You should see what I can do with this."

"I know. I watched you do that handstand, one-handed."

"I think you'll be equally impressed with this skill," she answered, wrapping her hand around his hard length.

Raz inhaled a sharp breath. "You might be right," he answered, then pressed his lips to hers.

They were relentless, both intent on bringing the other the maximum amount of pleasure. She worked him in long, fluid strokes, matching his pace as he massaged her sweet bud. Shades of blue and violet colored her gaze, cocooning them in a haze of sexual energy. This man's touch reached her on a cellular level. Her once frustrated, blocked chakras joined the rhythmic dance as they drifted into alignment.

This was the closest she'd been to flying over the edge and tapping into her O.

But she wasn't there yet.

She parted her lips, about to tell him she wanted him buried deep inside her. But before she could say the words, Raz read her mind.

"I want to feel you, Libby Lamb. I'm clean. I haven't been with anyone since I was last tested," he said, kissing a trail to her earlobe.

That was music to her ears!

"Tested. Clean. On the pill. Yes, magnificent cock now," she rattled off in a breathy bluster of words.

He took a step back, releasing her. She gasped at the loss of his touch. It must have only been a second, possibly two, before he gripped her by her hips and lifted her onto the washing machine in one swift motion. Instinctively, she edged forward and reached for him. "Don't do that again," she whispered, the words spilling out.

Concern clouded the lust burning in his eyes. "Do what, plum?"

She held his face in her hands. "Let go."

What did that even mean?

She'd never spoken to any of her partners like this—so raw, so vulnerable. But she barely had a second to think.

Without a word, Raz's deft, capable hands slid her forward another inch. She teetered on the edge as he settled the tip of his rock-hard cock at her entrance, then thrust his hips.

Shimmering light radiated between them. She cried out as the sheer power of this powerhouse of a man stretched her in the most decadent, deliriously delicious ways. All she could do was hold on as he filled her to the hilt with his thick, perfect cock. Her soft curves met his hard body, melding together, the yin and yang of opposites attracting, complementing each other as two became one.

His large rough hands gripped her ass, holding her close, holding her like he never wanted to let go. "I've got you," he whispered in that dirty British accent that seriously scrambled her brain.

Or maybe it unscrambled her mind.

She'd never felt more present, more alive than she did sitting atop a washing machine with this giant man's enormous cock inside her.

But it was his words that set the air on fire with flashes of blue and violet.

I've got you.

Three words.

The power of three bound them together with an invisible thread.

She wrapped her arms around his neck, and heart to heart, they moved together, awash in a sea of titillating pleasure.

Each drive of Raz's hard length and the impassioned friction sparking white-hot between them carried her higher and higher. Like a line of roller coaster cars ticking up the track, grinding and pumping, headed for the top of the highest peak, their lovemaking fueled the ascent.

"You're so close, plum. I can feel it," he bit out, dialing up his pace as the machine clicked into the spin cycle.

"Yes," she cried.

Hearts beating as one, she held his gaze. The blue and violet haze exploded to include every color of the rainbow. The brilliant hues flashed before her eyes. An energy, no, a force like nothing she'd experienced, flowed between them. Encased in tangible color, she bucked her hips as an awareness set in.

She was there, perched on the precipice of total orgasmic release.

There was no more searching. She'd reached the top of the peak. It was time to buckle up and enjoy the ride. A bead of perspiration trailed between her breasts. She didn't know if it belonged to her or Raz or if the intensity of their lovemaking had created a whole new weather system inside the laundry room that was about to drench them in a hot, steamy downpour. And then, even though they were writhing together, panting and moaning, not holding back, a stillness in her spirit took hold.

Sweet release, in three, two, one...

"Hello, orgasm, it's me, Libby Lamb!" she cried as her pleasure hit in a wild crescendo. The whoosh, the rush, the heat, and the unstoppable force of their bodies carried them careening down the good old track to Climax Town. Cresting and descending, they rode the rails of ecstasy, up and down, thrust after powerful thrust. Seventy-five days of pent-up sexual frustration exploded like a giant orgasm cake loaded with TNT.

And Raz never looked away. He never closed his eyes. He never left her.

He tightened his hold, gripping her ass and not letting up one single bit as he roared his release. Drenched in sweat, bodies slick, and their breaths coming fast and hard, they clung to each other, reveling in their shared bliss.

Had she ever been this present? Her mind, body, and spirit

had converged on one salient, dirty as hell thought: This man better keep screwing her brains out.

"She's back, Raz! My O, my sacral chakra hasn't glowed like this in weeks," she exclaimed, working to catch her breath in a fog of sex-charged erotic energy.

Raz watched her as a sated smile spread across his lips.

Yes, there was an edge of arrogance in his expression, but it wasn't that cocky twist of a smirk he'd launched at her seventy-five days ago. Now, tenderness wove its way through the man. She could feel it as much as she could see it. Cast in that brilliant blue and violet, he ran his fingertips down her jawline as wonder sparkled in his gray eyes.

"Wham, bam, look at that, Libby Lamb. You're sure that was your O?" he asked, the awe in his gaze changing into a mischievous glimmer.

She'd wanted to throttle the man when he'd hurled the *Wham, bam* line at her before she hurled the vibrators at him. But now, she found it oddly endearing.

She worked to catch her breath. "You know it was my O."

He nodded. "I have an idea."

"Oh yeah?"

"It's regarding the *curriculum*," he continued, then pressed a kiss beneath her earlobe.

"Go on," she said on a breathy sigh.

"If we want to do this right, like a real experiment, we should make sure this result wasn't a fluke. It's like my training. One day hitting every target isn't enough to say I'm ready for a fight."

"Are you suggesting we compile more data?"

Please. Say. Yes.

That cocky smirk returned. "What do you think?"

"That would be the most prudent course of action—especially since, from a purely metaphysical and psychic perspective, I can assure you that continuing the execution of dynamic energy is a beneficial prospect for revisiting climactic events," she gushed like a sex-crazed geyser.

That was one heck of a word salad, but it didn't stop Raz from grinning.

"And in my opinion, this climactic event study requires a softer surface, like, for example, a king-sized bed," he answered.

Sweet Buddha's belly, she liked hearing him spout sexy like an academic!

"When do you propose we complete another round of testing in a king-sized bed?" she eked out, her body trembling at the thought of round two with this man.

Raz's eyes glittered with lust. "Right bloody now."

NINE

LIBBY

LIBBY'S MUSCLES TENSED, and her nipples hardened as she hummed a deliciously dirty moan—a sound she'd gotten quite good at making over the last eight hours.

Yep, she'd been riding the Orgasm Express for eight hours—and counting.

Twisting the bedsheets in her fists, the morning sun streamed in through the windows. She loved watching the sunrise, but she'd had to pass on welcoming the day this morning thanks to the man going to town on her beneath the covers. She arched her back as Erasmus Cress teased her, bringing her to the cusp of release only to draw her back, then do it all over again.

She should be exhausted. She hadn't gotten much sleep last night.

Scratch that.

She hadn't gotten any rest, but she wasn't complaining.

Thanks to the beefcake, still working her body like he was born to do it, her O had returned like a Formula One race car, ready for action and raring to go.

"Raz, that's it! That's the spot," she rasped.

"You don't think I know that by now, plum?" he answered, his lips pressed against her quivering body.

Yes, there was a hint of maddening arrogance in his tone. But the man deserved some credit. He'd gotten quite proficient in the titillation department, and she didn't even mind him talking. He could read aloud the ingredients on the back of a box of cereal. His growly words sent a heady vibration that tingled from her head down to her toes, adding to the heightened sexual bliss that had her writhing on the cusp of orgasm number...

Sweet climax pie, she'd lost count.

After her glorious orgasmic awakening on the washing machine, Raz had carried her into his bedroom. From there, she rode him like a cowgirl on his king-sized bed, and had again welcomed her O in a sweaty state of orgasmic ecstasy. She'd bucked her brains out on his mahogany four-poster bed that looked like it had rolled right off the set of *Bridgerton*.

And God save the Queen! She'd never been so grateful for sturdy Victorian construction.

But their evening didn't end in the bedroom.

Exerting and maintaining that kind of erotic energy required fuel. Even the most meditative yogi required sustenance, and somewhere between reverse cowgirl and going at it doggie style while gripping one of the carved bedposts, she'd suggested they pop down to the kitchen for a snack. Thanks to the douchebag Derricks and their run-in with the Denver police, she'd missed dinner. By the time she and Raz had knocked out several more orgasms, with no intention of calling it a night, thanks to their dedication to the like-cures-like curriculum, they agreed to indulge in a brief time-out to procure nourishment.

And wouldn't you know it, Raz's grocery delivery had arrived earlier in the day, and his cleaning people had set a bowl of fruit on the center of the table.

What luscious fruit had they piled high into a glass bowl?

Here's a hint: With a deep purple hue, it's got skin so smooth all you want to do is run your tongue over the satin surface. In addition to that, the spherical delight sports a decidedly naughty trait. No one could deny that the fruit resembled a succulently tempting ass.

Yep, they walked into the kitchen, naked as the day they were born, and spied a bunch of plums.

She'd never considered any fruit sexy until Erasmus Cress plucked a plum from the bowl, sank his teeth into the flesh, then allowed the juices to run down his chin—and from there, his chest and abs.

And she could not let anything go to waste. She'd licked the sweet nectar from the man's body like she was the naughtiest kitten, and he was a vat of cream.

But two could play at the plum game.

After her abs-fest, she'd chosen a plum of her own. She'd barely taken a bite before Raz had her spread across the kitchen table.

How's that for a fruit plate special.

He'd kissed every inch of her before bending her over and taking her hard and fast. Sure, they'd knocked over the bowl of plums and sent the fruit tumbling across the hardwood floor. Seriously, who could concern themselves with tidying up when a sex god was doling out orgasms—and fruit.

It wasn't even a choice.

She was team sex god every day of the week!

But the fun didn't stop with the dirty plum incident. After the fruit frenzy, they'd defiled the stuffy chairs in the foyer. Then they'd made it halfway up the stairs before they did it again. They paused in the hallway to screw against one of the fifteen zillion doors before making it back to Raz's suite and his decadent four-poster bed.

During this time, she'd learned a few tidbits about Erasmus Cress.

The man not only possessed a magic cock and magic hands. He also had a magic mouth, and he knew how to use it.

And that's where she found herself in the early morning hours. She peered beneath the sheet to watch this Adonis drive her wild with lust. "Raz, I'm so close. Don't stop," she panted.

After last night, she should know better than to cajole him to keep going. He had the stamina of a comic book superhero and the harnessed tenacity of a school of salmon swimming upstream through a tornado. Okay, there probably weren't a whole lot of tornados near salmon spawning grounds, but if there were, and if Raz was a fish, he'd barrel through that wind and water like the colossal beast he was. An innate, near-tangible drive seemed to propel him forward. And propel, he did. He held her hips, controlling the pace as she threaded her fingers into his ash brown hair.

"You taste like the sweetest plum," the man growled, switching from working her with his mouth to massaging her sensitive bud with his hand as he prowled his way up her body. His hard length brushed against her thigh as he settled himself between her legs. "And now, I'll be making you call out my name with my cock buried deep inside of you. Do you like that, plum?"

This fruit-inspired dirty talk made her head spin.

"Yes, yes, yes," she cried, holding on to his muscled, beefy biceps, so eager to feel the power of this man as he thrust inside her.

He positioned the tip of his cock at her entrance when the distinct clap of a door slamming cut through their sex haze.

Breathless, they stared at each other.

"Could that be a draft? Did you leave a window open?" she asked.

Raz frowned. "I don't think so. And it better not be bloody Rowen and his merry group of wankers."

She giggled, smiling at this man, who looked back at her like she was just the plum he wanted to devour.

They waited, listening.

"Must be a draft," he said, laser-focused on her as he slid in slowly. She closed her eyes, absorbing the energy and savoring the sensation when a voice called out—and it wasn't Rowen or any of his merry wanker besties.

"Erasmus Cress, where are you, lad?" came a woman's voice with the same rolling British accent as Raz.

The man stilled. "Did you hear that, or am I starting to hallucinate from shagging nonstop?"

"I heard it. Who is that?" she whispered. Could it be a member of a cleaning crew or a cook or a scullery maid? Did she know what a scullery maid did or if that was even a job in the twenty-first century? No, but this giant English manor house probably required one or two.

At least, that's what she hoped. The alternative meant another heaping spoonful of mortification was on the way.

"Dad, are you home? Your car is out front," came a boy's voice.

A little boy.

It couldn't be Sebastian, could it?

"Bollocks!" Raz whisper-shouted. "They weren't supposed to arrive for another day."

"Are you sure that's not your gardener and her *lad*?" Libby offered, not sure where that *lad* came from. Could she have had so much sex with a sexy beast of an Englishman that she'd started speaking like him? Because if that was a thing, they'd probably hit the language swapping threshold. But there was no time to concern herself with semantics.

Raz scrambled off the bed, wobbling like a giant redwood

tree about to come down. "No," he whispered. "It's my granny, and the lad is my son."

"Your grandmother and Sebastian are downstairs in this house," she said, stating the obvious.

"Erasmus, Libby, it's Madelyn Malone! Wake up, wake up! I've got a surprise for you."

"And Madelyn's here!" he whisper-shrieked, sprinting to a chest of drawers and whipping out a pair of athletic pants.

"How is everyone able to get into your house?"

"Madelyn and her people have the alarm code. Remember, they brought your things here while we were..."

"At the police station. Yes, I remember." Libby stared down at her sex-flushed skin and very naked body. This was not the way to make a good impression. This might be the way to make the worst impression ever made in the history of impressions. Shock and mortification hit like a blast of arctic air. After the giant slice of humiliation pie she'd hoovered yesterday, one would assume she'd built up a tolerance to the unpleasant emotion.

They'd be wrong.

This situation—the granny, son, nanny matchmaker trifecta crashing her orgasm-fest with the orgasms being supplied by her new boss—might vault her to the top spot of the most humiliation experienced by a twenty-five-year-old in a twenty-four-hour period.

She searched the bedroom. "Where are my clothes?"

Raz pulled a T-shirt on over his head. "In the laundry room."

The laundry.

She grabbed a pillow and covered herself, well, the front of her body as she high-tailed it to the bedroom door. Peering out into the darkened hallway, her thrumming heartbeat slowed a fraction. The coast was clear. She inhaled a fortifying breath, then set off like a shot toward the end of the sprawling corridor. Charging into the laundry room, she flipped on the light and spied her clothes strewn about the floor. Like a little yoga ninja, she dressed at Mach-speed.

Granny panties?

Check.

White yoga capris?

A bit wrinkly, but no worse for wear, so...check.

Sparkly yoga-Barbie sports bra? Yes, ma'am, with sparkles intact!

She slid into that sucker, then gasped when she spied a hickey between her breasts.

To say things had gotten crazy in the kissing, hickey, and humping department might be the understatement of the century. Thankfully, the gold fabric concealed the red mark.

She plucked the aquamarine stone from the ground and slipped it into the hidden waist pocket on her yoga pants before sliding into her sneakers.

But she was missing something. What was it? Her sex-addled brain wasn't firing on all cylinders.

She caught a glimpse of herself in a mirror on the far wall.

She didn't have her pop of power. Her red wrap.

She studied the empty washing machine as jubilation washed over her.

When had they changed the laundry from the washer to the dryer? Had all those orgasms given her memory loss?

"Are you ready?" Raz asked, peering into the room.

"Who switched the laundry from the washer to the dryer?" she asked, opening the dryer door and separating her red wrap from his hoodie.

A cocksure grin spread across his face. "Pretty impressive, yeah? I heard the buzzer go off when I left the bedroom to get a few more plums. Remember, you wanted to eat them off my abs?"

Yep, she'd requested the pleasure of dining off his body.

"I don't think you can classify putting the wash into the dryer as an impressive feat. You're smiling like the King of the Jungle."

"I am the Lion."

"I don't even know what that means," she tossed back, taking in the smirk—the same smirk that had once driven her to bang gongs and now drove her to bang beefcakes.

But the expression was short-lived. Raz's conceited grin melted into a look of pure shock. "Plum, your neck!"

Her hand flew to her throat. "What about it?"

"You've got a love bite showing."

"Love bite?" she echoed. Was he a boxer or a vampire? "You mean a hickey?"

"Whatever you call it here in America—I can see it on your neck, which means—"

"Your family and Madelyn might notice." She threw on the wrap and held it closed at her neck like a Victorian schoolmarm. "Can you see anything? Is it hidden?"

"Erasmus, get your arse in gear, lad," his grandmother called. "You're not about to make an eighty-year-old woman with an arthritic hip climb this monstrosity of a staircase now, are you?"

"Granny is in rare form. She can be a right ball-buster. We better go," he replied, waving for her to join him in the hallway.

They sprinted past the myriad of doors before booking it down the stairs. Screeching to a halt, they froze as they hit the first floor and found three people staring at them—three people positioned within a few feet of her yoga tote.

A yoga tote filled with vibrators.

Why hadn't she put it away?

That was easy to answer.

She didn't know where to put it. She hadn't even set foot in her room. Having all that sex got in the way of a grand tour.

Libby's heart jumped into her throat. She observed the woman standing next to Madelyn. With her salt-and-pepper-colored hair twisted into a bun, that must be Raz's granny Fin, and the boy beside her had to be Sebastian.

Sebastian.

She parted her lips to greet the boy when Raz broke out into a bout of jumping jacks, right in the middle of the grand foyer.

"Libby and I are getting in some training," Raz huffed, knocking out those jacks like a champ, which he was, so it made sense. She still wasn't clear on why Raz had chosen the fitness ruse. Perhaps it had something to do with her sex-flushed cheeks. Whatever it was, she had to go along with it in hopes his family and Madelyn would buy it.

"It's never too early for fitness," she replied, upping the wattage on her grin. She glanced at Raz. She needed to get in on this fitness business—and fast. But she couldn't join him in his jacks-a-thon. Her wrap would fly open if she flung her arms into the air. She couldn't chance a hickey spotting. Instead, she parted her legs and sank into the splits.

A morning stretch never hurt anyone.

Because she was on the floor, she looked up to find everyone staring at her with their mouths hanging open.

Note to self: dropping into a splits position in a grand foyer with an audience of mostly strangers is not the best way to make an entrance.

Raz froze mid-jack. "Blimey, that's quite a trick, plum!"

"You know I can do the splits. Remember, in the hallway when we—"

"Were discussing yoga positions," Raz supplied.

Heat rushed to her cheeks. Her O might have returned, but

her chi, her inner balance, was as lopsided as ever. Was she about to reference sex with her boss...in front of his son and grandmother?

Libby Lamb, act like a professional—and not the lady of the night sort of professional! A fitness professional.

"Yes, that's correct. We were discussing yoga. This pose is called hanumanasana. That's Sanskrit for this position known colloquially as *the splits*."

And...crickets.

For the love of Buddha, get up!

No one said a word as she maneuvered to a standing position with the grace of a drunken sailor. Attempting to stand with crap balance while concealing hickeys was more challenging than it looked.

Madelyn gave them the once over. "How nice to see you both up, dressed, and raring to go."

Oh no!

Libby glanced at her outfit—the same outfit she'd worn yesterday. The outfit seen around the world and in outer space.

Maybe the matchmaker didn't notice.

Madelyn drank her in for a beat as the whisper of a grin pulled at the corners of the woman's lips.

Nope, she noticed.

"Let me make the introductions," Madelyn said, glancing around the room. "Libby Lamb, this is Finola Cress and her great-grandson, Sebastian."

"So, you're Libby Lamb." Granny Fin eyed her closely. With her salt-and-pepper hair piled into a bun, the woman couldn't be much more than five feet tall, but in the intimidation department, she'd easily hit Raz's height. The woman shared the same curious gray eyes as her grandson. And like Raz, she could dole out her fair share of intensity. "You're the spiritual advisor and the nanny?"

Was that an accusation or a question? She couldn't tell. And more than that—had Finola seen the viral video, or had Madelyn simply shared the whole spiritual advisor part?

"Miss Lamb?" Finola pressed like a seasoned interrogator.

"Yes, I'm both the nanny and the spiritual advisor," she stammered.

"Madelyn tells me you're good with children."

The woman didn't let up.

Libby tightened her hold on the wrap. "I've taught yoga to school-age kids. My degree is in elementary physical education, and I helped care for my younger brothers growing up."

Finola Cress narrowed her gaze. "This yoga business."

"Yes," Libby eked out.

The woman's iron demeanor dissolved. "Any suggestions for a cranky neck?"

Libby held back a king-sized sigh of relief.

"Yes, actually, there are quite a few exercises for cervicalgia," she blurted, happy to change the subject.

"Cer-vic-what?" the woman repeated.

"Cervicalgia. It's the medical term for neck pain. Here, watch me and do what I do. Roll your head over to your right shoulder, then allow it to fall forward. Now, over to your left shoulder. Inhale at your shoulder and exhale as you roll."

Granny Fin did a few more rolls. "Hmm," she hummed, a skeptical huff of a sound. "There's some relief. I'll admit that," the woman answered, then crossed her arms and turned to the matchmaker. "Are you sure about this arrangement, Madelyn?"

This couldn't be good.

"I am. Libby is the right match for Sebastian and Erasmus, Finola," Madelyn purred.

"We shall see," Granny Fin answered with a scowl. This woman was one tough cookie. And hopefully, one tough cookie who hadn't seen the viral video. She couldn't imagine that piece of internet infamy going over well with the ball-busting woman.

"It's good to see you, Granny. But what are you doing here? I didn't expect you until tomorrow," Raz said and pressed a kiss to the woman's cheek.

"Change of plans, dear. Didn't you get my email? It took me bloody forever to figure out how to send it. You know technology is no friend of mine. I even mentioned it to Callista and Calliope. Did they not tell you either? It was our friend Madelyn's idea. She suggested we leave a day early."

"Did she?" Raz asked, eyeing Madelyn.

The matchmaker smoothed her trademark red scarf. "Of course. With the arrangements made, I saw no need to delay. And Sebastian tells me he's quite excited to explore Rickety Rock, Colorado. Not to mention, Finola and I have plans here in Denver. I promised her I'd show her all the city has to offer, and we've got a few philanthropic pursuits to investigate."

Philanthropic pursuits?

"For the foundation?" Raz asked his granny, and she would have sworn there was a shake to his voice.

"Someone's got to keep an eye on it."

What was up with this foundation?

He crossed his arms, hardening his exterior. "So, you're not coming with us to the mountains, Gran?"

"I'll be along when I've taken care of things here. And there surely seems to be enough room in this house for six, possibly seven families. Who do you think you are, living in a place like this? A bloody duke? It must cost a fortune."

Raz released a weary breath. "Granny, we can afford it."

"But do you need it?"

"You'll be happy to hear that there's a one-story cottage on the property, Finola," Madelyn supplied. "I made sure it had everything you needed to be comfortable. It'll be perfect for you."

"That will suit me better," the woman replied, then patted Sebastian's shoulder. "Now, be a good lad, dear, and say hello to your father and your nanny."

"Dad, check out my jab-cross," the boy chimed in a refined British accent that sounded slightly different from Raz's and Granny Fin's rolling speech.

The child's expression grew laser-focused as he bounced on his toes and started swinging. She'd didn't know the first thing about boxing, but the kid's movements were sharp and precise. There was power behind those tiny fists and an unyielding balance in his stance. She could sense his centered energy. It radiated from his body, which was quite something for a boy of his age. She stole a glance at Raz, expecting him to be pleased. He wasn't—not even close. His expression hardened, and a muscle ticked in his jaw.

"I send you to that fancy school, and the first thing you have to say is, *check out my jab-cross?*" the man muttered.

The boy dropped his arms and slumped. "Did I do the punches right?"

"That's beside the point, Sebastian. You shouldn't be filling your head with boxing."

Hello, negative energy vortex. The intensity between these two could take out the city. She had to intervene before it got worse.

"Hello, Sebastian, those moves looked pretty great to me," she said, coming between the father-son standoff, but the child didn't respond.

"Manners, Sebastian," Granny Fin said under her breath.

The boy nodded to his great-grandmother, then lifted his chin. "Thank you. It's very nice to meet you, ma'am. I'm Sebastian Arcadia Cress. I'm six and three-quarters years old."

With ash brown hair and strong features, there was no doubt this was Erasmus Cress's son, but upon a closer look, she noticed the child didn't have gray eyes like his father and great-grandmother. No, his eyes matched the aquamarine stone Ida had given her.

"It's very nice to meet you, Sebastian Arcadia Cress. I'm excited to be your nanny."

At her admission, the boy's focus dropped to the floor.

Was he nervous about having another caregiver, or was it something else? Anders had been shy, too, when he was younger. Sometimes, all it took was a question or an observation to get him to come out of his shell.

She tapped her chin. "If you're six and three quarters, that means you've got a birthday coming up."

The boy brightened. "It's more like six and eleven-twelfths. That's a fraction with the eleven on top and the twelve on the bottom."

"Those are some amazing math skills," she answered.

"Being six years and eleven-twelfths means my birthday is really close. My granny Fin said I'll get to have my party in the mountains this year." He set his gaze on his father. "Will we live in Colorado now? Will I go to school here?"

Raz glanced away. "I'm not sure, Sebastian."

What was up with this guy?

"Will I get to live with you all the time in Colorado, or do you have two houses here, too?"

Two houses?

"I have one house, and you're here now," the man replied.

Good grief! You're here now?

That's no way to answer anyone, let alone a child.

Sebastian's light dimmed at his father's terse reply.

"I have a question for you, Sebastian," she posited, hoping to soften the blow.

"Yes, Miss Lamb?"

"You can call me Libby like my friends do because I am sure we'll be fast friends." She smiled at the boy, then glanced at Granny Fin and found the woman watching her—well, glaring was a better way to describe the woman's piercing gaze.

Don't blow it in front of the tiny ball-breaking grandma.

"Here's my question for you, Sebastian. I can't tell if your eyes are blue or green." She'd meant it to get the boy's mind off his father's callous comment, but when she caught Raz out of the corner of her eye, his expression hardened. Now she had the beefcake and the granny glaring at her.

The boy shifted his stance. "My eyes are the same color as my mum's, right, Dad?"

"And look at the time," Raz blurted.

And look at the time?

What was it with Raz? She wanted to throttle him.

He gestured toward a grandfather clock. "I'm late to train with Augie. I've got to go."

Was he kidding? His family had just arrived.

Libby's jaw dropped. "You're leaving?"

TEN

LIBBY

THIS COULD NOT BE HAPPENING.

Libby blinked. She had to be hallucinating. Perhaps it was an aftereffect of experiencing multiple orgasms after surviving a stint in a sexual wasteland.

But she wasn't.

Raz vibrated with jittery motion as he opened the closet and removed another hoodie. His energy was all over the place.

"Is this your bag, Dad?" Sebastian asked, excitement bubbling as he picked up the yoga tote. "Want me to carry it for you? I can put it in your car."

"No, Sebastian, that's Libby's bag. My gear is at the gym. I don't need any help."

The child obviously wanted his father's attention. Why was Raz giving the boy the cold shoulder? And then she remembered what was in the bag.

"Let me take that off your hands, Sebastian. My tote is filled with boring yoga stuff. Nothing inappropriate," she stammered, accepting the tote, then checking if it was zipped up.

Thank the cosmos, it was.

What would Granny Fin say about a nanny who schlepped around town with a bag chock-full of sex toys?

"Can I go with you to train, Dad?" Sebastian pressed, swinging his fists like he was pummeling the air.

"Not today. You understand, don't you, lad? I've got a big fight coming up. I have to concentrate." He didn't even give the boy a chance to answer before turning to his grandmother. "You know how it is, Granny, and I'm sure Madelyn can get you settled. I'd probably be in the way."

Granny Fin eyed her grandson. "Oh, I know what it's like, love."

Raz ruffled the boy's hair. "You can get to know Libby, your nanny," he finished, not even meeting her eye as he headed toward the door.

Giant, self-absorbed beefcake!

"I guess we'll see you when we see you," she called, restraining herself from hurling a few choice words his way. Raz glanced over his shoulder, and like seventy-five days ago—no, now it was seventy-six days ago, he looked through her, past her.

She was nothing to him—again.

For Pete's sake! She hadn't expected him to fawn over her, but a simple, civil acknowledgment wouldn't kill him. They had spent the last several hours naked and screwing each other's brains out—aka following the like-cures-like curriculum she'd suggested. Perhaps that's all it was. An exercise. A set of motions to elicit a physical response. That's how she proposed the sexual endeavor, right?

And then that little voice in her head returned.

You can't trust a man with your heart. They will always disappoint you.

Had she wanted to trust Erasmus Cress with her heart? The man was a self-proclaimed beast and, as far as she could tell, a giant creep of a father.

Could she have feelings for him?

The front door slammed, and Libby got her answer.

Feelings could not get in the way of their association.

Bottom line? She could not fall for the beefcake.

And honestly, he was helping her out in that department.

Raz had bolted from the house like it was on fire, and he'd demonstrated Deadbeat Dad 101 behavior.

He'd walked out on his son.

Sure, he claimed he had to prepare for his upcoming, larger-than-life boxing match.

A chill spider-crawled down her spine.

Raz was preparing for a Pay-Per-View fight that people would bet on.

There would be winners and losers.

And a good portion of the fallout would be cataclysmic.

A decent number of those losers would take a hit that would devastate their families.

Anger permeated every cell in her body, but she swallowed down the anguish. She couldn't let her mind go there—back to the days she longed to forget.

Get your head out of the past, Libby Lamb.

But the facts were the facts. Raz hadn't only given her the cold shoulder. He'd barely acknowledged the son he hadn't seen in months. She focused on the boy—a little boy she already wanted to protect. Sebastian's bottom lip quivered, but the kid didn't cry. Instead, his expression hardened.

She recognized the reaction. It was a child's desire to please only to be rebuffed again and again.

She was well acquainted with that dynamic.

Libby steadied herself. She understood soul-shredding disappointment better than most. And she knew what Sebastian needed: a shift in energy, a change of scenery, and a little distraction.

Manufacturing what she hoped was a pleasant expression, she checked the clock. "My friends Penny and Charlotte usually get together with their kids and meet at a playground near here on Saturday mornings. It's the same one I used to take my brothers to when they were about your age." She paused as the memory of her frail mother entering the community center adjacent to the playground materialized. She pushed the thought away and pasted a smile to her lips. "I'd love to take you there, Sebastian. You can meet Phoebe and Oscar. They're great kids, and they're six like you are. I know they'd love to play with you. Are you up for it?"

Sebastian didn't meet her eye, but the boy nodded as he stared at the front door. Libby could read the boy's mind, watching as the loop of his father leaving played over and over.

They each needed a distraction and the restorative power of the outdoors STAT.

Libby met Granny Fin's appraising gaze. "That is, if it's okay with you, Mrs. Cress."

The woman sized her up with those sparkling gray eyes for a beat, then two.

"What a glorious idea, Libby! It's a beautiful day," Madelyn said, chiming in and taking Granny Fin's arm. "I'm sure after that flight, Sebastian could use some time outdoors. And I can show you the cottage, Finola. We can put the kettle on like we used to do back in Chelsea. We must get you off your feet, dear. Travel by private jet is far better than flying commercial, but it still comes with jet lag."

Granny Fin nodded. "Agreed. I could use a cuppa, and a spot of exercise will do Sebastian good. Nothing like a bit of fresh air to clear the mind. Now, Sebastian, hug your old granny Fin."

The boy wrapped his arms around the tiny woman's waist.

"Libby," Madelyn said, lowering her voice as she left Finola's side. The two of them moved toward the door to give Sebastian and his great-grandmother some privacy to say their goodbyes.

The matchmaker slipped an envelope out of her purse. "My people were here last night before you and Erasmus arrived. I understand there was quite a welcoming party."

"Yep, the whole crew."

A sly grin spread across the woman's face. "Before your friends greeted you, my people parked your Buick in the garage and brought your things to your room. I'm sure you've seen them."

She hadn't seen diddly-squat.

Libby recycled that plastic grin. "That was very kind. Thank you."

"And I'll give you these," the matchmaker continued, reaching into the envelope. "Here are the keys to the vehicle, a Lamborghini Urus. The code to the gate is written on a slip of paper on the dash. And, of course, a credit card for any expenses you incur as Sebastian's nanny. Your trial period paychecks will be directly deposited. I'm sure you're acquainted with the process."

After watching Penny and Char go through the nanny grind, she was certainly aware of how this nanny match worked.

She stared at the key fob and bit back a grin, thinking of Harper's hilarious Lamborghini envy. Now the beleaguered piano teacher was the one without an Italian-made mid-sized SUV. But that lightheartedness switched to a sinking sensation. Unlike Penny and Charlotte, there wouldn't be a happily ever after with Erasmus Cress—or with any man, for that matter.

That wasn't the focus. Her crazy stint as a boxer's spiritual advisor would cover the cost of med school for Anders and Alec. That's what mattered. She could put the income she earned as a nanny into a savings account for her brothers. Med school had to come with extra expenses—advanced studies always did. It would give her peace of mind to know that the boys had a pool of cash to draw from.

And what of her dreams of opening her own center—a place where people young and old could connect to their deeper self through yoga and meditation?

Those dreams would slide to the back burner—again.

She thanked Madelyn, then slipped the credit card into the side pocket of the yoga bag when she spied her phone.

"Can we go, Libby?" Sebastian asked.

"There's one last thing. Mrs. Cress, would you like my cell number?" she asked, holding up her phone.

Granny Fin crossed her arms. "What for? I can tell you right now, I'm not one for that texting nonsense. Callista and Calliope make me right bonkers with that business."

Yeah, it was pretty evident Granny wasn't down with nonsense, period.

"I thought you'd like to have my number in case you wanted to check in on Sebastian."

Granny Fin gave her what must be at least the fourth appraising look. "I see. But you're the nanny, right?"

Was that a challenge?

She held the woman's gaze. "Yes."

"Will you look out for Sebastian? Will he be safe with you, Libby Lamb?"

Libby lifted her chin, feeling more balanced than she had in ages. "Yes, your great-grandson will be safe with me."

Madelyn surveyed the women. "I've got your number, Libby. I'll share it with my friend once we've got two steaming cups of Earl Grey before us. And here, dear," the matchmaker said as she removed her scarf. "You seem to have a chill. This should help."

Libby glanced at her white-knuckled hand, still gripping the red fabric at the base of her neck.

The hickeys.

"Yes, right, it gets drafty in these large homes," she stammered. She accepted the scarf and, with a quick flick of her wrist, hid the evidence of her night with Erasmus Cress.

"Listen to your nanny, Sebastian," Finola said, her gaze softening as it fell on the boy.

"Goodbye, Sebastian, dear, I'll see you soon," Madelyn cooed, threading her arm with Finola's, then leading the woman toward the back of the sprawling house. The tap of their footsteps grew faint, and then you could hear a pin drop.

"It's just you and me, Sebastian. Are you ready to head out?"

"May I take my sketch pad?" he asked, gesturing to a backpack in the corner of the room.

"Sure, the park is a great place to draw."

The child pulled a pencil and a thick pad from the bag, and the two headed out the front door where, lo and behold, a Lamborghini Urus was parked in the drive.

A Lamborghini Urus in the shade somewhere between blue and violet.

What an odd coincidence. That hue seemed to turn up everywhere.

"I like the color of your car," Sebastian remarked, opening the back door and settling himself inside.

She situated herself in the front and checked the boy in the rearview mirror.

Sebastian sighed and sank into the seat with a far-off look in his eyes.

"Is something on your mind?" she asked. The twins always opened up when they got in the car. Perhaps it was the hum of the engine or existing in that in-between place—away from home but having not yet reached the intended destination.

He strummed his index finger along the wiry spiral holding the sketchpad together. "Does my dad want me here?"

Libby willed her heart not to break.

"Yes, absolutely, Sebastian, but he's got a lot on his mind," she answered, internally cursing the man as she started the car. "We'll get to see more of him when we get to Rickety Rock," she added, not quite sure why she'd made that prediction, but it lifted Sebastian's spirit.

"Ms. Malone said we're going to get a donkey when we get to the mountains, and then we'll get to run around with it."

"Pretty exciting, huh?"

"Do you think my dad will let me run with the donkey?" Sebastian asked, staring out the window as they headed down the private drive.

"I'm not sure how it works with children and donkeys, but I bet we can work something out."

"I researched the donkeys on the car ride from the plane to the house," he continued, perking up. "I downloaded a whole book on them."

"Did you?" she queried as they exited Raz's estate and headed down the treelined street toward the Crystal Acres playground.

"They don't like rain."

"I did not know that," she replied, catching his eye in the rearview mirror.

"And they're smart." The boy leaned forward. "They have good memories. They don't see colors, and they have brown eyes. But not like yours. Yours are yellowy golden brown. Donkey eyes are dark, dark brown."

"You already know a heck of a lot more than I do. You can be the donkey expert."

"Yeah, I can do that," the boy said to himself, relaxing into the seat. "I like you, Libby."

"I like you, too, Sebastian."

"Want to know something else about donkey eyeballs?"

"Sure," she replied, stifling a chuckle.

"They have trouble looking up and mostly look down to eat. Sometimes they don't see what's right in front of them."

She nodded. That wasn't only true of donkeys—jackasses like Erasmus Cress also fell into that category.

She kept her gaze on the road as the park came into view. Situated near the community center, she caught a glimpse of a person with long white hair entering the building. A strange sense of déjà vu passed over her—or else it was her garbled chi. She brushed off the feeling and pulled up behind a cherry-red Urus, Charlotte's car, then cut the ignition.

"Do you want to know more about donkey eyes? I read a lot about them," Sebastian added.

She looked up and met the child's gaze in the mirror. "Can I ask you a question about your eyes, Sebastian?"

She couldn't stop herself.

"Okay, what's your question?" Sebastian asked.

Libby pushed the image of the mystery woman entering the community center out of her head. She focused on the boy. "You never got to answer if you thought your eyes were more blue or more green." She slipped Ida's gift from her pocket, then unclasped her seat belt and turned to face the boy. "They're the color of this stone. It's aquamarine. It's the Colorado state gemstone. It can be blueish or greenish or a combination of the two like this." She handed him the stone, and he rubbed his thumb across the smooth surface.

"This color makes my dad sad," Sebastian answered and returned the rock.

"Why would this color do that?"

"Because I have the same color eyes as my mum did. She died when I was little, but I have a picture of her. Do you want to see it?"

Raz was a widower?

Libby nodded. She shouldn't be this curious about the man's life. She had a job to do—and she couldn't allow her heart to get in the way. But as the thought crossed her mind, a breeze cut through the trees lining the periphery of the park. Out of the corner of her eye, she caught an aspen tree dancing in the air, almost shimmering, when Raz's words came back to her.

I should warn you. I'm a boxer. I'm better at breaking things than I am at putting them back together.

"I keep Mum's picture in my grandad's watch. I never knew him, but Granny Fin said she was sure he'd want me to have it." Sebastian reached into his pocket and removed a golden pocket watch. It caught her off guard. Kids these days usually carried handheld electronics, not antique clocks. Gently, he pressed a release, and the door clicked open. "Her name was Meredith, and she liked mint chocolate chip ice cream, twirling around in the rain, swinging as high as she could at the park, and drawing pictures in notebooks."

Libby concentrated on the image of the beautiful young woman. Caught in a slip of time, the photo captured the woman as a lock of dark hair blew across her pink cheek. Her gaze cast to the side as if she were smiling at someone she truly loved.

A lump formed in her throat. "Did your dad tell you those things about your mom?"

Sebastian focused on the photo. "No, Auntie Callista and Auntie Calliope used to tell me lots of stories about my mum, but then they got busy with uni. They're on the other side of the world teaching children how to speak English."

"Do you miss them?"

He nodded. "Granny Fin can't move around very well, so we spend a lot of time in the flat, just the two of us."

"What about your friends at school?"

Sebastian closed the watch and returned it to his pocket. "I don't have many friends. The boys want to fight me because they think I'd be a good boxer like my dad. They laugh at me and call me spaghetti arms when I try to throw a punch."

Poor kid.

"I'm not one for violence or fighting at school, but have you asked your dad to teach you?"

"He doesn't want me to be a boxer like him."

"What do you want?" she asked. "Sometimes, if I want something, I think about it and put a lot of energy into the thought. It's called setting an intention."

Sebastian squeezed his eyes shut. "I want my dad to be happy."

Her heart broke for the child.

She wasn't one for violence, but she sure wanted to kick Raz right in the balls for keeping his sweet boy at arm's length. And then her anger dissipated, and she felt a gentle energy coming off the child. It lapped and gurgled joyfully like a babbling brook.

Sebastian opened his eyes. "I put my energy into it. Could you feel it?"

She nodded, not sure what to say when a sharp knock on the window had her nearly jumping out of her seat. She turned toward the sound and spied a little girl with a hot dog headband and pink fairy wings fluttering in the breeze.

"Libby, you're at the park," Phoebe Gale announced. She jammed her finger against the window at Sebastian. "And who's that?"

Oscar ran to the car and held up his Polaroid camera,

framing a shot. "Hi, Libby! You're in the Lamborghini car club, too. That's awesome! And you've got a kid now."

These two were a riot.

Penny and Charlotte joined the kids, and their attention bounced from the car to the child in the back. Her friends stared at her as if she'd arrived in an alien spacecraft while Oscar and Phoebe stared in the window at Sebastian like he was an exotic animal on display at the Denver Zoo.

"These people look a bit dodgy. Is it safe to exit the car?" Sebastian asked, his nose touching his side of the glass opposite Oscar.

She could feel the waves of anxiety coming off the kid. "Yes, these are the friends I told you about. They seem excited to meet you. But before we get out of the car, try this. It's called a mudra." She raised her hand and touched her index finger to her thumb. "This is called the gyan mudra. It helps you feel calm."

Okay, that was a rudimentary description for the yoga practice that had been used for thousands of years, but she didn't have time for a grand explanation.

Sebastian raised his hands like a mini-Buddha and copied the pose. "I feel better, Libby."

"I'm glad, honey. Now, take a nice big breath and let it out slowly."

The boy complied. "Am I doing yoga?"

"You are. How do you feel?"

Sebastian returned his attention to the children outside his window. "I feel better, but I'm still a little nervous."

She smiled. "It's okay to be nervous. Being a little nervous allows us to be brave. Are you ready to get out of the car? Are you ready to be brave with me?"

The child inhaled, then exhaled a slow breath like a seasoned yogi. "Yeah, I'm ready to be brave, Libby."

They exited the car and were met by a barrage of hellos.

"Madelyn texted us. She said you were on the way here. Welcome to Team Lamborghini," Penny teased as they embraced.

"We're so happy to see you. You must be Sebastian Cress," Charlotte added, pinning the boy with her emerald gaze.

Sebastian glanced around. "Can I hold your hand, Libby?" the boy asked.

Understandably, he was still a bit nervous.

She took his hand in hers, and the connection between them solidified. She spent more than half her life taking the twins by their usually sticky hands, but this was different. Instantly, she understood this was exactly where she was supposed to be.

Charlotte grinned at Sebastian. "I'm Charlotte Ames, and this is Penny Fennimore. And the kids are Phoebe Gale and Oscar Elliott."

Phoebe and Oscar inspected Sebastian closely.

"It's very nice to meet you, Phoebe. You, too, Oscar," Sebastian said with a slight shake to his voice. He tucked his sketchbook under his arm as he reached out to shake Phoebe's hand. But the little girl stood there, frozen in place.

"Phoebe, are you okay?" Penny asked.

Phoebe stared at Sebastian, wide-eyed. "Say that again, new kid," she whispered.

"What would you like me to say?" the boy asked in his crisp British accent.

Phoebe gasped. "You sound like Harry Potter...and you sound like your dad. But more like Harry Potter. Are you a boy wizard?"

Sebastian looked himself over. "No, I'm just a boy."

"Say that again," Phoebe cooed. Little red hearts would have replaced her eyeballs if the child were a cartoon character.

"I'm just a boy?" Sebastian repeated, confusion marring his expression.

The little girl released a high-pitched squeal. "Say, hello, Phoebe, Princess of the Hot Dog Fairies, Bearer of Cookies, and Eater of Pizza."

Sebastian sucked in a tight breath. "Um..."

Oscar came up alongside the flummoxed child. "You should just say it, Sebastian. She'll keep asking you and asking you, and then you'll think you're ready to go nuts, and she'll ask you again."

Sebastian nodded. "Thanks, mate. What was it you wanted me to say, Phoebe?"

Phoebe looked ready to burst, but she held it together. "Hello, Phoebe, Princess of the Hot Dog Fairies, Bearer of Cookies, and Eater of Pizza."

"Okay, here goes. Hello, Phoebe, Princess of the Hot Dog Fairies, Bearer of Cookies, and Eater of Pizza," Sebastian repeated. "That's quite a name!"

"I'm quite a woman," Phoebe shot back, flicking one of her braids over her shoulder.

"Phoebe, why don't you and Oscar show Sebastian around the park?" Penny suggested.

"We love this park. It's got the best swings," Phoebe chimed.

"I don't have to call you by your title every time I want to talk to you, do I? You're not American hot dog royalty, are you?" Sebastian asked with a crease to his brow.

Mischief twinkled in Phoebe's eyes. "I sure am American hot dog royalty."

"Sebastian, you can call her Phoebe, like we do," Penny answered, biting back a grin.

Phoebe gave her soon-to-be Auntie Penny a dose of stink eye, then tapped her foot twice.

"Those taps better be for *o-kay*," Penny chided, barely keeping it together.

Sebastian stared at Phoebe's foot. "What do the taps mean?"

"Butt—" Phoebe began when Oscar wrapped his hand around her mouth.

"Yep, Phoebe was tapping out *o-kay*. Come on, Sebastian," Oscar called, pulling the self-proclaimed pint-sized hot dog fairy princess along by one of her pink wings. "Phoebe and I can show you the swings and teach you how tap talking works."

Sebastian looked down at his sketchbook. "Will you keep this safe for me, Libby?"

"Absolutely," she answered, accepting the item.

Sebastian released her hand and ran off to play with Phoebe and Oscar. Libby watched the trio go, her heart bursting in her chest. Sebastian had pushed past his anxiety and embraced bravery. It was also reassuring to watch Phoebe and Oscar take to Sebastian so quickly. The boy stopped and spun around and waved to her. She waved back, then gave him a thumbs-up.

"Let's grab a bench," Char suggested.

Libby nodded, but not before staring at her hand and missing the warmth of Sebastian's little fingers wrapped around hers. How could a little boy she'd known for less than an hour already own a piece of her heart?

They settled themselves on a bench not far from the play structure and looked on as Sebastian, Oscar, and Phoebe stood in a circle. Phoebe tapped while Oscar spoke, and a wide grin stretched across Sebastian's face.

This is exactly what the boy needed.

"I adore that hot dog devouring tiny human," Penny declared, shaking her head as Phoebe danced around the boys, tapping out God knows what.

"When Phoebe turns twenty-one, we're taking her out for margaritas," Char remarked.

"She'll probably drink us under the table, then get arrested for hacking into the FBI database. She's quite a little coder herself these days. She truly is Rowen's niece."

"Speaking of getting arrested," Char said with a glint in her eyes. "How's it going with Raz?"

Penny and Char zeroed in on her.

How's it going with Raz? Good question!

Libby tried to conjure some serenity, but she must have maxed out her positive energy reserves with Sebastian. She pinched the bridge of her nose. "Girls, you know how I feel about negativity."

Penny raised an eyebrow. "I feel a *but* coming on."

"But," Libby lamented. "I am ready to open up a can of karmic whoop ass on the man."

Penny touched the red scarf. "Would that be before or after he gave you another hickey?"

Holy hot love bites!

Libby reached for the scarf that must have loosened since she'd twisted it around her neck like the scarlet fabric was all that kept her head attached to her body.

"That's not one of Madelyn's scarves, is it?" Char asked.

Libby adjusted the scarlet fabric. "Yes, it sure is."

"Does it have secret powers?" Char asked, touching the corner.

"Not that I can tell. Red is the color of passion and power," she answered, wishing it did have the secret power to make beefcakes act like actual caring human beings.

"That is her thing," Penny remarked, taking her turn to stroke the luxurious fabric. "When did she give it to you?"

"She offered it to me this morning while Raz's grandmother was sizing me up. Madelyn, Sebastian, and Raz's granny Finola arrived at the house while Raz and I were..."

"Were?" Charlotte said, stretching out the word.

Libby looked between her best friends. There was no sense in holding back now—not with the hickeys giving her away.

"They arrived while Raz and I were going at it like sex

maniacs," she answered, slumping, then cradling her head in her hands.

"Libbs!" Penny exclaimed. "Did your O return?"

Libby closed her eyes. Her skin tingled at the thought of Erasmus Cress pumping his hips as he brought her over the edge, again and again.

"Libby, are you there?" Penny asked.

She blinked. "What?"

"You spaced out. Were you getting in a little spontaneous meditation?" Char teased.

"No, I was replaying all the sex I had last night through my head. There was a lot."

Char lowered her voice. "How did it happen?"

"I told him about my messed-up chi and my missing O, and he volunteered to help. I've tried everything, and then I remembered a holistic school of thought that supports the idea of like curing like. I figured, if Raz was the cause of my missing O, he could be the cure."

"Did it work? I mean, you've got hickeys, and you've copped to sleeping with the man, but that doesn't mean you were able to orgasm," Penny reasoned.

Libby leaned back and remembered the man's abs, his strong hands, and those eyes owning her every moan. "Oh, I had an O. Actually, I had so many Os I lost track."

"Are we talking five Os?" Penny pressed.

Libby shook her head.

"Ten Os?" Penny whisper-shouted.

"The man knows how to use his mouth and his hands, and let's just say, he's got the right equipment below the belt."

"So, more than ten Os?" Penny pressed.

"That's a lot of Os," Charlotte added with an impressed whistle.

Libby's skin tingled, and her core clenched. Her body ached for more Os.

"Have you tried masturbating to see if your O is back for good? You do have, as everyone on the internet knows, sixteen vibrators in your possession," Penny continued.

"That's the next step we agreed upon."

"The next step?" Penny and Char questioned in unison.

"I set up an O curriculum. First, we tested my ability to have an O with him. Next, I'll try to knock one out on my own, and the final test will be to pick out another man, a sort of test subject, to see if I can have an O with another partner. Raz agreed to it, but I'm not so sure we should keep sleeping together."

"Why not? You like him, right?" Char pressed.

Libby shook her head. "No, I don't like him."

Lie. Lie. Lie.

Her brain was furious, but her treacherous body wanted more hickeys. And what about her spirit, her soul? The man had aligned her chakras with one kiss. When he looked at her, the connection between them practically sparked. Energy flowed between them as seamlessly as two rivers coming together to become one. But he certainly wasn't that man this morning.

"Why don't you like him? I figured you'd be doing cartwheels across the park after more than ten Os," Penny remarked.

"Everything changed the minute his grandmother and son arrived. You should have seen him. He barely interacted with Sebastian and bolted the second he could without a backward glance. I also hardly know anything about him. Sebastian told me his mother had passed away. Raz is a widower. Did you guys know that? Do Rowen and Mitch know about Raz's wife?"

"The guys are oddly protective of each other when it comes to their pasts," Char answered as Penny nodded.

"It's sweet. I'd never say this to Rowen, but it's like they're their own support group, even though half the time they're messing with each other. The truth is, they're there for each other when it matters."

"Penny and I try to honor that," Char added, "but now that you're working for Erasmus, I think we can get a little dirt on the man without feeling like we're snooping around his personal life."

"Already on it," Penny announced, tucking a blond lock of hair behind her ear as she concentrated on her phone. "I'm on his wiki page. Wife, Meredith Holmes Cress, died unexpectedly three years ago. It also says here that Raz learned of her death moments after winning his last heavyweight championship fight. And, oh, this is heartbreaking."

"What is it?" Libby asked, leaning in.

Penny held out her phone. "There's a picture."

Bloody and glistening with sweat, Raz stood in the center of a media circus with Augie next to him. The glittering championship belt hung limp in Raz's hand while he pressed a cell phone to his ear with the other. Libby enlarged the photo and stared at his face. Tears trailed through the blood on his cheeks. Her breath caught in her throat and a heaviness set in as she took in Raz's hollowed-out expression—the gut-wrenching look of a man learning he'd lost everything.

Steadying herself, she read the paragraph below the image. "A year later, it says he was a no-show for his next fight, then he disappeared until reemerging now to fight the current champion, Silas Scott."

"I wonder what brought him back?" Char mused.

Libby stared at the image of a broken Erasmus Cress. "I don't know."

Penny scrolled down, revealing a picture of Raz, Meredith, and Sebastian, when the boy was just a baby, then passed her the phone. Libby studied the image. With Sebastian in his arms, holding a paper butterfly in his tiny fist, Raz smiled down at Meredith as she cut a ribbon.

The caption read: Erasmus Cress and his family donate to local community centre. Photo courtesy of the Cress Family Foundation.

Cress Family Foundation.

"Will Raz stay in Denver after the fight?" Penny asked.

Libby handed the phone back to her friend. "I don't know that either. But I do know that I need to do whatever I can for Sebastian. He deserves to be happy."

"What about you, Libby?" Char asked.

She shrugged. "My O is back, at least for the time being, but my chi is still whacked out. Except for when Sebastian's grandmother asked if I'd keep her great-grandson safe."

"Of course, you'll keep him safe," Penny remarked. "You're great with kids."

Libby shook her head. "The energy inside me went beyond wanting to keep Sebastian safe. It was weird. The same thing happened just now when I held his hand. It was like he was mine—like a force brought us together for a reason."

"And what about Raz?" Char pressed.

"Thanks to that stunt outside the gym, we're stuck together for sixty days," she answered. "And you know all about the whole spiritual advisor business and Anders and Alec's tuition. The agency paid half now and will pay the other half after the fight."

"Covering the boys' tuition takes a huge burden off your shoulders," Char offered.

Her friend was right, but it didn't diminish the weight entirely. It complicated things even more.

She was well and truly stuck with boxing's Lion.

Penny leaned in. "What happens now?"

Libby sighed. It was as if she'd lived a thousand lives in the space of a day. She needed something to ground her, something to even out her erratic energy. Then she remembered the stone. She removed the smooth aquamarine gemstone from her pocket and rubbed her thumb along the polished surface.

"I haven't seen that in ages," Charlotte said, staring down at the stone.

Libby glanced from the object to her friend. "What do you mean? I just got this."

"Didn't you have one like it when we were kids?" Char asked, studying the blue-green object.

Libby stared at it, turning it over in her hand. "I don't think so." Then again, there had been something familiar about Ida, or that could have been her wobbly chi leading her astray.

"New subject," Penny announced. "When are you headed to that town near Aspen? What's the name again?"

Libby returned the aquamarine stone to her pocket. "It's called Rickety Rock. A perfect name for someone with rickety, unsteady chi."

"Maybe you and Raz will click there. A change of scenery might be good for you guys," Charlotte offered, sharing a look with Penny.

Libby knew that look. "I might be a vibrator throwing crazy lady, but I see what you're doing. Just because you two ended up with Mitch and Rowen doesn't mean I'm destined to be with Erasmus Cress. You know that's not in the cards for me. It never will be. And you both know why."

"Oh, Libbs," Char chimed. "Not every guy is bad news."

She sighed as her heart ached. "I can't take the chance."

Libby scanned the playground. Sebastian, Oscar, and Phoebe had migrated to the swings. She observed Sebastian as he pumped his legs. The boy leaned back, sailing through the air, laughing with his new friends.

"Have you heard from your dad lately?" Penny asked gently.

Libby stared up at the sky. "You mean, has Connolly Lamb called to ask his daughter, who also happens to be putting her brothers through school, if he can borrow a few hundred bucks to tide him over because he's got a tip to hit it big?" She twisted the edge of Madelyn's scarf. "No, I haven't heard from him in a while, which is for the best."

Penny and Char each took one of her hands.

"If Harper were here," Char said, then bumped her shoulder playfully, "she'd tell you she'd happily kick your father in the nuts."

"Or drop a cup of hot coffee on his lap," Penny added, bumping her other shoulder.

Libby nodded, blinking back tears.

What would she do without these women?

"Just keep an open mind," Penny continued.

"You never know. People can surprise you," Char added.

Libby squeezed her friends' hands. They wanted the best for her, but no man was going to surprise her. In fact, despite her heart breaking for the beefcake over the loss of his wife, Raz's disappearing act today solidified her position. "Mark my words, girls. Unless there's a cataclysmic shift in energy, and the beefcake undergoes a metaphysical transformation, in fifty-nine days, Erasmus Cress will be nothing more than my former employer."

She'd said the words, now she had no other choice but to believe them.

ELEVEN
ERASMUS

RAZ GRIPPED the steering wheel and kept his gaze trained on the road. It took everything he had to focus on the simple task of driving a bloody vehicle.

Irritation prickled through his veins.

Augie would label this state of mind as acting like a wobbly twat who wasn't batting with a full wicket. Or perhaps his trainer would fall back on barking out that he looked as steady as a thirteen-year-old who just hoovered his first pint. The thing is, as an athlete training for the fight of his life, he hadn't touched a drop of alcohol in months. And as far as the wicket slang for acting like a deranged lunatic, it wasn't that far off the mark.

No, this state of discombobulation was of his own making.

And the reasons for his cockeyed state of mind sat mere inches away.

This was the first time he'd been with Libby and Sebastian in over a week. He glanced at the nanny in the passenger seat. She and Sebastian were passing a book back and forth. Chatting and laughing, the cadence of their voices drifted through the cab of the Hummer. Still, he couldn't concentrate on the content of their conversation or even enjoy the breathtaking mountainous scenery that stretched before them as they headed down the interstate to Rickety Rock for the summer.

This day seemed to arrive in the blink of an eye. One minute, he was balls deep inside a woman who'd awoken a burning desire inside him. The next, searing guilt that cut bone-deep laced with a prickling frustration engulfed his entire life.

Set to his default of arrogant beefcake mode, he'd been running on autopilot for the last ten days.

Wake up before dawn.

Train for hours on end.

Return home and collapse into bed after the house was dark.

Ignore the world. Ignore everyone.

Repeat. Repeat. Repeat.

A dreary exhaustion washed over him. If there was such a thing as a zombie boxer, he was it.

And like a bloody zombie, despite his self-important facade, he'd gotten slower, sloppier. The set of Aug's jaw was enough to know that London's Lion looked more like a headless chicken in the ring.

Good boxers understand the difference between speed and power. The great ones, the champions, know exactly when to turn that dial to find the sweet spot. Over the last ten days, one singular notion had become abundantly clear. He couldn't find the bloody dial if he were hooked up to GPS and had a trail of breadcrumbs to lead him there.

He was utterly lost. What had once come as second nature, that rhythm, that steady tempo, had vanished, and in its place had left this wobbly, off-kilter joke of a boxer.

It was as if the picture of himself as that boxer faded with each passing day. The energy he'd once easily tapped into the moment he gloved up grew fainter with each passing hour. Like a song on the tip of your tongue that you can't quite remember, the words are there, stuck deep in your brain, but no matter how hard you try, you can't access the melody, can't touch the magic.

The Lion was lost in a maze of his own making. And every passing minute had taken its toll as three conflicting emotions tore at his heart: desire, doubt, and dread.

He desired to be with Libby and Sebastian, but his doubt in his abilities fueled his obsessive need to train. And then there was the dread—the emotion that sucked the energy from his soul.

And what did he dread?

He feared they'd see him for who he really was—a man whose own actions cost him the person who had meant everything to him.

He had one way left to honor Meredith. He couldn't fail her again.

He'd timed his comings and goings these past ten days, making sure Libby and Sebastian were asleep when he'd get home and still in bed when he'd left before dawn.

But he couldn't ignore them. He could feel their presence the second he set foot in that bloody enormous house.

Each night, he'd slip into Sebastian's room like a ghost. The boy would be curled up on his side like he used to do as a toddler and would have one of two things clutched in his little palm, the pocket watch with Mere's picture or Libby's blueish green gemstone—the rock she'd thrown at him. And every night, he'd unfold the boy's hand and place the trinket on the bedside table. The six-foot-five fighter who couldn't be missed in a crowd hid in the cover of night, bobbing and weaving among his demons.

And then there was Libby's room. He didn't dare open that door, but the signs of her presence were littered throughout the house. A yoga mat in the kitchen. Two empty mugs in the sink.

Her red wrap, along with Sebastian's trousers and T-shirts, resting in a basket on top of the dryer. It was a bloody miracle he could maintain his hardened exterior when he entered the space where they'd made love for the first time. Each night, one grating question circled through his mind.

What was he hiding from?

Was it Granny Fin and her knowing gaze?

Was it Sebastian begging to be a boxer?

Or was it Libby Lamb and that pulse of tantalizing energy that passed between them?

Alone in his room, before he'd succumb to sleep in a fit of fatigued muscles, he'd whisper her name.

Libby Lamb.

Try as he might, he couldn't turn off the nanny reel in his head. She was bloody everywhere. From the ruby-red punching bag to his jet-black gloves hanging on a hook in Aug's gym, every color screamed her name. And speaking of every color. He'd caught the arc of a rainbow after an afternoon downpour, and even that made him think of her—and her bag of vibrators.

But when he closed his eyes, he only saw one color, amber.

The image of her sparkling amber eyes never gave him a moment's peace. Aug would call out a combination, and before his gloves hit the bag, she was there. His body called out to her. Her memory took up every inch of space in his consciousness. Touching her, kissing her, holding her in his arms as he dissolved into a sea of pleasure. There was no escape. And it wasn't only the sex and the thrill of making her come hard that had his mind reeling.

Despite the insanity of their vibrator calamity, Libby grounded him. She steadied him. Those amber eyes teased him with the promise of home—a home for his battered heart. He'd recognized the sensation well. He'd experienced it before, and he'd known it for more than a decade.

He recalled the day fate knocked the breath right out of him.

East London, eighteen years ago.

He was a fourteen-year-old lollygagging around Aug's boxing gym.

It was another rainy day in the city. He'd grabbed his bag, preparing to head back to Granny Fin's place to make dinner and to help her with the twins. It was another ordinary day at the gym until that average Tuesday turned into the day that changed everything. Two bolts of lightning scorched the sky, and in the space of those charged flashes of light, the door to the gym swung open. Like something out of a movie, the prettiest girl he'd ever seen dashed inside to get out of the rain.

Meredith.

Had she left her house ten seconds earlier, or had she walked more quickly, or had a million other tiny insignificant things crossed her path, she would have popped into the shoe store one door down from Augie's gym or maybe gotten a little further and entered the sweets shop.

But she hadn't.

She'd slipped into the gym, sopping wet. She wiped the rain from her cheeks, then looked him square in the eyes and grinned like she knew her life was about to change.

Those two flashes of lightning cracked open a new chapter in his life. All that faffing around, toying with the idea of becoming a boxer, hemming and hawing like a rudderless boat, solidified into a drive to be the best—for her and his family. Money was tight. They were barely getting by, living off his grandfather's pension. He was the man of the house, and at that moment, he manned up. He devoted himself to the sport and put his faith in Aug to train him to become a champion. Augie held the candle, but Meredith was the spark.

And that begged the question, if Mere had captured his

heart with two strikes of lightning, could Libby Lamb have done it with two strikes to her gong?

Had that infuriating clanging sound pulled him back from the edge?

Could he love again?

He tightened his grip on the steering wheel, internally berating himself. He was a daft mug to moon over a proposition like that.

He couldn't have Libby. He didn't deserve anyone.

No true north existed for Erasmus Cress anymore.

He'd have to get his head in the game on his own. But the more he tried, the worse he got. His sprints were rubbish—his timing, absolute shit. He'd tried to shut out the noise and silence, the gnawing questions rattling around his mind. He'd barely looked at his mobile. After an onslaught of emails and texts from Briggs droning on about bloody promotional bullshit, he'd turned the blasted thing off, effectively divorcing himself from everything in his professional and personal life.

Well, saying he had a personal life was a bit of a stretch.

He was the definition of an absent parent and an indifferent grandson.

What was he to Libby?

Oh, that one was easy. He was the cocky beefcake.

Case in point, he'd barely said two words to her since they got in the car.

Be the beefcake.

Harden your heart.

"Did you say something, Raz? Something about your heart?"

The breath caught in his throat at the sound of her voice.

"No, Libby," Sebastian countered. "I don't think my dad said *heart*. It sounded like he said *fart*. Did you fart, Dad? Granny Fin says you shouldn't fart in a car. But if you do, you should roll down the window." Sebastian tilted his head, sniffing the air. "I smell a fart."

Libby leaned forward and gave the air a sniff as well.

"I didn't fart," he roared.

"Are you sure? I smell something bad. It's okay if you're a car farter," Sebastian replied.

Car farter?

"It's not my fart," he answered gruffly, feeling his cheeks heat.

God's sake!

He was teetering on the edge of a breakdown, working himself into knots over the upcoming fight. He didn't have the emotional energy to defend himself from being labeled a car farter.

"Do you have a sour belly, Dad?" Sebastian continued.

"Sebastian, my belly is fine, and I didn't fart." He could feel Libby's eyes on him, but he didn't dare look her way.

"If you did fart," Sebastian droned on, "Libby could show you how to move around in circles to make it better. It helped me after Phoebe dared me to eat three hot dogs in one minute. Americans like to eat a lot of food quickly. I thought I might puke after. We did yoga to make it better."

"You're doing yoga with my son?" he asked, eyeing the woman.

She threw a glance toward Sebastian in the back. "Yes, and he's been showing me a few boxing moves. It's too bad your busy schedule precludes you from taking part in family activities. If you had been around the last ten days, you would have seen that Sebastian and I practice yoga every morning and in the evenings. But of course, you're so very busy."

Venom dripped from her words.

Libby Lamb might not know a damn thing about boxing, but she sure could land a punch when she wanted.

"Yeah, I can do the tree and the warrior," Sebastian chimed, lowering his voice as he extended his arms. "Right, Libby? I hardly wobble at all."

"You are a yoga machine," Libby replied, reaching back to high-five the boy, then each went into a prayer position. "Namaste, Sebastian."

"Namaste, Libby," the boy replied with a bow.

"What the bloody hell was that?" he barked.

"We're honoring each other's life force. Yoga is an excellent way to reflect, build endurance, and increase focus in children." She sat back and threw a few eye daggers at him. "It also helps with indigestion and relieves symptoms that cause one to break wind. You know, your car farting condition."

This woman!

Anyone who could say *break wind* and *car farting* in the same breath without cracking a smile was well and truly pissed. If the whole fart business clearly hadn't lightened her up, that had to mean he was doing a bang-up job of projecting the arrogant beefcake persona she despised. He should take comfort in that. She wasn't for him. But that didn't stop his bloody heart from aching.

"Libby and Granny Fin do yoga, too," Sebastian added.

His jaw dropped. His gran wasn't one to waste an hour, or even a quarter of an hour, for that matter, to sit on a mat and twist around. He wasn't even sure the old bird could get herself down to the floor. She was more of the type to bustle around the kitchen, slapping him on the backside for drinking out of the milk jug or riding his sisters to do their homework.

"You have my granny Fin doing that splits business?" he asked.

"No," Libby replied curtly. Her tone was cordial, but irritation simmered beneath her singsong voice. "I showed her a few restorative yoga positions to help with her arthritis. You might have noticed if you'd been able to spare us a moment."

And the punches kept coming.

He had to do this. There was no other choice than to make her despise him—again. But as the realization hit, the image of her naked and biting her bottom lip as she hummed the dirtiest of moans invaded his mind. Their bodies had moved together, pumping and thrusting as they rode wave after wave of delirious ecstasy. The hum of energy that had flowed between them and the depths of her amber eyes had him craving a life that was not for him. A life he didn't deserve. A life he had to forfeit. Libby's tenderness only fueled the fever dream that he could be anything more than a fighter. He'd failed as a husband. He was failing at being a parent. Boxing was all he had left.

Mere had sacrificed too much for him to fail in the ring.

"Now that we'll be together in Rickety Rock, we'll get to see my dad every day, Libby. You won't have to ask me so many questions about him because he'll be with us," Sebastian chimed, and now Libby was the one blushing.

"You've been talking about me with my son?" he asked, lowering his voice.

Libby shifted in her seat. "Just normal nanny questions."

"What did you want to know?"

"She wanted to know what you and I used to do in London," Sebastian answered crisply before Libby could conjure a reply. "I told her we didn't do much of anything because you were training a lot back in England, too."

Shame scorched through his veins. He glanced at his white-knuckled grip on the steering wheel. It would be a miracle if he didn't rip the damn thing clean off the dash.

The kid couldn't be right, could he? The two of them had to have done something together in the recent past.

Or maybe not?

After Mere's death, his time in London blurred into a parade of one-night stands that only ushered in more loneliness. He released a pained breath when Sebastian cut into his tormented thoughts with an elated whoop.

"We're here! Look, it's the sign for Rickety Rock, and it's got a donkey on it—a donkey next to a big boulder. I wonder if that's our donkey. I can't wait to meet the donkey. Did you know that a male donkey is called a Jack, and a female donkey is called a Jennie?"

"Sebastian's read a lot about donkeys and pack burro racing since he got to Colorado. He's even made a few sketches in his book," Libby said. He didn't have to look at her to hear the smile in her voice.

"See," Sebastian called, holding up a drawing of a donkey's head. "I drew you with a donkey, Dad."

"He's excited to spend time with you now that we're out of the city and training for the Ass-in-Nine," Libby added in a hushed voice. The venom in her tone had been replaced with a hopeful lilt.

Too bad he was about to disappoint her again.

"You know that I'm still going to be training for the fight, right, mate?" he said, meeting Sebastian's eye in the rearview mirror. "This donkey race isn't such a big deal compared to a championship fight that millions and millions of people are going to watch."

"Yeah, I know, Dad," the child answered, deflating into the seat.

"But you'll have those camps and activities with your mates," he said, trying to find the bright side. "You'll be so busy you won't even miss me."

Had more hollow words ever been spoken?

What was wrong with him? He was better off keeping his gob shut.

"Yeah, Dad, camp with Phoebe and Oscar will be cracking," the boy answered flatly.

Bloody hell.

Libby glared at him, her amber eyes blazing.

If she had a vibrator, she'd surely chuck it right at his head.

Silently fuming, she didn't say a word as they exited the interstate. The GPS barked directions as they entered the tiny town of Rickety Rock. The place looked like something out of an olden day's movie. There was a quaint downtown area with a mix of one- and two-story brick buildings lining the main drag, coupled with hanging baskets of brightly colored flowers. He took in the shops and raised an eyebrow at their interesting names. There seemed to be a theme to this town—an odd coupling of two categories: donkeys and discombobulation.

Sebastian rolled down his window and craned his neck. "Burro Café, Ass You Are Western Wear, The Mule and Donkey Saloon, Jack and Jennie's Bookshop, Wobbly Hardware, Loopy Scoop Ice Cream Parlor, Askew Market, Crooked Zen Rocks and Fortunes, Rickety Rock Visitor Center and Vortex Resources," Sebastian called out, reading the names of the various eclectic shops.

Bloody brilliant! He'd be training in a lopsided town that had a bizarre affinity for donkeys and mystical bullshit. Libby should be over the moon. There must be spiritual yoga people coming out of the woodwork here. This was not his scene in the least, which may be a good thing. What he needed was some bloody peace and quiet to train. Hopefully, Madelyn had worked her magic to secure decent lodging for them in the peculiar mountain town.

"There's a bunch of little houses down the side streets. And look, there's the post office, a library, a community center, and a town square," the boy continued, like a mini tour guide. "Where's our house? Is it close to here?"

"It's off Falling Stone Road," Libby said, glancing at the GPS display. "Up there," she added, pointing toward a cluster of structures in the distance.

At least they'd have some privacy.

They continued up an uneven gravel road that zigged and zagged until the mountain foliage cleared, and the large structure that he'd spied from the town below turned out to be a grand Victorian mansion. One would assume an English-style home would stick out like a sore thumb against the rocky, mountainous terrain, but it worked.

"Wow," Libby breathed.

He parked in front of a set of stone steps that led to the front door. They exited the car and inhaled the clean mountain air.

He surveyed their summer lodging.

The place looked like an elaborate dollhouse come to life.

Painted a crisp cream with plum paint outlining the windows and highlighting the fish-scale shingles, the three-story structure rose into the air with a pointy, pitched roof and a tower-like portion with a turret jutting into the sky like a witch's hat. Several windows were fitted with square glass panes in every shade of the rainbow. A path lined with white stones curved along the wraparound porch. It meandered past three more structures. The first appeared to be a two-story five-car garage, the second a barn, and the third, tucked closer to the back of the main house, was a small cottage built in the same Victorian style.

"Can that be my room?" Sebastian asked, perking up as he pointed to the third-floor window of the grand Victorian below the triangular turret.

"I don't see why not," Libby answered, smiling up at the house. She was trying to keep her features neutral, but the awestruck look in her eyes couldn't be ignored. It was a look he quite fancied. He liked seeing a smile on her face.

Do not concern yourself with her happiness.

"What's that stack of rocks for?" Sebastian asked, pointing to eight stones stacked from largest to smallest next to the trail leading to the other structures. It wasn't that big—less than a foot tall.

"That's an outdoorsy thing, like a signal. It's a sign to let you know you're on the right path. Hikers leave them for others, so they don't get lost in the wilderness," Libby answered.

"Brilliant," Sebastian cooed, studying the stones.

Raz turned away, working to even out the competing emotions welling in his chest. He rubbed the tense muscles at the base of his neck and studied the landscape. While it was no substitute for Libby's captivating beauty, the view still took his breath away. He could see the whole town from here, nestled in the valley between two majestic rocky peaks. Ranches dotted the mountainside with grazing animals moving across the mountainous backdrop. Wildflowers peppered the land. Vibrant reds, yellows, and periwinkle-colored flowers spread across a vast ocean of rocky greenery.

And there was bloody more.

A creek stretched as far as the eye could see, and a lake, or possibly a reservoir, glinted blue-green in the afternoon sun.

If there was ever a time to extend your arms and belt out lyrics from *The Sound of Music*, this was it—not that he'd ever bust out singing like a bloody fool on a mountainside.

Sebastian sprinted down to the garage and threw open the side door. "It's a whole gym, Dad!" he cried. "There's even a boxing ring in it."

"Don't touch anything, Sebastian," he instructed.

The boy closed the door, and his shoulders slumped.

Bloody hell! Could he get anything right?

"Why don't you head inside and find your room," he said,

softening his tone. "It should be open. Madelyn's people knew we were arriving today."

The boy nodded and trudged up the stairs leading to the front door.

"You could let your son be a little excited about having a boxer for a father," Libby chided as she came up beside him.

A heady mix of lust and loathing had him feeling as rickety as this town's name. Their ten-day separation hadn't sat well with her. He didn't have to be a rocket scientist to figure that out. The thing is—most people weren't bold enough to give him shit. Crikey, who was he kidding? She'd never been intimidated by him. In fact, with her in his arms, naked and bloody gorgeous as she rocked against him, he was the one ready to surrender.

Get your head in the game, mate.

"Sebastian doesn't know how to use any of the equipment. He could get hurt," he explained, but the sharp twist of her lips told him she wasn't buying that excuse.

"I wonder why he doesn't know how to use any of it?" she huffed, throwing more eye daggers his way. Thank God she didn't have a gong. He could picture it now. Libby, in a rage, chasing him down the mountain in a flurry of clangs and jarring bangs.

"The door is unlocked. And there's a note taped to it for you," Sebastian announced from the porch.

He waved for the boy to go on ahead of them, then turned his attention back to the nanny. "Sebastian is my son and my responsibility."

"He's my responsibility, too. I promised your grandmother I'd keep him safe. And I'll have you know, I don't break promises," Libby shot back, then set off for the house before he could reply.

The nerve.

He followed behind, fuming. Did she not understand what

was at stake for him? He could quite literally see red as he charged through the door.

He grabbed the note and skimmed the text. It was from someone named Maud, writing that she'd left two sets of keys on the hooks by the door for them and that she would be by later to say hello. He folded the sheet in half and stuffed it into his pocket. She was probably a real estate agent or the house's caretaker. He looked up and glanced around their temporary home. And bloody hell, he was no interior design aficionado, but even he could appreciate the décor. The house was stunning, welcoming, and cozy like a bed-and-breakfast, and the agitation prickling through his veins subsided. He stopped and studied a painting of two pack burros.

"Donkey art," he mused.

"Are you okay?" Libby asked and cocked her head to the side.

Jesus, what was wrong with him? Donkey art? Was the elevation draining his brain?

Forget the home furnishings and bloody lace doilies, you daft wanker.

Again, Libby didn't wait for his response and stomped her way up the stairs. If she could stomp, so could he. He had a lot on his mind, too, and he plodded along behind her like the beast he was. The bloody staircase whined and creaked beneath their feet as if the house itself was begging them to ease up and mellow out.

There wasn't a snowball's chance in hell of that happening. The frantic energy pulsing between them was enough to knock a man twice his size on his arse.

"I found my room. It's on the third floor. The ceiling is a triangle," Sebastian hollered from higher up in the Victorian.

"Good, lad," he replied, but his mind was elsewhere. He focused on Libby's jet-black ponytail swishing wildly from side to side. She'd worked herself up into a right fit. "Why are your knickers in such a twist, plum?" he whisper-shouted as they stepped onto the second level, the old floorboards continuing to creak beneath their feet like the house itself could sense the tension. "Is it your O?" he asked, enunciating the letter like the arrogant arse he was. "You can't have it without me, eh? Are you angry with me for not following the *curriculum* and hitting those *benchmarks* this week?"

She turned on her heel and grabbed a fistful of his T-shirt in her ridiculously firm grip. Like a pint-sized bouncer, she pulled him into a bedroom and slammed the door. "What did you say to me?" she hissed, pressing his back to the wall.

His heart hammered in his chest. He'd taken the arrogant beefcake act too far this time. The question was, what was his raven-haired captor going to do about it?

TWELVE

ERASMUS

"HOW DARE you bring up my O," Libby bit out.

The energy coming off her might just blow the top off this Victorian.

And not only that.

This whole tough yoga nanny business was one hell of a turn-on.

"You seem keyed up like you're desperate for release," he answered, his voice sounding a hell of a lot huskier than he'd expected.

A sexy blush colored her cheeks as her chest heaved. "That's what you think this is about? My O?"

Steady, mate. Put on the beefcake mask. Karma won't help you now.

He manufactured a smirk. "It's kind of my O, too. It only comes out for me."

"It is absolutely not *your* O," she whisper-shrieked, pushing up onto her tiptoes. Her breasts grazed his chest, and a titillating buzz penetrated every cell in his body.

"Have you been able to..." he trailed off, losing a fraction of his cocky edge. He was genuinely interested. Plus, the heat of her nearness had scrambled his brain, and if she leaned in any closer, she'd feel what he had going on in his trousers.

"Have I been able to do what, Erasmus? Masturbate to completion? Have I jumped into bed with another guy and spent the night in a state of orgasmic bliss?" she tossed back, eyes blazing.

Her touching herself was one thing. The image of this woman spread out on a bed with her hand between her thighs, working her sweet spot, had him rock-hard in a bloody second. But the thought of her with another man was a different story. He shouldn't care what or who she did in her spare time. She wasn't his, and she never could be. But that didn't stop his jaw from clenching as he gnashed his teeth together. They'd be dust if he didn't get the notion of Libby Lamb screwing some idiot bloke out of his head.

She huffed. "Not that it's any of your business, but no, I haven't attempted any of the benchmark activities. I haven't had time."

"Busy with your nanny life?" he bit out, keeping his emotions in check. He couldn't let on how bloody relieved he was that she hadn't been with anyone else but him.

He held her gaze as the blush on her cheeks intensified. He'd hit a nerve.

"Yes, as a matter of fact," she answered, gathering more of his shirt into her fist. She jerked his head down to look her straight in the eyes.

Crikey, she was strong!

"I've been extremely busy caring for your son, and I've loved every minute of it. I don't think you've noticed, but you have an amazing kid—a kind and intelligent soul. And you can't spare a second for him. Do you know how much he wants to be like you?"

The fire in his eyes matched hers.

"Yeah, I do," he rasped, the words tasting of ash and iron.

"And he misses his mother. He thinks he makes you sad because he reminds you of Meredith."

Every muscle in his body tensed.

She'd gone there.

He figured Sebastian would have mentioned his mum. The boy carried that picture of her in the watch everywhere he went. But he didn't have the emotional capacity to discuss his wife—not with Libby and not with the fight of his life looming over his shoulder. A fight he had to win for Meredith.

"Don't bring her up," he growled. This was the voice he used in the ring when he wanted to instill a shit ton of fear into his opponent. It worked every time, except bloody now.

Libby lifted her smug little chin. "It's your son's mother's name. You can't banish the memory of her. It's not your call."

He leaned in and could feel her breath against his neck. "You want to know about Meredith?" he dared—was he challenging her or himself? Christ, he didn't know.

She held his gaze. With her lips pressed into a hard line, she gave him space to talk.

He swallowed past the lump in his throat. "I loved her. She believed in me. We came from nothing. She worked two jobs so I could train full time with Augie. I owe her this win. It's an affront to her if I fail." He glanced away. He should button up his gob and shut the hell up. He had to hold back the emotions he'd kept locked inside.

"Erasmus," she whispered, and her voice, her angelic voice, opened the floodgates to his heart.

"I've only ever been good at one thing, plum. That's putting on gloves and knocking men down." He steadied himself because he couldn't stop if his life depended on it. He exhaled a slow breath. "I'm fighting for Meredith. I do it so Sebastian can have a better life. That's what Mere and I wanted for him."

Yeah, he'd dropped one hell of a truth bomb, and with the emotional turmoil in the air near palpable, he'd expected that to be the end of it. That's what she wanted, right? A sad, pathetic excuse to explain his failings? A little insight into his cracked psyche. But her expression didn't soften. No, the fury in her eyes burned brighter.

"You're hiding behind that excuse. That's not why you're fighting. Do you think no one can see behind that smug beefcake exterior? News flash, I can."

The breath caught in his throat. Could she see everything? He'd wondered the same thing when she'd charged into Aug's gym a few months ago. And he knew the bloody answer. Those damn eyes saw into his soul. But he wasn't about to cop to it, and he sure didn't need her take on why she believed he fought. He couldn't budge, and he couldn't waver—too much was at stake.

What would he do if he were in the ring, knowing that his opponent was about to steal the advantage?

He'd turn the bloody tables.

"Speaking of excuses," he snarled. "You've got some nerve to call me out."

Confusion marred her fierce expression. "What are you talking about?"

"You've walled your heart off, Libby Lamb. Somebody hurt you. That's why you've written off love and relationships. You're no different from me. No, that's not right. You're worse."

Her bottom lip trembled, just slightly, but he caught it. It was her tell.

"Worse?" she shot back. "You don't know anything about me."

He'd gambled and was right. She'd been hurt badly. Was he a bastard for coming at her weakest point? Yes, but that's what he did in the ring, and that's what he'd have to do if he had any chance of getting out of this damn funk and getting her out of his head.

Now it was time to go in for the knockout.

He cupped her face in his hands. "You're worse, Libby Lamb, because you hide your pain behind a mask of serenity. My pain and aggression are out there for everyone to see. You pretend like yours doesn't exist."

Her lips parted, and she stared up at him, those pools of amber threatening to swallow him whole. The raw honesty in her gaze cut right to his heart. The fight to hold himself back from her weakened. His defenses shattered. He'd started this tête à tête with his gloves up. Now, completely exposed, his hands were at his bloody sides.

They were back to this place—a place where he knew better than to lose himself, but he couldn't gather the resolve to pull away. The energy, the force propelling them toward each other, was too powerful. She gripped his shirt with both hands, holding on to him. Had she done it to stop herself from using her free fist to clock him in the chin for mouthing off like a bloody prick? It wasn't like he didn't deserve it. Or had she done it to anchor herself to him?

That was it.

Deep within, he knew this to be true, but it didn't change the fact that he couldn't have her. He should take her hands and remove them from where they rested against his chest, but that blasted violet-blue haze was back, clouding his vision, muddling his thoughts. No, that wasn't it. What he'd tried to peg as confusion wasn't confusion at all.

It was clarity.

A terrifying clarity.

He wanted her. He wanted her like he'd wanted...

"Raz, you're right, I..." she whispered, but he couldn't allow her to go on.

He drew his thumb across her bottom lip, and she trembled at his touch. His arrogant exterior was no match for her words—words that resonated with such searing honesty that he had no other option than to make it stop. There, in an unfamiliar room, in an unfamiliar town, time stood still, and every reason to turn away from Libby's light disappeared. In a desperate move to quell the ache in his chest, he crushed his lips to hers, silencing her with a kiss that calmed and shattered him all at once.

And he was home, bloody home. He teetered on a precipice, playing with fire, gambling with his heart. He knew better, but he couldn't stop.

Libby parted her lips, and he deepened their connection. His mind emptied of all rational thought as an overpowering sensation took over.

Don't stop kissing Libby Lamb.

Hot, sweet, and wet, she tasted like the forbidden fruit, and he wanted to make her juices flow.

She sighed a sexy sound—a sound that went straight to his cock. He slid his hands into her hair, wrecking her ponytail as he twisted the silky locks between his fingers. This earned him another lusty sigh from the raven-haired beauty. Each kiss fueled his desire. He'd fought his feelings so viciously these past ten days that the relief of giving in felt more like a victory than a defeat. She skimmed her hands beneath his shirt, and he inhaled a tight breath as she explored the expanse of his muscled torso. Her tender touch was almost unbeatable. It gutted him while making him want more of her, all of her.

"You taste so sweet, plum," he whispered against her lips before dropping a kiss to the corner of her mouth. She smiled a honeyed smile against him, humming her delight. Sweeter than a summer day, she'd cast a spell on him. His mind stopped spinning. His nagging thoughts drifted into the distant corners of his mind. The second-guessing dissolved as he trailed his fingertips down the petal-soft skin of her neck, past her shoulders, and settled his grip on her hips. Lifting her into his arms, he turned swiftly and pressed her back into the door as she wrapped her legs around him. Fused together, they released a collective sigh laced with relief and desperate longing. He gripped her supple arse and his palms melded around the perfect globes. They moved together as if one completed the other—two halves becoming a whole.

She held his face in her hands, and her thumb brushed against his earlobe. He'd never bloody thought about his damn earlobes until now. But he'd give up every penny he'd earned to lock that feeling in a bottle.

Kiss after kiss, the energy flowed between them, rhythmic and harmonious. She rocked her hips, grinding into him, teasing his hard length. A frenzied friction kindled between them. He was so much bigger than her. She wasn't wrong with the beef-cake moniker, but they met as equals when their bodies came together.

Spiraling deeper and deeper, he ran his tongue across the seam of her lips when a squeak and a faint rattle nudged his consciousness. He blocked it out, then slid his hand inside her shirt. Massaging her breasts through the lace of her bra, he drew his tongue down her jawline. Tasking himself with tasting every exposed inch of skin, he kissed her neck, licking and sucking the sweet skin—claiming her.

She bucked against him, gasping as they fell into a rhythm that had them breathing hard. He was on the edge, ready to shrug out of his trousers and rip her leggings off. Every impulse screamed for him to thrust inside her, rocking and bucking until he couldn't see straight. He shifted her weight to his left hand, ready to use his right to free his weeping cock, when that bloody squeak and rattle returned. It had to be the old Victorian, but that assertion vanished when a sharp knock cut through the sensual blue-violet haze.

Libby went rigid in his arms, and they stared at each other. She bit down on her kiss-swollen bottom lip as they remained stock-still. Limbs entwined and chests heaving, they listened.

"Are you in there with my dad, Libby? Are you doing noisy yoga? Is noisy yoga a thing, or are you doing punching yoga? You sure are making a lot of sounds in there."

Sebastian.

Bollocks.

Libby's eyes went wide as the color drained from her cheeks. Her mouth opened and closed a few times before she was able to form a sentence. "Yes, I'm in here with your father doing him." She shook her head. "We're doing a special boxing yoga. We're doing this because I'm his spiritual advisor, and that's part of my job. Advising him spiritually with my body and doing it noisily."

She winced.

Yeah, that was about as cringe-worthy of a reply as one could muster—but at least she could talk. All he could do was stand there rocking a giant boner.

"That's what I told the people outside that I thought you were doing." The doorknob rattled as Sebastian turned it from the other side. "Is the door broken? I can't get it to budge."

"It's just...stuck. We'll try to open it from our side. Now, what's going on outside?" he asked, finally able to speak.

"I told you already, Dad. There are a bunch of people here."

It could be that Maud woman who'd left the note, but why would she have a bunch of people with her? A jolt of anxiety rocketed through his body. Bloody Briggs had sent a slew of emails with *Rickety Rock PR Events* written in the subject line.

Had he bothered to open them? No, and that was a decision he was beginning to regret.

"And what are they asking for, Sebastian?" he called, waiting, trying to get a handle on what the hell was going on outside. He held his breath. A thousand bloody lives could have been lived in the few seconds it took for the boy to answer.

"They're asking for—"

"For me?" he interrupted.

"No, Dad, they want Libby."

THIRTEEN

ERASMUS

WHAT IN THE bloody hell was going on?

"Who would want to speak with me? I don't know a soul in this town," Libby said with a crease to her brow as he set her down.

That was his question, too.

"They asked for Libby, you're sure?" he called to his son on the other side of the door.

"Yeah, Dad, that's what I said. I decided to check out the barn since it sounded like you and Libby were busy doing noisy yoga, and I didn't want to bother you. And when I opened the front door, I saw the people with the cameras."

Cameras?

"One posh guy knew my name," Sebastian continued. "He said, 'Hello, Sebastian.' And I said, hello, posh bloke, if you want my dad and Libby, you'll have to wait because they're busy doing noisy yoga, or they could be doing noisy tummy yoga because my dad farted in the car. And yoga helps if you've got a sour belly."

Bloody hell.

"Want me to tell them that you're coming?" Sebastian asked.

Libby gasped.

What was wrong now—aside from completely losing themselves in frenzied passion.

"What is it, plum?"

She ran her hands through her tangle of hair, working to fix her now lopsided ponytail. "If there's press here," she said, lowering her voice, "I don't think you want your son to run onto the porch to tell them we're upstairs, locked in a bedroom, doing noisy yoga, and *coming*."

She was right!

He cleared his throat. "Sebastian?"

"Yeah, Dad?"

"No matter what you do, do not go outside and say that I'm coming with Libby."

"Well, Dad, who else would you be coming with?" the child lobbed back.

This had to stop.

"Want me to see if any of the people outside can help open the door? Maybe that posh guy?" the boy offered.

It had to be Briggs.

"No, don't go out there. I can manage the door," he answered, then swung the creaky thing open. He met Sebastian's gaze, and the kid cocked his head to the side and frowned.

"You're wrinkly, Dad," the boy observed before scanning Libby from head to toe. "What's wrong with your lips?"

"My lips?" she exclaimed, covering her mouth.

"They're puffy and red. And your neck. You got another one of those bug bites."

Bug bites?

He glanced at Libby's neck. He didn't see any bug bites, but he did spy a love bite.

Bloody hell. Why did her skin have to taste like honey?

Libby ran to the center of the bedroom and scanned the space.

"What are you looking for?" Had she lost her mind? Had they both?

"That," she announced and pointed to the curtains.

He took a page from Sebastian's playbook and cocked his head to the side.

Yep, that kissing had done them both in.

He stared at the flowing curtains with tiny black birds embroidered on the fabric. They were blue and violet like the rest of the room—which he hadn't even noticed. They could have been in a broom closet for all he knew. Too much blood had left his brain and had headed south thanks to their hot and heavy make-out session.

And speaking of hot.

If he wasn't in such a tizzy about the house being bombarded by the press, he'd need to subject himself to the coldest shower known to man. After that, he could sure use a sparring partner to clock him in the head a few times. He studied the heavy wooden door. Perhaps he could bang his head into it and knock some bloody sense into him.

What was he thinking?

That was the problem. He wasn't thinking—at least not with his brain.

Distract yourself, you bloody fool!

He gave the frilly purply-blue room another look. There were little bird figurines everywhere—creepy little buggers— staring at him from every corner. Even the crows on the curtain seemed to be eyeing him.

"How are window coverings supposed to help?" he pressed.

"I'm repurposing them," she replied, then removed the

fabric from the rod and looped it around her neck. "It should cover my bug bite, so it doesn't get..."

"Infected?" Sebastian offered with a weary bend to the word, clearly not quite sold on the whole curtain scarf idea.

"Yes, exactly, Sebastian! You're a genius," Libby exclaimed, and the boy lit up.

"Now that I'm looking at it, I quite like it as a scarf," the lad chimed. "I like birds, especially crows."

"You do?" he asked his son, raising an eyebrow.

"Yeah, sometimes I draw them in my sketchbook."

"I liked birds when I was a kid, too."

Sebastian grinned from ear to ear. "I didn't know that, Dad. Do you hear that, Libby? My dad likes crows like I do."

Raz's chest tightened as the hole in his heart expanded. Despite giving his son the best this world had to offer, he didn't know much about who the lad was. What made the boy tick, that is, besides wanting to learn about boxing? He honestly didn't know.

"Look at that," Libby answered as she checked her appearance in a mirror. "Everyone here is a fan of crows. Crows are special birds. Some say they can see the future."

"A crow pooped on your shoulder the day before we met, right, Libby?" the child pressed.

"Yes."

"I wonder if that crow knew you'd be meeting me and that I'd be living in a house with my dad, and you'd be with us?" the boy pondered, wide-eyed.

"Maybe it did," Libby answered, slightly awestruck.

Raz ignored the emptiness in his chest. This wasn't the time to go over his faults as a father, and they needed to drop the crow chatter. Now that they had the love bite situation under control, he had to deal with whatever was waiting at the door asking for Libby. He paced the length of the room. "This shouldn't be too bad—probably a PR thing."

Why, why, why hadn't he skimmed over Briggs's emails?

Libby smoothed her makeshift scarf as she swallowed hard. "What do you think? Do I look okay?" she asked with a shake to her voice, edging out the momentary astonishment.

She was nervous, and he didn't blame her.

The press could be vicious. Briggs had given them an excuse for the vibrator situation, but he couldn't figure out why they'd be asking for her now. There was only one thing to do—the one thing that used to be offered to him when the whole world went topsy-turvy.

And that lifeline was unwavering reassurance.

He softened his expression and stared at her reflection in the mirror. "That curtain actually works as a scarf. Sebastian's right. The crows look...nice. They match your...hair."

He sounded like a moron.

He was a boxer, not a stylist, but he had to say something.

She turned from side to side, watching the fabric flow in the mirror. "Are you sure? You know what happened last time I was in front of the press." She gave him a weak smile, the nerves getting the better of her.

He came up behind her, assessed the material, and smoothed the fabric at the nape of her neck. His fingertips brushed against her soft skin. A shiver tingled down his spine. It was torture to refrain from kissing her, but he held back. She caught his eye in the mirror and watched him closely as he went back to work adjusting the scarf. His throat tightened as a strange sense of déjà vu came over him. This moment felt more intimate than their kissing frenzy against the door. Adjusting her scarf was a simple gesture, but one he hadn't done for another in over three years. How many times had Mere asked him to zip her up or clasp a necklace? He lowered his hands, holding Libby's gaze. "It was twisted. I fixed it for you."

She didn't answer. Instead, she leaned back the slightest bit, and her body grazed his chest. Did she even know she'd done it? Had she felt her shoulder blades brush a whisper-soft kiss to his torso? The movement was so slight, it was hardly detectable. But there was no mistaking her touch. Was it that pull between them? That maddening sensation drew him to her like two halves of a whole.

"Thanks," she whispered, her voice a raspy scrape of sound. She stared into his eyes, and in that blissful slip of time, there was no fight to prepare for, no PR blitz, and no silly donkey race. It was just the two of them, trying to decipher what came next.

What did he want?

"I'll tell them you're coming," Sebastian called, popping the hazy Libby Lamb bubble. The boy turned on his heel and bounded down the staircase, his rhythmic descent clomping against the creaky boards.

Ready or not, it was time to face the press.

Raz stepped back and ran his hands down his face. "So much for the lad not mentioning the whole dirty coming bit." He met Libby's gaze in the mirror and found her staring back at him, her jaw on the floor. "Not like there was any dirty coming-coming. We were simply caught up in the moment, or maybe it could be the altitude," he offered like a right twit.

He was grasping at straws. But he wasn't the only one who seemed like a fish out of water.

Libby twisted the curtain scarf around her index finger and nodded vigorously. "Yes, it's probably that pesky altitude. We've got to be up at around ten thousand feet—possibly higher. That can do things to people—kissing things and dirty coming things. Oh gosh, we should stop saying, coming. You know, the sexytimes type of coming. Not the, hold the elevator, I'm coming-coming kind of coming."

If this kept up, the press would eat her alive.

They'd had a few awkward back-and-forth exchanges, to say the least, but this one was taking the cake. Granted, it seemed as if she was also keen on blaming the mountain air for their lip-lock situation. Brilliant, they were on the same page. That's what it had to be. They'd ventured into a new town, and each had new endeavors on the horizon. It was bound to feel a bit unsteady.

It took time to get one's bearings, right?

Oh, who was he kidding?

It didn't matter how high up they were. He would have kissed her if they were ten thousand feet beneath the sea.

She turned toward him. With those sparkling eyes and kiss-swollen lips, an urge that had nothing to do with the altitude had him cupping her cheek in his hand. "Try not to worry about the media, plum. I'll be out there with you. You won't be alone." His emotions were all over the bloody place—that is, until he touched her, and the energy that flowed between them smoothed out his jagged edges.

"Okay," she whispered when the chorus of creaks and foot-steps caught his attention, and they pulled apart.

"Augie and Luanne are here," Sebastian reported, grinning from ear to ear, clearly amped up from the activity. "I met Luanne. Augie says she's his friend, but I think she's his girlfriend."

"That's enough of that, lad," Augie teased in a dry tone, coming up the stairs with Luanne by his side.

The addition of Aug and Luanne begged another question.

What the hell were they doing here, and what exactly had Briggs scheduled?

Again, he wanted to punch himself in the mouth for

blowing off those emails. He took in Aug's rosy expression. The man hated pressers. He'd gotten damn good at them over the years, but that was only because everyone loved an old sourpuss. But today, he had a bona fide grin on his face. Then again, he'd never had Luanne by his side at one of these dog and pony shows.

"Briggsy's about to blow a gasket. How much longer will you make them wait?" Augie harped.

There was the piss and vinegar trainer.

"Oh, give him a break, honey," Luanne said with a pat on Augie's arm. "How are you, Erasmus?" the woman continued. In khaki pants and a blue tunic with a straw hat covering her silver hair, Aug's girlfriend looked the part of a seasoned geologist ready to venture into the field.

He embraced the woman. "It's good to see you, Luanne. It appears you've met my son, Sebastian."

"I showed Luanne Libby's gemstone, and she knew it was aquamarine right off the bat," Sebastian chimed, tittering with delight. "She didn't have to look in a book or on the internet or anything. She said I was a budding something or other. What did you call me, Luanne?"

"A budding rockhound," the woman replied, gifting Sebastian with a grin. "You'll love this part of Colorado. There are rock and mineral treasures just about everywhere you look."

Libby reached out to shake Luanne's hand. "We haven't met. I'm Libby Lamb the..."

"The spiritual advisor slash nanny," Luanne interjected, sharing a look with Augie before shaking Libby's hand. "Yes, Sebastian was telling us about this special yoga you two are doing up here."

Special yoga? More like sucking face like horny teenagers.

It could be worse, though. At least Luanne didn't ask if he was up here nursing a sour belly and farting up a storm.

"Yes, the special yoga! So very, very special," Libby replied through a blush.

And the awkward meter had skyrocketed through the roof again.

He had to shift the subject from this *special yoga* to literally anything else. But what? His mind had gone blank.

Fall back on formality. You're English. Use your bloody manners.

"Libby, you remember Augie from the night we agreed to..."

He shot a look at Sebastian, then met Libby's gaze.

Crikey, so much for relying on pleasantries to introduce a neutral topic!

He should have asked about the blooming weather. Brits could go on and on about that subject. He sure as bloody hell couldn't mention the whole vibrator debacle with Sebastian standing two feet away.

"Yes, I remember Augie," Libby said, swooping in. "We met the night you and I agreed to represent Denver's first responders in the Ass-in-Nine pack burro race. An event we absolutely weren't coerced into doing under threat of prosecution."

Oh, sweet Jesus.

"Well," Luanne said, amusement sparkling in her eyes, "you both should be commended for caring about the community."

"We're happy to help," he answered, plastering on a grin.

Yep, that's it.

It was run with jackasses or face time in the slammer.

And, of course, Luanne knew everything. He'd be a fool to think Augie hadn't mentioned the whole insane story to the woman. Then again, she'd probably seen the vibrator encounter. Most of the human race and a decent number of astronauts had viewed the viral video.

It was time to move on.

With the introductions made and no one dropping any

vibrator talk, he turned to Augie. "What's going on out there? Did Briggs tell you to be here for a PR thing?"

Aug and Luanne had left for his place in Aspen a few days ago, leaving him to train alone in Denver. The two hadn't spoken in a few days. Still, the man hadn't mentioned anything about coming to Rickety Rock today.

"Are you not reading those emails from Briggsy?" Aug huffed. "Why am I not surprised? It's like you've been on another planet this past week," the man shot back when, speak of the posh devil, Briggs Keaton sprinted up the stairs, mobile in hand.

"The mountain air is quite invigorating," Briggs announced, sporting the least-mountainy outfit in his trademark three-piece suit as he surveyed the group. "Excellent, you're looking terrific, champ. Aug, you don't mind sitting this one out, do you?"

"I do not," the trainer answered.

"And, Libby," the agent continued, his attention bobbing between the nanny and his mobile. "It's so good to see you. There's already chatter, thanks to Sebastian, here. Social media is blowing up after only a few minutes."

Social media's blowing up?

He better not be trending because his son blurted out his dad was a bloody car farter!

"What do you mean? We just got here," Libby asked, confusion marring her expression.

"It's about you, Miss Lamb. Let's walk and talk," Briggs said, gesturing for the group to head downstairs.

Sebastian was the first to hit the steps, followed by Luanne and Augie, but Raz hung back to keep an eye on his agent. The man was ogling Libby like she was made of money. Granted, as a sports agent, Briggs's job was to make deals and rake in the cash. He gave the guy a fair share of shit, but Briggs Keaton was good at what he did. Nevertheless, when it came to Libby, all he wanted to do was protect her from the glare of this world.

"Per my email," Briggs began, "we're here for a little meet and greet. The mountain west is excited to have a heavyweight champion training in their backyard. But the big names got wind of it and sent crews. You know how it goes."

"I actually don't know how it goes," Libby replied, looking more and more anxious by the second as they gathered in the first-floor entryway.

Sebastian jumped up and down. "Just look outside. There are people everywhere. They left their cars on the road and walked up," the boy called, hopping into the sitting area adjacent to the entry. The child plunked himself on the picture window bench and pressed his nose to the glass to peer out at the media circus.

"Sweet Buddha's belly, that's a lot of people," Libby whispered, glancing out one of the windows near the front door.

"It's an exciting time in the world of boxing," Briggs began, sounding like a game show host. "The odds are in the Lion's favor, but it's very much in flux. Everyone's scrutinizing this fight, looking for who to put their money on."

"Money?" Libby breathed.

"Yeah, you know, online gambling and betting on the outcome. It's part of the whole show. It's a billion-dollar business," the agent explained as he hammered out a text, oblivious that the color had drained from Libby's face.

"What is it, plum?" he whispered.

"I absolutely loathe—"

"Sorry to cut you off, Libby," Briggs said, nearly vibrating as he pocketed his mobile. "It's go-time. ESPN and Box Nation arrived." The sports agent fixed his gaze on the nanny. "Welcome to the big leagues, Miss Lamb."

Bloody hell, what had Briggs done?

FOURTEEN

ERASMUS

"WHAT DO you mean ESPN and Box Nation arrived?" Raz hissed.

"What's Box Nation?" Libby asked.

"They're a boxing network that broadcasts in the UK," he said, answering Libby's question as he pinned Briggs with his gaze. It was one thing for Briggs to promise a meet and greet with him—he was the professional athlete. But throwing Libby into the fire was unacceptable. Major media outlets meant major, global coverage, and that came with brutal scrutiny. Sure, there was the damn viral video, but putting yourself out there to spar with the media was a whole different animal.

"This is too much, Briggs," he said through gritted teeth. "I'll go out alone."

"Champ, they want Libby," Briggs answered. "If you go out there, they'll wait until they can see her. This way, we're in control," the man replied, then let out a self-congratulatory harrumph.

"What's that for, Briggs?" What did the posh bloke have to be harrumphing about?

"I threw that spiritual advisor mumbo-jumbo together on

the fly. It could have flopped. The press could have called our bluff. But no, they're buying it, and they want more. I quite deserve a pat on the back."

"For lying to the press?" Libby asked.

Briggs shook his head. "I didn't lie. I crafted a narrative around an unfortunate set of events. Honestly, Miss Lamb, I thought you might be deranged. What an amazing turn of fate that you're not completely off your rocker. And, thanks to Sebastian, the press knows that you've been using your spiritual yoga skills to help train the Lion." Briggs beamed, doing a little jig—a bloody jig. The guy was positively buzzing with excitement.

Libby twisted the corner of her curtain scarf nervously. "About the whole spiritual advisor position..."

"Just be yourself, Libby," Briggs interrupted, "but at the same time, bring your A game. We've got major sports media outlets here."

This was too much.

Raz shook his head. "Briggs," he hissed, getting in his agent's face. "Libby didn't sign up for this. This is my world. This is my fight."

"Listen, Raz," the man answered, raising his hands defensively. "I understand, but in this business, you've got to be able to pivot at a moment's notice. That's what I did after the incident in front of Aug's gym, and that's what we have to do now. This was supposed to be a quick photo shoot with you and Aug in your mountain training location. Then your son mentioned a special yoga regimen, and the press glommed on to it—hook, line, and sinker. We need to go with it. I'm sure there are people out there still skeptical about us calling that event outside Aug's gym a new-age training technique. Today, Libby controls the story. They want her."

He hated to admit it, but Briggs had a point.

"They're not expecting me to throw things at Raz, are

they?" Libby asked. "I brought the *devices* with me, but I don't think it would be appropriate to use them in front of Sebastian. And as we learned back in Denver, it's a crime to throw sex toys in public. I don't want to get arrested again."

Raz's jaw dropped. "You brought them? You packed sixteen vibrators?"

"I wasn't about to leave them in Denver," Libby whispered, wide-eyed. "What if someone found them? What if your grandmother or some of Madelyn's people saw them? What would they think?"

"I get it. I get it," Raz conceded.

Briggs waved them off. "It's no secret that you've got them. Astronauts reenacted that scene in space—great exposure, by the way. Masterful PR! Pay-Per-View sales spiked like I've never seen. Thanks to the show you put on outside the gym, the championship fight between the Lion and the Snake may be the most-watched TV event ever. And like I said, the online betting alone is astronomical."

Libby crossed her arms. "Listen, I'm willing to help in whatever way I can, but I won't go out there and throw vibrators at Raz to improve gambling."

"We're not doing that, Briggs," Raz said, picking up on the shift in Libby's energy. Her uneasiness had changed to simmering anger.

"Forget throwing things. That's not even what they want to see. Show them the yoga techniques Sebastian mentioned. That is what you were doing locked in that room, right?"

"Right," he and Libby chimed in unison.

"Brilliant! Demo that. But only give them a sneak peek. Don't give too much away. We don't want Silas Scott's people to pick up any tips," the agent added.

Raz pinched the bridge of his nose. This would be a bloody

terrific idea, aside from the fact that the special noisy yoga Sebastian announced to the press didn't even exist.

"About that special yoga regimen I'm implementing with Raz," Libby began, but Briggs had checked out of the conversation. The man swung open the front door to an onslaught of reporters lobbing questions.

"Raz, what do I do?" she asked, but before he could respond, Briggs gestured for them to exit the house.

They left the confines of the Victorian. Luckily, the porch was enormous, allowing them to hang back in the cover of shade as Briggs addressed the media from the front steps.

"Thank you for waiting so patiently," the agent crooned. "We don't want to cut into the champ's training time too much, but we're thrilled to give you a taste of the Lion's mountain training regimen. As you know, Erasmus Cress is taking a multifaceted approach to prepare for the upcoming fight. Working with his longtime trainer, Augie Bimston, and his spiritual advisor and private yogi, Libby Lamb, the Snake, Silas Scott, doesn't have a chance against London's Lion. Now enough of me, I give you the Lion and the Lamb," he announced like a bloody carnival barker.

Libby's shoulder brushed against him, and with that brief skin-on-skin contact, the primal urge to wrap his arms around her and shield her from the sea of cameras nearly overtook him. He knew this game. He'd played it for years, but there was something very different about what was happening now. He reined himself in and looked on as confusion and shock welled in her eyes.

He understood her reaction. What was she supposed to say to the press? He wanted to help, but he was the last person to counsel her on yoga and spirituality. As far as he was concerned, it was a colossal waste of time for a boxer to indulge in stretching and screwing around with gongs.

And time wasn't exactly on his side.

The fight was a little more than six weeks away. That was barely a blip when it came to training. A knot formed in his stomach, and his pulse kicked up.

He didn't have time to bullshit around.

But what choice did he have? Briggs had broadcast to the world that he'd immersed himself in this unorthodox training.

What the hell were they supposed to do?

No, that wasn't the question. He was in this on his own. What he should be asking is how was he going to beat Ireland's Silas Scott. How would he regain the title for Meredith?

He'd watched the man's fights. The Snake was the perfect moniker for a slippery fighter who delighted in having fouls called on him. The guy played as close to dirty as he could without getting booted from the ring.

He'd done his homework on the man. But he hadn't settled on a strategy to win.

What was his game plan? Aug tossed out idea after idea, but nothing clicked, and nothing clicked because of his off-kilter, distracted energy.

All these questions tormented him day and night.

This is exactly why he'd spent the last ten days holed up in the gym, ignoring the world. He needed to focus and train. He had to tune out the noise and tighten up his punches and perfect his footwork. He should be eating, breathing, and sleeping boxing.

Then again, he'd done that. He'd cut off contact, and everything had still gone to hell.

Just like last time.

His heart thundered in his chest. He could hear the blood whooshing in his ears. Adrenaline coursed through his veins. He stared at the sky. Gray ominous clouds had rolled in.

He blinked, and his stomach flip-flopped.

Everything went blurry.

What was wrong with his vision? Was it the shift in the weather or the drain of mental exhaustion?

He tried to breathe, but there wasn't enough air—there wasn't enough of anything.

He wasn't enough.

Bloody soul-sucking doubt.

It was as if this crush of frantic energy was on the cusp of swallowing him whole. His thoughts spiraled, and he was no longer in Rickety Rock, Colorado.

And then it was bright—so bright it exposed every crack in his facade. All that existed was the glare of the lights illuminating the ring, the battering *click, click, click* of cameras, the stench of sweat and blood and bodies closing in, crowding around him, suffocating him, and the doctor's voice coming through the mobile pressed to his ear.

I'm sorry, Erasmus, she's gone.

He sucked in a sharp breath, but the air couldn't get to his lungs. Was he about to pass out?

Would he skip out on this fight, too?

Was it all for naught?

That would be it.

Another failure.

The boxing world would surely write him off. Everything Mere had sacrificed would be for nothing. He'd be labeled a head case—a has-been fighter who'd lost his nerve. He could see the headlines and hear the commentators clucking away. *The Beast has lost his bark. The Lion is no king of the ring. Erasmus Cress is not a champ. He's a chump.*

He looked away from the sea of cameras and squeezed his eyes shut. He couldn't let them see him like this. People had wondered why he didn't show for the fight the year after

Meredith died. Of course, the boxing world speculated that it was the grief that had made him a no-show.

And they weren't wrong. He was grieving. He was still grieving.

But it was one thing to speculate.

The truth, the ugly, debilitating truth, was a whole different story.

The press hadn't seen him on his knees, hyperventilating, trapped in the moment when he'd learned she was gone. No one had witnessed the tears streaming down his cheeks or could comprehend the punishing flood of guilt that kept him on that floor, shivering in a heap of pain and regret, unable to live up to the fighter Mere had helped him become.

He was a damned fool for responding to Silas Scott's juvenile taunts, but when he'd replied, it was as if she'd wanted him to fight, like she was there, leaning over his shoulder.

Or maybe that was a load of crap, and he'd accepted the challenge for his own selfish ego.

One thing was for certain. There was no way he was about to untangle his thoughts standing on the porch, steps away from a herd of reporters. He turned, ready to bolt inside the house when the noise stopped, and there was only warmth. The incessant thrum in his head quieted as heat spread over his body. Tender and calming, a gentle peacefulness soothed his battered heart. He opened his eyes and found the source of the heat—a hand pressed to his chest.

Her hand.

Libby's hand.

"Erasmus Cress, look at me," she whispered, and he complied, grateful for the direction. "You're going to ground yourself in this moment, and your breath will hold you together. It doesn't feel like it can right now, but it will. Put your hand on top of mine."

He stared into her eyes and pressed his hand to hers.

"Feel that rise and fall? That's your breath. That's your chi. That's your pulse slowing down as you return to your body."

He inhaled, becoming one with his breath as the storm of chatter cleared, and a weight lifted with his exhale.

How did she stop his panic attack with simply a touch and a few words?

"There you go. There you are," she said, then slipped her hand out from beneath his. "We should address the press." She adjusted her curtain scarf. "It's more like *I* should address the press."

"What will you say, plum?" he asked, still in awe of what she'd done to him.

She gave him a weak smile. "I have an idea, but I might need you to chime in and help me with some boxing terminology. Can you do that?"

"Yeah, I can," he answered smoothly. Was he under her spell? Had she psychically hijacked one of his chakra thingies and reset him? Whatever she did, he felt like a new man.

"I can help, too," Sebastian called, wiggling between them.

When did Sebastian come out onto the porch?

"No, Sebastian, wait inside with Augie and Luanne," he directed, not meaning for the words to bite, but they clearly had, and the lad's shoulders slumped.

Dammit.

"Actually," Libby said, wrapping her arm around Sebastian's shoulders, "if it's okay with you, Raz, I'd like to have Sebastian close by. He's the one who gave me this idea."

"Me?" the boy asked.

"Yes, remember when we were being silly, and we modified some of those yoga moves."

"Yeah, I do."

"I've got an idea, and it might work," Libby said, no longer messing with her scarf or mustering weak smiles. She had some sort of plan, and as long as it didn't involve vibrators, he was for it.

"Libby, can I do something first for my dad?" Sebastian asked.

"Sure."

The lad removed the aquamarine stone from his pocket and rubbed his thumb across the smooth surface, then he rested the stone on his palm and held it up. "Here, Dad, this will make you feel better."

The old Erasmus Cress would have waved the kid off, but he didn't. He accepted the gemstone, taking it from the boy's small hand. He was no believer in rocks and crystals altering behavior. That being said, when he accepted the stone and rubbed it with the pad of his thumb, a strange sense of empowerment mingled with the serenity vibe Libby had imparted into him.

"Do you feel better?" Sebastian asked.

He returned the stone. "Yeah, I do. Thanks, son."

With a wide, proud smile, the lad shared a look with Libby and slipped the stone into his pocket. Then the child reached out, first taking Libby's hand before reaching out to him. Raz swallowed past the lump in his throat, not realizing how much he'd missed this.

He wasn't always the absent father. When Sebastian was a tiny thing, bright-eyed and babbling with chubby legs, they'd spend hours playing in the garden. Sebastian was so curious. He used to toddle into their home gym and wrap himself around his leg while he was knocking out pull-ups. Mere used to call it the boxer's version of a carousel. Oh, and how the boy would laugh and laugh as he went up and down with each rep.

"Ready, Dad?" Sebastian asked.

He stared at the boy, his boy, the lad with Mere's eyes. "Yeah, I am."

Linked together as one, the three of them joined Briggs on the top step, and he surveyed the sea of reporters and news cameras blanketing the grounds. He hadn't noticed the swarm of media that wrapped around the side of the house. This was absolute insanity. He waved Briggs in. "This is what you call a little meet and greet?"

"They're chomping at the bit to see Libby in action. My phone's been blowing up ever since that video. The media requests are through the roof. We've got promo events lined up that coordinate with the Ass-in-Nine burro race and the festival that goes along with it—not to mention the usual promo before the fight. This is the best kind of buzz we can get."

"Do we need all that, Briggs?" he pressed.

The agent dropped his syrupy smile as his expression grew earnest. "This is what you want, Erasmus. You win this fight, and it'll be worth it. You'll be the champion again."

That was what he wanted, right—to be the champion?

Briggs nodded to him, then gestured to Libby. "The floor is yours, Miss Lamb," the man announced and stepped aside.

"Hello, I'm Lib—" she began when a slight man in the front of the group cut her off.

"Libby Lamb, the Irish Snake, Silas Scott, commented about you on social media," the reporter called out, holding up his mobile.

Oh shit!

"And what did Mr. Scott say?" Libby asked.

"He writes, I doubt that deranged chick Libby Lamb knows the first thing about yoga or training athletes—but I'd sure do her." The reporter lowered his mobile. "Silas Scott's words, not mine, ma'am."

"He said that?" Libby shot back.

The man nodded. "There's more. He goes on to say, real fighters don't waste their precious training time touching their toes and twisting around like a pretzel. Do you have a reply, Miss Lamb?"

Bloody Silas Scott! That little twat.

A muscle ticked in his jaw. It was one thing for the Snake to go after him. That was part of the show. But to say that about Libby? The bloke just signed his own death warrant.

"Bloody Silas Scott can go right to—" he began when Libby cut him off.

"I most certainly do have a response to Mr. Scott," she answered brightly, flashing him a serene smile as she slipped off her trainers.

Why the hell was she taking off her shoes?

"And what is that reply?" the reporter prodded, glancing at the woman's bare feet.

Libby pressed her hands into a prayer position. "I'm sending him peace and love."

"Peace and love?" the reporter shot back.

"Yes, my heart goes out to the man. From the sound of Silas Scott's post, I'm picking up a distinct energy. In my professional opinion, as a certified yoga instructor, I'm getting the vibe that Silas Scott is a man with tiny chakras—very, very, very tiny chakras. One might need a microscope to find them."

Bloody hell! Libby could handle herself. She was ripping the Snake apart with a smile.

"That's your reply?" the reporter asked, biting back a grin.

"It is. Now, let's forget about the man with the teensy tiny chakras and clear his negative energy," she said, stretching from side to side, which looked a little nuts in a crowd of reporters.

"What are you doing, plum?" he asked under his breath. She couldn't be warming up to throw her trainers at him, could she? Better shoes than vibrators, sure, but he'd rather not have anything chucked at him—again.

"I'm connecting to Rickety Rock's energy. There's something special about this place. Something is different. I can feel it," she whispered back—straight-faced.

Bollocks! Maybe it would be better if she threw her shoes at him.

He glanced at Sebastian and reared back.

What the bloody hell was going on?

The boy untied his trainers and kicked them to the side of the porch, joining his nanny in the crazy-barefoot-in-the-mountains bit.

"Don't worry, Dad. Libby and I have done this before. We're good at connecting to the earth."

He nodded and gave the lad a weak grin. Bloody perfect. Not only would he have an off-her-rocker spiritual advisor. The press would also report that his son was a few slices short of a loaf.

"It's time for punchy yoga!" Sebastian announced.

Punchy yoga? What the hell was that?

Several reporters chuckled at the boy's enthusiasm while scribbling in pads and tapping away on mobiles and laptops. Whatever this punchy business was, it was about to go viral.

"Miss Lamb, what is punchy yoga?" a tall woman asked, jotting furiously on a pad of paper.

And thank you, madam reporter! That was his question, too.

Libby and Sebastian walked down the steps, and the press parted, making way for the pair like Moses parting the Red Sea.

"I'd like everyone to set down your phones, notepads, and cameras," Libby said as she and Sebastian stood with their hands pressed in a prayer position.

"We're the media, ma'am. We can't do that," a man in the back replied.

Libby smiled at the guy. "You can. I give you permission." She gestured to the rock stack on the path leading toward the other structures. "Those stones are a sign that you're on the right path. You are exactly where you're supposed to be, doing exactly what you're supposed to be doing. So again, let me reassure everyone here. You can disconnect from your responsibilities for the next few minutes."

The reporter cocked his head to the side. Raz waited for the guy to start laughing or huff a haughty breath, but that's not what happened. Miraculously, the reporter shoved his mobile into his messenger bag and set it on the ground. Like dominoes falling, Libby and Sebastian stood quietly as every member of the media abandoned their pads, cameras, and devices.

Akin to a celestial being, who happened to be barefoot and clad in a crow scarf, Libby walked through the swarm of people frozen in place, their attention trained on her. "Pun-chi yoga is and isn't what it sounds like."

Oh, sweet Jesus!

"Raz, do you know what she's talking about?" Briggs asked in a frantic hushed tone, his million-dollar smile faltering.

He shook his head. He didn't answer. He wasn't trying to be a dick, but he couldn't speak. He could only concentrate on the mesmerizing woman gliding past hardened sports journalists.

"The *pun* part is short for punch," Libby explained. "But the second syllable is spelled *c-h-i*. Chi."

Chi.

She'd called him a chi thief or a chi scrambler. He honestly couldn't remember. All he knew was that he'd screwed up her chi. But nothing appeared off-kilter with her now.

Libby raised her hands as if she were holding two invisible orbs. "Chi is our life force, the energy that flows through you and everything around you. Chi connects our minds and our bodies, and it's where we start with Pun-chi yoga. Observe." She pressed the sole of her foot into her upper thigh. "This is tree pose. You try it."

Raz surveyed the group and could barely believe they were following along. Big guys teetering. Little guys wobbling. Men and women collectively working to stay upright.

"If you can't get your foot up that high, you can do it like this," Sebastian instructed as the lad pressed his foot to the side of his calf, doing a modified version of Libby's stance.

"Rest your gaze on something in the distance. Doing this will help you maintain balance," Libby instructed.

Raz stared ahead at the two forms directly in front of him.

Libby and Sebastian. And there it was—that lovely blue-violet tint to the light, and a stillness settled upon the group.

"Now, this is where we incorporate the punching part. We can do this one that's called a..." Libby focused on Sebastian, and she started throwing hooks while balancing on one foot.

"Those punches are called hooks," Sebastian supplied.

"Or some of these," Libby continued, throwing some damn good jabs.

"Those are jabs," his son answered correctly.

"And then we can mix it up." She threw a jab, a cross, and a hook. "This is called—"

"Jab, cross, hook combo," he answered, coming down the steps, unable to stop himself. Could it be something with the energy here? Whatever it was, it drew him to her.

She looked over her shoulder and winked at him. And blimey, she was radiant! The brightest star in the universe had nothing on Libby Lamb.

"Go ahead and stand tall on two feet with your chin up and shoulders back while I demonstrate an advanced element," she instructed.

As if they were in a daze, the throng of media did as they were told, standing like soldiers eager to please their general.

"In Pun-chi yoga," Libby continued, tucking the tails of her scarf into her T-shirt, "we build a stable foundation by grounding ourselves. Stability and ease of motion come through repetition. And then we practice something called non-attachment, where we learn to let go. Long story short, you have to be strong and centered before you can release what holds you back." Libby hinged forward and drew her legs up into a handstand.

And he knew what was coming next.

Gracefully, like she wasn't on uneven, rocky ground, she raised her hand and busted out the same move that shut him up in the police chief's office. Her legs parted into a wide V, and she started punching with her free hand.

The press gave a collective gasp as every pair of eyes remained locked on the woman defying the laws of gravity.

"Uppercut, jab, jab, cross, jab, uppercut!" Sebastian exclaimed, labeling each punch as Libby threw punch after punch and barely wobbled in the process.

He stood beside Sebastian to get a better look, and his boy waved him down.

"See, Dad, it's punchy yoga."

"Yeah, I see," he answered, catching Libby's upside-down gaze.

"Is it okay if we get some tape of you demonstrating Pun-chi yoga, Miss Lamb?" a voice called, but Libby didn't acknowledge the reporter. She kept her attention on him and Sebastian. With a sparkle in her eyes, she gave them an upside-down grin, then tossed him a wink—another bloody wink—before turning her head toward the woman asking the question. "Go ahead, you can film me and take as many photographs as you like," she answered and began throwing punches again as Sebastian labeled each one.

He took several steps back to give them some space, and Briggs strolled up to his side with his million-dollar grin intact.

"She's brilliant, champ," he exclaimed in a hushed voice. "Who would have thought that a lunatic banging a gong and throwing sex toys at you could charm this hardened lot? Did you know she was this good?"

Raz shook his head, his gaze trained on the raven-haired lunatic. "No, I didn't."

"You're one lucky bloke," Briggs replied, relief coating the words. "At least for the moment, she's PR gold, and you only have to stick with her until the fight. I already have the press release ready to go when you part ways."

Raz's posture stiffened. "Part ways?"

"You know, mutual respect, blah, blah, blah. Wish you well, blah, blah, blah."

Raz parted his lips, but nothing came out. All he could do was ignore the tightness in his chest and let Briggs's words sink in.

The man was right. Despite the pull between them to tear each other's clothes off, she couldn't be his. She'd made it clear that a relationship wasn't in the cards for her. Their professional split should be a no-brainer, and yet his lips still tingled from her kiss.

"Miss Lamb," a reporter called, pulling him from his thoughts. "Can you tell us any more about the Pun-chi yoga moves you're using to train Erasmus Cress?"

"We'll chat more later, mate," Briggs whispered, pulling out his mobile. "I need to listen and make sure Libby doesn't say anything bonkers."

He nodded to his agent, hardly able to make heads or tails from his reaction to the thought of parting ways with Libby Lamb.

"As you observed," Libby began, returning to a standing position, "Pun-chi yoga incorporates elements of boxing and yoga. The practice can be either smooth, where one flows from pose to pose, or punctuated, akin to quick bursts of movement," Libby explained, glancing away. He caught the hint of a blush on the apples of her cheeks—the seductive blush that sent his blood supply south.

"Were the quick bursts of motion what we saw on the viral video?" a reporter called out, and thoughts of raging hard-ons vanished from his mind.

Bollocks! They'd never discussed how they would address the viral video topic with the media.

Libby glanced over her shoulder at him, then clasped her hands in front of her. "Yes, I think we can all agree that the Pun-chi session viewed by many in the viral video motivated Erasmus Cress to move very, very quickly."

That was a brilliant answer.

Cheeky but accurate.

"How about you, Lion? What are your thoughts on Pun-chi yoga?" a short gentleman in the front asked.

Raz came to Libby's side. Every cell in his body wanted to reach out and touch her. But why? Why was there this incessant need to claim her—to let the world see... See what? She wasn't his. He cleared his throat and kept his features neutral. "I'm getting used to Pun-chi yoga."

"Do you think it's something you'll keep in your training regimen after the big fight?"

After the fight?

His mind couldn't go there. "We're keeping our options open."

That was a bloody lie.

The PR word salad he'd regurgitated wasn't the answer he wanted to give.

But he couldn't bring himself to admit the truth about what he wanted.

"Will you be throwing other objects at the Beast?" another reporter called, blessedly taking the focus off him.

Libby looked up and caught his eye. "Only if he makes me mad," she answered, and the press loved it. Every damn person on the property chuckled at her response as they hammered away on their devices and scribbled into notebooks.

"Like I said, PR gold," Briggs said under his breath as he came up alongside them. "We're going to wrap it up, but I do have dates and pertinent information, so listen closely," the man announced.

Raz and Libby gave the man some space and walked over to where Sebastian, Augie, and Luanne stood on the porch.

Raz leaned in toward Libby. "Did you make all that up on the fly?"

She looked up at him, eyes sparkling. "I expanded on a game Sebastian and I came up with. But yes, I BS'ed my way through the demonstration."

"What made you do the crazy upside-down move, plum?"

She bit her bottom lip as pure mischief glinted in those gorgeous amber eyes. "It worked on you, didn't it?"

Sweet blooming Christ, it had.

"Final announcements," Briggs continued, then glanced up at the dark clouds rolling in. "I'll be quick, so no one gets caught in the storm. You should have received an email with the schedule of events with Erasmus Cress and Libby Lamb that line up with the Ass-in-Nine Festival in a few weeks. We're raising funds for the town of Rickety Rock and several of the charities housed in the mountain town. Please share with your readers and viewers that one lucky person who donates will get to jump into the ring with the champ for some good old-fashioned boxing fun. We're calling it Spar with the Beast, and

Erasmus Cress's team, along with the town, would be most grateful."

"Did you know about that?" Libby whispered.

"No, but I've missed a few emails. You don't mind, do you? I can tell Briggs to call it off if you do."

"No, don't do that. It's for charity, and I'm sure the organizations will appreciate it. And I'll get to see you in action."

And there it was—that Libby Lamb smile that could light up the night sky.

"And don't forget about my birthday, posh bloke. It's coming up, too. I'll be seven years old, and my friends Phoebe and Oscar say that if I stay in Colorado, I'll be in second grade with them," Sebastian called out to the delight of the press.

Raz stared at his son. He'd never seen the boy so happy.

"After the Ass-in-Nine race and Sebastian's seventh birthday," Briggs continued with a nod to the boy. "The countdown begins for the fight of the century. I don't need to remind you that this is the highest Pay-Per-View event ever recorded, and it's just weeks away. This is truly a moment in heavyweight boxing. And with that, I think the weather will allow for one last question for the Lion and the Lamb."

The Lion and the Lamb.

Just as the man finished talking, a muddy white truck pulling an equally muck-covered trailer gunned it up the drive, then hit the brakes. Pebbles skipped across the rocky land as a swirl of dust welcomed the visitor, and an older, portly gentleman in a cowboy hat with a bushy white beard emerged from the vehicle.

"Can we help you, sir? Do you have a question?" Briggs asked.

The man surveyed the media spectacle. "Oh, I have a question."

"And what would that be?"

The newcomer removed his hat and stared directly at Libby. "Do you know him, Raz?" Libby asked under her breath.

"I have no idea who he is."

For an old-timer, the bloke looked bloody intimidating, like a hardened Colorado cowboy.

Just as he answered, the man took a few wobbly steps forward and pointed to them. "You two," he called.

"Yes, sir?" Libby answered, coming to attention.

"I need some answers," he barked.

"About what, sir?" she eked out.

The man's bushy white beard twitched as he leaned against the dusty truck. "Which one of you is going to tell me what's really going on with Beefcake and Plum?"

Raz's jaw dropped as he caught Libby's eye. Dumbstruck, she shook her head, looking as clueless as he felt.

Who was this old codger?

FIFTEEN

LIBBY

BEEFCAKE AND PLUM?

Libby blinked as the dust settled, and she drank in the older gentleman. The crusty senior citizen, dressed in boots and head-to-toe denim, looked like he'd moseyed on out of a Wild West saloon.

Was she hallucinating? Was this discombobulated state the karmic response to creating an entirely new school of yoga on the fly? Had she tipped the cosmic scales and descended into a catatonic meditative state?

She wasn't sure. All she could do was stare at the new arrival.

As if he were made of stone, the bearded man kept his gaze trained on them as the press remained silent. Good to know that even mouthy sports journalists found the guy formidable. Honestly, after the last ten days, she was lucky she could put a coherent thought together. And the events of the last hour hadn't helped. It was as if her chi had gone from being mixed up, to leveling out, to getting thrust into a super-charged spin cycle, to now being scrutinized by a salty character in a Western flick.

The man cocked his head to the side, continuing his silent assessment as the reporters' gazes bobbed back and forth between where she, Raz, and Sebastian stood and the gentleman with a cantankerous air. No, cantankerous wasn't the correct description. The man's energy wasn't angry. He had more of a steady, no-nonsense vibe, and there was something strangely familiar about him.

Then again, who was she to interpret anyone's vibe?

She was still flying high from the Pun-chi yoga demo. Yes, it had started as a bunch of make-believe yoga babble. Still, somewhere between leading the horde of reporters in a five-minute yoga class and busting out into the one-handed handstand to rock some punches, the overarching concept of Pun-chi yoga solidified in her mind. There appeared to be merit to marrying the vastly different concepts of yoga and boxing.

"We seem to have a local in our midst," Briggs whispered as if the dude who rolled up was from another planet.

And maybe he was from another galaxy.

How in the world could some random person in Rickety Rock, Colorado, have known their nicknames? She'd called Raz a beefcake in the viral video, but this local didn't look as if he spent his days glued to social media. Not only that—there was no way he could have known that Raz called her plum.

Plum.

She'd never had a nickname before Raz blurted the term of endearment in the heat of her cosmic vibrator-laden meltdown. But the audio on the viral video hadn't picked up that exchange. There was no way anyone could know about the moniker. Should she have put a stop to the man calling her plum? Yes, of course! But something inside her liked it when he randomly dropped the sweetly satisfying syllable—like they had a secret connection that went beyond a forced partnership and great sex.

No, not great sex.

It was out-of-this-world sex.

No, that wasn't right either.

It was more like toe-curling, eyes rolling back in your head, wondering if your soul will ever return to your-body while riding the orgasm-of-all-orgasms kind of sex.

Yep, that was it.

With that admission, a hot blush bloomed on her neck and chest. Dark clouds had rolled in along with a breeze, and the temperature seemed to have dropped, but was it getting hotter now? Was she in the path of a solar flare cutting through the clouds and heating her to a sex-obsessed boil?

Stop.

After Raz's ten-day MIA-fest, she'd promised herself she'd keep up her guard when it came to the handsome beefcake with his magic mouth, perfect cock, and dexterous hands. She tensed, forcing herself to think of anything other than Erasmus Cress's hard abs and muscled arms.

Buddha, give this woman strength.

Why had she pulled him into that bedroom? Why had she kissed him? Why had she moaned the dirtiest of sighs as he ran his tongue across her skin and tasted her neck? Did she enjoy receiving hickeys? Was she on team hickey now? Was there even a team for that?

No, no, no!

Forget the hickey master and focus.

There was a gruff cowboy not twenty feet away.

Who was he, and why was he here?

She needed answers, and she needed to get her mind off kissing the beefcake. So, answers it was.

Granted, the slightly wobbly-on-his-feet old cowboy pulling up with a trailer and using their secret-ish nicknames wasn't the craziest thing that had happened to her since she'd become Raz's nanny and spiritual advisor. Scratch that. She was a spiritual advisor in name only. She hadn't done anything in the spiritual advisor department with the man.

No, that's not entirely true.

When Raz started spiraling, she'd sensed it immediately. She'd watched him gasp for breath as he fell into the clutches of a panic attack. Unable to stop herself, she'd known exactly what to do. Like muscle memory, but the spiritual kind, when she rested her hand on his heart, it was as if a force had raised her arm and pressed her palm to his chest. And it had worked. For that brief slip of time, a steady thrum of energy bound them together, two halves coming together as one spiritual whole. The vibe was a combination of pure glowing kindness and a grounding, solid serenity with the gentle whisper of quiet consent. Warm and comforting, she'd never connected with a man in that way before. There was something else there, too. Something she couldn't quite identify. Could it be the fresh energy of this town, the rush of adrenaline, or even a silent, knowing presence?

She couldn't say—but it had been there, in them, and with them.

"Are you sure you don't know this man, Libby? He's looking at you like he knows you," Briggs pressed, snapping her out of her daydream. "You are from Colorado," the agent added, his voice rising an octave.

"That doesn't mean I know everyone in the state," she replied as she studied the bearded gentleman closely.

Did she know him?

No, she couldn't. She'd never stepped foot in Rickety Rock, Colorado.

What still didn't make a lick of sense was why he'd called them Beefcake and Plum.

One thing was for certain. She had to get it together. They were surrounded by the media, and the last thing they needed was another viral video. She wasn't about to give those astronauts another clip to reenact in zero gravity.

"You don't think Silas Scott's people sent this guy as a stunt, do you?" Briggs whispered to Raz before turning to her. "You landed quite a blow to the bloke with the tiny chakra talk. Brilliant, by the way, using yoga verbiage to insinuate the chap wasn't packing anything in his trousers. Bravo! After this nanny spiritual thing runs its course, you could work in PR. That little ditty is already making the rounds on social media."

Okay, there was a lot to unpack in the agent's statement. Was Raz's team already planning for her exit? Was she okay with that? Was Raz? And holy karma pie! She'd dropped her whole love-and-light vibe to insult a man's testicles for the world to see.

Was it kind to send out such negatively charged energy?

No.

Can chakras be teensy-tiny?

Not really.

They're energy centers, but she couldn't help herself from getting in a little dig. She still wasn't a fan of fighting, but if there was ever a man who sounded like he deserved to be punched square in the jaw, it was that snake of a boxer.

And what should she do about Briggs's comment—the after the nannying and spiritual advisor stint ends business? A lump formed in her throat, but she had to shelve her emotions. Could she imagine life without Sebastian? She glanced at her barefoot partner in crime. No, she couldn't. Could she imagine life without her beefcake? She couldn't go there either. On that sticky matter, her head and her heart weren't in agreement.

"It can't be Scott's people," Raz countered. "There's no way they could have anticipated what Libby would say. And it's too soon. He won't want to take away from the weigh-in."

"The weigh-in?" she repeated.

"It's when the boxers meet in front of the media to juice up the publicity and weigh-in on the official scale to qualify for the fight," Raz explained. "They're choreographed events. The press wants to see the tension between the fighters. It's too soon for that. Silas Scott is a snake, that's for sure, but he knows how to use the media for maximum exposure."

"All right, so he's probably a curious local. I'll take care of this. I thought of something brilliant," Briggs said and cleared his throat. "Sir, you with the hat and the dirty truck, about the word beefcake."

"Yeah?" the man shot back, eyeing the agent.

Briggs puffed up. "If that's what you thought you heard on the viral video, which was a piece of the eclectic training regimen Mr. Cress is following, you're mistaken. Libby didn't say that. She was counseling Erasmus Cress not to *eat cake. Beefcake. Eat cake*," the man continued enunciating each syllable, then scanned the swath of media, watching them gobble up his explanation like hungry vultures. "Do you see how they have a similar ring to them?" the agent finished.

"Eat cake?" she whispered as Raz cocked his head to the side and stared at the sports agent.

"Did you get hit on the head with a rock?" the old man asked Briggs. "You gotta watch out for those in these parts. Why do you think this town is called Rickety Rock?"

Briggs gasped and stared up into the cloudy sky as if he anticipated an onslaught of incoming boulders.

"I said rocks, not meteors," the bearded man corrected.

Flustered, Briggs smoothed his sport coat as he studied the ground. "No, I haven't been hit in the head with a rock."

"Are you sure? You're not making any sense, and I need to know what's going on with Beefcake and Plum," the old-timer repeated.

"Do you think we're Beefcake and Plum?" she asked, gesturing to herself and Raz as her pulse skyrocketed.

She caught Raz's eye and gave him a look that said *that old cowboy can't know about our nicknames, can he?*

Raz's eyeballs replied with *bloody hell, who knows! This place is bonkers.*

Her beefcake wasn't wrong. Everything about this day had been bonkers.

The old man slapped his hat against his leg and broke out into a full belly laugh. He was a tall man, fit for his age, but he did have a bit of a tummy on him. His entire body, from his beard to his rounded abdomen, jiggled as he cackled with amusement. "Are you asking me if you two are a pair of asses?" he got out through another cascade of laughter.

What was so funny? This had to be a hallucination.

She turned to Raz. "Is this happening?"

Everything about the last hour could have been a scene in a crazy dream. Maybe she'd been hit in the head with a rock. She could have gotten out of the car and *wham*—an actual runaway rickety rock, straight to the noggin.

"I was wondering the same thing," Raz replied.

"Bob," a woman in a cowboy hat exclaimed, exiting the passenger side of the truck.

And hello, second Western movie extra.

Libby gasped. She hadn't even noticed there was someone else in the vehicle.

"Don't go joking with these poor folks—especially when they have company," the lady cowgirl chided gently, gesturing to the throng of media when a high-pitched bray followed by a jarring hee-haw cut through the air.

"The donkey," Sebastian cried. "You've got a pack burro in your trailer, don't you?"

"Not *a* donkey, young man. We've got *two* pack burros," the woman answered.

"Two!" Sebastian exclaimed like he'd won the donkey lottery.

"Yes, their names are Beefcake and Sugarplum, but we call the female Plum. That's what I've been trying to tell you," the man explained, returning his hat to his head.

"Beefcake and Plum are donkeys?" Raz repeated.

Good idea to double check.

The old man shared a look with his white-haired companion. The pair looked close in age and shared similar features, and again, she had the feeling she'd seen them somewhere.

"These city folk are never that quick on the uptake, are they, Maud?" the man mused.

The woman waved off the surly cowboy's comment. "Yes, Beefcake and Plum are donkeys. I'm Maud. I left a note for you. My brother Bob and I run the Rickety Rock Donkey Rescue Ranch. I told you we'd be by. Thanks to the livestream, we knew you'd arrived."

"This is being livestreamed?" Libby exclaimed, then glanced over her shoulder at the myriad of reporters holding up their phones.

Raz leaned over, his breath warm against the shell of her ear. "It's because of the upcoming fight. Anytime there's press or even someone with a mobile, it's safe to say it's being livestreamed," he explained with an apologetic bend to his whispered words.

She nodded. "Good to know."

"And that's the problem," Bob announced, his features hardening.

"What's the problem?" Briggs pressed.

"There are too many people here. We don't want to spook

Beefcake and Plum. You only have one chance to make a first impression on a donkey."

"Is that true?" Raz asked.

"Donkeys are smart animals, Dad," Sebastian chimed. "They can remember things that happened to them for lots and lots of years. If they get scared now and think you're dangerous or unfriendly, they may not want to race with you."

"So, the donkeys have to like us to run with us?" she asked the boy.

Sebastian nodded. "Yep, if they trust you, they'll do what you want. They're happiest when they are part of a group and when you run with them, you say *hup, hup* if you want them to go faster."

"I see someone has been reading up on pack burros," Maud said with a tip of her hat to the child.

Sebastian beamed. "I've got three books on donkeys, and I can't wait to meet them. I know about their eyes and what they eat." The boy surveyed the crowd. "I'll take care of the people with cameras so the donkeys can come out," Sebastian said with his hands on his hips and a crease to his brow.

"What's he doing?" Raz asked.

Libby shook her head. "I don't know."

Sebastian ran over to one of the larger boulders and climbed on top. "May I have your attention?"

Libby startled. Ten days ago, Sebastian was skittish about a playdate at the park. Now, he was corralling reporters.

"It's time for the press conference to end and for you to go home so I can meet my new donkeys," the boy called. "When donkeys are introduced to a new environment, they need it to be calm so they can acclimate. The word *acclimate* means to get used to their new home. I read that in a book about donkeys. So, as my granny Fin would say, off you go, you dodgy plonkers."

"The lad can take charge," Raz commented as the hint of a grin pulled at the corners of his mouth.

Was that pride in Raz's voice?

Her heart was ready to burst with affection, like what she felt for her brothers. But this feeling was different. It harkened to a deep devotion she'd never experienced.

"We've got quite a kid," she replied, and oh, no! What had she said?

Raz stared at her. His expression hardened as his gaze went ice cold.

She swallowed past the lump in her throat as a knot tightened in her belly.

She'd crossed the nanny boss line—big time.

LIBBY TWISTED HER CURTAIN SCARF.

We've got quite a kid?

What was she thinking?

Stupid mixed-up chi!

She had to fix this. She could not have Raz thinking she wanted to take Sebastian's mother's place.

Say something not crazy!

"*You've* got quite a son. Sorry, I misspoke." The heat coming off her cheeks could fry an egg.

Raz didn't respond, and that only made it worse.

She had to be careful about how she spoke to Raz about his son.

His son, not hers.

She'd be smart to remember that.

"Sebastian is correct. It's time to conclude the presser," Briggs announced to the members of the media and blessedly shifting Raz's attention from her. "We appreciate your time. You've received the information on upcoming press events, and we'll be in touch."

"And feel free to go on down to Rickety Rock's town

center," Maud said to the men and women packing their equipment. "We've got Rocky Mountain oysters on the menu at the Burro Café, and the people of our little abode would sure appreciate your business."

"What are Rocky Mountain oysters?" Raz asked as the donkeys started braying and calling out.

Okay, at least he was speaking to her. But before she could answer, Sebastian called to her.

"Libby, we get to meet the donkeys!" The boy beamed, then ran over to peek inside the trailer. "I can see them. One is gray and white, and the other is bigger, with a dark brown body and a white nose. And they already like me. I can feel it."

"You've got a perceptive boy," Bob said, ambling over to them, cautiously traversing the uneven ground.

"Do you need a hand?" Raz asked, reaching toward the man.

"I'm good." Bob pulled up his left pant leg and revealed a silver rod. "I make do. I lost my leg from the knee down in a pack burro race back in eighty-eight."

"You lost your leg in a donkey race?" she asked.

"Rockslide," the man said, smoothing his pant leg. "I was able to get my burro out of harm's way, but a big one got me good. They don't call this place Rickety Rock for nothing. And then there's the vortex."

"Vortex?" she echoed.

Maud nodded. "Many have said that Rickety Rock sits on an energy center of sorts. We'll get birds flying in circles, cars that seem to roll uphill, and big rocks rolling down the mountain crushing people's limbs."

"Does that happen often?" Raz pressed, surveying the mountain.

Bob shrugged. "From time to time."

Sweet Buddha's belly. What was up with this town?

"Oh, Bob, don't go scaring these nice people. We haven't had a rockslide like the one that took your leg in years. And we're pleased as punch to have a sports celebrity competing in the Ass-in-Nine Race. The town could use some good press to shine a light on our little mountain community. Now, let's do this right. We haven't been properly introduced. You're Libby Lamb and you're Erasmus Cress, right?"

"Yes, we are," Raz answered.

"I'm Maud Askew, and that there is my older brother Bob Askew—or Wobbly Bob, as he's known in these parts."

"And by older, she means that I'm the oldest by seven minutes," Bob added with a sly twitch to his beard.

"You're twins?" Raz asked, looking between the pair.

"Triplets, actually," Maud answered.

Libby nodded. She could sense the connection between Maud and Wobbly Bob. But something was missing. "Does your other sibling live in Rickety Rock, too?"

Maud shook her head. "Our sister travels quite a bit and goes back and forth between the mountains and the city when she's in Colorado. Out of the three of us, she's more of the free spirit, but she gets to Rickety Rock when she can."

Libby grinned at the siblings. She couldn't help but ponder the off-kilter terminology in this place. Rickety, wobbly, askew, and a vortex? At least her loopy chi would be in good company. But it was more than that. Despite the climate of unsteadiness, she got a good vibe from the donkey rescuers. Their golden auras gave her the impression they cared for their animals and their community. And while she couldn't pinpoint exactly what was familiar about their energy, it soothed her, nonetheless.

"This is my son, Sebastian, and my agent, Briggs Keaton," Raz added, then peered over his shoulder as Augie and Luanne came toward them. "And that's Augie Bimston, my trainer, and his girlfriend, Luanne Stone."

Libby zeroed in on the agent, who'd turned a dishwater gray. "Are you okay, Briggs?"

"I've got a small issue with the landscape," the agent said, wearily surveying the side of the mountain. "We can't have Erasmus crushed by a boulder. He's got a fight coming up, and he'll require all his limbs."

"Don't you worry, Mr. Fancy Pants. Nobody's been hit by a rock in years," Wobbly Bob answered, then paused. "Well, there was that time back in ninety-four."

"And then in twenty-fifteen," Maud commented.

"That's not exactly comforting," Briggs mused.

"You worry about PR, and I'll focus on *winning*," Raz said with an edge to his voice, emphasizing the winning part. Was that little dig meant for her—a reminder that their time here in Rickety Rock couldn't serve as a distraction?

"Ah, well, brilliant," Briggs replied, still looking troubled when his phone pinged. He scanned the message. "Unfortunately, I do need to be on my way. I have a flight to catch to Kansas City. We're opening an office there and having a few staffing issues. It was lovely to meet you all." He turned to Raz. "I'll be in touch. You dodge those boulders, mate. You need to go into this championship fight the best you've ever been. Everything is on the line for this one."

Raz's posture stiffened. She understood the importance of this fight. But there was something else weighing on her beefcake—a heaviness. This fight went beyond winning and losing.

"Are you ready to meet the donkeys?" Maud asked as Briggs headed down the gravel road with the last of the reporters toward the myriad of cars and vans parked down the mountainside.

Sebastian gasped. "First, Libby and I need to put on our trainers." The boy ran toward the house, scooped up their shoes, and returned. "You should always wear shoes around donkeys. I never saw any pictures of barefoot people in my donkey books," he explained as they laced up.

"What else have you learned?" Wobbly Bob asked.

"I watched a video tutorial on how to brush a donkey, and I learned they like to have their whiskers scratched. It makes them smile."

Maud patted the child on his shoulder. "Beefcake and Plum are lucky to have you around, Sebastian. And I'll have you know, these donkeys love whisker rubs."

"Maud, are Beefcake and Plum brother and sister, like you and Wobbly Bob?" the boy asked.

"They're not brother and sister, but they are inseparable. They were rescued together. We usually keep the Jacks and the Jennies apart. But not these two. They balance each other out. And Beefcake is a bit protective of his Plum."

"I quite like that. They're best friends," Sebastian commented.

"This is pretty great, don't you think?" she said to Raz as Sebastian followed Maud and Wobbly Bob to the back of the trailer.

"Maybe," he stammered.

She could feel a fresh wave of anxiety engulf the man. "Maybe?" she questioned, sharpening her tone.

He rubbed his eyes. "I have a lot on my mind, Libby. Sure, rescue donkeys are brilliant," he grumbled, which set off a charge of irritation prickling through her body.

Couldn't he see his son's excitement? Would it kill him to show an iota of interest in the boy's passions? She stared at the man, anger simmering in her belly. If she had a vibrator, she would have thrown it at his thick skull. Yes, he had a fight, but that was one fight. It would come, and it would go. But his son was his forever. Could he not see that the boy adored him—idolized him? She knew what was in store for him if he continued to disappoint his child.

"Libby, Erasmus," Maud called. "You need to be here when we open the doors."

"We'll give you some space and watch from the porch," Luanne offered.

Augie nodded. "It'll give me some time to go over your schedule before we start training out here." He concentrated on Raz. "We've got to get your head in the game, mate."

"Yeah, I hear you, Aug," Raz answered as the frantic energy swirling around the man amplified.

What a pair they made! His chi was no more stable than hers.

"Dad, Libby, come on," Sebastian called, hopping from foot to foot.

"Let's get this over with," Raz mumbled.

The infuriating beefcake!

The group gathered around the back of the trailer. Gentle stomps and muffled grunty brays drifted out of the metal enclosure. Anticipation hung in the air, sweet and expectant. Sebastian came to her side and took her hand, and she gave him a gentle squeeze.

"They want to meet us. You can feel it, too, can't you, Libby?"

"I can," she answered. It wasn't a lie. There was a distinct pull between these animals and this place.

Wobbly Bob rested his hand on the latch of the trailer door. "Here's how this is going to go. Erasmus and Libby, you'll lead your pack burro out of the trailer. Plum is the gray Jennie, and Beefcake is the big brown Jack."

"And where should we store the donkeys?" Raz asked.

Store the donkeys?

"It's the three of you in the big house, right?" Bob tossed back, eyeing the giant Victorian.

"Yes."

"Then you've got a couple of extra bedrooms."

"You want us to give the donkeys actual bedrooms?" Raz shot back, wide-eyed.

"Oh, don't take Bob too seriously," Maud said, shaking her head. "The donkeys will stay in the barn. There's a fenced-in area for the burros to move around and graze. We've got it ready for them. The feed schedule is tacked to the wall, and our donkey rescue volunteers will keep you stocked."

"The donkeys are staying here with us?" Raz asked.

Wobbly Bob cocked his head to the side. "How else will you bond with them? It's the most important thing a burro racer can do."

"I thought we just ran with them," Raz mumbled.

Bob gazed down the mountainside into the valley. "There's a lot more to burro racing than running."

"What more is there?" the man asked.

Wobbly Bob's expression grew pensive. "The donkey knows."

"The donkey knows what?" Raz repeated.

"Like your boy said, donkeys are smart animals. They're your teammates in the burro race, and they're also spiritual creatures. They understand what you need to do to be the best version of yourself. The trick is learning to listen."

"That's your area, right, Libby?" Maud asked. "You're the spiritual advisor."

"Yes, I guess I am."

"It'll have to be both your areas of expertise," Bob added. "And yours, too, Sebastian, since you'll be living here and caring for the donkeys this summer. The connection between a pack burro and their team is essential. You ever heard the phrase as stubborn as a mule?" the wobbly man asked, looking squarely at Raz.

And rightly so!

If anyone was acting like a stubborn ass, it was Erasmus Cress.

"Sure," the boxer barked.

"If you and your donkey aren't on the same page," Bob continued, "you're not moving forward. That pack burro weighs close to five hundred pounds, and in the race, you run with thirty-three pounds of mining equipment. You only move forward if you do it together."

"It's about trust," Maud added.

"Trust?" the boxer echoed.

"When you bond, you become the animal's home," Bob explained.

Raz looked past the Victorian toward the barn and the garage. "But the barn is their home."

Bob studied Raz. "That's the physical enclosure. Home is created through bonding. Home is your heart."

"The donkeys already have a home in my heart," Sebastian crooned.

Raz crossed his arms and looked away. "Yeah, okay, I get it."

"Word to the wise," Maud added, leaning in. "You've got to watch Plum. If you're on the trails and she catches sight of a butterfly or a bird, she can wander off the path."

"So, you're saying Plum can be a little spacey in her own world?" Raz asked, injecting a touch of beefy arrogance into the question.

"She can," Maud agreed.

Libby pasted a plastic grin to her lips. She was out of line with her comment about Sebastian being their kid, but that didn't give Raz the okay to act like a put-off prick. He needed to be taken down a peg.

"What about Beefcake?" she pressed, playing it breezy but going in for a punch. "Is there anything we need to watch with him?"

Maud grimaced. "Lord, help me! Where to start with Beefcake? He can be willful and a little bit of a showoff."

Libby gave Raz the once-over. "Is that right? A stubborn, cocky showoff, you say?"

"And if Beefcake happens to get into the wild alfalfa," Bob added, waving his hand in front of his face. "I'll warn you now. His farts are strong enough to knock a man into next week."

How's that for karma!

She didn't even have to look at her beefcake to know what he was thinking.

Luckily, Sebastian perked up.

"Beefcake farts like you, Dad! My dad's a car farter, Wobbly Bob. He farted in the car on our drive here. Did you eat wild alfalfa before we left?" The child cocked his head to the side and scratched his chin. "What is wild alfalfa?" Sebastian mused sweetly as Raz's cheeks burned crimson.

Maud and Bob chuckled. Libby wanted to high-five the boy, but she restrained herself.

It served the sourpuss beefcake right!

If anyone deserved a little ribbing, it was Erasmus Cress.

Raz cleared his throat. "For the record, there was no car farting—especially, not by me. And now that we've cleared that up, we'll be sure to keep Beefcake away from the wild alfalfa."

Bob jiggled the latch. "All right, here we go. We're about to see if you've got what it takes."

Slowly, Bob lifted the latch. With the metal door creaking, the donkeys called out, stomping and shuffling. They knew the drill. The burros whinnied as he opened the gate, and then they were eye to eye with the animals.

"Wow." Sebastian breathed. "I've never had pets before."

Maud climbed into the trailer, hushing the restless creatures as she untied the ropes that kept the burros from moving around.

Libby studied the animals. How long had it been since she'd seen an actual donkey? It wasn't like you could find them traipsing around downtown Denver or in the ritzy streets of the Crystal Creek neighborhood. It must have been years ago before her mother had gotten sick. They used to visit a petting zoo in the city—when her father still acted like a father and when the man used to gaze lovingly at her mother. It was almost incomprehensible how much he'd changed since those days.

She tucked the bittersweet memories away and observed Plum. The animal had a gentleness about her, a knowing stillness Libby had once recognized in herself.

"Libby, take the lead rope and guide Plum out of the trailer. This sweet Jennie has done it before. She knows the way," Maud directed.

Libby focused on the animal as Maud handed her the rope. Plum regarded her with soulful, curious eyes and snow-white eyelashes.

Bob glanced up at the darkening sky. "We may be getting some weather, so Plum might be a bit hesitant with the shift in the temperature. Little things like that can throw her off. Be firm but gentle, Libby. Patience is the name of the game when it comes to getting a burro to comply. Frustration won't get you anywhere. Remember, the donkey knows."

The donkey knows.

"Let's get you out of this trailer, girl," Libby cooed, tugging on the lead. The burro turned her head and brushed her nose against Beefcake like she didn't want to leave without him. "He's coming, too, but first, you need to walk this way," she said, reassuring the animal. Plum looked her over. It was as if the donkey was reading her and assessing her energy. "You've got this, Plum. Let's do this nice and steady," she said, taking one step back, then two, then three.

With her hooves poised at the edge of the trailer, Plum nodded as if the animal comprehended the request. It was a slight movement. Perhaps, it meant nothing. A fly could have buzzed by, and that was the donkey's natural reaction, but it felt like more, like an understanding had passed between them. And with a deft *clip-clop*, Plum emerged from the trailer.

"Wham, bam, check out Plum and Libby Lamb," she whispered, stealing Raz's phrase, as a heady sense of victory had her beaming.

"You did it, Libby," Sebastian chimed and patted the donkey's neck.

"That felt incredible. So empowering!" she declared, scratching between the burro's ears.

"You did good, kid," Bob said with a tip of his hat. "There's nothing like passing that first test."

Libby's expression dimmed. "That was a test?"

"I'd reckon everything is a test when it comes to working with animals. They see right into your soul. Sometimes the connection happens immediately. Other times, it's like dancing with a new partner. You've got to feel each other out a bit. But I'd dare say that Plum's taken a shine to you," the man replied with an approving nod.

"I've certainly taken a shine to her. How old is she?"

"We estimate Plum is six or seven years old," Maud said, patting the Jennie on the rump.

"Like me," Sebastian replied. "What about Beefcake? How old is he?"

"Our best guess is that he's a bit older—or maybe it's his crankiness that makes him seem like an ornery old beast," Maud answered as the large Jack released what could only be described as one cranky whinny.

"We think he's eight or nine," Bob added, then turned to Raz. "You're up, Erasmus. Now, be careful. Maud was right about Beefcake. He's a beast."

"My dad's a beast, too. They call him the British Beast. He's a really good boxer," Sebastian bragged, staring at his father like the man could do no wrong.

Libby observed Raz. The moody beefcake barely cracked a smile at his son's adoring words. If this kept up, she'd be having words with the human beefcake—and there wouldn't be any gentle coos or reassurances. No, she'd lay into him.

"We read about your dad on the internet. Are you ready to see these two beasts meet?" Maud asked the boy, gesturing from the British beefcake to Beefcake.

"I am. Are you excited to meet your donkey, Dad?" Sebastian asked when Beefcake released another shrill call.

"Sure," Raz answered, cringing as he stared at his donkey equivalent.

"Move slowly but deliberately," Bob cautioned. "Beefcake is no fan of riding in the trailer. I can't say I blame him. You try staying upright in a metal box that's bouncing around."

Maud handed Raz the lead rope, and the man gave a sharp tug. But Beefcake wasn't having it. The burro shrieked and reared back. A muscle ticked in Raz's jaw as the donkey stomped, pounding the floor.

Look at that. The asses were two of a kind.

"Did you say something? I heard you mumble," Raz grumped.

She patted her donkey—the donkey she expertly guided from the trailer. "It appears you're having some issues with your Beefcake. You both seem to share similar qualities," she replied sweetly.

He parted his lips, but good old Beefcake, the donkey, beat him to it and let out another shrill donkey complaint.

"It's not about strength Raz," Bob said, intervening their little tête-à-tête. "It's a balance of strength, patience, and determination. Climb up into the trailer and start there. Remember, the donkey knows."

"The donkey knows," Raz muttered skeptically as he entered the metal enclosure. Beefcake gave another round of foot stomps, then stilled as Raz approached.

"There you go," Raz said, throwing her an arrogant grin when an echoing *BLAARRT* cut through the air.

And then came the smell—or more aptly described as the stench.

"Whoa," Bob called, nearly falling over.

Libby and Maud turned away.

"Did you fart, Dad?" Sebastian pressed, moving away from the trailer.

Raz's cocksure demeanor faded as he pinched his nose. "That was not me, Sebastian. It's the blooming donkey."

"Are you sure, Dad?"

"Yes," he grunted, pulling on the lead rope, as the two beefcakes battled in a foul-scented game of tug-of-war.

"The donkey isn't your opponent, Erasmus. You're on the same team. Maybe in the boxing ring, you're on your own, but in burro racing, you've got to trust your partner," Bob instructed.

"How is trust supposed to get this beast to budge?" Raz bit out, pinching his nostrils with one hand while pulling with the other.

Wobbly Bob and Maud shared a concerned look when a voice called out.

"Easy, there, Beefcake. Your buddy Zen Dougie is here."

Zen Dougie?

It was as if a whole new donkey had emerged. Beefcake brayed a cooing, lovesick sound as his long ears perked up. The animal stopped fighting and allowed Raz to lead him out of the trailer. The beast craned his neck, looking past Erasmus. Libby followed the animal's line of sight and turned to find a strapping man in a cowboy hat with a bouncing mane of blond hair striding up the drive toward them.

Where did he come from?

With the appeal of a rustic runway model, the man had to be around Raz's age. He wore a plaid shirt and jeans that might have been a size too small and looked as if he'd walked off a photo shoot for *Handsome Cowboy Weekly*.

"Who's that?" Sebastian asked.

"Bob's grandson, Doug," Maud answered brightly as the new arrival embraced the woman.

"People in town call me Zen Dougie," the man said, pressing his hands into a prayer position and bowing. "Namaste. You must be Libby."

Libby shifted her stance. "Namaste, yes, I'm Libby Lamb."

"They also call Doug the donkey whisperer," Bob added, clapping his grandson on the back. "He's the reigning Ass-in-Nine champion. He's got three wins under his belt, and he'll be racing again this year."

Doug shrugged off the compliment. "I'm a *jackass* of all trades," he said with what sounded like a practiced chuckle. "I'm here for the summer teaching yoga classes at the resorts over in Aspen and helping my grandad and great aunt before heading off to Tibet."

"Tibet?" Libby blurted.

"Yes, I take my spiritual journey seriously. May I?" the man asked, then gestured toward her hand.

"Okay?" she answered warily.

He lifted it to his lips and kissed her knuckles. "I've decided to continue my meditative practice there. I must say, I could feel your energy at the base of the mountain."

"Really?" she shot back.

Doug studied her palm. "I first connected with you when I saw the viral video of your training session with Erasmus Cress. Oh, hey, dude," Doug said with a nod to Raz.

"Did you?" she asked, then glanced at Raz. The man looked ready to tear Zen Dougie apart. She heard a low-pitched growl, but neither Raz nor Beefcake, the donkey, were the source of the sound. She turned to her left. Sebastian stood next to her with his arms crossed as he sized up the donkey whisperer.

What had gotten into the kid?

"Truly mystical stuff," Doug continued, seemingly oblivious that a man whose fists were most likely considered deadly weapons, along with a pretty pissed-off six-year-old, were shooting eye daggers at him. "I felt the vibration of our connection through my phone. That's some cutting-edge energy, Libby. From one yogi to another, I must say, I'm impressed."

She gently removed her hand from Zen Dougie's grip. "Thank you, Doug," she stammered. "My approach isn't conventional, but there are many ways to balance chakras and clear the subconscious mind for optimal performance."

There! At least she was able to put together a little yoga babble.

"So true," the donkey whisperer agreed. "You're here for the summer, right?"

"Yes," she began, gesturing to Raz and Sebastian. Both father and son had the same scowl glued to their faces. "We're here to compete in the Ass-in-Nine and for Erasmus to train for his upcoming fight."

Doug nodded, then peered at her left hand. "You coach him in the ring, but you're not wearing one."

"Wait, what?" she stuttered as another round of Sebastian's growls peppered the air.

"You two aren't together?" Doug asked, nodding to Raz. "I thought I sensed something between you guys on that video."

She glanced over her shoulder at her beefcake, who raised an eyebrow in response.

What was that supposed to mean? Was that a challenge? Was he angry? She couldn't read the infuriating man.

"I'm his nanny, his spiritual advisor, and..."

And the woman who rode his cock like a dirty cowgirl on their first night together and the gal who was sporting a hickey and had kissed the guy into oblivion in a blue-violet sex haze, but she wasn't about to mention that.

"We should meditate together," the man mused. "We can watch the sunset on the Rickety Rock lookout, then meditate during the sunrise."

Sweet Buddha's belly!

Was Zen Dougie hitting on her?

Was he insinuating sleeping together with his family and two scowling Brits ten feet away?

"Libby meditates with me, boyo," Sebastian snarled.

Hello, Cress family resemblance.

She zeroed in on the pint-sized badass.

"Hear this, Dougie," the boy called. "Libby is her own woman, making her own choices, and she chooses to meditate with me," Sebastian added, laying down the law like a mini beast.

She glanced at Raz, expecting the man to say something. Instead, the big beast remained silent as that maddeningly sexy smirk—the arrogant expression that had wrecked her chi, high-jacked her O, and could entice her to rip off his clothes—graced his lips.

"I see," Doug answered warily, taking an unsteady step away from her.

"And for your information, Doug," Sebastian continued, clearly not finished laying down the law. "My friend Oscar has a Charlotte. He calls her *my Charlotte*, and now I have a Libby.

My Libby or *Mibby*. She's my Mibby, boyo, you got that?" the boy finished, losing his prim British cadence and taking on his father's grittier accent.

Wide-eyed, Libby stared at the kid. That was quite a mouthful, and the whole *Mibby* business was new to her. When had he come up with it? Then again, she manufactured Pun-chi yoga out of thin air. Who was she to judge anyone for coming up with something slightly insane on the fly? And she had to admit, she quite liked the *Mibby* moniker. She hadn't been with Erasmus and Sebastian for a month, and they'd each already given her a nickname. A warmth filled her chest, but as she was about to let this feeling swallow her whole, it receded as quickly as it had risen.

Plum and Mibby might be charming names, but they had a shelf life. A shelf life that expired in a matter of weeks.

Focus, Mibby, Libby! Whatever!

Thunder rumbled, and the intense sound of the approaching storm added to Sebastian's formidable air. Unflinching, the boy stared down Zen Dougie. "Do we understand each other, boyo?" the boy pressed.

Holy karma clash, they would soon be having a little chat about speaking kindly to others. The child was in her charge. She couldn't have him *boyo-ing* every guy who looked her way.

"We better be heading out. We should get back to our animals at the ranch," Bob remarked, breaking the *boyo* versus Sebastian stalemate. "Everything you need for Beefcake and Plum is in the barn. We even tacked some tips and tricks on the wall. We'll be in touch, and we'll start the official burro race training in a few days."

A few days?

"You're leaving us with two donkeys and a few instructions? Two donkeys we need to keep in one piece. Well, two pieces." She shook her head. "You know what I mean."

"You'll be fine. Just follow the instructions," Maud replied, heading for the truck.

It was donkey time.

Libby released a shaky breath as her frenzied chi whiplashed through her body. She'd barely set foot in the town, and she'd already made out with her boss, invented a new school of yoga, been propositioned by a cowboy yogi, and watched a little boy strong-arm a grown man. And now she was supposed to care for two donkeys. She observed Plum and Beefcake munching on whatever grows on the ground in the mountains. And news flash: she had no idea what they were eating. Was it mountain grass or fart-inducing alfalfa?

"I'm not sure we're ready for this," she added, staring at the lead ropes trailing along the ground as the animals grazed.

When had they dropped their ropes?

No bother.

Plum and Beefcake weren't going anywhere and seemed quite content chomping on whatever the heck they were eating.

"Follow your intuition. You and Erasmus got the burros out of the trailer. Now, you need to take the bonding walk," Maud instructed. She pointed downhill toward a trail that snaked around the mountain. The path cut across a few steep points, then traversed the creek and rounded into the valley.

"That's the Crooked Mine Loop," Bob continued. "It's the course you'll be running in the Ass-in-Nine race. Some trails splinter off and some of the inclines can get a bit hairy. You've got to keep your wits about you. As long as you keep passing the rock stacks, you'll know you're on the right path."

"We'll let you get acclimated," Maud said, then turned to Doug. "You can ride back with us, dear."

This was happening! In addition to her other temporary occupations, she'd become a donkey nanny!

"Libby, Erasmus," Bob called.

"Yes?" they answered as another bout of thunder rumbled.

The man sniffed the air. "I'd suggest you get that walk in sooner rather than later."

"Absolutely," Maud added, sliding into the pickup. "The walk is essential in building the human donkey bond. You've got to do it now."

"I hope the universe brings us together soon, Libby," Doug said with a tip of his hat, then tossed a wary look at the still scowling Sebastian before settling into the truck next to Maud.

The skies darkened to a ripe purplish-blue, and Wobbly Bob waved goodbye as he circled around and maneuvered the truck and trailer down the road.

"I don't like that Zen Dougie. He's a knob-headed plonker," Sebastian remarked.

Libby gasped. "I don't know what a knob-headed plonker is, but it sounds awfully bad. I'm sure your granny Fin wouldn't approve, and you shouldn't say that about anyone."

Sebastian puckered his mouth like he'd been sucking on lemons.

"Libby's right, lad," Raz said, but there was still a hint of maddening arrogance in his tone. "You were slightly off. That Zen Dougie bloke is a right knob-headed mug of a plonker-loving twatwaffle."

"Erasmus!" she exclaimed.

"Fine, you can call him a blooming wanker, son. Blooming wanker is the gentler version of knob-headed mug of a plonker-loving twatwaffle."

"Erasmus Cress," she called again, her jaw hitting the ground.

"Is that okay, Mibby? Can we call Zen Dougie a blooming wanker?" Sebastian asked earnestly, again beaming at his father.

She glared at the pair of British beasts, but she couldn't stay mad. Of course, she'd wanted them to bond—just not over slang she could barely decipher.

"How about this? You can think it, but try not to say it," she offered, trying to find the middle ground.

"Zen Dougie is a blooming wanker. I quite like it," the boy whispered. "Oops, I said it. It's hard to just think it because the guy is the biggest wanker on the planet."

"Do your best to say it softly if you can't keep the sentiment in your head," she conceded as one giant raindrop, then another landed on her arm. She glanced at the ominous sky. Were they supposed to walk in the rain?

She was about to pose the question to Raz when the sky exploded. Rain pummeled the land. Sebastian ran to her side, and she wrapped her arm around his shoulder.

Wow, the wild weather blew in fast!

Lightning pierced the air as not one, but two flashing bolts seared the sky and met in a furious crash not twenty feet from them. The donkeys let out a cascade of shrieks and calls before charging down the trail.

"No! Stop, Plum! Stop, Beefcake! Don't run off," Sebastian cried as the animals disappeared into the foliage.

"Raz," she called, swiping the pouring rain from her cheeks as she held Sebastian back from chasing after the animals. The man looked as if he'd seen a ghost. "Erasmus Cress," she called, and he slowly turned his head.

What was wrong with him?

This was no time for the man to zone out. All she could picture were wet trails and the steep drops Maud had mentioned—steep drops that could surely prove treacherous for two out-of-control animals.

She waved her hands. "Snap out of it, you infuriating slice of British beefcake! We have to save the donkeys."

SEVENTEEN

ERASMUS

HE STARED AT LIBBY. Her mouth was moving. Her arms were flailing, but between the pound of the rain, the rolling thunder, and the crack of lightning, he couldn't move. He could barely breathe. It was as if he existed in two places at once.

Lightning had struck twice—twice—just like the day he'd met Meredith.

And just like that time, he knew his life would never be the same.

Two bolts.

Two blasts of bright white followed by a glimmer of violet-blue haze. It couldn't have lasted more than a fraction of a second. But he'd witnessed the dueling lines of light fuse together as they struck—not a London lamppost—but a large rock upon a mountainside in Colorado. He inhaled, then exhaled, living in slow-motion.

Raindrops fell in lazy streams as a vibrant indigo mist shimmered across the landscape. He closed his eyes, but the colors remained, brilliant and searing, beautifully punishing while astoundingly liberating.

"Mere?" he rasped, barely forming the syllable when he opened his eyes to find Libby waving her hands in front of him.

"Raz, can you hear me?" she cried.

He stared at her. *Shit!* He had to get it together. This was an emergency.

"Blimey, are you three okay?" Augie called as he and Luanne jogged toward them.

"We saw the strikes from the house," Luanne chimed, shielding the rain from her face.

"The donkeys! They got scared and ran. We have to get them back," Sebastian sobbed as another violent cluster of thunder and lightning played out in the sky.

Raz turned to his trainer. "Can you bring Sebastian inside? I'll go after the animals."

"I'm coming with you," Libby said, determination coating the words.

"I'm the fastest. You'll slow me down. Stay at the house. It'll be safer for you there," he said, unable to look her in the eye.

"No, you're not going alone," she replied sternly, leaving no room for him to protest, then kneeled in front of Sebastian. "It'll be okay. Your dad and I will find the donkeys and bring them home. Go inside with Augie and Luanne. Dry off, and then you have an important job to do."

"I do?" the boy asked and sniffled.

She nodded. "After the thunder and lightning pass, check the barn and make sure everything is ready for Beefcake and Plum. You won't have to wait long. Summer storms in Colorado rumble in and are gone before you know it. I'm sure the donkeys will be grateful for a dry, comfortable place to relax after their adventure."

The lad swiped his tears away and lifted his little chin. "Yeah, I can get the barn ready for Plum and Beefcake. You can count on me, Mibby."

Mibby.

My Libby.

That word was a salve to his battered heart and sucker punch to his gut all at once.

"Do you have the aquamarine stone with you?" she asked.

"Right here," Sebastian answered, pulling it from his pocket.

"Rub it with your thumb and think positive thoughts. The donkeys will be safe and happy. We'll manifest our best destiny to make it happen."

Manifest their best destiny? What the bloody hell did that mean?

But it worked. Sebastian brightened.

"Okay," he answered as the pound of the rain intensified. "I'm sending love and light to the donkeys."

Augie patted Sebastian's shoulder. "Come on, now, lad. Let's get back to the house."

"You'll bring the donkeys back, right, Dad?" Sebastian asked with such trust in his tone.

"We'll find them. Mind Augie and Luanne. Off you go," he said, holding his son's blue-green gaze.

He couldn't let the kid down.

With Luanne on one side of the boy and Aug on the other, the trio navigated the front yard's uneven terrain and made it to the safety of the covered porch. Sebastian stood at the railing, calling for them to hurry.

The urgency in his son's voice cut right to his heart.

"Sebastian's safe! Let's go," Libby called, taking off like a shot.

He followed a step behind, trying to get hold of himself. Sure, he was concerned about the animals, but that wasn't the only thing on his mind. He couldn't seem to untangle the memories of Meredith that swished around in his brain, colliding with images of Libby and Sebastian.

In the blast of light, it was as if Mere was there. He'd half expected to see her, standing on the mountainside, giving him that smile that meant it would be all right—that there was nothing they couldn't do if they did it together.

His pulse kicked up, and it wasn't because he was sprinting down a mountain trail, dodging slippery rocks, water-logged ruts, and protruding branches. No, he was a bloody mess, thanks to the insanity that had ensued from the second they'd arrived in this mountain town.

Whatever remnant of balance he'd had left had been obliterated.

From the pun-chi-yoga pandemonium to his stubborn donkey farting up a storm to watching the plonker Zen Dougie drool over Libby to two bloody lightning bolts damn near hitting them, he wasn't sure if he could discern up from down or left from right. What he did know was that he had to pull himself together and find the donkeys. What the hell would he say to Sebastian if the animals were injured, or God forbid, killed? Ice crackled down his spine.

The donkeys had to be okay.

Sebastian didn't deserve more heartache.

Mere, show me the way.

He'd never asked her for anything from the great beyond. He'd barely allowed himself to indulge in her memory. But he couldn't let Sebastian down—not for what must be the millionth time.

"We can do this, Raz. We'll follow their hoof prints. And look, the lines from the lead ropes are there, too," Libby called, then glared at him from over her shoulder. "Is that all you've got, beefcake? Can you pick up the pace? We can't let the donkeys careen off a cliff."

Is that all he had?

Was that a challenge?

He barked an arrogant laugh and did what he seemed to do best, morph into beefcake mode.

Was it a jerk move?

Absolutely.

But who did she think he was, some couch potato? Some weekend gym warrior? He was bloody Erasmus Cress—a professional athlete, a heavyweight champion.

He was no knobby slowpoke wanker.

A surge of jealousy laced with a confusing sense of betrayal worked its way into his bloodstream. Anger permeated his every heated breath. Who was he mad at? Himself? Libby? Dougie, the yoga wanker?

Yeah, it had to be the yoga wanker.

Hardening his expression, he kicked up his speed and matched Libby's pace as they sliced by a wall of fluttering aspen trees, dancing in the pouring rain.

They passed one of those stacks of rocks, indicating they were on the main trail, and she glanced at him. "I can feel beefcake waves coming off of you."

"Are you sure it's not you, plum? You might be hot and bothered over your yoga-loving Zen Dougie?" he fired back, giving her the full beefcake treatment.

"What are you talking about?"

"You didn't seem to mind *Dougie* hitting on you?" he bit out, and bloody hell, Libby Lamb kicked up her speed. Forget the notion of her having trouble keeping up with him. This woman could run like the wind.

"That's why you've been acting like a giant jerk? You're mad about Doug inviting me to meditate with him?"

She was no idiot. She had to have known what the wanker was doing.

"He wasn't talking about meditating, and you know it. Even

Sebastian picked up on the guy's sleazeball factor," he replied between tight breaths.

They passed another stack of rocks that accompanied a slew of hoof prints.

They were in donkey hot pursuit—but the pursuit had nothing on the crackle of agitated energy ping-ponging between them.

"You could show a little gratitude," she replied as another bolt of lightning punctuated the sky.

"For Zen Dougie? You want me to be grateful for that twit!" he exclaimed.

"He helped you get Beefcake out of the trailer," she shot back, barely winded. Maybe there was something to her Pun-chi yoga regimen. She had killer endurance and an amazing body. She was a beast wrapped in tiny yoga pants that hugged her in all the right places.

Don't imagine her perfect backside in those leggings.

He focused his agitation on the Zen cowboy. "I didn't ask that wanker, Dougie, for any help. I was doing fine on my own," he lobbed back as they side-stepped, left, right, left, down a steep incline.

"Zen Dougie's arrival doesn't account for why you couldn't show a speck of interest in your son's excitement to care for the donkeys."

There they go. With that remark, she'd opened the flood gates.

"Are you bloody joking?"

"No, he was so excited about the burros, and you just stood there, rebuffing his enthusiasm."

Did she have a point? Had he been acting like a sullen git? Perhaps.

But he wasn't about to cop to it.

"Plum, like I said, I have a lot on my—"

"You have a lot on your mind, blah, blah, blah. I'm the fancy boxer Erasmus Cress, blah, blah, blah," she interrupted, prancing from foot to foot like a nimble jaguar to avoid a slick spot in the center of the trail.

"It's the truth," he answered, sounding like a surly schoolboy.

"You sure seem to have room in that beefcake brain of yours to obsess over Doug."

"So, you do like him?"

She glared up at him. "I don't dislike him."

He ran his hand through his hair, swiping back the errant dripping locks as the trail curved around a sharp bend. They pushed past a cluster of evergreens, and the needles scratched his forearm as he lifted a low branch for Libby. As if they'd been tandem running for ages. She buzzed under his arm, then leaped over a trio of large roots crossing the length of the trail.

He needed a zinger worthy of the most beefcakey of the beefcakes. He copied her jump and ran alongside her as the path widened and a whopper of a retort shot out of his big mouth. "Dougie should be your final Mr. Benchmark screw."

Bloody hell! What had he unleashed?

"My what?"

A muscle ticked in his jaw. There was no going back now.

"The guy you pick to see if some random bloke can get you off," he tossed back and shit. In a grand effort to be an asshole, he'd bloody cut off his nose to spite his face. The thought of Zen Dougie laying a hand on her had his blood boiling. Surely, she'd tell him he was crazy.

Her posture stiffened as she flitted across a series of flat rocks. "That's not a bad idea. Maybe Doug should be the final benchmark test subject. You're already planning to get rid of me. What would you care?"

Yes, he was an arrogant, selfish ass, but he'd never mentioned sacking her.

"What are you talking about?"

"Briggs said I should go into PR after you're done with me as your spiritual advisor and Sebastian's nanny. I assumed he's got a plan for us parting ways. Am I right?"

He could feel the heat coming off her, or perhaps it was the frantic energy they created when their emotions ran hot—when he didn't know if he should kiss her into oblivion or work out his frustration on the heavy bag, punching until his knuckles bled and his mind emptied of all things Libby Lamb.

"Briggs plans for everything. It's his job."

She stopped, standing on a large rock protruding from the side of the trail where the route broke off into two pathways. A slim stack of rocks was piled next to her as she pegged him with her fiery amber gaze.

He concentrated on the stones—the marker of the right path.

Too bad that didn't translate into real life.

He didn't know what the right path was supposed to be—only that he had to walk it alone.

"It's settled," she bit out. "Doug will be the benchmark guy. I'll wait until after the Ass-in-Nine race to seduce him. He said he's leaving for Tibet at the end of the summer. It'll be a one and done."

Was she serious?

Then again, this was entirely his fault. He'd offered up the flowing-haired yoga plonker.

He hardened his features. "Sounds like you have a plan."

"I certainly do," she shot back with the tiniest shake to her voice. It was subtle, but he caught it. Unable to reply, he stared at her as the rain cascaded down her cheeks. Her long wet hair hung past her shoulders in tangled waves. With the blustery sky and the rich greenery glinting in the rain, it was like staring at a woodland nymph. She parted her lips, and he couldn't help but hope she'd take it back. It made no sense—knowing he couldn't have her but not wanting her with anyone else was selfish and utter madness. Nonetheless, he wanted, no, needed her to reject the yoga cowboy.

Say you don't want anyone else.

Say you don't want to sleep with Zen Dougie.

"I don't—" she began, her eyes trained on the ground.

"Say it," he rasped, his heart in his bloody throat.

She cocked her head to the side and swiped the rain from the apples of her cheeks. "I don't know which way the donkeys went. Their trail ends here. You see, the path changed. There's not as much mud and gravel. It's too rocky, and there are so many pine needles on the ground, I can't make out if they stayed on the main trail or took the offshoot."

Beefcake and Plum.

The bloody donkeys!

With the thought of her with Zen Dougie dominating his mental capacity, he'd nearly forgotten they were on a donkey rescue mission.

Buck up and focus!

He studied the trail. She was right. There weren't any hoof prints past this point nor the winding line from the donkeys' leads.

He peered down the two trails. "The donkey knows," he whispered.

"Did you say what I think I heard you say? The donkey knows?" Libby shielded her eyes from the rain, staring at him like he'd sprouted donkey ears.

He shrugged. "I'm trying to do what Maud and Bob told us —you know, channel the donkey. The donkey knows."

"Do you know which way they went?" she pressed skeptically.

"No, but I'm trying to think like a donkey."

"That shouldn't be difficult for you. You've got acting like an ass down pat," she murmured.

He'd walked into that one. And blimey, she was properly pissed off at him.

Bloody brilliant.

He wasn't walking sunshine either.

He needed a pithy retort—something that could counter her sharp wit, but before he could get a word out, the bray of the donkeys floated through the air.

She stilled, and the irritation in her gaze vanished as another round of donkey noises cut through the blustery rain and wind. "Did you hear that, Raz?"

"Yeah, I did."

"The sound came from this way. They've left the main trail, but we've got to be close," she said, setting off down the narrow path.

He followed a few paces behind her as the trees grew thin and a rickety barn emerged on the edge of the slope. It had to be abandoned. Several planks from the roof were missing from the sun-bleached shelter, and the door was nowhere to be found.

"I see them. They're in the barn!" Libby called, sprinting up the side of the mountain. "Hey, Plum! Hey, Beefcake!"

He caught up to her, but as they approached the pair of burros, Beefcake let out a great shriek, baring his big teeth and maneuvering his massive body in front of Plum.

Libby took a step back. "I don't think they're happy to see us."

He scanned the space. Weeds grew in the corners of the weathered structure, but that wasn't what Plum and Beefcake were munching on. They'd stumbled upon something far sweeter. "They found a wild strawberry bush," he said, craning his neck to see the ruby-red fruit amid the tangle of leafy greens.

The male donkey stomped his foot, and he couldn't help but

chuckle at the loudmouthed beast. He knew a thing or two about putting on a puffed-up testosterone show. He met the animal's eye. "We're not here to interrupt your meal, Beefcake," he said, taking a step toward the donkey with his hands raised. "But we can't have you gallivanting around a mountain during a lightning storm."

The creature's fierce demeanor dialed back.

"That's a good donkey. We'll take this nice and easy." He turned to Libby, who watched him with a curious glint in her eyes. "I'm going to get hold of Plum's lead. It's closer," he said, gesturing with his chin toward the ropes resting on the ground amid the old planks.

She chewed her lip. "I don't know if Beefcake will like that."

"What does he care what rope I pick up?"

She pressed her hand to her heart and closed her eyes. "I'm getting a vibe."

"From the donkey?" he shot back.

Her eyes fluttered open, and she glared up at him. "Yes, from the donkey. Just like humans, animals can forge deep, spiritual connections."

He glanced at Beefcake, currently sniffing Plum's ass. "Yeah, I can see that," he deadpanned. "But I think I'm good to grab hold of Plum's lead." He took another step forward, picked up Plum's rope, then tugged. The gray Jennie released an alarming cry and tugged back, triggering Beefcake to dart toward him, baring those bloody giant donkey teeth.

"Raz, be careful!" Libby called.

He dropped Plum's rope and raised his hands above his head.

This Beefcake was worse than any bloke he'd faced in the ring. But now, he understood the beast. Cooing and sweet talk wasn't the way to make his point.

That's not how beasts communicated.

He had to change tack. It was time for a meeting of the beefcakes.

He paced across the barn as the pound of rain against the roof slowed to a gentle pitter-patter. "All right, all right, I get it, Beefcake. You don't want me messing with your girl, you wanker burro. I see where you're coming from." He caught Libby out of the corner of his eye. With her jaw nearly hitting the floor and her head cocked to the side, she observed as he bantered away with Beefcake like they were two chaps in a pub. A tingle ran down his spine. He liked having her eyes on him. He puffed up a little more, getting into character. "You see, mate, I can't leave you here untied. You can eat the bloody strawberries. Your girl can, too, but I'm going to tie your lead to that post. Are we seeing eye to eye, Beefcake?" He glanced at Libby. "You want to add anything? Any vibe you're picking up?"

"No, I think you've conveyed the message clearly," she answered, looking mighty impressed—or maybe gobsmacked. Either way, he'd become the bloody beefcake whisperer.

Take that, plonker Dougie.

"Come on," he coaxed, tugging at Beefcake's rope. The animal complained, but it was no different than asking some cantankerous bloke in an East London hole in the wall to move down a stool. "There," he said, tying the lead to the side of the barn. "Now we both win, you arsey ass."

The donkey looked him square in the eye and nodded.

Now that's the way beefcakes get it done.

"Looks like there are two donkey whisperers in Rickety Rock. Zen Dougie's not the only one with mad donkey skills," he said, adding a little swagger to his step as he pinned Libby with his gaze.

He'd expected to find her beaming at him. He had charmed the donkey into compliance. Instead, she scowled. Leaning against one of the beams supporting the structure, she stared out the opening. "There are blue skies in the distance. We can go when the rain lets up. This will be over soon," she added with an irritated edge.

What had set her off? Was it something he said?

"What do you suggest we do while we wait?"

"I plan on distracting myself with thoughts of my benchmark night with Doug," she answered sharply. Yes, there was sarcasm in her biting tone, but that didn't mean he found it humorous.

With the animals secured and feasting on the berries, he zeroed in on the raven-haired woman, who drove him bloody crazy. His steps devoured the ground between them.

Crunch, crunch, crunch.

His trainers cut into the pebbled ground as his pulse hammered in his throat. Libby held his gaze, scrutinizing his every step. Most people shuddered when he set his sights on them. He was an imposing man. When he turned it on and asserted his dominance, fighters quaked in their boots.

But not this woman.

She wasn't easily intimidated. He knew that better than anyone. Thanks to the viral video, the bloody world knew it, too. He stopped mere inches away from her, but the woman remained undisturbed and seemingly unaware of his little peacock display, save for one barely perceptible behavior. She inhaled a quick, shaky breath. Oh, she could try to pretend that his presence didn't affect her, but she sensed his nearness. His fingertips tingled at the prospect of touching her, and his cock took notice of her wet T-shirt, voluptuous breasts, and the points of her hardened nipples pushing up beneath the soaked garment. Every muscle in his body tensed. The attraction between them sparked electric. They were two live wires pulsing with energy, and the desire to have her focus her energy on him, and only him, was too strong to resist.

He bit back a grin.

He knew how to push her buttons and shift her thoughts away from Dougie the Plonker and onto him.

He leaned in. "I remembered something."

She kept her gaze trained on the view outside. "Oh yeah?"

"You're not ready for a benchmark night with the Rickety Rock yoga wanker."

She abandoned the scenery and studied him. "And why is that?"

A cocky grin spread across his face—the expression he saved for her. "You haven't completed the second benchmark objective, plum."

Her smug expression evaporated. "Masturbation," she whispered.

"You said you hadn't done it yet, thanks to being so busy."

She lifted her chin and twisted the tail of the soaked curtain scarf. "I'm sure when I have a moment to myself, it'll happen."

He rested his forearm against the beam above her head, caging her in from above. "But you don't know for sure."

"Officially, no, I don't."

"I know what you *won't* be thinking of when you find a moment to touch yourself," he purred.

"And what *won't* I be thinking of?" she snarled.

"The plonker Zen Dougie."

The charged air that filled the slice of space between them hummed. A cocoon of rousing exhilaration wrapped around them.

"I could think of him. He's quite handsome. He's got nice...chakras."

Raz shook his head, zeroing in on her. "You won't be

thinking of his chakras because you'll be fantasizing about mine."

"That's not true," she lied—he knew it from the depth of his soul.

"Do you think Zen Dougie can make you purr and moan those sexy little sounds you make when I thrust inside you? Do you think he'll find that rhythm that drives you to call out my name and come so hard you can't remember the name of this funny little town?"

"It's Rockety Rick. I mean, Rickety Rock," she blurted, then schooled her features. "You're a knob-headed plonker if you think that I can't resist you."

He bit back a grin and gave her a self-assured little shrug. "You also called me infuriatingly handsome back at the house."

Fire blazed in her amber eyes. "I had to say something that would kick-start the arrogant beefcake to get you to snap out of it. It was an act of desperation to save the donkeys. Nothing more."

"You don't want me to kiss you, then?" he rasped.

Why was he doing this?

That was a stupid question.

The answer was simple.

He couldn't stop.

Now that he had her to himself, every reason to ignore her melted away, and the cautionary whispers in the back of his mind were instantly silenced by the haze of violet-blue that engulfed them each time he hovered on the brink of losing himself in her.

Teetering on the edge of spellbinding recklessness, he brushed his thumb across her lips. "Do you want to kiss me?" he pressed as she trembled beneath his touch.

He undid her scarf with his free hand and allowed the damp fabric to fall to the ground. Slowly, he drew his fingertips along her collarbone, then rested his palm on her neck. Her pulse thrummed against his skin, betraying her mask of indifference.

"Your heart's about to beat itself clean out of your chest, plum. Your body wants me to kiss you. It's begging for it."

She ran her hand down the side of his torso before slipping it between them and palming his rock-hard cock. "Are you sure it's not you who wants to kiss me, beefcake? Your body is doing more than just begging."

He leaned in closer, anticipation driving him mad as her touch removed the last shred of his restraint. She tightened her hold, stroking him through his soaked trousers. Her warm breath against his mouth fed the carnal drive burning within him. Hot, wet, and near delirious with the need to kiss her, he walked the tightrope between knowing he should pull back and the delicious bite of the all-encompassing yearning to claim her mouth with a searing kiss. A kiss that would capture her, body and soul. A kiss that would taste as sweet as a ripe, juicy—

"*Plum.*"

Raz stilled, so close to kissing this raven-haired yoga goddess until he couldn't see straight.

But there was one major obstacle.

Despite his spiraling thoughts and lust-fueled desire, he wasn't too far gone to comprehend that neither he nor Libby had uttered the word. And now, one poignant detail couldn't be ignored.

They weren't alone.

EIGHTEEN

ERASMUS

RAZ ENTERED THE COZY ROOM, tucked away on the third floor, and set a glass of water on Sebastian's bedside table.

Was he a bloody waiter now?

No, but he needed to do something to quell the frantic energy flowing through his veins. And even more than that, he had to quiet the thoughts that whirled through his mind like an out-of-control carousel.

What sort of thoughts had him shuffling around the Victorian with his head in the clouds transporting cups of water?

The type of thoughts that transported him back in time—back to the patter of mountain rain tap dancing on the roof of a ramshackle barn, which happened to be the location of his berry-scented, almost-kiss with Libby Lamb.

Aptly described as an *almost-kiss* thanks to his son's arrival.

He stared out the window and was met with a sea of twinkling lights set against a midnight blue backdrop.

At least he'd made it through the first day.

Well, he'd almost made it.

It wasn't over yet.

But it was Sebastian's bedtime.

Once the lad was asleep, it would be himself and Libby, face-to-face with no loquacious lad buffer between them.

They hadn't had a moment to acknowledge what had almost happened in the barn. Add that near indiscretion to the Rickety Rock arrival make-out session in the blue and purple crow curtains room. He was doing a shit job of keeping his hands off the nanny. And to say that there was a whole lot of awkward fizzing in the mountain air tonight was an understatement.

What was he supposed to say to the woman?

My bad for going full-on beefcake?

Sorry for kissing you, then almost kissing you again?

Here's the thing.

He wasn't sorry.

At that moment, with the light taps and scrapes of hooves on wood and the calming neighs and gentle whinnies of the donkeys indulging in the wild berries, he'd wanted to kiss her. But when he'd heard his son's voice, the bubble had popped. He'd barely had two seconds to pull away from Libby before Sebastian got an eyeful. Luckily, the pair on the verge of ripping each other's drenched clothing off wasn't what caught the child's eye. Sebastian had zeroed in on the burros before noticing them. And the boy wasn't alone. Augie and Luanne were only seconds behind. And with the trio's arrival, the weight of his folly set in.

He'd done it again. He'd lost his head and crossed the line.

It shouldn't be that hard to comply. There was one rule to follow.

Do not kiss the bloody nanny.

He should have it tattooed to the inside of his eyelids.

It was a close call. It was simply dumb luck that Beefcake had whinnied as Sebastian approached the barn.

He couldn't allow himself to stumble again. He had to put Libby, with her dark hair, alluring eyes, and lips he could kiss until his last breath, out of his mind. And thank bloody Christ, he'd had a bit of a reprieve since they'd returned to the Victorian.

Sebastian had provided a kind of respite these past few hours.

After he and an equally quiet Libby listened to the boy go on about the care and feeding of pack burros during dinner, he'd informed the nanny and his son that he would check the grounds and lock up the house—otherwise known as a hyper-masculine bullshit excuse to get away.

And why did he need the escape?

Because he didn't want to escape.

Because if he were a different man, a worthy man, he'd deserve Libby and Sebastian. He could sit at that table and allow the joy of simply being near them to fill his heart.

But he couldn't.

He'd forfeited that pleasure the day Mere died.

After checking the animals, who'd settled into their luxury barn digs quite well, he puttered around, locking doors and closing windows, while listening to the Victorian's creaking floorboards above. Libby and Sebastian's muffled voices floated down from upstairs like leaves falling dreamily from a tree.

The two already had a rhythm—a pattern they must have picked up in Denver while he'd been holed up at the gym. The chipper cadence of his son's voice, then Libby's gentle tone, then laughter played out over and over as the pair moved from the bathroom to the boy's third-floor bedroom with the quaint, sloped ceiling. Somewhere between listening to the whoosh of water from the draining bathtub work its way through the Victorian's old pipes and the patter of feet trekking down the hallway, he'd left the confines of the house. He'd purposely moved slowly, taking ten times longer than it should to check on the donkeys. Had he not left and blocked out the sweet murmurs of their sounds, he would have surely gone mad.

He'd recognized the voices and rhythm. Once upon a time, he'd been a part of it.

But he couldn't hide out for the entire night.

The second he'd made it back to the house and closed the door behind him, Sebastian had called to him and requested a glass of water.

And that's where he was now, standing in the bedroom, his head nearly hitting the sloping triangular ceiling like a bloody useless third wheel. With nothing left to do other than fall back on his water boy gig, he picked up the glass of water and set it a few inches closer to the boy, listening as his son held Libby's mobile and chatted away with Phoebe and Oscar on a video call.

Perhaps, it was another respite of sorts.

This situation allowed him to pretend to attend to the child while watching Libby like a hawk from the corner of his eye. He wasn't one for evaluating energy or giving much credence to the hocus-pocus chakra stuff Libby ascribed to. Still, he couldn't ignore the anxiety coming off the woman in crashing waves. If he was the water boy, then she was the laundry lady. He'd observed her fold, unfold, then refold Sebastian's shirt and track pants half a dozen times since he'd joined them.

"So, you're a real donkey rescuer, Sebastian?" Phoebe questioned, her curious voice weaving its way through the tension-filled room.

Sebastian leaned against a wall of pillows in his new bed. Lit by the golden glow of the bedside table and fresh from the bath, the boy beamed. Drops of water from his still-damp hair dotted his pajama top as he stared at the mobile's screen.

"Yeah, Phoebe, I'm a real donkey tracker. The two strikes of lightning had them running as fast as race cars. After the rain stopped, I begged Augie and Luanne to let me help my dad and Mibby find our donkeys."

"Mibby?" Oscar repeated.

"That's what I'm calling Libby now. You know, like you call Charlotte, *my Charlotte*. Well, Libby is my Libby, but I didn't copy you, mate, so I shortened it up to Mibby."

Raz glanced across the room at Libby, who'd stopped folding and froze at Sebastian's declaration. She caught his eye but looked away as quickly as she'd met it before returning to her folding routine.

Bloody hell! He couldn't even pinpoint what she was most worked up about. Between offering up Zen Dougie as her benchmark screw, then falling back onto beefcake mode, he'd cocked up an already mucked up situation.

"Mibby! I love it, Sebastian. It's a blooming brilliant name," Phoebe sang out in the worst British accent he'd ever heard. Still, despite the whirlwind of emotions hitting him harder than any boxing rival ever could, he chuckled at the child's remark and caught Libby doing the same.

Okay, maybe they could get past this uncomfortable strain.

"How did you know where your donkeys went?" Oscar pressed, his voice, thankfully, not in a grating British accent.

Sebastian schooled his features and squared his jaw, looking properly formidable. "First, I tracked their prints. Then, when the hoofprints disappeared, I told Augie and Luanne that I thought the donkeys may have strayed off the main trail. Donkeys are smart. They like to explore new places. And I was right. I found the donkeys in an old barn on the side of the mountain, eating wild strawberries. My dad and Mibby were there, too, but they were busy."

"What were they doing in the barn?" Phoebe demanded, her accent now sounding like an uppity French maître d'.

"Libby got an itchy bug bite on her neck, and my dad was helping her scratch it," Sebastian explained.

Raz flinched. He'd come up with that crock of shit on the fly.

"Do you know what that makes me think of?" Phoebe replied, sticking with the French maître d' voice.

Libby inhaled an audible breath. And he was right there with her. God only knew what was about to fly out of the child's mouth.

"What?" Sebastian queried.

"Bergen Summer Adventure Camp in Aspen. The camp you, me, and Oscar get to go to," the girl spouted, going back to her normal voice.

Libby released her breath as he did the same. There's one crisis averted.

"The Bergen part is the same name as me and Oscar's teacher, Mrs. Bergen," Phoebe explained. "But I don't think she'll be at camp. I think teachers stay in their classrooms over the summer. Why would they want to leave? School is the best."

"Camp is great, too," Oscar added. "Remember Outdoor Lab in Telluride, Phoebe? You scared all those boys and made them give you their cookies at lunch every day."

Phoebe sighed. "I really love camp."

"My Charlotte showed me the brochure for the camp we're going to," Oscar continued. "They've got woodworking, and we get to decide if we want to build a picture frame or a little step stool."

A stool.

Raz's heart twisted in his chest as the image of a boxing ring with two stools crystalized. He stared at the ground and willed the picture away.

"That gives me an idea," Oscar chimed. "Your birthday is coming up, right, Sebastian?"

"Right-o, mate! My birthday is a few days after the donkey race," Sebastian answered, puffing up, then paused. "Dad," the boy whispered, waving him to the bed.

"Yeah?"

"I asked Augie for the dates to make double sure you could come to my donkey birthday party. Remember last year. You had to train."

Shame came at him from every corner of the room. "I remember. I'll be there," he answered, his voice a tight rasp.

Sebastian flashed him a toothy grin, then got back to his friends. "What's your big idea, Oscar?"

"You know how I'm a photographer like my Charlotte?"

"Yeah, mate, you take a real banger of a picture."

"I'm going to make you a picture frame for your birthday. If you go back to England, I'll put a picture of me and Phoebe in it, so you can remember us."

Raz shifted his stance.

Were they going back to England?

"I don't want you to go back to England, Sebastian. You're the only one who calls me Phoebe, Princess of the Hot Dog Fairies, Bearer of Cookies, and Eater of Pizza. I made Oscar try to say it, but it sounds better when you do it."

Raz chanced a look at his son. The boy wasn't looking at the screen. The kid had fixed his gaze on Libby.

There was that pang in his heart again. He didn't need to be awarded Father of the Year to know what the lad was thinking.

He didn't want to give up his Mibby.

Too bad it wasn't that easy.

He could buy the child anything—except what the lad truly wanted.

"I'm making a stool," Phoebe announced, pulling Sebastian's attention back to the screen. "And then," the girl mused, "I'm going to give it to my almost aunt, Penny. She's always asking my uncle Row to get a book off a high shelf for her. And it's always in a room where the door is locked."

"Phoebe," came Rowen's voice, laced with exasperation, and Raz chuckled. Despite the turmoil in his chest and the buzz of electricity he simply couldn't turn off between himself and Libby, he couldn't help but smile. The nerd had his hands full with his firecracker of a niece.

"It happens everywhere," the girl continued, ignoring her uncle. "In our Denver house, on our big boat, in our Aspen house, and our California house. How many more houses do we have, Uncle Row?" the child bellowed.

"It's bedtime, Phoebe," Rowen called. "Say good night to your friends. And do I smell chocolate? Do you have cookies hidden in your room, Phoebe?"

Libby smiled and shook her head as he did the same, delighting in the sweet craziness that was Phoebe Gale. Libby met his gaze, and all he could do was relish the warmth in her amber eyes. In this seemingly mundane parenting moment, on the surface, it was nothing, but experiencing it with Libby felt like home.

"Grimy, I'm busted again!" Phoebe whisper-shouted, switching back to her grating English accent.

Grimy?

"It's blimey, Phoebe," Sebastian instructed, grinning at the mobile's screen like he'd won the lottery.

And maybe he had. Granny Fin had mentioned more than once that the lad didn't have any mates at school. Could Oscar and Phoebe be his first real friends? He turned his attention to the glass of water and swallowed past the lump in his throat.

"Right-o, tally-ho, cheerio!" Phoebe called, reverting to the French maître d'.

"Bye, Sebastian!" Oscar exclaimed. "I can't wait for your donkey birthday. My dad and I are going to bake you a cake. I'd bring popsicles, too, but every time I see them in the freezer, they're gone by morning. My dad and my Charlotte are popsicle maniacs," the boy added as Mitch's audible, mock-hotheaded, grouchy groan echoed in the background as the children waved to each other before logging off.

He chanced another look at Libby.

He should have kept his focus on the glass of water.

He'd caught her gazing at Sebastian, eyes shining like she was so happy she wasn't sure if she should laugh or cry. He knew that look well. It was the same way Mere used to gaze at the boy when he was just a little thing.

Bloody memories.

He ground his teeth together, the muscles in his jaw tightening, then startled when Sebastian cleared his throat.

The boy stared up at him. "Do you need to fart, Dad?"

Fart?

Raz almost fell over. "No, of course, not. Why would you ask?"

The boy studied him closely. "Your face is pinched like you're holding in a giant whopper of a fart. Beefcake made the same face before he farted in the trailer."

What was it with boys and farting? Never mind. Part of being a little boy was remarking on farts. Still, he was no child, and he sure as hell wasn't making a fart face.

"I don't need to fart," he announced, then glanced at Libby. Pink-cheeked, with a playful glint in her eyes, she'd pressed her fingertips to her lips to keep from laughing. It was better than watching her fold-a-thon but still blooming embarrassing for him.

"You think it's funny now, Libby Lamb," he teased. "Just wait until Sebastian starts asking you about farting."

"I don't have to ask her, Dad," the child replied as quick as a whip. "Mibby farts. I heard her. It echoed in the room."

"What?" Libby exclaimed, wide-eyed.

"Yeah, when you were on your yoga mat a few days ago, bending over to touch your toes. I heard you fart," Sebastian clarified.

Libby's lips parted, then they opened and closed like a fish out of water. "That must have been my...bare feet...sliding across the surface of the mat. It can make a squeaky, fart-like sound."

Sebastian didn't look convinced. "It wasn't a squeak, Mibby. You farted."

Libby's gaze bounced from him to the boy, her cheeks growing pinker—and he loved every adorable second of it.

"If I did fart," she began, not quite conceding, "and I'm not saying that I did, passing gas is a natural bodily function."

"Your fart sounded like a loud mouse fart, Mibby. Like *eeeeeee!*" the boy shrieked, close to breaking windows and cracking wineglasses with the high-pitched nanny-fart demonstration.

"Time for bed," Libby announced, her cheeks a rosy scarlet as she cut off the boy's mouse farting impression.

"I need my treasures," he called and reached beneath his pillow to retrieve two items.

Raz stared at the smooth aquamarine stone—the same stone his son had offered up as comfort when he'd been on the brink of a panic attack. And then there was the second treasure, the pocket watch with Mere's picture. He rubbed his thumb across the stone, then opened the watch. "Good night, Mum," he said softly. He closed the timepiece with a gentle click, then set the items on the table next to the forgotten glass of water. Wiggling into the pillows, he sank onto the bed and closed his eyes. "I'm ready, Mibby."

Ready for what?

"Take a nice big breath and let the air out of your lungs,"

Libby instructed, settling herself on the edge of his bed. "Picture a time when you were truly happy. Hold that feeling inside your chest, close to your heart."

What the bloody hell was this?

"I'm on the swing set," Sebastian answered with a resolute nod.

Raz crossed his arms. "What are you doing?"

"Guided meditation, Dad. It settles the mind," Sebastian answered, eyes closed.

"Oh, okay," he answered, witnessing yet another facet of the Sebastian-Libby connection he'd missed these last ten days.

"You're on the swing," Libby continued. "It's sunny. Can you feel the sun shining on your face?"

"Yes," the boy answered as the ghost of a grin graced his lips.

"The wind is whooshing through your hair, and your legs are kicking back and forth."

"And my mum and dad are here. They're pushing me," Sebastian added, his smile widening.

Libby smoothed a lock of the boy's ash brown hair as his features relaxed beneath her touch. "You're happy and safe, and I bet you're giggling."

"Yeah, and I want to go higher and higher," Sebastian answered, his voice a dreamy slur of syllables.

"Now, focus on the breeze as you swing back and forth, watching the trees sway back and forth, back and forth..." she whispered as Sebastian's head rolled to the side, and the lad conked out.

How could Sebastian remember swinging in the garden?

Emotion welled in his chest. The lad was barely three years old when he and Mere used to push him on the toddler swing. He wanted to ask what else his son had mentioned about life before his mother died, but he didn't. He couldn't form the words. "That was fast," he whispered instead, listening to Sebastian's slow, even breathing.

"He's had quite a day. He doesn't always drift off so quickly, but he likes the guided meditations," Libby answered, adjusting the covers before coming to her feet.

"He'll be out for the night. He's a good sleeper," Libby shared, coming to his side.

"Always has been," he answered when his mobile pinged an incoming text. "Bloody hell," he whispered, hurrying from the room. Libby joined him and closed the door behind them as they made their way down the stairs leading from the third to the second floor. Before he'd made it down, he stilled and read the text.

"Is everything okay?" she asked.

"It's a text from Aug. He sent my training schedule." He held out his phone for her to see.

"Augie writes your schedule out on notebook paper, then takes a picture and sends it to you?"

He studied the image of Aug's chicken scratch writing. "He's old-school like that. It's a miracle he can text at all. I remember watching Briggs teach him how to record his voice mail greeting years ago. You've not seen comedy before you've watched a posh private school millennial and an East London old-timer huddle over a piece of technology barking at each other like Chihuahuas."

She laughed that laugh he wished he could bottle up and save for a rainy day, but the amused expression didn't last long. Her smile disappeared, and her countenance grew serious as she slipped the mobile from his hand and stared at the screen.

"What is it?" he asked, his voice barely a whisper.

"Pun-chi yoga is written on the page."

He'd seen it there and had been surprised, too.

"Yeah, you must have impressed Aug with your demonstration."

She bit her lip, still focused on the screen. "Or he feels like he has to add it because I shared it with the press."

"Aug's not like that. Not when it comes to training. If it's on the sheet, it's because he believes it's exactly what I need to do to win. It means he trusts you with my training."

That curious glint in her amber eyes returned. "It's amazing to think that my idea is part of anyone's training protocol. It's ironic, actually," she answered, sinking to sit on the bottom step.

"How so?" he pressed, joining her.

There was an oddly lovely equilibrium between his large, muscled legs next to her toned, smooth ones. They'd had to change their clothing after the rain-soaked donkey adventure. He'd slipped on a pair of mesh athletic shorts and a T-shirt. She'd done the same—well, the ladies' version. Sebastian had taken it upon himself to assign them their rooms, and Libby had emerged from the bird-inspired blue and violet bedroom in a pair of fitted runner's shorts and a simple white tank top.

He relaxed onto the step, taking comfort in her company. There was something calming about sitting on the staircase. It held a purgatory-like quality as if anyone who remained on them existed in a middle ground, a neutral plane. Sitting there with Libby, he didn't have to decide if they were coming or going. They were simply together, and he liked it, liked the relief of not having to prepare for what came next.

She returned the mobile to him, then leaned forward and rested her elbows on her knees. They sat for a spell before she spoke. "Remember that day—the day with the gong and the vibrators?" she asked, then leaned back and pretended to throw an invisible sex toy at his head as the rosy hue returned to her cheeks.

He played along and dodged the make-believe dildo. "It's

safe to say I will never forget that day."

She angled her body toward him. "I was supposed to pitch my fitness business concept to a venture capitalist group."

"The fake meeting? The guys who were doing it for kicks to meet girls, right?"

She'd mentioned it before. And like then, he had the urge to seek out those wankers and throw a few well-placed punches straight to their guts.

She nodded. "Yeah, that's the one."

"What made you think of that?"

She played with one of the green beads on her bracelet. "The plan I'd put together was solid but not unique. As crazy as it sounds, Pun-chi yoga is a remarkably effective way to build more strength and cardio into a typical yoga practice. And kids love it. Well, I'm not sure if every kid does, but your son enjoys it."

He leaned in but didn't speak, giving her room to continue, which was odd for him. Anytime the topic of Sebastian and boxing came up, he usually bristled. But this time, he didn't.

"Sebastian likes pairing yoga and boxing moves," Libby explained. "It happened by chance the first time he asked me to show him how yoga worked."

"He asked you how to do yoga?" He'd never pictured the lad barefoot on a mat. Then again, he didn't know the boy that well. Whenever this fact was thrown in his face, he'd close himself off and disengage. But again, like with the boxing comment, he didn't. Listening to Libby talk about Sebastian didn't feel like a vice tightening around his heart. It was the opposite reaction. It was as if his heart expanded in his chest with her every word.

A warm, knowing grin bloomed on her lips. "Sebastian's curious like that, and it's like he's built for both yoga and boxing. He's got extraordinary balance and physical strength for someone his age. I'd bet you were the same way as a kid."

He was. Athletics had come easily to him.

"It's funny," she continued. "I thought the day I confronted you at the gym would go down as one of the worst days of my life. Instead..." she trailed off and peered over her shoulder at the door that led to Sebastian's third-floor bedroom, and there was no second-guessing what she was thinking about. "He's a terrific kid, Raz," she added softly.

A slip of silence sealed them in the safety of the staircase. They sat together, two people pausing on a step. He shifted slightly, and his knee grazed hers, changing the energy. He sensed her tense in response to his touch. She was about to stand and bring their impromptu stair conversation to a close. He could feel it, but he wasn't ready to leave this perfect purgatory.

"What made you want to be a yoga teacher?" he blurted like a bloody BBC reporter.

She watched him for a beat, then released a slow breath, her shoulders lowering and her body relaxing again as she settled in on her half of the step. She gave him the saddest smile. "My mom."

"Was she a yoga teacher?"

He'd used the past tense, remembering the other tidbit Briggs had rattled off.

Libby's mum, Aurora Lamb, was deceased.

"No, she was a librarian. She stopped working after my brothers were born. She passed away from cancer when I was thirteen."

"I'm sorry." Death was another topic he avoided, but the power of this place softened the blow. Usually, the mention of death brought him face-to-face with the ghosts of his past. But tonight, he wasn't as burdened by his, and more than anything, he wanted to learn more about hers.

Libby's eyes shined, and she blinked away the emotion.

"Did your mum like taking yoga classes?" he prodded gently.

"The funny thing is, I don't think she ever took an actual yoga class. She did take a meditation and stretching class for women going through chemotherapy at one of the community centers in Denver. I used to babysit my brothers at the park right outside while she took the class. And while she didn't practice yoga, she was a spiritual person—quite intuitive."

"How so?"

A warmth radiated from Libby, lighting her up in a comforting golden glow. "Like me, my mom knew things about people—like when the twins were about to wake up from a nap or if I'd had a rough day at school and could use a hot fudge sundae. She'd give these feelings colors, and I could see them, too. I didn't think much of them until I began studying yoga and learned that we were reading people's energy and perceiving their auras."

"Like how there was all that blue and purply-violet around us in the police car?" he asked.

"I was surprised when you told me you noticed the colors."

She wasn't the only one.

He sat back, recalling the intensity of the night and the powerful yearning to kiss her. "I think me seeing colors has to do with you and me. It happens when I'm around you. And it's usually the same hue—violet and—"

"Blue," she finished. "It's violet and blue when it comes to us."

"Yeah, do you know what it means?"

He'd never believed in auras, visions, or vibrations controlling people's fate, but that assertion had been more than challenged since Libby entered his life.

"It could mean a lot of things," she considered. "Blue signifies intuition and peace. Blue could also represent having the blues and feeling down, but I don't get that with us. Sadness isn't the driving force. Yes, it's there, but the blue I see reads more like healing."

"And the violet?" he rasped.

Mischief sparkled in her amber eyes. "Power."

"Well, that makes sense for me," he joked as the mood lightened.

"It can also be a sign of becoming one, a kind of coming together to heal and grow spiritually," she added, and her words stopped him right in his tracks.

Was that even possible for someone like him? Could he heal? Did he want to heal?

He ignored the questions. "Does seeing auras run in your family? Can your dad see them?" he asked, and the offhand comment fell from his lips like a grenade.

And bollocks!

Why did he mention her father?

Then again, maybe it wasn't such a sore topic.

Nope, it was.

Libby's serene expression dissolved as her features hardened, and his gut churned. If at that very moment a genie had offered him one wish, he'd ask to erase his careless words. He'd felt her energy shift when the cops had asked if she'd known of Connolly Lamb. Even then, in the insanity of that situation, he'd perceived her disdain for the man.

"The only thing my father can see," she seethed, "is the direction that points toward selfish, self-serving choices."

Double bollocks!

The last thing he wanted to do was upset her and throw off this beautiful equilibrium they'd created on the step.

He had to fix this.

And the only way to do it was to come clean.

NINETEEN

ERASMUS

"YOUR DAD'S name is Connolly, right?" he asked, knowing damn well that was her father's name.

He'd had a feeling the man was bad news the night the officers asked her if she knew a Connolly Lamb, and she'd said no. He'd known she was lying. He didn't understand why...until now.

Shock pierced Libby's face. "How do you know that?"

Dammit! He hadn't meant to sound like a stalker. Then he remembered bloody Briggs.

"Briggs mentioned it. Remember when he recited your background in the police chief's office?"

"And the policeman asked me about him," she added, palpable pain coating her words. "I wasn't sure if you caught that—or remembered it."

"Yeah, I caught it. I got the feeling you knew him even though you told the cop you didn't. I didn't know he was your father until Briggs mentioned his name. I could tell whatever it was between you and your dad—it was strained."

"Strained is one way of putting it, but he wasn't always a train wreck of a father," Libby offered with a heavy sigh. "He didn't handle my mom's illness well. And after she died, it got worse. He stopped working and started having run-ins with the police. Nothing major. He drinks too much at bars to numb the pain because he's usually bet everything he's got on..."

"Sports," he supplied, putting two and two together. When Briggs had mentioned the enormity of online gambling for his fight, he'd felt her demeanor change.

"Yes, he's got a gambling addiction."

"And that's why you're the one caring for your brothers, helping them pay for uni?"

"I'm the oldest. I promised my mother I'd watch out for the twins, and it's my sankalpa."

"What's that?"

"Sankalpa is like a sacred promise or intention you make to yourself. Mine is to be there for my brothers."

"Your dad's not so good at that?"

She huffed a humorless bite of a laugh. "If making and breaking promises was a contest, my dad would win first place. He'd promise me and my brothers that after one more big win, he'd stop gambling. But one win became two, then three. Something always came up—some setback. Then he'd move the goalposts, and the cycle of broken promises would continue. Winning at gambling was more important to the man than his kids, and I learned at an early age that Connolly Lamb wasn't a man I could rely on."

"So, you stopped relying on men completely?"

Her no-strings approach to dating made a hell of a lot of sense now.

"Yes, it's the best choice for me." Her bottom lip trembled as she spoke. It was a slight movement, but he caught it.

"Do you see him much?"

Libby sighed. "Any time he comes around now, he has a big story about a great sports tip or this guy who knows a guy who might be able to pull a few strings to get him a job. There's always some tale that leads to him on the cusp of wealth and greatness if he only had a little more cash to get in on the scheme."

Raz nodded, anger thrumming through his veins. Sure, he was no saint of a father, but he wasn't a burden either.

"What did he do before your mum passed? Does he have a profession?"

"He's a facilities manager. He makes sure buildings run correctly. Heating, cooling, plumbing, electric—that type of thing. It's good work, but it's not the sort of job you can flake out on. He'd go on a bender, gambling and drinking, and those traits do not make for a reliable employee. But his behavior helped me find yoga."

He frowned. "I'm not following. I thought it was your mum?"

She sat back and gazed at her bracelet. "I guess they both played a part in pointing me in that direction. After my mom passed and my dad started going out almost every evening, I'd wait up for him to come home. Sometimes, I'd wait all night—and even into the early morning. I'd keep the television on for the background noise."

She paused, but he didn't say a word. There was more, and he wanted to hear it, wanted to know as much as he could.

"At five in the morning," she continued, "after the infomercials, this lady would come on the public TV station. She looked the part of the sage, elder yogi. She had this wild flowing hair with a flower tucked next to her ear, and she stood on a beach next to a yoga mat." Libby paused as a gentle serenity returned to her expression. "There was a swing hanging from a tree next to her with the ocean in the background. Her name was Shandra, and she was on the Hawaiian island of Moloka'i. That's what it said in the credits. The entire program was hypnotic.

Her rich, peaceful voice, the swing swaying in the breeze, and the rhythm of the ocean left me captivated. And even though I hadn't slept, it left me feeling renewed."

He nodded, giving her space to keep going.

"To me," she continued, "the practice of yoga, of moving with breath and intention, was like entering a dream world. Shandra's little island seemed so far away—a place of calm and joy. But it was more than that to me. For an hour, Shandra offered me an escape from my worries. And then, one day, I stopped sitting there watching her, and I started doing the moves along with her. From that minute on, I learned how to cope. The show went off the air, but I never stopped doing yoga." She paused again, then pressed her hands together in a prayer position. "At the end of each class, Shandra would look into the camera and say, be the light, and always remember, love is stronger than any force holding you back." Libby rested her hands on her lap. "It must sound corny to you, but—"

"It's not corny," he said, emotion coating his words.

She held his gaze. "That was probably more than you wanted to hear, but yoga gave me a way to cope with my dad's choices, and it makes me feel closer to my mom."

"Boxing makes me feel closer to Meredith," he said, barely able to believe the words had tumbled from his lips.

"Sebastian talks about Meredith quite a bit," she replied.

"What does he say?" He'd never talked to his son about Meredith. He'd left that to Granny Fin, Calliope, and Callista—a choice that, for the first time, he regretted.

"He told me she liked mint chocolate chip ice cream, drawing in notebooks, twirling in the rain, and swinging as high as she could on the playground," Libby replied.

"The lad's right." He pictured Mere in the garden with a little Sebastian on her lap as they glided through the air, swinging and laughing as the chains on the swing set emitted a jovial creak with each pass.

Libby pinned him with her amber gaze. "Was Meredith the reason you started boxing?"

He chuckled. "No, my granny Fin is responsible for that. I was falling in with a bad crowd after my parents passed away, and she was done putting up with my teenage nonsense."

"Your parents died at the same time?" Libby asked.

He pictured his mum and dad. Kind and generous, John and Isabelle Cress had loved him and his sisters.

"They'd gone to the sea on holiday for their anniversary. My mum got caught in a riptide, and my dad swam out and tried to save her. That's what the other people on the beach said. Somebody called for help, but it didn't arrive in time."

"I'm so sorry, Raz. That had to be difficult."

"It was a shock, and it wrecked me to the bloody core, but my granny is the hallmark of keep calm and carry on. And that's what she did. She kept us going. Callista and Calliope were only toddlers when my parents passed, so she didn't have time to have a delinquent grandson on her hands. After the first call from the headmaster for skipping school, she signed me up at Aug's gym."

"Is that where you met Meredith?"

"Sort of—with help from lightning."

"Lightning?" Libby repeated.

"I was at the gym, and it was raining something fierce when I glanced out the window and saw two bolts of lightning hit a lamppost. I had never seen anything like it in the city. Meredith was walking down the street when it happened. It freaked her out, and she ran inside to get out of the rain. She'd never stepped foot in the gym before."

"That's quite a cosmic meeting."

"I guess you could say that," he replied. "From that moment on, we were together."

"Was she a fan of boxing?"

"No," he answered, recalling Mere's expression the first time he brought her to a fight. "She never liked watching me get hit in the head till I fell down. So, I told her I'd become so good that no one could do that to me. And I kept my word. She gave me focus and clarity. We got married when we were eighteen. She worked two jobs to support us before I started winning big money. She believed in me. She put her hopes and dreams on hold to be there for me. After I'd won my first title, she started a charity to give back, the Cress Foundation. She loved volunteering, loved going into tough neighborhoods and helping kids. She dragged me along a few times. We even took Sebastian. She wore him in one of those baby carriers while she scooped ice cream and handed it out." He could see her laughing and chatting with the kids.

"What happened with the charity?" Libby asked.

"Aug and my granny took over." He stilled. He'd cut himself off from that part of his former life. It hurt too damned much. "I'm not sure if it's even active anymore."

"Meredith sounds like an incredible woman."

His throat grew thick with grief. "Yeah, she was."

One would think talking about a dead spouse with someone you'd slept with and pretty much wanted to kiss into oblivion twenty-four seven would be awkward. It probably should be awkward, but it wasn't. Libby had an open quality about her that drew him in like a beacon guiding a wayward boat through tumultuous waters.

"What happened to Meredith?" Libby asked, and the beacon's light dimmed.

Could he tell her?

He'd never spoken the words.

There hadn't been a reason to rehash the gut-wrenching tragedy. His sisters knew what had happened. Aug had been on the phone with his granny Fin and had spoken with Briggs. All the players in his life who needed to know did know, and he wasn't about to go blabbing to the media. Even Briggs didn't push him on that.

He concentrated on a spot on the Victorian's hardwood floor. He should stop talking, stop dredging up the past. He tapped the stair with his hand like he was testing the strength of it—checking to see if this perfect purgatory could endure the tale of Mere's passing.

But as he touched the wood, it became clear.

He wasn't testing the strength of the steps.

It wasn't the stairs at all.

The support he truly required wasn't made of wood. It had amber eyes and jet-black hair.

He allowed his gaze on the wood plank to grow blurry as the words spilled from his lips. "Mere died of sepsis—blood poisoning. Her appendix had burst a few weeks before my championship fight, and she needed emergency surgery. She hated making a fuss and cutting into my training. She kept telling me to get back to the gym, get back to Aug. And after a few days when she seemed to be on the mend, I did. She had my sisters and Granny Fin to help with Sebastian, but her health started going downhill. She'd blamed feeling poorly on a slow recovery and looking after a toddler. We left it at that. She'd always been a healthy person. She rarely got sick. We didn't have any reason to believe her fatigue was anything more than her body trying to heal."

He paused, recalling the last time he'd kissed her goodbye. She'd been in bed with Sebastian curled up next to her, sleeping. He exhaled a slow breath, then continued. "The night of my fight, she stayed home. She said she needed to rest, but the pain got so bad that my granny insisted on taking her to hospital. By the time they got there, she was in major organ failure. The nurses told me she was in terrible pain, but she still made them put the fight on the telly. She passed away seconds after the bell rang—just as the ref raised my hand and declared me the winner."

He sat there, dumbfounded. The story had churned and grated beneath his mask of arrogance. He'd finally spoken the words that had tormented him for years.

"I saw a picture of you after that fight," Libby said, pulling him back.

"The one right after I won, where I was holding Aug's mobile to my ear?"

He could feel the crush of people, the blaring music, and the doctor's voice slicing through it like a scalpel. He knew exactly which photo she'd seen. The bloody image had made it around the globe before he'd set foot inside the hospital.

"Yes, it was that one."

He ran his hands down his face. "I should have been with her. I should have made her go to the doctor when she started feeling bad. I live with that every day. Now, all I can do for her is make her sacrifice worth it by winning, by being the fighter she helped create. I cannot fail. I can't be a no-show for this fight. I got a pass, being the grieving widower, last time. It had only been a year since her death. But this is different. This is my last chance. I'm thirty-two years old, plum. I either go out a champion or fade away as some flash-in-the-pan mental case who couldn't get it together after his wife died. I owe it to Mere to be the champion."

The weight was back, heavy and gnawing. It hung around his shoulders, dragging him down like stones descending to the bottom of the sea. The spot he'd been staring at had become blurrier. He blinked, needing a new focus. He chanced a look at Libby and got it.

He'd expected to see pity in her eyes after his sad-sap story, but he didn't.

She cocked her head to the side, her neutral expression not giving anything away. "Can I tell you something, Raz?"

"Sure."

"I feel awfully bad about calling you a beefcake," she deadpanned.

For two measured beats, neither said a word. And then, like magic, the gloomy dam in his chest broke, and he laughed, and God help him, it was the release he needed.

How did she know that?

Was he easy to read, or was it something else? Was it that thread that formed between them the moment he'd set eyes on her months ago when Rowen had dragged his arse, along with Mitch and Landon, to nerd-stalk Penny at that dodgy bar?

He shrugged, playing along with her mock aloofness but so damned grateful for choosing this brand of humor. "I can't blame you. Beefcake is probably the nicest thing you could have called me under the circumstances."

"Oh, don't worry," she answered, gifting him with the ghost of a grin. "I called you other names, too."

"The obliterator of orgasms, the sinister chi thief, and the climax crusher," he replied like one of those commercial movie voice-over announcers hyping up a film.

"Climax crusher? That's a good one," she chimed as a more playful energy thrummed between them.

Beyond their sexual chemistry, this new sensation of peeling back his layers and revealing himself left him raw but lighter. They sat quietly as a comfortable silence descended on the house when a muffled donkey bray floated in through one of the windows he must have forgotten to close.

"It's a little mind-blowing that the donkeys are named Plum and Beefcake," Libby noted as another soft bray fluttered in on the breeze.

"It threw me for a loop, too," he confessed.

She leaned in toward him, and her leg brushed his, but she didn't tense this time. This touch felt natural, almost expected, like the force that drew them together had strengthened, and there was no use resisting it. "What do you think the chances of that happening are?" she asked, her breath tickling his chin.

He moved closer and rested his hand on her knee. "Probably the same as lightning striking the same place twice."

"And you've seen that happen two times," she whispered.

He'd been twice blessed with a phenomenon most never experienced.

Could it mean more? Could it be a sign?

"Why didn't you show up for your last fight, Raz?" she asked.

Just like Mere's death, he'd told himself he wouldn't talk about that day. He'd gotten good at putting on the arrogant mask and pretending nothing could touch him. But it came at a cost— a cost that ate away at his soul. A price he didn't want to pay anymore. He stared into her eyes, those deep pools of amber that calmed his spirit. "It was like what happened today but on a bigger scale."

She rested her hand on top of his and gave it a gentle squeeze. "You experienced a panic attack?"

He nodded. "When it was time to leave for the fight, I couldn't get off the floor. I couldn't do anything but lay there, frozen." He focused on their hands and allowed the soothing flow of energy to pass from her to him. "How did you do it, plum? How'd you stop it today?"

She threaded her fingers with his and stood, guiding him up

with her. "I offered your heart another choice," she said, like that made all the bloody sense in the world.

"Another choice? What does that even mean?"

She led him toward the door to her room. "I can show you. It's easier if we have more space."

"You want me to come with you to your bedroom?" he asked, like an idiot.

She pressed her palm to the door to her room and stared at it like they were communicating. "The room has good energy. The whole house does. But there's something about this room. I think it's the colors. They complement our energy."

If someone had mentioned a room having good energy before, he would have laughed his arse off. Today, he couldn't help but agree.

"Yeah, okay," he answered, his voice squeaking like he was fourteen. He cleared his throat. "I'm down with the violet, blue, and the crows," he tried again, making sure to add a low, gravelly quality to his response to counter his initial teenage squawk. But Libby didn't seem to notice his walk down puberty lane. She opened the door, and they entered the space. Lit by the glow of a lamp across the room, the space invited him in like a confessional. Dropping his hand, she fluttered around, removing the pillows from the bed, and making a little violet and blue nest on the rug.

"Is this part of it?" he asked, not sure if he should take part in the pillow party.

"Yes, we'll be on the ground. You have to sit first, cross-legged, please," she instructed. "And take off your shirt," she added as she slipped her tank top over her head, revealing that gold sports bra.

Bloody hell.

A tingle worked its way down his spine at the sight of it.

"Sure, shirts off works for me."

"And shoes and socks," she continued, slipping off her trainers.

Blimey, if this was the karma-licious yoga remedy for panic attacks, he was beginning to like the idea of adding yoga to his training schedule.

He sank into the cottony-soft nest and crisscrossed his legs. "Is this right?"

She played with her hair, letting it loose from the bun on the top of her head, and shook it out into soft waves before assessing his position. "Yes, that's excellent. Now, close your eyes and take three slow breaths."

He could do that.

One.

Two.

He was about to take his third when she rested her hands on his shoulders. Lowering herself, she sat in his lap, chest to chest, with her legs wrapped around his waist. And bloody hell, his cock took notice.

"I...um..." he muttered.

"Don't apologize. I'm using my shakti on you. An erection is a natural reaction to my energy."

He stared at her wide-eyed.

She made the word erection sound hot.

"What's a shakti? Is it a type of sex toy?" he asked, trying to sound sophisticated, but that damn puberty voice struck again.

She chuckled. "No, shakti isn't a sex toy. Think of it as my womanly vitality."

"Huh?" He chewed on that for a second. At least he could comply. Pretty soon, he wouldn't be able to think of anything other than her womanly vitality—especially with her in his lap nearly naked. "Right-o, womanly energy," he answered with a British accent worse than Phoebe Gale. And he was an actual Brit, who'd been talking this way for his entire life. He cleared his throat, going back to the gravelly tone. "I understand."

Get ahold of yourself, man.

"This is the yab yum position," she explained.

He cocked his head to the side. He'd need a pad and a pen to keep up with the terminology. "Yab yum?"

"Yes."

"Are you making this up like you did with Pun-chi yoga? Yab yum sounds like bubble gum or a type of candy floss."

She giggled, and the sound, along with the majority of his blood supply, went right to his cock.

"This isn't candy, Raz. These methods have been around for thousands of years. Are you ready to begin?"

He shifted slightly, relaxing as best as a man could while sporting a giant hard-on. "I think so."

"Today, when I touched your chest, I didn't press my palm to your heart. I pressed my wrist—my pulse point. I was nervous at the time. My heart was racing, too. But I had a feeling yours was skyrocketing."

"It was. I thought I might pass out," he answered. It wasn't like him to be vulnerable. It wasn't in the persona of a fighter. But with Libby, vulnerability didn't feel like a weakness. With her, it was a strength.

She nodded. "My sort-of-steady heartbeat spoke to yours. It sent a message, asking your heart to mirror mine and slow down. I suspect the breath work also helped. If this ever happens again and you're alone and feel like you're losing control, lead with your breath, and your heart will follow."

Lead with your breath, and your heart will follow.

Again, had he not lived through today, he would have discarded her spiritual mumbo jumbo as utter bullshit. "My body got your message. I felt the change instantly."

She grinned. "I know. I felt it, too."

He gazed into her amber eyes. "What happens now?"

She moved in closer, wrapping her arms around his neck. "We press our hearts together and align our breathing."

That boner was going nowhere.

"What should I do with my hands?"

"Rest them wherever it feels natural."

Without giving it a second thought, he gripped the globes of her arse, then dropped his hands. "Sorry, that just...happened."

She tightened her grip on him. "Put them back. Nothing is wrong or off-limits," she whispered into his ear.

It was as if the room were closing in on them, but not in a terrifying way. This closeness mimicked a cocoon, a safe harbor.

He returned his hands to her taut arse, and she rocked her hips.

He might have that boner for the next twenty years.

He inhaled a tight breath as her tiny shorts slid up, revealing her bare arse and—

"You might notice that I'm not wearing any underwear," she supplied, reading his mind.

Might notice?

His rock-hard cock twitched in his track shorts. "Yeah, I'm noticing. I'm doing quite a bit of noticing."

She pulled back to meet his gaze. "In this position," she said, her voice growing breathy, "our focus narrows as our alertness increases."

"I don't think I've ever been more alert than I am right now, plum," he confessed.

"Good, you'll feel the shift as our chakras align."

"Do my chakras seem okay? They're not tiny, are they?" he bit out, recalling the sassy barb she threw at Silas Scott.

She swiveled her hips and bit her lip. "Your chakras align with mine perfectly."

They moved together, rocking slowly, so slowly.

"You may experience some tingling," she added, followed by a dirty little moan.

"Yeah, I'm getting that," he replied as she arched into him.

With their breath and heartbeat in sync, a flood of words came to him, and he couldn't hold back.

"I don't think it's any secret that I want you. But the more I want you, plum," he began, sliding his hands beneath her shorts, "the more beefcakey I seem to become. I act like an arrogant prick, and I don't want to be like that to you. I want you, Libby Lamb. I know I should fight this impulse. But I can't. You don't do relationships. I get it. I don't do them either. But I need you. Can I have you, for now, here in this crazy donkey town?" He grimaced. "Sorry, I don't know where that came from."

She cupped his face in her hand. "It came from your heart. And I agree with you. There's an attraction between us that can't be denied, and—" She dropped her gaze.

"And?" he gasped, praying she'd agree.

She returned her focus to him. "And we did commit to following the like cures like program to remedy my lopsided chi. We also agreed to the exercises and benchmarks regarding the loss of my O," she said, making slow, grinding circles with her hips.

"Yep, I remember," he answered as the friction between them nearly drove him mad.

She closed her eyes and hummed a sexy little sound. "And we've made progress in assigning a benchmark test subject."

She was damn good at sounding smart. It took everything he had to not flip her onto her back, drive his cock inside her, and screw her brains out in this pile of violet and blue with birdie figurines watching.

He stilled as his last two working brain cells pieced together what she'd said.

"What's a benchmark test subject?" he got out. It was a

miracle he could still speak.

"Doug."

"Doug?" he repeated—thanks to the dwindling blood supply.

"Yes, Doug appears amicable to spending time with me and would be an appropriate final benchmark subject. And until the race, we could gather more data on the like cures like method and call everything you and I do up until that point spiritual development."

He liked the sound of gathering more data. Even in his state, he understood that meant sex. What he didn't like was the thought of the Zen douche donkey whisperer touching Libby.

"How about this," he posited, his words taking on a possessive bend. "We put the final benchmark in the hands of the universe."

Look at that. He could sound yoga-smart, too, when properly motivated.

"What are you proposing?" she asked, rolling her hips.

Focus, man.

"If Doug beats me in the Ass-in-Nine race, we follow the benchmark plan and treat him as a test subject. But if I win, Dougie is out. You don't let him lay a finger on you," he growled, the beast emerging.

"How will we know if the like cures like regimen worked without a final benchmark guy?" she pressed, their bodies grinding together.

"I'll figure it out after I've got a little more blood in my brain," he answered, tightening his grip on her backside with one hand and sliding the other into her hair.

He was bloody done talking.

He brought her to him, and their lips met, parting instantly and giving way to what must have been the hottest kiss ever shared between two human beings.

Electricity crackled.

Colors hummed.

He devoured her softness, and the hunger of his need shattered any last threads of resolve. Fueled by desire, he gave himself over to her, over to the passion that could not be restrained. Frenzied and urgent, a surge of titillating vibrations consumed him. He lifted her high enough to free his cock, then pushed the crotch of her shorts aside and lined himself up with her entrance. His tip indulged in her sweet wet heat as his mouth captured kiss after kiss. He had to get closer. He needed all of her. Her kisses sang through his veins, calling out to him.

Take me. I'm yours.

He was so close to thrusting his hips—so close to forgetting what they should and shouldn't do. As much as he'd tried to banish her from his mind, his body remembered the beautiful ecstasy of the first time they'd made love. Searing anticipation tore through him. His heart was ready to beat itself out of his chest when Libby stilled.

"Wait, Raz, we can't. Not yet."

"What is it?" he asked, searching her expression.

She twisted away from him and reached toward a bag—her yoga tote—and pulled it over. He hadn't noticed it.

"What are you looking for? Condoms?" His addled mind couldn't put together what she was doing.

"We don't need condoms. We need a rainbow."

He could do a lot of things. He was as strong as an ox and resourceful as hell—but a rainbow?

"Plum, I know we've got the whole bright energy thing going on. I feel it, too. But it's nighttime. It's pitch-black outside."

"I've got it covered." A dirty smirk stretched across her lips as she held up the Rainbow Screamer.

He stared at the multi-colored vibrator. "You're not going to throw that at me while we..."

"No," she answered. "I'm going to use it on myself, and you're going to watch."

His mouth hung open.

Bloody hell, he loved yoga.

"The benchmark, remember? Before we have sex, we should test if I can have an orgasm by myself."

"Yeah, I'm happy to watch you pleasure yourself—for the purpose of the program and chi and orgasm reclamation," he blathered.

He sounded like an idiot, but he didn't care.

Had he ever been this horny?

Never.

Was he ready to explode?

He was damn close, but he had to keep it together.

"Should I move?" he asked, glancing around the masturbation nest.

"No, I want to do it like this—with your energy around me."

"Yeah, okay, cheers to that," he stammered. Bloody moron!

She twisted the device, activating it, and a heady buzz filled the room. Sliding the vibrator between them, she worked it against her most sensitive place. It was a tight fit with their bodies wrapped around each other. He held her close as a rousing realization hit.

Well, not *hit* but *buzzed*.

The vibration didn't just touch her. The slim sex toy hummed against his cock. He'd never felt anything like it. Unable to control himself, he reclaimed her mouth, swallowing her breathy moans as she slid the device up and down. Leaning back, she rocked against his cock and the vibrator as their kisses dissolved into an exquisite symphony of moans and breath and primal cries. It was as if he'd entered her consciousness, knowing she was close, so close to meeting her release.

"You're there, plum. I feel it. Surrender to it," he bit out as she bucked and writhed, owning her do-it-yourself orgasm, not like a meek lamb but like a lion, taking and consuming as she rode the waves of her pleasure.

Breathing hard, she rested her head on his shoulder as he removed Mr. Rainbow Screamer from her grip and tossed it aside. He'd be taking care of her next orgasm.

"I did it," she rasped, her sated smile touching his heart.

He'd never wanted her more.

"Yeah, you did. And you did it like a bloody champion, plum. Forget about me being the beast. You're the lion of Rickety Rock."

Her countenance grew cat-like, and she looked him up and down—his female apex predator. "I think you're right," she purred, pushing onto her knees, then pressing his chest hard enough to have him flat on his back.

She shimmied out of her golden bra, then whipped off her shorts, and he shrugged out of his clothing in time for her to climb on top of him. He stared up at the raven-haired beauty cast in a hue of violet-blue.

Their energy.

Their aura.

"You are spellbinding, Libby Lamb," he professed, his gaze locked with hers as she sank down, welcoming his weeping cock.

And that's when their energy aligned—when the force that had him ready to take her hard and fast dissolved into the colorful haze.

There was no past or future, only the here and now.

He held her hips but allowed her to set the pace. With her palms pressed to his chest, she rose and fell, riding his cock. Her breasts heaved with every thrust, and like their first time, eye to eye, he lost himself in her. This wasn't who he was—well, it wasn't who he'd become. For years, sex was simply sex—a carnal release. There was no connection beyond where his cock entered their bodies.

Libby held him, mind, body, and soul. Their very beings spiraled, around and around. There was no end, no beginning, only the balance of their bodies moving together.

The sensual slap of skin on skin resonated, providing an erotic soundtrack that had him teetering on the edge. But he wasn't about to plunge into orgasmic bliss without her.

A bead of sweat trailed between her breasts, and as much as he enjoyed the show from this vantage point, his heart needed hers. He held her in place, then sat up as they returned to the yab yum position. Upright, his hard chest melded with her soft, smooth curves and the beat, the steady thrum that called out to him, set the tempo. His lips hovering above hers, his breath was her breath. His energy was hers. A circle of ethereal light encased them, holding their heat, kindling their desire into an inferno of raw need. He shifted his hips, altering the angle to work her tight bundle of nerves as his cock filled her to the hilt.

"We go together," he bit out between kisses.

"Always," she breathed, her lips meeting his as they careened over the edge. But there was no falling, only flying, gliding on the waves of energy. Pleasure held them in a rush of delicious rapture. He pistoned his hips like a well-oiled engine, lengthening their release until they collapsed into the pillows.

He tightened his grip on her body. "You're mine, plum."

For now.

But he couldn't say those two words.

She turned in his arms and caressed his cheek as unspoken understanding passed between them.

He got the message loud and clear.

There wasn't a forever for people like them.

There was only *for now*, and she wanted it, too.

TWENTY

LIBBY

"COME ON, Plum! Come on, Beefcake! Let's do this!" Sebastian called over his shoulder, laughing as he pedaled his mountain bike up the rocky incline on the meandering Crooked Mine Loop.

The trail, which would double as the Ass-in-Nine racecourse a week from today, was busier than usual. Competitors and their four-legged donkey friends had begun descending on Rickety Rock for the festivities that started up that evening. And it appeared many participants had decided to scope out the course and slip in a practice run before the sun went down.

Libby couldn't blame them. She surveyed the trail and the picturesque landscape. In the late afternoon light, the land came alive.

Who would want to be inside with views like this?

It was late July and summer was in full swing in the mountain town. Wildflowers blanketed the sides of Rickety Rock Mountain. They'd doubled or even tripled since she, Raz, and Sebastian had arrived. And they hadn't been spared the splendor across the valley in their Victorian on Falling Stone Road. Over the last few weeks, their little slice of heaven had become a feast for the senses. Vibrant shades of red, violet, and an array of golds and yellows burst through the mountain greenery. They cast the swaths of rocky terrain in a rainbow buffet of colors and scents.

"What do you say, Beefcake, you beastly wanker?" Raz teased, his tone breathy as he ran beside his donkey partner. "I know we've got this, mate. Do you think Plum and Libby can keep up with Sebastian?"

This man.

She acknowledged the challenge with a slight nod, and he tossed her what she used to call his infuriating beefcake smirk. Now the expression that once made her blood boil had her hot under the collar for a decisively different reason.

Did his handsomely self-assured face still make her want to throw vibrators at the mountain of a man?

Not exactly.

The urge to hurl sex toys at the boxer had subsided, but they hadn't completely forgotten about the sixteen vibrating projectiles.

When the lights went out, they'd found a better use for her devices that had nothing to do with her aim and everything to do with orgasmic bliss.

She shook her head, knocking some sense into her sex-addled mind.

Eyes on the trail. This was still a training run.

Libby tightened her hold on Plum's lead. She gave a sharp *hup-hup* and clicked her tongue, signaling to her Jennie that it was time to kick up the pace. She could not be distracted by thoughts of sexytimes with her beefcake. "Plum and I know what to do," she answered through shallow breaths as they rounded the bend. She clicked her tongue again, adding more speed.

Alongside Raz and Beefcake, they flew past a smattering of

aspen trees and a marker that indicated they were two miles away from the trail's technical descent. From here, they'd traverse the inclines, working their way up and down until they crossed the shallow part of the creek, dissecting the nine-mile Crooked Mine Loop.

She kept her gaze up, making sure Sebastian was a safe distance ahead of them on his bike, then chanced a look at Raz and found him stealing a glance at her. His smirk had been replaced with a grin that was only for her. There was nothing cocky or arrogant about it. This smile was boyish and heartfelt and resonated with stolen kisses and nights spent tangled in each other's arms. Sure, he could be the beast, but there was a tender side to the man—a gentle giant dwelling in his rock-hard, muscled body.

A breathlessness took over that had nothing to do with sprinting and everything to do with thoughts of their secret nightly rendezvous.

This had become their life in Rickety Rock.

They'd fallen into it like puzzle pieces clicking into place.

Augie would arrive at dawn, and he and Raz would spend six hours in the gym training hard. They followed a strict schedule. Augie had arranged for sparring partners to come to the house, and the trainer kept Raz on his toes with drills and weight training sessions. She and Sebastian didn't rise quite as early, but they'd take their breakfast outside onto the porch where they could watch and listen in on the training sessions.

And Buddha, help her. Gobbling down cereal next to her favorite almost seven-year-old while watching a shirtless Erasmus Cress move with raw power, his muscles slick with sweat and glistening in the morning light, was one cosmically sensational way to start the day.

Putting aside the fact that the man was truly a thick slice of hotness, her beefcake was athletic poetry in motion.

His focus and dogged determination were visible with every punch, every rotation of the jump rope, and each clang and bang of weights. Sounds that once made her want to bang the living daylights out of her gong now signified the man's resolve to win.

But that didn't mean she'd become professional boxing's biggest fan.

She still didn't like the idea of fighting and certainly didn't condone gambling as a pastime, but she viewed the sport differently now. With Sebastian explaining the maneuvers and breaking down the intricacies of the combinations, what once looked like a pair of men begging for brain damage had become a technical dance—a choreographed combat that required as much mental strength as physical prowess.

But her pint-sized partner in Pun-chi yoga wasn't always by her side. Sebastian attended the Bergen Summer Adventure Day Camp twenty minutes away in Aspen with Phoebe and Oscar during the weekdays. The trio were as thick as thieves, laughing and chatting as they waited to be picked up each day. And that led to another part of her day that put a smile on her face. There was nothing like watching the boy spot her in a crowd of parents, grin that sweet toothy grin, then run toward her, arms wide open, ready for a hug.

But she wasn't only the nanny.

She wore two hats in this household.

The frilly-sounding position of spiritual advisor Briggs had invented had morphed into the role of Pun-chi yoga coach.

And these sessions were no joke.

Augie had scheduled an hour a day of the budding practice, and she wasn't about to let him or Raz down. What had started as a game with Sebastian had become an offshoot of traditional yoga that literally and figuratively packed a punch. The practice fostered balance, core strength, and endurance, and she challenged Raz every day, training him to use his breath to channel his focus.

And he did.

He not only followed her instructions, but he also suggested punches for different yoga poses. On the surface, yoga and boxing appeared to be two diametrically opposed types of exercise.

But they weren't.

Not anymore—not with the two of them collaborating.

She'd lead him through a yoga flow, and Raz would suggest boxing elements.

This balanced approach had ushered in a balance within her—a centering of her chi that she welcomed like a long-lost friend.

Was it simply a tweak to her usual yoga regimen that had stabilized her life force, or was it something else?

Could it have been the power of three, the harmonious trifecta of energy created between herself, Raz, and Sebastian, that evened out her life force?

Or could it be the man who gazed into her eyes and spoke the words that set her body aflame?

You're mine.

With that statement, he'd stripped her soul bare and touched her heart, but the proclamation came with an unspoken caveat.

She would be his...until she wasn't.

Their stint in Rickety Rock would end in a matter of weeks.

What did the future hold for two self-professed loners in love?

She didn't have a clue.

All she had was this time in this place, and she wasn't about to waste a single second worrying. There would be plenty of time for that later. Luckily, their days were jam-packed, rarely giving her time to dwell when the questions arose in her consciousness.

And speaking of jam-packed days, the training didn't stop after their midday Pun-chi yoga session.

There was no time to lounge around after lunch.

That time was donkey time.

Maud and Wobbly Bob had shown them the pack burro racing ropes. Never in her life had she pictured herself jogging alongside a donkey. But now, she couldn't imagine hitting the trail without her sweet Plum. Sebastian was right. Donkeys were remarkably smart, undeniably affectionate, and exceptionally fast when they wanted to be. She and Plum had clocked a seven-minute mile—and they'd done it running uphill.

But it wasn't always an effortless walk in the park—or run on the trail, for that matter. Bob was on the mark with his *"the donkey knows"* words of wisdom.

The donkey really did know when it wanted to move, and it also knew when it didn't. But Plum, with her gray face and a fondness for chasing butterflies and Beefcake with his occasional bouts of passing foul-smelling gas, had brayed their way into their hearts.

Yes, even Raz's beastly boxer heart had opened to the animals.

Similar to the Pun-chi yoga sessions, Augie had worked the donkey runs into Raz's training schedule, and truth be told, this had become one of her favorite parts of the day. Raz and Beefcake shared an alpha energy like no other, and the banter between the beefcakes had her in stitches. Of course, Beefcake couldn't speak, but his grunts and whinnies communicated his bullheaded nature. These two loved to go at each other, which had educated her in the wide world of British insults, thanks to Raz's colorful language.

She cleared her throat as she formulated a zinger. "What do

you say, my sweet bird?" she sang in her best British accent. "Ready to splash out and show these plonkers what a proper burro racer looks like?"

"Nice one, Mibby!" Sebastian called, glancing over his shoulder.

Here's the thing.

She might be all about love and light ninety-nine percent of the time, but a part of her lit up when faced with a challenge. Not to mention, it was great fun to toss around the saucy British barbs.

The Brits could really craft an insult.

"Don't exert yourself too much, *Mibby*," Raz chided, going big bad boxer. "You've got to save some energy for our noisy yoga session tonight. You know how demanding the practice can be."

Her cheeks, already warm from running, now burned.

Yep, it didn't take a genius to figure that one out. Noisy yoga was the codeword for knocking boots.

If the daylight hours were for training time, the night was for like cures like benchmark maintenance, otherwise known as hot and dirty, noisy yoga.

Forget about red rooms with whips. They had nothing on the delights of crow figurines and shades of blue and violet.

It was safe to say that her O was back. And little Miss O had returned with a vengeance.

Now, the gal who'd fallen prey to an O hiatus was living on the apex of ecstasy and banging out Os almost as fast as Erasmus Cress could knock out a set of one-handed push-ups.

But fantasizing about what Raz had up his sleeve for tonight's noisy yoga sesh wouldn't get her through this training run. She lengthened her stride and sized up her beefcake.

It was time to throw a little shade his way.

"When it comes to exertion, we both know which one of us

is spent at the end of a noisy yoga session. News flash, it's not this plum," she tossed back.

And there it was, the back and forth—the playful banter that had her grateful she could go toe to toe with this beefcake of a boxer.

"It's almost time to cross," Sebastian cried as the creek came into view, and they began the descent down the trail's steep grade.

"Take it slow," Raz called. "We've got the Spar with the British Beast charity event in town. You'll get to see your old man dance around the ring, and you don't want to be soaked when you see your friends."

Her stomach did a little flip-flop. Raz's PR people had coordinated with Rickety Rock, and their friends were coming to town to check it out. Of course, she was happy to support the town and visit with her friends. But tonight was also a reminder that this time was quickly coming to an end.

"Got it, Dad."

Libby took a second to take in her fresh-from-the-trail mud-speckled legs. Luckily, Rickety Rock wasn't ritzy like its neighbor city, Aspen. Showing up on Main Street in muddied running gear was par for the course around here.

She kept an eye on Sebastian as they passed a mile marker. This stretch was the final leg of the Crooked Mine Loop. Once they crossed the creek, it was less than a mile to downtown Rickety Rock, which would serve as the start and the finish of the big race.

"*Hup-hup*," she called, signaling for Plum to pick up the pace, when another *hup-hup* rang out from behind. She looked over her shoulder as Doug, and his donkey racing partner, Ace, sprinted their way.

Oh no!

She glanced at Raz, but she didn't have to see the man to

read his reaction. She could feel the agitation rolling off him in crashing waves.

Raz hadn't exactly warmed to the guy.

"Bloody Dougie," he muttered under his breath.

"Namaste," Doug called, coming up alongside them. "Can you feel the pull of the vortex? It's giving Ace a little spring in his step." The man gave Raz and Beefcake a once-over. "Is everything okay with your burro? Did he get into the alfalfa?" Doug continued as his blond, flowing hair bounced like a shampoo commercial with each stride.

"Beefcake's fine, and we haven't given him any alfalfa. Why?" Raz grouched.

"He looks a little sluggish, that's all. Donkeys can pick up on your energy and mirror it. Just a little tip from your local donkey whisperer."

"More like donkey wanker," Raz grunted.

"What's that?" Doug called.

"I said—" Raz began when Plum emitted a well-placed whinny and cut him off.

"This day's got great energy," she chimed, ignoring the fierce vibe coming off her beefcake.

With Raz and Beefcake on one side and Doug and his burro on the other, she and Plum were stuck smack-dab between her benchmark guys.

"And the energy will be even stronger after the Ass-in-Nine race, thanks to the full moon that night," Doug continued.

"Oh yeah?" she replied, stealing another look at Raz and Beefcake. Both the donkey and the man were throwing eye daggers at Doug and Ace.

Hello, powder keg of psychic energy.

She could only hope it didn't blow.

She couldn't concentrate on the karma kinetics. She and Plum had to slow down. Besides the incline that came after crossing the creek, leading straight into Rickety Rock's town square, this was the second trickiest stretch of the loop. This section of the trail included a steep incline that, in the blink of an eye, dipped into quite a downhill run. It leveled out for the creek crossing, but it would be easy to lose control with the dramatic changes in grade and terrain.

"I have a question for you, Libby," Doug continued, his breaths coming hard and fast as the three racers ran side by side.

"What's that?"

"Do you have plans after the Ass-in-Nine? I wanted to see if we could hang out, just the two of us."

Really? Doug had to pick right now to hit on her?

She liked the guy. He was harmless—and clueless when it came to the whole benchmark situation. But she needed to focus on her footing, not play verbal footsie with the man.

Raz growled—the beast. But what did he have to growl about?

If anyone should be growly, it was her.

Erasmus Cress was the architect of the like cures like final benchmark. He was the one who'd suggested Doug. Sure, he looked like he'd swallowed a lemon when he'd done it, but it was his idea. And what was she supposed to say when he reversed course and threw out the twist of putting the defining bench-mark into the universe's hands? She appreciated the sentiment. She allowed the universe to guide her path every day. That was how she lived her life, but this Zen-Dougie-or-bust situation was like something out of a medieval romance.

If Doug wins the race, he wins her for the night.

If Erasmus wins...to be decided.

Ugh.

And nothing had been decided. Raz hadn't weighed in on the TBA O limbo situation. It had been easy to put this crazy proposition out of her mind when the race was weeks away. But here they were, seven days out, and neither had breached the topic...until now, thanks to Doug's invitation.

She caught Plum's eye and would have sworn the donkey cringed.

Could donkeys cringe?

If there was a time to wince, it was now.

"I haven't made any concrete plans for after the race," she bit out, her thighs burning from the exertion. They should be going slower, but Raz and Beefcake had picked up the pace, and Plum had followed suit.

Raz growled again.

The Lion needed to cool it.

She hadn't lied to Doug. And what did he want her to say?

Hey, Zen Dougie, if you win, I'm going to use all my womanly charms to sleep with you to see if you can rock my world and bring on the Os. And by the way, the growling beast running with Beefcake was the one who offered you up.

Yes, she wanted to make sure her O was back without the assist of Erasmus Cress and his magical cock.

Wait...

Or did she?

Everything had changed since she'd gone to the gym, and Raz had looked through her as if she didn't exist.

Now, when he looked at her, he devoured her with his eyes as if he were counting the hours until they were alone.

She and Raz had revealed the darkest parts of their souls to each other. She'd connected with the man on a level she'd never thought possible. She couldn't deny how happy she'd been these last few weeks. But it wasn't a forever happiness. She'd known this the moment after they'd made yab and oh, so yummy love. She'd looked into Raz's eyes and saw the truth. He wanted her, but there was still pain in his gaze. A pain that held him back. She wasn't that different. And yet, nannying for

Sebastian, creating Pun-chi yoga, learning to run with a donkey, and playing house with the man had felt like a life, a real life.

But it wasn't.

This was a transaction.

Her situation hadn't changed from the night she and Raz were arrested.

Raz had agreed to help her find her O, and she was here to care for his son while he trained.

This was about her needing a job and Anders and Alec needing tuition money.

It was a business deal.

A deal that had an expiration date.

"After I win," Doug continued, breaking into her thoughts, "we could take a hike up Rickety Rock Mountain."

Sweet Buddha's belly!

Doug dropped the *W*-word.

Win.

The rush of frenzied energy coming off Raz amplified tenfold. He'd gone from run-of-the-mill surly to super-charged beefcake mode in the blink of an eye. This wouldn't be pretty. It was one thing for Doug to ask her out. It was a whole different ball of cosmic wax to throw a competition wrench into the mix.

"You seem pretty sure about winning," Raz shot back, not missing a beat, as Beefcake quickened his pace.

"It's in my blood. My family's been racing burros here in Rickety Rock since the race started. And Ace is a strong partner. We shouldn't have trouble clenching the title," the man answered, patting the burro as they got closer to the creek.

"Are you up for some friendly competition now?" Raz tossed out. She could tell that he was going for nonchalance, but she heard the edge in his voice.

"Ace and I are up for it," Doug answered.

"We race to town. One mile. Go as hard as you can," Raz answered, setting the terms.

They had to be running a swift six-minute mile by this point. How much harder could they go?

"Do you want to put a wager on this?" Doug asked, lengthening his stride as she bristled. "Perhaps a kiss from the lovely Libby as the prize?"

She was no prize. Plum, sensing her irritation, released a huff of a cry as Libby parted her lips, ready to tell Zen Dougie where he could kiss her when Raz caught her eye. They shared a look—one look that spoke volumes.

I've got you, plum.

She could hear it as if she could read his mind.

"No bets, Doug. We do it for the glory. We'll go on your count, Libby," he answered, then gave her a glimpse of that boyish grin.

If they weren't rocketing down a mountain with donkeys, she would have kissed him.

"Thank you," she mouthed.

"I'm not always a beast," he answered.

Her pounding heart skipped a beat.

He wasn't.

"Are we going?" Dougie bit out, dialing up his pace.

Raz glanced past her, tucking away his sweet smile and sizing up his competition. "Absolutely."

The crackle and pop of air between the men couldn't be denied. She should tell the guys to knock it off. This was a training session. But psychic energy, like kinetic energy, was a curious thing. Often, it took less effort to let it work itself out rather than try to restrain it. And there was no holding back Raz and Doug now. Even their burros, breathing hard and gazes locked on the trail, seemed to sense the intensity of the moment.

Libby pulled her attention from the guys and scanned the

trail for Sebastian. He'd stopped not far from the creek bed. They'd taught him to never cross without them.

"Move to the side of the trail and wait for me, Sebastian. Your dad and Doug are going to pick up the pace," she called.

"Waiting on you, plum. We go on your call," Raz said, back to flashing her that secret smile—that expression that said, you're mine.

And again, the question hovered in her mind. Could she be his?

"Plum?" he rasped as time seemed to slow down.

Was the universe about to give her the answer?

She glanced from side to side.

The energy coming off the guys could melt iron.

Here goes everything.

"Ready," she called.

The men edged ahead of her.

"Set."

Raz peered over his shoulder and tossed her a cocky wink. With determination written on his face, she couldn't deny that the trait that had once driven her to bang gongs and throw vibrators was now quite the turn-on.

She tossed the man a little wink of her own, then let loose. "Go."

In that split second, the anticipation in the air shifted. The raw desire to win erupted, and the men were off.

TWENTY-ONE

LIBBY

STONE CHIPS and bits of dirt rose from the trail as the men took off, rocketing toward the creek.

Hoofs and feet pounding, the race was on.

Ace and Beefcake released a chorus of hee-haw battle cries as Raz, Doug, and the hyped-up burros charged past Sebastian. The men hit the shallow part of the creek with a force that sent sprays of droplets above their heads and splashes of water pelting their legs.

"Go, Dad! Go, Beefcake!" Sebastian cried. "And Dougie, the wanker, you can—"

"Sebastian," she called, cutting him off as she and Plum jogged up to the child.

"Sorry, Mibby, that's the *pun* in me getting riled up."

"The pun in you?" she repeated, biting back a grin and guiding Plum toward the shallow water as Sebastian got onto his bike and rode alongside her.

"The *punch* part of pun-chi yoga. That Doug makes me want to kick things and punch my dad's heavy bag."

Like father, like son.

"Are Dougie and Dad racing?"

She stared down the trail and the dust settling behind the burros. "Something like that."

"Do you think Dad will win?"

Her silly heart wanted to say yes—yes to not only him winning, but yes to a yearning she had to ignore.

And she knew what Raz was doing.

This wasn't any old race.

The man was testing the waters, or in this case, the burro racecourse, to get some insight into his opponent.

Did he want to win because it was his nature, or was it more? Was it the prospect of her and Doug together, or simply her and anyone else that got him hot and bothered?

"Oh, no!" Sebastian exclaimed before she could reply. His mini beast scowl had changed to a look of surprise.

"What is it?" she asked. Now on the other side of the creek, she led Plum onto the trail, watching the boy closely.

"Dad and Beefcake will be wet. They ran across the creek like they were being chased by a bear, and water went everywhere."

Thanks to the slight increase in elevation, crossing the creek at this point was akin to trudging through a puddle. But anyone who's seen an excited child dash into a shallow body of water knew exactly what could happen. She looked ahead as the half-soaked men, side by side, disappeared into the heavy foliage.

"Yep, they're pretty wet. But they'll dry out," she commented.

"But we weren't supposed to get wet because we're meeting everyone in town to watch my dad pummel some bloke in the ring."

Spar with the Beast.

She'd almost forgotten they were expected in the town square—and their friends would be there to greet them.

"Luckily, it's so dry in Colorado, he'll probably dry out pretty quick."

She checked her watch.

They'd purposefully timed their donkey run so they could arrive in town a little before the boxing event. They wanted some time to say hello to everyone before Raz was expected on stage, or in this case, in the mock ring Briggs had constructed. Despite being twenty minutes away from where Penny and Rowen and Charlotte and Mitch were spending the summer with Phoebe and Oscar, the hectic training schedule she and Raz had to keep had kept her from spending time with her girls. A quick text, here and there, was all she could manage over the last few weeks.

"I wonder if Dad's going to knock the bloke out?" Sebastian mused, dismounting from his bike and pushing it along as he walked beside her.

"It's not like that, Sebastian. Your dad won't be knocking out anyone. This is for fun to raise money for Maud and Wobbly Bob's donkey rescue. Your dad will be in the ring with the person who donated the highest amount to the charity. It's not a fight but more of a photo op."

Sebastian patted Plum's neck, and the sweet Jennie nuzzled the boy with her nose. "We'll have to give the donkeys back to Maud and Wobbly Bob, won't we?"

She could hear the sadness in his voice.

"We'll have them for your birthday party. That will be fun."

"But then it will end. We don't get to keep the house or the animals, do we?"

It was as if a stone had dropped in her belly. "I don't think so. All we can do is be grateful for the time we have," she replied, trying to infuse optimism into her reply but falling short.

"Can we stop walking, Mibby?"

"Are you tired? Do you need a break?"

"No, I need to put an intention out to the universe. You know, like we do after morning yoga," the child answered, resting the mountain bike on the ground.

"Okay," she replied as the boy's expression grew serious.

Sebastian closed his eyes, raised his arms, and touched his thumb to his index finger on each hand, creating a mudra. "You and me and my dad belong here with the donkeys. I'm making this my almost-seventh-birthday birthday wish slash intention. I'm bundling them together." Sebastian squeezed his eyes closed like he was mustering up as much psychic energy as he could. "And one more thing, universe. I'd like to keep Mibby. If I had to put my intention wishes in order, I'd say I'd want Mibby, then Plum, then Beefcake. Beefcake's last because he farts so much, but I still love him like I love Plum and Mibby. What do you think of my intention?" Sebastian asked, opening his eyes.

Libby swallowed hard, not sure if sweeter words had ever been spoken. But how was she supposed to answer? She'd fallen head over heels for the boy. It wasn't hard. He was a terrific kid. Their connection had been immediate. The car ride over to the park had solidified her feelings for him. From that moment on, Sebastian Cress had occupied a place in her heart, but she didn't have an answer to the what-came-next part.

"Mibby, what do you think? Do you think the universe heard it?"

She nodded, willing her eyes not to tear up. "I do."

"And do you think that means we'll stay together like we are now?" he pressed as his stomach rumbled.

Saved by the belly.

"I think this mountain biking has made you hungry," she replied instead of answering. "And if I remember correctly, Maud mentioned there would be a hot dog tent in the square tonight."

At the mention of food, Sebastian's pensive countenance brightened. "Phoebe's gonna go right bonkers over that."

She tapped his nose playfully. "Yep, I think you're right. It's a good night for eating hot dogs." It wasn't as if she wanted to brush off Sebastian's earnest intention or evade his question. It was that, despite knowing better, a piece of her heart wanted the same thing.

They continued down the trail quietly, listening to the gentle clop of Plum's hoofs meeting the path.

"Hey, Mibby?"

"Yeah?"

"Why were my dad and Dougie racing? When they ran past me, my dad looked scary. He was making his boxer lion face, and Dougie was puffing his cheeks like he was giving it all he's got."

Another doozy of a question.

How was she supposed to answer this one?

In a quest to find my lost O, your dad and I are in a physical relationship to maintain the quality of my sexual response, and Doug is the final test to see if my O decides to stick around.

Um...there was no way she was dropping that explanation.

"A butterfly," Sebastian remarked, and again, she was saved from formulating another answer.

Plum, bless her donkey heart, noticed the butterfly and tugged on the lead.

"Let's follow the butterfly, Plum," Sebastian suggested, getting back on his bike and pedaling beside the donkey as they picked up speed.

"Easy, girl," Libby said, patting the Jennie's neck. They'd gone from a meandering walk to a brisk running pace in a matter of seconds. She clucked her tongue, trying to get the burro's attention, but Plum had locked in on the insect. A gust of wind thrust the butterfly forward, and the motion elicited an enthusiastic cry from the burro. They picked up more speed, chewing up the trail.

Left, right, left, right.

Libby concentrated on the rapid beat of her feet striking the ground.

Slow down.

"I've never seen Plum move so fast," Sebastian called, pedaling furiously.

Neither had she.

She tugged on the lead, beckoning the donkey to slow down but to no avail. They flew down the trail, passing couples out for an evening walk. Gaining more and more speed by the second, panic flooded her system as they rounded a bend, and the lights from Rickety Rock's town square came into view. Complete with a makeshift boxing ring for the night's event, the place was packed with people milling around, securing their donkeys, and coming and going from the many food tents scattered on the periphery of the square when a realization hit.

If she didn't get her donkey under control, their entrance wouldn't be pretty. There was a good chance they'd careen into the crowd like a freight train.

She eyed the butterfly. "Fly away, little insect. Go find a nice flower." She wasn't one to wish harm on nature's creatures. Still, she'd be A-OK with a crow swooping in and picking off this renegade butterfly riding the breeze like a fluttering kamikaze paraglider.

"Easy, Plum. Slow down, girl," she called to the burro, her voice going up an anxious octave.

But the Jennie didn't stop. Dust built beneath them as the burro team sliced down the path.

"Sebastian, steer clear. I can't get Plum to stop," she said. The one saving grace was that the trail had widened, giving ample distance between herself and the child.

"Make way!" Sebastian yelled. "Runaway donkey coming through!"

Truer words had never been spoken.

Libby tightened her grip as the breeze died down, and the butterfly flitted away into a smattering of golden sunflowers. She tugged the lead, but Plum gave no indication of slowing down.

Think, think, think.

She couldn't let go of the lead and allow Plum to charge into the crowd, but she sure wasn't doing much to slow her down. She glanced around. There weren't any trail offshoots they could take to give the donkey more space to run. There was nowhere to go but down into the bustling square.

Stay on your feet, Libby Lamb.

Her pulse raced, and her breathing grew ragged and uneven. She dropped her gaze, focusing on the rocky trail. There was nothing left to do other than hold on and pray people would see them and get out of their way. But what about the children? There was a kids' tent right next to a hot dog tent. She parted her lips, prepared to start screaming at the top of her lungs when a rolling British accent that sent a tingle down her spine cut through the crunch of hoof and foot meeting rock and gravel.

Her frazzled nerves calmed a fraction at the sight of Raz sprinting toward her.

"Sebastian," the man called to the boy, who had dutifully stayed by her side. "Ride ahead. Your friends are at the bottom of the hill. I'll help Libby with Plum."

"Righto, Dad," the boy answered as Raz slipped his hand around Plum's bridle.

"Wham, bam, where you headed in such a hurry, ma'am? This is some real speed racer action," he cooed, peppering the air with his infuriating *wham-bams* as he ran alongside them.

"Are you talking to Plum or me?" she got out between sharp breaths.

"The question's for both my girls. I didn't think my plums would be so desperate to see me. I've only been gone a few minutes," he teased.

And, hello, this was not the time for making jokes!

"We could use a little help putting on the brakes. A butterfly caught her eye, and I can't get her to slow down," she bit out as tents with the words Jumbo Hot Dogs and Kids' Crafts emblazoned on the sides grew closer by the second.

They could not collide with a hot dog booth.

The last thing she needed was another viral video containing her and cock-shaped items.

"All right, old girl, ease up. Take a breath, inhale the peaceful mountain air, and exhale your butterfly mania," Raz cooed—actually, cooed. "Focus on your breath, donkey. Balance your chi. Clear your subconscious. The donkey knows," he purred, rattling off the yoga-infused burro speak. But it wasn't his words that mattered. It was the pleasing cadence of his voice. It washed over her, steadying her pounding heart.

And she wasn't the only plum affected by Raz's voice. The burro whinnied as he whispered sweet donkey nothings in her ear. Plum's swift gallop slowed to an easy walk as she gave Raz a saucy little bray—the flirt.

"There we go," Raz said, scratching between the donkey's ears.

Libby stared at the intact tents and breathed a sigh of relief as the adrenaline in her veins had begun to recede. "You certainly charmed Plum."

"I guess that makes me a plum charmer," he tossed back.

The man wasn't wrong.

"You see," he began with a cocky glint in his eyes. "I've been studying yoga. That's where I got those fancy words to calm the beast."

"Is that so?" she replied, playing along.

"The teacher must be rubbing off on me," he added, flashing a panty-melter of a grin.

She cocked an eyebrow. "She must be some teacher to rub off on a beast like you."

"She's the best thing that's happened to me in ages." He looked away. "I mean, I'm glad you're all right. You're okay, yeah? You didn't twist your ankle or stub your toe?" he asked, dropping the cheeky cocky act.

"I'm fine, thanks to you." She tried to get a read on him when a familiar voice called to her.

"Wow, Libby, you can really move with that donkey!" Phoebe Gale called, skipping toward them with a hot dog in each hand and another tucked under her arm. "You were running faster than Raz and that golden-haired guy."

"Debatable," Raz uttered, trying to play the role of the self-assured joker, but he couldn't hide the look in his eye that gave him away. The man was shaken, even off-kilter. He'd flown in like her white knight, but now something was off.

"And who got to town first, Phoebe? The golden-haired guy or Raz?" she asked.

In the runaway donkey melee, she'd almost forgotten about the impromptu battle of the donkey beasts.

"Go on, Phoebe, tell Libby what you saw," Raz said with a slight shake to his voice.

She looked him over. "Are you okay?"

He nodded as Phoebe waved the hot dogs.

"Here's what happened. I was eating my third hot dog," the girl whispered, then glanced around as if the hot dog police might jump out at any moment. "And then, I looked up and saw them. They were zooming down the trail super-duper fast like they had rockets hooked up to the donkeys."

"And..." Raz coaxed.

"And Raz was the first one off the trail."

If she wasn't shaking from the donkey catastrophe, she would have done cartwheels across the square. Instead, she adjusted Plum's bridle. "I see. And where's Doug?"

"He needed to get back to the donkey rescue since Maud and Bob are helping with the festivities," Raz answered.

"Did you part on good terms?"

Raz shrugged.

That was a no.

"Raz was smiling when I came up to him, and he let me give Beefcake a hot dog bun." Phoebe's expression darkened. "And then he looked up and saw you and got really scared."

"Did he?" Libby asked, studying the man.

"Yeah, he was happy, and then he turned the color I turn when I eat too many cookies. But Raz didn't throw up like I always do. He started running up the trail."

Raz cleared his throat. "It wasn't quite like that."

Phoebe took a bite of the hot dog. "Yeah, it was, and you said more. You said, I'm not losing my girl again. And I said, Libby's not your girl. You have a boy named Sebastian."

My girl?

She glanced at Raz. He was doing his best to hide it, but the runaway donkey situation really frightened him.

No, it was more.

The thought of her in harm's way had scared him.

"Where is everyone, Phoebe? Where's your uncle and Sebastian?" she asked, drawing the focus away from Raz.

"They're with Beefcake, over by the place where there's water and stuff for the donkeys. When Sebastian zoomed down on his bike, he saw Oscar and rode over."

Libby checked the donkey corral and spied Sebastian, safe and sound, with their friends. The group had missed the excitement and were chatting with Maud and Wobbly Bob.

"Would you like to lead Plum over to them, Phoebe?" she asked, needing a moment alone with her beefcake.

Phoebe stuffed the rest of one of her hot dogs into her mouth to free up a hand. "Yeah, I can do it," she answered as she chewed.

"We'll be over in a minute," she said, handing the child the leads, then turned her attention to Raz. "I didn't mean to scare you."

"I'm fine, plum," he said, shifting his stance.

He didn't look fine—not even close.

He cleared his throat. "Be careful, all right? I can't..."

"I'm okay," she said, trying to meet his eye, but he kept his gaze trained on the ground.

"What would have happened if I didn't see you? It's dusk. It's getting darker here in the shade of the mountain, and it's even darker on the trail. I can't be everywhere, Libby Lamb."

"I know," she answered, pressing her palm to his chest. His heart thundered beneath her touch.

Her beefcake released a heavy breath. "Plum, I couldn't take it if—"

"Look who decided to show up," Mitch called, cutting Raz off.

She glanced past Raz. The group was headed their way. She dropped her hand from Raz's chest. With his back to the crowd, no one could have seen her touch him. And she didn't want to give Sebastian the wrong impression.

"I told you they were here," Sebastian chimed.

Libby surveyed the group. Penny and Charlotte were here with their plus twos, Rowen, Mitch, and of course, the kids, but Harper didn't seem to be with them.

"Can I go get a hot dog?" Sebastian asked.

"I'll take care of this," Phoebe announced, taking Sebastian by one hand and Oscar with the other. "I'll make sure the boys eat."

"And how many hot dogs have you had, Phoebe?" Rowen asked, raising his eyebrow skeptically.

"Not enough to vomit," she replied, hauling the boys toward the tent.

"We'll drive home with the windows open," Penny said gently, patting her fiancé on the back as he held his head in his hands.

"Are you okay, Libbs?" Charlotte asked. "Sebastian mentioned you and Plum were having some trouble slowing down."

"I'm fine. Plum loves to chase butterflies. She got caught up in the moment chasing one. That's all, but we're both safe and sound," she answered, chancing a look at Raz. A muscle ticked in his cheek. The runaway donkey episode scared him more than he was letting on.

"Are you sure it wasn't Raz's face that scared the donkey?" Mitch commented with his signature Mitch smirk in place.

Raz puffed up. "Don't you start, you cheese toastie eating wanker."

"Mitch has a point," Rowen added with his own nerdy grin in place. "I don't know how Libby can stand to train you every day. And what's that about?" the man asked, gesturing to Raz's mud-speckled legs.

And just like that, Raz's darkened aura lightened.

"It's called training, and it's something you can't do with your arse in a chair, staring at bits and bobs floating around on a screen," Raz tossed back, loosening up as she felt his energy shift.

Yep, thanks to Rowen and Mitch, Raz was coming back from a dark place.

Rowen stared at the boxer, then studied the donkey corral. He tapped Penny's shoulder. "I have an idea for a new video game."

Penn gasped. As the head video narrative writer at Gale Gaming, the nerd spoke her love language. "What is it, honey?"

"Erasmus Cress, Donkey Boxer," Rowen announced.

For a beat, no one said a word until Raz doubled over, laughing as he waved off Rowen.

"That would be a hell no, mate! Not a chance of that happening. Donkey Boxer? What'll it be? Donkeys, standing on their hind legs with boxing gloves?"

"Now that's a terrific idea," Penny beamed, pulling a notepad from her bag and jotting down the idea.

"I was kidding," Raz stammered, looking positively dumbstruck, but Penny and Rowen pushed on.

"I could definitely write a compelling story about a donkey, and maybe Harper could help with the music—Landon, too," Penny exclaimed, scribbling away.

"Babe, type the notes on your phone. Then I can see them," Rowen suggested, eyeing the pad as if Penny were writing on a stone slab.

"Sometimes, my brain requires paper and pen," Penn replied, chewing her bottom lip as she continued with her notes.

Libby chuckled. She loved seeing her friends in their new love-filled lives, but thoughts of Penny and Rowen evaporated when Raz touched her arm and moved in closer.

"Are they serious? Donkey boxing?" he asked under his breath.

"Who knows," she answered, grateful to get the words out. With Raz's hand at her elbow, every cell in her body screamed for her to lean into him like they did when the house was quiet, and it was just the two of them.

"Where's your friend with the mouth and snappy comebacks?" Raz asked, glancing around the square. "I'm sure she'd have something to say about donkey boxing."

Libby surveyed the square. "Yeah, where is Harper?"

"I've been texting her. We invited her up, but she never responded," Char replied.

Penny dropped her pad into her tote and nodded. "It's like pulling teeth to get her on the phone these days. I'm not sure what's going on."

"Is it her grandma?" Libby asked.

"I texted her asking just that last week. She said her grandmother was doing as well as could be expected. But that was the last time she responded," Char answered.

Mitch wrapped his arm around Charlotte's shoulders. "It's been the same with Landon. I even checked to see if there was a boy band former teen heartthrob event happening in the city. But I came up with nothing. I don't know what's up with the guy."

"He hasn't responded to my calls either," Rowen added. "So, I made a bot that scanned every Landon Paige fan club page to see if there was a recent sighting."

"You made a bot searching for Landon Paige?" Mitch asked, raising an eyebrow.

Rowen cocked his head to the side and stared at Mitch. "Yeah, how else do you find things?"

"I'm just saying, that's a lot of effort," Mitch replied.

A smug grin graced Rowen's face. "How long did it take you to search the internet and read a few posts?"

Mitch shrugged. "I don't know. Twenty minutes. I might have spent ten of that reading about Landon's hit records. The guy's had major success in pop music. Not my thing, but people seem to love him."

Rowen adjusted his glasses. "It took me five minutes and nineteen seconds to scour three point two million sites. And while the bot was deployed, I read a fascinating article about Landon's record sales. Years ago, the guy was considered the top pop heartthrob in Eastern Europe and Italy—they love him there."

"Bullshit," Mitch blurted.

Rowen pulled out his phone, tapped the screen, presenting the results.

"Landon Paige Eastern European and Italian Pop Heart-throb," Mitch read. "Huh, who knew?"

Penny crossed her arms and pegged Char with her gaze. "I'd say my nerd wins the Landon Paige search competition."

Charlotte copied the movement and lifted her chin. "I disagree. It's about effort, and Mitch spent twenty minutes researching because he cares about his friend."

"You may be pushing the whole friend part, babe," Mitch uttered.

"I have to respectfully disagree with you, Char," Penny tossed back, ignoring Mitch. "It's about efficiency, and Rowen got it done, quick and dirty."

"Mitch likes to savor the experience," Charlotte countered with a sly grin.

Okay, that got naughty fast.

Libby met Raz's gaze, and he leaned in toward her. "They're talking about..."

"Yep, knocking boots," she whispered back, stifling a giggle.

"Yeah, I can't let my mind go there," he whispered. "I'll take care of this, plum," he added, giving her that sweet, boyish smile.

She looked on as the man sauntered over to stand between the dueling women.

"Okay," Raz said, eyeing Penny and Charlotte. "I genuinely like you, ladies. You've got fight in you, and I can respect that, but I can barely stomach your fiancés. These blokes are a bunch of wankers, and the thought of them..." Raz cleared his throat.

"Thought of them doing what, Raz?" Charlotte asked, sweetly observing the boxer.

"Yeah, Raz, what do you think we're talking about?" Penny chimed.

Libby pressed her fingertips to her lips, trying to hold back the tumble of laughter. She could watch her girls take Raz to task all day long.

"Well," her beefcake began with another nervous throat clearing. "Libby thinks you're talking about..."

"Now you're bringing me into this?" she teased. Libby stared down the mountain of a man as Char and Penny came to her side.

Raz tugged at his collar, then turned to Mitch and Rowen. "They're tiny, but they're bloody scary when they gang up like that."

"You haven't figured that out yet? These women are a force to be reckoned with," Mitch answered as he mooned over Charlotte, gazing at her like she'd invented grilled cheese sandwiches.

Libby glanced at her girls, taking comfort in their presence, then felt Raz's gaze slide back to her.

That beefy dreamboat of a smile teased the corners of his lips. "I'm starting to see that."

And...swoon.

And hello, ethereal blue-violet aura. The color pulsed in the air. Light and flowing, it connected them. Raz's gaze shifted, and he scanned the empty space around her. Sweet disbelief registered on his face. He saw the color shimmering in the mountain air. She wasn't one to bet, but if she were, she'd put everything she had on that assumption.

"Good, you're here," Briggs grunted, lurching forward and holding his stomach. "The winner of the Spar with the Beast has arrived, and Maud and Bob are ready to start."

"Are you feeling okay, Briggs?" she asked.

He removed a handkerchief from his pocket and blotted his forehead. "I ate something that might not be sitting well with me. It was so delicious. I couldn't stop eating."

"What was it, Briggsy?" Raz asked, assessing the man.

"Seafood, Rocky Mountain seafood," the agent replied, then released a breathy burp.

Mitch cocked his head to the side. "We don't have seafood in this part of the country."

Briggs scratched his chin. "I don't understand. I ate three platefuls of what Maud and Wobbly Bob called Rocky Mountain oysters. They were fried and had an odd sort of taste to them for seafood."

Mitch sucked in an audible breath. "Buddy, that wasn't seafood. You ate three plates of deep-fried bull testicles."

Briggs stood there, wide-eyed. "Pardon me, but it sounded like you suggested that I consumed the testicles of a bull."

"Yeah, you did," Mitch replied. "Those are Rocky Mountain oysters. They're a delicacy out here."

"But oysters are in the sea," Briggs whimpered, turning greener by the second.

"Not in Colorado, they're not."

Briggs covered his mouth and convulsed a few times. "I need to return to my room. Can you handle this event without me, Erasmus? It's only local press—none of the heavy hitters are here."

"Yeah, no problem."

"Just jump in the ring, smile for the cameras, and play nice. No funny business," the agent cautioned.

"When in the bloody hell have I ever done anything remotely close to funny blooming business? There's nothing funny about me," Raz tossed back, going into beast mode.

"There was the incident with the devices," Briggs answered, waving her way as he stammered between convulsions.

Raz shrugged. "Right, that."

"Be the benevolent lion. This is good PR. Silas Scott's been —" The agent burped, stifling his statement.

"Been what?" Raz growled.

"Just mouthing off. It's not your concern. Your job is to train. I'll take care of the PR circus. That is, after I..."

"Get rid of three plates of bull testicles?" Mitch asked with a wry grin.

"Something like that," the agent sputtered. Doubled over, the man staggered through the crowd.

"Will he be all right?" Raz asked as the group watched the sports agent disappear.

"Yeah, he'll be fine. Rocky Mountain oysters are delicious. I wouldn't hoover three plates of them. It's probably the shock of consuming mass quantities of bull testicles," Mitch answered.

"Honey, you should probably stop saying *bull testicles* so loudly," Charlotte cooed, patting Mitch's cheek as the screech and blare of speakers coming to life reverberated through the square.

"Hello, folks! Welcome to our first Ass-in-Nine event happening here in Rickety Rock's town square. I'm Bob Askew, and this is my sister Maud," Wobbly Bob announced from the center of the ring, then handed the microphone to Maud.

"We're excited for tonight's event, Spar with the Beast. We'd like to thank the former heavyweight boxing champion and soon-to-be burro racer, Erasmus Cress, for agreeing to this charity event."

The crowd erupted into cheers as Raz nodded to Maud and Bob.

"That's my dad," Sebastian called. He, Phoebe, and Oscar had positioned themselves up high on one of the carts holding the donkeys' hay. Double fisting hot dogs, the trio had a terrific view of the ring.

"And before we bring up Erasmus," Maud continued. "I'd like to introduce the individual who donated twenty-thousand dollars to Rickety Rock Donkey Rescue."

A young man emerged from the crowd with blond hair. The guy sported a T-shirt and a stylishly bro-tastic wannabe GQ haircut she recognized. He slipped through the ropes and climbed into the ring.

A chill spider-crawled down Libby's spine.

It couldn't be.

The man turned, the lights hit his face, and Libby gasped.

It was him.

"What is it, plum?" Raz asked. "You look like you've seen a ghost."

Her jaw dropped, and disbelief coursed through her veins. "It's him, Raz. It's—"

"Meet our winner, Derrick Dawson," Maud announced, cutting her off. The four syllables of the man's name rang out like water hitting hot coals.

Libby stood there, speechless.

"Tonight, Derrick," Maud continued, "you'll spar with the beast."

TWENTY-TWO

LIBBY

LIBBY STARED into Raz's eyes and watched as the realization sank in.

"That's him?" Raz said, gesturing with his chin. "That's one of those Derricks—the fake venture capitalist blokes?"

"Yes, and the first thing he asked me to do when I walked into the conference room was to turn around and bend over," she uttered, the words tasting like dirt. Memories of the sheer mortification of that day flashed through her mind. She seethed, recalling the Derricks' stupid smug faces—a trio of spoiled bros, toying with the hopes and dreams of young women in the quest to meet hot chicks. The absolute creeps. At least she'd scared the hell out of them with her power of three curse and gong skills. But it didn't make the humiliation pill any easier to swallow.

"Oh my gosh, Libby! That's the guy?" Penny asked.

Libby scanned the area around the ring and got another unwelcome surprise. "Yeah, and those guys with their phones out are the other two Derrick bros." She turned to Raz, expecting to find the man stone-faced or a little ticked off.

Oddly enough, he wasn't.

He grinned like an idiot, but there was a fire, or perhaps mischief, behind his twinkling eyes.

"Raz?" she said, concentrating on his bizarre expression.

"Yeah, plum?"

"What are you going to do?"

His grin widened. "Charity work."

What did that mean?

Libby shared a look with Penny and Char. Her friends stood there, wide-eyed, still staring at the Derricks.

"What are the chances?" Charlotte uttered, shaking her head.

"Want me to hurl a spatula at them?" Mitch asked, eyeing the food tents.

"Or I could hack in and ruin their credit or put them on the FBI's most wanted list," Rowen offered.

Libby swallowed past the lump in her throat. "You guys know about this, too?"

"We told them, Libbs," Penny answered. "They were as upset about it as we were."

"We're ready to tear these guys apart for you, Libby. Say the word," Mitch added, craning his neck to investigate another food tent, presumably in search of spatulas.

"Or if you think ruining their credit would be going too easy on them, I can pull out my phone and arrange for them to be sent to a Siberian prison camp," Rowen added.

Libby's gaze bounced between Mitch and Rowen. "You guys aren't fooling around."

A wicked smile bloomed on Mitch's lips. "I spied a spatula. There, in the rocky mountain oyster tent."

"No need for scrotum cooking utensils or high-tech cyber hacking skills, Mr. Nerd and Mr. Spatula-Obsessed Chef," Raz countered, as cool as a cucumber. "While I'm sure Libby appreciates the sentiment, you, my bloody prick chat mates, can sit this one out. The beefcake can handle it."

"I told you he called it that," Rowen said under his breath.

"I call it man chat," Mitch murmured.

"Do you really?" Rowen asked. "I never thought to name our group text."

"Yeah, keep it simple, but add an emoji for a little pizazz. I like the middle finger. It's edgy," Mitch continued, pulling out his phone.

Libby shook her head. She didn't have time to focus on the men's adventures in texting, not with Raz's statement swirling in the air.

The beefcake can handle it.

It didn't sit well with her.

"Raz, I don't need you to fight my battles."

She watched the man crack his knuckles, clearly not taking heed of her statement. The beefcake! Didn't he understand? She was an independent woman. She'd built her life around *not* needing a man in her corner, and she couldn't have him getting in trouble either. This was a charity event. And despite Derrick being a colossal asshat, he had donated to the donkey rescue. She pressed onto her tiptoes, gathered the fabric of Raz's T-shirt in her hands, and pulled him toward her. He needed to know that she meant business.

"This isn't your fight, Erasmus."

He cocked his head to the side. "Your fights are my fights, plum."

"Wow," she breathed. She wasn't expecting that.

Could he mean that?

And more than that.

If he did mean it, could she accept it?

Could she trust in him?

Was that what was going on here?

She stared into his gray eyes, and while there was a touch of homicidal maniac glinting in there, she saw something else that scared her even more.

Devotion.

The emotion radiated around them in a blue-violet cloud.

"You can't maim him or leave him requiring immediate medical attention," she whispered-shouted.

He made a sourpuss face. "I can't?"

"Of course, you can't!"

"I'm teasing, plum. He'll be fine, more or less."

More or less?

"I'll let the universe guide me," he added as euphoric energy circled him like a psychic tornado.

"Erasmus Cress, will you join us in the ring?" Maud called, her voice echoing through the square.

"Duty calls," the man crooned, then tucked a lock of hair behind her ear.

She tried to order her thoughts. "Wait, you should know one more thing about those guys—the Derricks."

"And what's that?"

"They're betting on Silas Scott to win. News of your fight being broadcast on Pay-Per-View pinged on their phones while I was with them. They started talking about it. I didn't know what they were going on about at the time, but now…"

He nodded, and his syrupy smile widened. "They're fans of the Irish Snake. Good to know, plum," the man mused, nodding like he was cooking up something wicked.

She chewed her bottom lip. "Maybe that wasn't the smartest thing to tell you when you look like you're pondering bodily harm."

"Libby Lamb," he said in that voice that made her core clench.

"Yes?"

"Namaste," he purred. And sweet Sanskrit, the word had never sounded dirtier.

"Namaste, and please try to channel healing into your metaphysical orbit to counter your cosmically crazy vibe. Remember, there's a vortex in this town. There's a good chance it can amplify emotional responses," she said, sounding downright crazy herself with that word salad.

He flashed her that arrogant grin, and hello to another round of core clenching! "I don't know what half of what you said means," he replied, then tapped the tip of her nose. "But I like hearing you say it."

This beefcake!

"This isn't a joke, Raz."

"I'm well aware. I told you, the beefcake can handle it."

That was one heck of a to-be-determined statement.

She released his shirt and looked on as he sauntered toward the ring like a jaunty gunslinger traipsing into a Wild West saloon.

Okay, universe, throw this gal a bone.

The last thing she needed was another viral video.

She turned to her friends. "So...I'm not sure how this will play out," she offered, working to put a bright spin on the bizarro situation.

Mitch stared up at the ring. "I can tell you one thing. This night got a lot more interesting."

That was one way to put it.

Libby looked over her shoulder and caught Sebastian's eye. He jammed a bite of hot dog into his mouth, then waved to her, and she breathed a sigh of relief. Raz wouldn't do anything monumentally bad to the douchebag donkey donor in front of his son.

He wouldn't.

He couldn't.

But her beefcake was generating a psychic truckload of alpha-infused energy.

Anything was possible with an aura like that.

No wonder they called him the Lion. There was no missing his King of the Jungle vibe.

Was it what she usually went for?

Not at all.

Her usual guy was more of a Zen Dougie type.

Was it hot as hell to feel those alpha vibes crash over her like she'd driven into a pure male magnetism car wash with the top down?

Every tittering chakra in her body said, oh, yes!

"Let's move in closer," Penny said, taking her hand.

The group worked their way to the front of the crowd and snagged a spot against the side of the ring. From here, they could see and hear everything. Libby's heart beat a mile a minute as Raz helped Maud and Bob exit the ring, and more and more people gathered around for the show.

Raz picked up the mic. "Good evening, everyone, I'm Erasmus Cress. I'd like to thank my sports agency and Maud and Bob Askew for putting the Spar with the Beast charity event together. It's been a pleasure spending time in Rickety Rock. The donkey rescue is a worthwhile organization, and I am thrilled to help support it."

Libby's hammering heartbeat slowed a fraction.

So far, so good.

Raz was in his element. This is what he did. He was a professional athlete. He knew how to walk the walk. He could play the game.

Raz retrieved two pairs of boxing gloves from Maud then helped Derrick put his on.

"I figured Raz would jump in the ring and punch the guy's lights out," Char whispered.

Libby nodded. "Me too."

She surveyed the large crowd gathered around the ring. Many held up phones, filming and taking pictures.

She had to get used to the fact that any moment could go viral.

Raz slid on his pair of gloves, then set his sights on Derrick Dawson. "You donated twenty thousand dollars to the donkey rescue, mate. Is that right?" he asked, circling the man like a shark.

"Twenty grand is nothing for me," Derrick crooned in reply.

Libby listened to the banter, hanging on to every word. It was a good idea to move up close to the ring. This way, if it went sideways, at least she'd know thirty seconds before the rest of the world did.

She set her sights on Derrick Dawson. The bro ran his glove-covered hand through his expensive haircut and sported a self-satisfied grin, blissfully unaware that there was a good chance he'd leave the ring with a limp. He glanced at his friends, then paraded around like a guy who'd never set foot inside a boxing ring.

"So, you're a philanthropist?" Raz asked, baiting the man.

Derrick's swagger lost a little steam. "It wasn't exactly my money. My dad's company donated in my name. You know how it goes. He wants the best for me."

"I do know how it will go. I know exactly how it'll go," Raz replied like the Cheshire cat, luring Derrick in. "Are you ready to get your money's worth and spar with the British beast?"

"I was hoping that for donating twenty large, you'd let me land a shot or two," Derrick said, hamming it up for his friends by bobbing around like an over-caffeinated buffoon.

"Those your mates?" Raz asked, eyeing the Derricks.

"Yeah."

"How are you boys doing?" he asked, then scanned the

crowd and found her. He grinned that slightly insane smile and tossed her a wink.

She tried to read him but couldn't.

Was that a *see-I'm-playing-nice* wink, or was it a *just-wait-and-see-what's-going-to-happen* wink?

She was about to find out.

The two Derricks tittered and whooped, jostling between pointing their phones at Raz and then at themselves. In the space of ten seconds, they had to have taken three hundred selfies.

"How about this, *Derrick*," Raz announced as the crowd grew still, hanging on the boxer's every word. "I won't move my feet, and you can have two free swings at me. But in return, I get one shot at you."

"Are you guys getting this?" Derrick called, vibrating like an electrified toddler.

"Focus, Derrick. Take the punch," Raz chided, planting himself in front of the man.

Wild-eyed, Derrick Dawson pounded his gloves together, reared back, then let loose.

And what did he hit?

Nothing but thin mountain air.

With the grace of a Prima ballerina, her giant, muscled beefcake angled his shoulders and deftly dodged the first punch.

"Come on, spaghetti arms. You've got to have more than that," Raz goaded.

Derrick Dawson's features hardened. He shot a glance at his friends, then raised his gloves. Back to bobbing like a buffoon, the guy threw not one, not two, but three rapid-fire punches.

Swish, swish, swish.

Derrick missed again, and again, and again.

Libby watched with bated breath as a lightness took over, and a tantalizing tingle popped and fizzed in her chest.

Maybe she was a boxing fan.

She knew one thing for sure.

Derrick Dawson was simply no match for Erasmus Cress, and she liked it.

A lot.

Like, a lot, a lot.

Butterflies erupted in her belly.

She could watch Raz knock the bro down a few pegs all day long.

The noodle-armed Derrick swung again and again, grunting with exertion.

But it was no use for the grand Derrick douche canoe.

Her beefcake had gone into champion boxer mode. As if he were channeling a Zen master, Raz's torso glided side to side, flowing with his chi as he evaded the punches. She couldn't take her eyes off the pair. It was as if she were watching the scene play in slow motion.

Raz be nimble.

Raz be quick.

Derrick Dawson's ass, Raz, please kick!

Her beefcake was the epitome of boxing perfection, and she was there for it.

"Let him have it, beefcake!" she howled, banging her hand on the ring's padded floor as Penny, Char, Mitch, and Rowen joined in.

Derrick Dawson pouted like the spoiled bro he was. All he needed now was a sad trombone rendition of the *wah, wah, wah, wah* disappointment soundtrack. At his pathetic failure to land a punch, his jaw dropped, along with his gloves, and his cheeks grew scarlet.

Raz tossed her a mischievous smile, then set his sights on the man. "Hey, Derrick?"

"Yeah?"

"How's the venture capitalist life treating you?" he growled.

"What?" Derrick shrieked, confusion marring his features.

And that's when Raz went in for the punch. In the space of a breath, he got the guy right in the solar plexus.

Pop!

It wasn't a hard hit. She'd been watching him train. The tap he administered to Derrick Dawson would barely sway the heavy bag. Still, the bro stood there, frozen with the wind knocked out of him, as the crowd expelled a collective gasp.

"Ooh," Wobbly Bob said with a wince.

Yeah, ooh, was right.

Raz grinned at the audience. "Don't you worry. Derrick's only playing around, aren't you, boyo? All he got was a tap to the diaphragm. What a great sport you are, mate. Look what twenty grand gets you. This man knows how to spar with the Beast," Raz finished as cameras flashed, illuminating his shit-eating grin.

Derrick tried to nod, but the man was well and truly stunned—and chasing his breath to boot.

Raz met her gaze, then leaned over like he was listening to something Derrick had to say. He nodded, then took a stroll around the ring. "Listen to this, folks. Derrick has a request. He wants me to invite my Pun-chi yoga coach into the ring to demonstrate a few of our moves. It turns out he's a huge yoga fan. What a banger of an idea!" he exclaimed, slipping off his gloves.

And sweet chakra pie, what did he say?

She stared at the man. "No, Raz, I can't," she whispered.

"You've got this, Mibby!" Sebastian cheered.

"It is for charity," Charlotte offered, biting back a grin.

"Do it for the donkeys," Penny added. "And give me your phone. I'll hold it for you and take some pics for Anders and Alec. They'll get a kick out of this."

"Go on, Libbs!" Charlotte coaxed.

Libby peered at Sebastian, grinning and whooping. "Yeah, okay," she answered, still dazed as she handed over her cell and took in the surreal situation.

What choice did she have?

She glanced at the array of people with their phones out, snapping pictures and taking videos. Her gaze bounced between Raz and the winded Derrick Dawson. Wide-eyed and still sipping shallow breaths, he couldn't speak a word.

Raz leaned in toward Derrick again. "What's that, Derrick? You and my coach Libby Lamb are old chums?"

Old chums? Raz was laying it on thick.

The boxer turned to the crowd. "Let's give Libby a nice welcome. Libby, Pun-chi, Libby, Pun-chi!" the man chanted. And sweet Buddha's belly, everyone in the square joined in.

"Go on, Libby," Bob called, his white beard twitching as he waved his hat in the air.

"Okay," she answered nervously as Raz slipped out from under the ropes. He took her hand and helped her into the ring.

"You can thank me later. Let's see some wham, bam, Libby Lamb fireworks," he whispered.

This man.

"What do you think you're doing?" she whispered.

He shrugged. "You know how Madelyn calls herself a facilitator of fate?"

"Yes."

"Tonight, I'm keen on being a facilitator of karma," he answered, that rolling British accent massaging the hell out of the words and sending a bona fide zing through her body.

"Karma," she echoed. She stared at Derrick, who glowered at her.

"She's the yoga bitch who cursed me and my friends," the guy rasped. It was faint, but she'd heard it loud and clear.

Even gasping for breath, the guy was a certified spoiled brat.

However, this nugget of knowledge ushered in a dose of divine insight.

Like a haze dissolving into the night air, Derrick Dawson's wellbeing no longer took center stage. If anyone on the planet could use a dose of his own medicine, it was this entitled jerk.

A heady sensation took over. It was time to join Raz and get in on facilitating a karma whiplash.

The universe was all in for unleashing her off-the-cuff power of three curse.

And who was she to argue with the metaphysical?

Like a yogi with a grudge, she inhaled serenity and exhaled sweet revenge.

Sensing her shift in energy from meek yogi to conniving super villain, Raz puffed up and manufactured his signature cocksure smirk. "Our Derrick Dawson is in for a treat," he began, addressing the crowd. "As practitioners of Pun-chi yoga, it's our sacred duty to assist this fine gentleman in achieving inner balance and harnessing his chi. It's the least we could do after the man donated so generously to the donkey rescue ranch."

The crowd roared, eating it up.

Raz circled the ring, then stopped behind her. The palpable pulse of energy between them and the heat coming off his body lit a fire in hers.

"We're doing him a favor, plum," he whispered. "You can give him a chakra tune-up or a cosmic kick in the balls. It's your choice."

A cosmic kick in the balls?

This man was speaking her love language.

With her chi balanced and her energy centers purring, she'd never felt freer and more deliciously devious in her life. But she had to play to the audience and maintain the appearance of the consummate yoga professional.

"I agree. It's the least we can do." She tapped her chin theatrically. "Derrick's energy is quite off-balance. Pun-chi yoga to the rescue," she announced, then waved in her boxer. "And you, Mr. Beefcake, get bonus points for using that fancy yoga lingo."

"You can show your appreciation during our noisy yoga session tonight," he tossed back.

That heady sensation working its way through her bloodstream morphed into a naughty tingle.

"Now, Miss Pun-chi Yoga, you've got a demo to do," Raz said, his breath warm against the shell of her ear. "And you need to get moving, plum. Derrick will be able to catch his breath soon, and I have a sneaky suspicion, he'll be a runner once he can get a little more oxygen."

It was payback Pun-chi or bust time.

She took a knee, looked Derrick straight in the eyes, then channeled her inner beefcake, flashing the winded bro her best shit-eating grin. "Namaste, venture capitalist. I've come to deliver on that curse."

TWENTY-THREE

LIBBY

CALL in the four corners and hold on to your hat. Miss Wham, Bam, Libby Lamb, the gong banging, donkey racing, spiritual guru was about to conjure up a karma cleansing.

Derrick Dawson groaned, his eyes relaying what his mouth couldn't.

He was completely and utterly mortified.

And even better than that. He was the one on display this time.

She turned to the crowd. "Since Derrick was so kind to donate to Maud and Bob's donkey rescue ranch. I'd like to demonstrate a Pun-chi yoga movement inspired by our dear donkeys, Plum and Beefcake."

Raz leaned toward Derrick, his hand to his ear, pretending to listen. "Derrick says, let 'er rip!"

Libby came to her feet, positioned herself in front of the winded man, and pressed her hands into a prayer position. "This Pun-chi yoga move is one of my favorites," she began, eyeing the two Derricks in the crowd. The bros stared up at her, completely gobsmacked. "It incorporates balance as well as an array of punches and even packs a special donkey surprise."

She glanced over her shoulder and looked Derrick Dawson dead in the eyes. Before he could protest, she hinged forward, executing a round of sharp jabs. She lifted one leg, bent her knee to a ninety-degree angle, then rocketed her foot into the air. Leading with her ankle, she executed a quick donkey kick movement—a movement that had her heel rocketing through Derrick's open stance and grazing his Rocky Mountain oysters.

"Oops!" she remarked as Derrick attempted to suck in a breath, his eyes bulging and his cheeks blooming scarlet.

"Oy, mate! You're supposed to move out of the way," Raz coached, slapping the guy on his back. "Dodge and evade, *bro*. And protect those Dawson family jewels. Don't you know anything about survival in the ring?"

Libby scanned the throng of onlookers. Penny and Charlotte held on to each other, shaking with laughter as Rowen and Mitch gave her two thumbs-up. The crowd whistled, clapped, and roared their appreciation. Even the donkeys took notice, braying and calling out. Raz raised her arm into the air—the victor. She hollered a hearty hee-haw, channeling her inner badass. Grinning like a psychic psycho, joy permeated every cell in her body. She caught Sebastian and Phoebe waving their hot dogs in the air as Oscar pointed his Polaroid camera her way and snapped pictures.

"How about your buddies?" Raz asked, waving for the two Derricks to come up as the cheers died down. But the men didn't move. Raz pointed to his ear again and pretended to listen to Derrick speak. "What's that? Your friends' daddies want to donate ten thousand apiece to the donkey rescue?"

The crowd went wild as a beaming Maud entered the ring. "What a demonstration. And what a night for jackasses. Rickety Rock Donkey Rescue thanks you, Derrick Dawson and your friends for your kind donations," the woman exclaimed for everyone to hear.

Libby clapped along with the rest of the crowd, absorbing the euphoric vibes.

Blame it on the moon. Blame it on the vortex. Blame it on the fierce blue-violet energy bouncing between herself and Raz. But whatever the trigger, a true cosmic reckoning had taken place.

But it wasn't over.

A quick flash of black from above caught her eye. She looked up as a crow sailed above the ring, gliding on the night breeze...and *splat*.

Derrick Dawson stared at his bird-crap-covered shoulder as a look of pure, repulsed horror marred his features.

"Karma can be a real bitch sometimes, can't she?" Libby cooed, then shifted her focus from the bro to the boxer. She stared into Raz's twinkling eyes, delighting in the rich violet and blue shades shimmering in the air.

"There it is," the man said, pride shining in his eyes.

"What?" she breathed.

"The fight. It's hidden beneath the love and the light, and, might I say, with a bit of bloody sexy psycho."

A wry grin bloomed on her lips. He wasn't wrong. She'd tapped into a vein of gloriously liberating crazy.

"You've got a lion vibe mixed in with your lamb," he added.

"You're just now noticing?" she tossed back when Derrick Dawson staggered forward. The man groaned as his friends helped him out of the ring, sliding him under the ropes like a limp noodle. The Tri-Derricks looked ready to bolt, but Raz jumped the ropes and blocked their exit.

"I believe you owe Ms. Lamb an apology," he said, his voice low and gravelly.

She climbed out of the ring and stood beside her beefcake. Solid and as balanced as she'd ever felt, their energy mingled, yin and yang, creating an impenetrable whole.

"Sorry," the Derricks lamented in unison like a trio of sullen schoolboys.

"For..." Raz coaxed.

The two Derricks stared at Raz and swallowed hard, sweat glistening on their brows, while Derrick Dawson moaned, holding his oysters.

"Let me help," Raz began, taking a step toward the men. "You're sorry for mistreating women and acting like a bag of dicks."

Libby raised an eyebrow.

Not bad.

Concise and to the point.

"Now say it," Raz demanded.

"We're sorry for mistreating women and acting like a bag of dicks," the two Derricks, who could breathe, parroted as Derrick Dawson nodded.

"Can we go?" Derrick Dawson eked out, staring at the poop on his shoulder.

"All we need is a credit card for the two bonus donations," Maud chimed.

"Toodel-oo, thanks to the jackasses for supporting the jack-asses," Raz sang out, waving as the Tri-Derricks followed Maud to one of the tents.

Libby eyed her boxer. "Toodel-oo?"

"I'm British," he offered with a cheeky shrug. "I can throw a *toodel-oo* out, here and there. It balances out the bag of dicks part."

She chuckled as the rush of the moment ebbed, and her hammering heart slowed. "I don't know what to say besides thank you."

He waved her off. But he still looked awfully full of himself. "I'm two for two."

"What does that mean?"

He held her gaze, and his perceptive gray eyes swallowed her whole. "I beat Zen Dougie in our practice race. And then I found myself uniquely positioned to help my spiritual coach exact some duly deserved vengeance. The universe seems to be telling us something, plum."

She could feel it, too. And the question she'd been grappling with danced in her mind.

Could she believe in it?

"And what do you think the universe wants us to know?" she asked, her words airy like flower petals carried on the breeze.

They stared at each other, and she tried to read him as his words echoed in her heart.

Your fights are my fights.

She shouldn't want that to be true.

"Mibby, Dad," Sebastian moaned, popping their angsty, universe-induced bubble. The boy's jovial demeanor had disappeared, and he rubbed his belly.

"What's wrong?" she asked, taking a knee in front of the child alongside Raz.

"It's a hot dog situation," Penny said as she and Char wove through the crowd.

Rowen arrived with Phoebe in his arms, and Mitch came up with Oscar in his.

"What happened, Sebastian?" Raz asked.

"Americans really like to eat a lot of hot dogs, and I couldn't resist either," the boy moaned.

"How many hot dogs did you eat, son?"

"Seven, because I'm almost seven," the boy answered, followed by a meaty belch.

"Come on, you," Raz said, lifting Sebastian into his arms.

"It's all fun and games until the hot dog situation goes awry," Penny remarked and rubbed Phoebe's back.

"We know that better than most," Rowen added.

"Yep, it's time to call it a night," Charlotte said, slipping Oscar's camera strap from his neck.

"I have something for you, Libby," Oscar mumbled wearily through a yawn, holding out a Polaroid. "I got a shot of you kicking that guy in the balls."

"Thank you, honey," she said, staring at the photo. He'd caught the moment the top of her heel grazed Derrick's naughty bits. With bulging eyes and a look akin to Edvard Munch's painting, The Scream, the man's expression was pure comedy gold.

Char peered at the picture. "Yep, that sure captures the evening for me."

"Never let me eat hot dogs again," Phoebe lamented, the back of her hand pressed to her forehead like a soap opera actress.

"We should head home, too, Libby," Raz added, pressing his hand to her lower back.

The contact sent a different kind of vibration through her— a natural comfort that bound them together. They were three people, ready to turn in for the evening, but the everyday simplicity of his words and the ease of his touch cracked open the door to the hopeful part of her spirit she'd kept hidden away.

This must be what it's like to click into a life so seamlessly.

"Do you guys want us to give you a lift?" Mitch asked.

Raz waved him off. "No need. There's a trail that leads straight to the back of our Victorian, and a little air will do Sebastian good. Not to mention, we have the donkeys with us."

"What about my bike, Dad? I think I'll puke if I try to ride it," Sebastian added through a whimper.

"It'll be here in the morning. Nobody will nick it in Rickety Rock. These aren't the mean streets of London," he teased as the boy rested his head on his father's shoulder.

"Oh, I almost forgot. Here's your phone, Libbs," Penny said, passing it over. "A couple of emails came in from a C.L. Investing while you were doing your demo. Is that a new business prospect?"

Libby replied with a skeptical huff. "It's probably more fake venture capitalist bros. Thanks for holding onto my cell, Penn."

"We'll see you in a week for the Ass-in-Nine," Charlotte called as she headed out with Mitch and Oscar.

"Nice job tonight, Libby. Good to see you, Raz," Penny added before joining her crew and disappearing down the block.

"We can't forget Plum and Beefcake," Sebastian mumbled, his sleepy words slurring together.

"Who could forget Plum and Beefcake?" Raz answered, rubbing the boy's back as he caught her eye.

And the real magic of the night revealed itself.

Sure, kicking a spoiled misogynist in the balls was a fantastic rush, but it didn't hold a candle to these quiet moments when it was the three of them.

They said good night to Maud and Bob, untied the donkeys, contented from chomping away on a buffet of fresh hay, and headed for the trail that led to the Victorian. It was another perfect Colorado night. The gentle burro whinnies combined with the echo of their steps crunching along the path and Sebastian's sleeping breath made for a peaceful lullaby. She stared ahead, and in the glow of the moonlight, she spied a stack of rocks off to the side of the trail.

"We're on the right path," Raz said softly, taking note as they passed the marker.

Was he talking about the trail or about them as a couple?

"We are," she replied, not exactly sure which question she'd answered when her phone pinged, cutting through the quiet.

"Do you need to check that?" Raz asked.

"I better look. It might be Penny or Charlotte." She slipped her cell from her pocket and frowned. "Never mind, it's nothing. Another email from C.L. Investors. I'm sure they're as legit as the Tri-Derricks." She peered at the screen and noticed the other emails. "Penny mentioned a few messages came in from them while I was in the ring with you and Derrick. It's probably another group of creeps," she answered, tucking the phone away.

"Who knows? You are Libby Lamb, Pun-chi yoga creator and spiritual advisor to arguably the best boxer who's ever lived."

"You forgot that this boxer is also the humblest athlete on the planet," she teased as Beefcake whinnied.

"Thanks, Beefcake. I appreciate the support, mate," Raz replied, shifting Sebastian to one arm so he could scratch the burro's neck.

The back of the darkened Victorian came into view, and the man chuckled.

"What is it?" she asked.

"If someone had told me ten years ago that I'd be spending the summer learning how to race donkeys through the Colorado Rocky Mountains, I would have bet everything I had that they were dead wrong." He paused. "Sorry, plum, I shouldn't have put it like that."

"It's okay. I understand what you mean," she replied as the door to the part of her heart containing that grain of hope cracked open a little farther. He got it. He got her. For Pete's sake, he masterminded the whole kick-Derrick-in-the-balls situation. That alone meant the world to her.

"I truly never thought I'd be doing anything like this, plum." He shifted Sebastian in his arms and pressed a kiss to the top of the boy's head. "I didn't think I could be this person," he added with a slight shake to his voice.

She understood him completely.

"They don't race burros across the London Bridge after teatime?" she asked, lightening the mood.

"Teatime?" he repeated, amusement infused in the word. "I didn't grow up in an episode of *Downton Abbey*. Sorry to disappoint you."

"No?" she asked, feigning mock curiosity. "Your granny Fin didn't have the servants ring a gong to inform you it was time to dress for dinner?"

"You and those bloody gongs," he said, shaking his head. "We didn't have much growing up, but we had enough. Granny Fin thinks this fame and fortune is a little over the top," he answered, gesturing in front of them as the back of the grand Victorian came into view.

"And what do you think about where you are in the world?"

She hadn't meant to ask the question. It slipped from her lips, and the words hovered in the sweet mountain air.

He glanced at her, and the moonlight highlighted his strong, angular jawline. "I'm beginning to think those stacks of rocks might be right."

What could she say to that? Her heart had one answer, but her head had another.

Shrouded in a comfortable silence, they followed the path that led to the barn. It didn't take long to remove the donkeys' bridles and secure them for the night. Plum and Beefcake sniffed the sleeping Sebastian, bidding the boy the donkey version of sweet dreams, then settled into their temporary lodging.

"Love you, donkeys," Sebastian murmured as they left the darkened barn. Like ghosts in the night, the trio silently passed the cottage, then made their way up the steps leading to the Victorian's back entrance.

She opened the door and held it for Raz, patting Sebastian's back as they entered the darkened house. Falling into step, they ascended the two sets of stairs that led to the boy's third-floor bedroom. Raz removed Sebastian's shoes and socks as she opened his window, allowing the wildflower-scented air to cool the space—the familiar nightly ritual as soothing as a mindful meditation. And it was a type of mindfulness—the three of them existing in a perfect bubble of mountain harmony. She remained by the window, admiring the moon as the curtains tickled her arm, fluttering like that renegade butterfly who'd sparked quite an adventure and had brought her beefcake sprinting to her rescue.

Sebastian mumbled something about hot dogs in his sleep as Raz tucked the boy into bed, and a single question percolated in her mind.

How would a guy and a gal, who'd each sworn off relationships, navigate the muddy waters of what came next? There was no doubt they shared lightning-hot chemistry. The question was, could they look past the for-now quality of this arrangement? Or was she foolish to imagine he'd want more beyond their like cures like experiment?

"I can hear you thinking from across the room," Raz said softly, coming toward her, the old floorboards giving a weary whine beneath his step. She pressed her hands to his chest, reveling in the solid wall of muscle when a cell phone rang, and a voice from below floated in on the breeze.

A voice she recognized.

"What is it, Tony? I'm waiting for my daughter. I can't be on the phone. I'll be back in Denver late tonight. We can talk over a beer in a couple of hours."

A pause.

"I wasn't lying. My daughter is working with Erasmus Cress. You saw the video and heard his fancy agent go on about it. I'm at their place now. They should be back any minute.

There was some event in town. It gave me a chance to peek around their training compound. It's something, Tony. The guy's got a state-of-the-art boxing facility here. Once they're back, I'll work the old Connolly Lamb charm and see what else I can learn about what he's been doing to prep for the fight."

Libby held Raz's gaze as the voice—her father's voice—grew quiet. Raz's expression hardened, and the man turned to leave, but she held on to his arm, keeping him in place. She sensed her dad's call wasn't finished. And as much as it hurt to listen to him cluck and boast about exploiting their relationship, she needed to hear every selfish word. A few seconds passed, and like she'd thought, her dad was back at it.

"Now, come on, Tony. You said if I gave you the inside scoop, you'd loan me a grand to put on the fight. I told you, my daughter's living with the guy and training him. I'm sure I can get her to introduce me to the Lion. Then I'll let you know if I think he's making a real comeback or not. Either way, we're making money off this fight. I can feel it."

A thousand stones sank in her belly, and the weight of being Connolly Lamb's daughter hung heavy, like an anchor pulling her down, down, down. She closed her eyes and did what she used to do as a girl. She pictured a beach on a Hawaiian Island with the swing swaying in the breeze. She could almost hear Shandra's voice cueing the next move in the yoga flow, gentle and reassuring, a balm to her broken heart.

Be the light, and always remember, love is stronger than any force holding you back.

Inhale peacefulness and exhale stress. Inhale love and exhale forgiveness.

Libby opened her eyes. She wanted to take Shandra's advice, but she couldn't exhale forgiveness.

Not for her father.

It was one thing to call and ask for cash, but coming here to spy on them was next-level duplicity. And she wasn't about to stand for it.

Ditching the mantras, she hurried past Raz, leaving Sebastian's room like a gathering storm, and flew down the stairs to the second floor.

"Do you want me to take care of him, plum?" Raz asked, taking the steps two at a time behind her. A muscle ticked in his jaw as his energy darkened—or maybe that was her vibe overshadowing his. She couldn't tell.

"He's my father. I'll deal with him."

"Then I'm coming with you."

She shook her head. "You heard him, Raz. He's here to snoop around. You don't have to give him the satisfaction of getting to tell his friends he got to meet the champion, Erasmus Cress. No, I won't do that to you. I'll tell him to leave on my own."

"Yeah, you can tell him, but I'll be by your side when you do it," the man answered, as stubborn as a mule.

She blinked back tears. "I don't want you to see this. I don't want you to think that I'm anything like him."

And there it was, the searing humiliation and the thunderous anger she'd carried for more than a decade. The burning resentment snarled and popped in her chest.

He ran his hands down the sides of her arms. "I know you're not like him, plum. I know who you are."

"But you're still coming with me, aren't you?"

He tipped her chin. "I meant what I said. Your fights are my fights."

There was such comfort in his words that his kindness alone nearly brought her to tears.

"Okay, but let me do the talking."

Without a word, he nodded, then gestured toward the staircase. Step by step, she gathered her resolve, hardening her heart.

When she reached the first floor, she was ready for battle. She flicked on the outdoor lamps and glanced through the window. In response to the blast of light, her father cried out, flailing his arms as a cascade of cracks and thuds added to the flurry of movement. She swung open the door, stepped onto the porch, and observed her dad bent over and working furiously to balance the stone stack he'd knocked over.

"There's my girl. I've been waiting to surprise you," her father said, glancing over his shoulder toward the gravel road that led to the Victorian. He must have assumed it was the only way to the house.

She crossed her arms and observed the man. It had been several months since she'd last seen him. He'd lost weight, and his clothes fit awkwardly on his slight frame. He smoothed his hair and straightened like a child gearing up to ask for something. She knew this song and dance well.

"We were in town and came in through the back. You must not have heard us."

"I sure didn't," he answered, shifting his stance nervously as the pile of rocks teetered, then tipped over again.

What a perfect analogy for the man.

Raz joined her on the porch, and immediately, she wanted to melt into his embrace and erase this part of the night from her memory.

"Well, look at that. It's Erasmus Cress. Hello, I'm Libby's father," her dad exclaimed, doing a crap job of faking surprise as he gawked at the man. He'd already started collecting intel for good old Tony, whoever the hell he was.

"Nice to meet you, sir," Raz said, his tone negating the nice part, but her starstruck father didn't notice.

"Oh, it's Connolly Lamb, but Connolly is fine," he blathered.

Connolly Lamb.

C. L.

It hit her like a wrecking ball.

Was this visit part of a grander scheme? Would he try to pump information out of her by pretending to be an investor?

Would he sink to that level of deception?

Would he?

He already had.

She'd heard him admit it on the call.

"What are you doing here, Dad?" she asked, her tone razor sharp. This was his chance. If he admitted he'd come to glean info on the championship match, it would turn her stomach, but at least it would be the truth.

"Your brothers mentioned you were spending the summer here. They told me about your new job working with Erasmus Cress."

Translation: He'd called Anders and Alec to fish for details about her situation.

"And?" she bit out.

"And...I was passing through town. I'm headed south. I'm on my way to Albuquerque for a job. Well, not so much a job... but an opportunity. A facility management position opened up, and a buddy of mine knows the owner."

Translation: The man was using all his tricks to butter her up.

There was no job opportunity in Albuquerque, Timbuktu, or in a galaxy far, far away for Connolly Lamb.

She would have known this even if he hadn't blabbed to his pal that he'd be back in Denver late tonight.

She stared at the man. "Are you the *C.L.* in C.L. Investing, Dad?"

Her father's brow crinkled. Confusion replaced his plastic smile as his attention bounced from her to Raz. "Libby, I'm here to see you. Can't a father stop by to visit with his only daughter?"

Each lie cut into her like a lash.

"Do you see that window on the third floor?" she asked, pointing to Sebastian's room. "I'm willing to *bet* you didn't notice it went from closed to open a few minutes ago."

She'd chosen her words carefully, speaking the only language her father understood.

He swallowed hard, the muscles of his throat constricting. "No, I didn't notice. I was...uh...checking the ball game scores on my phone. You know how I love sports."

Oh yes, she knew.

"And then your phone rang, and it was Tony," she continued.

Her dad stared at the pile of fallen rocks. "Sweetie, I..."

"Please don't call me sweetie," she interrupted. "I know why you're here. And I'll make another wager with you. I bet you'll be leaving empty-handed. It's such a shame you'll have nothing to share with Tony."

Venom dripped from her tongue.

How dare he lie to her face. Then again, why would she expect anything different? The good man, the man he'd once been when her mother was alive, had withered away. Each bet and every broken promise had transformed the man into a ghost of the father who used to give her piggy-back rides and take her to the petting zoo. She was ready to let him have it, to tell him to lose her phone number when Sebastian's cry quelled the rage churning in her belly.

"Mibby," he called, his sleepy voice cracking her hardened facade.

"Is that the kid? What's his name? Sebastian?" her father rattled off, excitement glinting in his eyes like he'd finally happened upon a morsel of information to feed his friend, a faux feather in his cap of lies.

Did the man not understand she saw through him? All Sebastian was to him was something to gloat about. She could see the whirlwind of questions whipping around inside her father's mind.

Was the boy getting in the way of the Lion's training?

Was that distraction enough to tip the scales and secure a win for Silas Scott?

She balled her hands into tight fists.

His piqued interest in Sebastian was the last straw.

"Don't say his name," she bit out, adrenaline firing through her veins.

"Mibby," the boy called again.

"He needs you. Go on. I'll be up after I see your father to his car," Raz said, his tone even as he pointed to where her father had parked his sedan, hidden behind a cluster of blue spruce.

She held his gaze—his remarkably steady gaze.

"It's all right, plum."

Without another glance at her father, she entered the Victorian, hurried up the stairs, and found Sebastian, twisted in his covers. The boy pushed up onto his elbow, blinking as the light from the hallway entered his darkened room.

"I'm here, honey. What is it?" she asked, kneeling as she untangled his leg from the bedsheet.

"I'm not in my pajamas," the boy slurred, half asleep.

"It's okay for tonight. Lie down and close your eyes."

Sebastian sank into his pillow. "Can we do the happy thoughts meditation?"

She nodded. She could use some happy thoughts right about now, too. "Here we go," she began, working to keep the shake out of her voice. "Take a deep breath, and picture a time when you were truly happy. Hold that feeling inside your chest, close to your heart."

"I'm riding my bike with you and Dad and Plum and Beefcake," he answered, the corners of his mouth turning up at the thought.

"Are you now?" she whispered as a torrent of emotions threatened to break through.

"Yeah, and I feel the happiness in my heart," Sebastian mumbled, pressing his hand to his chest.

She smoothed his hair, then rested her hand on top of his. Within seconds, the boy drifted back to sleep. His chest rose and fell as his features relaxed, and she exhaled the heavy breath she hadn't realized she'd been holding.

What happened next?

What would she say to Raz?

And what about her dad? The man had broken her heart time and time again, but he was still her father. She watched Sebastian sleep, taking solace in the peacefulness when her dad's voice cut through the quiet.

"You aren't calling the police, are you, Mr. Cress?"

What was Raz doing?

"No, of course, not."

"Then why did you take out your phone? I'll leave. I didn't mean to make any trouble."

Anguish coated her dad's words.

But it was a good question. What would Raz need his phone for?

"I'm sending a text, Mr. Lamb."

A text?

"Now give me your phone, sir," Raz directed, his tone curt but not cruel.

"Are you worried about pictures? Because I didn't take any. I swear. You can look. I'll show you right now."

She wasn't sure what was worse, her father's deceptive ways or the gut-wrenching desperation in his voice.

"I'm not looking for pictures. I'm putting a note in your phone. If you know what's good for you, you'll call the number and do everything the man on the line tells you to do."

"Who do you want me to call?" her father asked, his voice shaking.

"Just give the person your name, and he'll handle the rest."

"Mr. Cress?" her father blurted, his voice thick with emotion.

"Yes."

"Tell Libby I'm sorry. I haven't been the father she deserved. You see, I've burned a lot of bridges in my life, and I don't have many options. Aurora, Libby's mom, made me better. I know I've let her down. I know I've let everyone down, but I tried. I tried to do right by my kids."

She squeezed her eyes shut, holding back tears.

Did he know she could hear him?

Was that speech for her, or was that Connolly Lamb trying to save face and garner sympathy?

The truth is, she'd never know.

Still kneeling at Sebastian's bedside, she focused on the aquamarine gemstone and timepiece on the side table when a memory flickered. It was an image of her mother outside the community center, slipping a stone similar to this one into her pocket.

Or maybe it wasn't a stone.

It very well could have been her keys or a pack of gum. Her addled mind couldn't focus. It couldn't order the onslaught of emotions.

She released a shaky breath and listened.

And...nothing...until an engine turned over, and the grind of tires meeting gravel hung in the air, fading away.

Her father had left.

The front door slammed, and all she could hear now was the thump of Raz's footsteps.

It was over.

She pressed a kiss to Sebastian's forehead.

"Night, night, Mibby," he mumbled, turning onto his side.

She rose to her feet. With her body trembling and her heart racing, she started down the stairs. But after three steps, she stopped, afraid her wobbly legs might turn to Jell-O. Holding the rail, she lowered herself onto the step and cradled her head in her hands when the blue-violet aura edged out the darkness. She touched the smooth plank of wood where Raz had sat a few weeks ago. They'd opened their hearts to each other here, sharing their shards of pain. But it was one thing for her to tell Raz about her father. It was a whole different story to experience the man in the flesh.

Why couldn't he do it? Why couldn't Connolly Lamb have been the father she and the twins had needed?

The stairs creaked, and she glanced up to find Raz coming toward her.

"I'm sorry about that. My dad must be desperate," she said, staring at the floor. "He usually calls. It's never a good sign when he shows up."

"It's not your fault, plum."

She forced herself to look up. "I heard what you said to him."

He nodded and sat down next to her. "I figured you did."

"Who do you want him to call?"

"It doesn't matter."

"It does to me." She watched him closely.

"It's an opportunity to become a better version of himself."

What did that mean?

She couldn't work it out, not now, not with the cocktail of

humiliation, exhaustion, and frustration surging through her veins. And that's when the dam holding back the flood of pain and disappointment broke. Tears trailed down her cheeks, and she turned away from Raz just as he stood.

Was he leaving?

Was this too much for him, or perhaps he wanted to give her some privacy?

But he didn't go anywhere.

Before she could wipe the salty tears from her cheeks, Raz lifted her into his arms and held her close.

"You don't have to hide your tears from me, plum," he said, carrying her into her bedroom.

They'd spent every night in this room, limbs tangled and bodies writhing. But something was different in here tonight.

The energy had shifted.

He lowered her onto the bed, then went to the window and pushed the one crow curtain aside, allowing the light of the moon to bathe the space in a blue glow. She couldn't take her eyes off him as he shook out a quilt folded at the foot of the bed, slid in next to her, and covered them.

She rolled onto her side, and he mirrored her movement. They stayed like that, safe under the warmth of the quilt, staring into each other's eyes. Her heart swelled in her chest as she gazed at her beefcake, the former thorn in her metaphysical side who was now the man she...

Stop.

She couldn't go there—not now, not ever.

Raz cupped her face in his hand, then kissed the tears on her cheeks. "Picture a time when you were truly happy."

"What are you doing?" she whispered, swallowing a sob.

"What I listen to you do with Sebastian every night. I decided to add kissing to it. Do you mind—the kissing, that is?"

This man.

Fresh tears trailed down her cheeks, and he kissed them away.

"You don't have to do this, Raz. I'll be okay. I'm used to being disappointed by my dad. It just happened when I was feeling so..." she trailed off.

"What were you feeling, plum?"

How was she supposed to explain it?

One minute, she dared picture what a real life with him and Sebastian could be like. And the next, the universe had served up her father on a platter.

It had delivered the man to her doorstep.

But it wasn't her doorstep.

It was the doorstep of a rental home—a rented respite from the worries of making rent and supporting her brothers.

Sometimes the universe communicates silently through vibes and rhythms. Sometimes, it whispers its plan in the air. And then sometimes, it drives up to your house, snoops around, and breaks your heart.

Think of a time when you were truly happy.

"We know what happens if Doug wins the Ass-in-Nine. What happens if you win the race? You've never told me."

Why had she chosen this moment to ask him that? After the train wreck of an encounter with her father, she shouldn't care what Raz thought should or shouldn't happen. She couldn't entertain thoughts of making a life with this man or any man, not when the universe had just served up the ultimate reminder of why she had to guard her heart. But she couldn't quiet the little voice in her head, or maybe it was the pull of her heartstrings, the faint whispers asking one poignant question.

What if she could trust her heart to another?

The competing thoughts went back and forth in her mind like a game of mental tug-of-war.

Come on, chi. A little balance could help right about now.

"No," she breathed, pressing her fingertips to his lips. "I shouldn't have asked. You don't have to answer."

"I do. I owe it to you because the answer is you, Libby."

"Me?"

He stroked his thumb across her bottom lip. "You trust the universe, right? You believe it guides our paths?"

"Yes."

"Then we leave it there. If I win, you're meant to be mine."

The breath caught in her throat. Did he mean it?

"And if you lose?" She had to ask. They were in dangerous waters—at least, she was.

He tightened his hold on her, determination flashing in his eyes. "I thought you knew the answer to that by now."

"And what is the answer?" she whispered.

That self-assured beefcake grin spread across his lips. "I don't lose."

TWENTY-FOUR

ERASMUS

CAMERAS FLASHED, and Raz turned up the wattage on his grin. He glanced at Libby, sharing the spotlight with him today, and his heart swelled in his chest like a lovesick schoolboy.

But there was no fighting this feeling.

They'd made it to race day.

It was Ass-in-Nine or bust, and everything was on the line.

He couldn't have made it clearer. If he won, Libby would be his.

Had they discussed the nuts and bolts of what that actually meant?

Not exactly.

Over the last week, neither had brought it up, choosing instead to live in this perfect dreamworld where all that mattered was himself, Sebastian, and Libby.

But their time was up.

Today, they'd see if the universe was on their side.

Was he a fool to set the stakes so high?

Was he even capable of trusting himself with another's heart? And was Libby ready to give her heart to him?

He couldn't let those questions consume his thoughts—not minutes before the race.

He glanced at Libby, smiling as a photographer moved in for a close-up. She leaned in and nuzzled Plum for the shot. There was no denying that the woman handled the media like a pro. Then again, who couldn't help but fall under her spell?

He caught Briggs out of the corner of his eye. The man checked his watch. With the big fight less than two weeks away, the entire PR team descended on Colorado, and the group was working overtime to promote the event. "We've got a few more minutes for questions and photos," the agent announced to the mass of media clustered in the square.

"Mr. Cress, Ms. Lamb, turn this way so I can get the Ass-in-Nine starting line banner in the shot, please," a photographer called.

"Then look this way. We need a photo for the Denver Post."

"And here for BBC. Big smiles, and if the larger donkey wouldn't mind turning his head this way, I'd very much appreciate it."

Raz surveyed his beast of a burro. "The larger donkey's name is Beefcake, and good luck getting this beast to do anything he doesn't want to do," he said, patting his donkey's rump. Unfortunately, Beefcake had other things on his mind besides posing for the cameras.

He and his donkey had the same thing on their minds—well, sort of.

Currently, Beefcake had his sights set on Plum. The demure gray and white burro stood next to Libby as photographers and reporters surrounded them, snapping shots and peppering them with questions.

He used to find these events tiresome, but not today, not with Libby by his side. He could feel the positive energy coming off her in soothing waves, and he couldn't help but grin like an idiot, taking in the scene.

This London boy had grown quite fond of mountain life.

The town of Rickety Rock had gone all out for the big day. Ass-in-Nine flags in every color of the rainbow emblazoned with burros waved from lampposts, and a grand banner marking the start and finish of the loop swayed in the breeze. Race participants were scattered about, warming up with their burros, surveying the map of the Crooked Mine Loop, and getting in a final snack before the big event. Families milled around the square eating ice cream, taking in the animals, and participating in the flurry of kids' activities as a band played a jaunty tune setting a jovial tone. Anticipation crackled in the air, or maybe that was just him, ready for the universe to confirm what he already knew.

Libby was his.

He'd fallen arse over elbow for the raven-haired beauty, and he couldn't deny it any longer.

And hopefully, he wouldn't have to.

After he won, he wouldn't hold back. He'd even rehearsed a little speech.

Wham, bam, Libby Lamb, you're mine.

P.S. I plan on being the only man giving you Os from here on out.

P.S.S. Dougie is a right knob-headed mug of a plonker-loving twatwaffle.

P.S.S.S. Feel like having an O now? I'm game.

It wasn't poetry, by any means, but it got the job done.

After the incident with her father, his protective instinct had gone into overdrive. He'd shortened his training sessions with Augie to spend more time with Libby and, in turn, his son. Pun-chi yoga went from an hour a day to three. Their donkey runs turned into day-long hikes with Sebastian and a picnic in tow. They explored the trails, especially those that didn't have stacks of stones lining the sides of the path. They'd gone off the usual route and investigated weather-beaten barns, rundown mining structures, and picked wildflowers under the Colorado sun while the donkeys munched on wild grasses, birds sang out, and bees and butterflies crossed their path.

Yes, the British Beast, Erasmus Cress, bloody enjoyed frolicking in nature as well as arranging bouquets of fragrant bluebells, larkspur, and Columbine wildflowers.

He'd become a man of many talents this week.

But it was more than a shift in his schedule and his newfound appreciation for fauna and flora that had him walking on sunshine.

It was the remarkable company he'd been blessed to keep.

When he sat on the creek bank and looked on as Libby and Sebastian had a splash fight, his cheeks hurt from smiling. And in the evenings, when Libby put the boy to bed, he'd stand outside his son's door and listen for those precious words.

Picture a time when you were truly happy. Hold the feeling inside your chest, close to your heart.

There, in the darkened hallway, he couldn't help but follow along. With his hand pressed to his chest, thoughts of days spent with Libby and Sebastian bolstered his spirit. The man who'd once pegged yoga and meditation as a crock of shit now joyfully busted out a downward-facing dog and projected a positive aura.

Here's the thing.

Pun-chi yoga was no bloody walk in the park. He'd come out of the sessions covered in sweat with his limbs trembling.

But the heat he and Libby generated on the yoga mat was nothing compared to the raging inferno that burned once Sebastian was fast asleep.

He could barely wait to have Libby naked and beneath him.

Tangled together, writhing in ecstasy, he disappeared into the woman. All it took was one kiss, one touch, and the pain he'd carried these last three years evaporated into the sex-infused air. Sliding inside her, slowly filling her to the hilt, and the sweet, grinding rhythm of their bodies quieted the nagging voices in his head. With this powerhouse of a woman by his side and in his bed, he didn't have to face the ugly truth. Her brightness drowned it out. That blue-violet aura masked his darkness.

It was as if he were living an alternative life, and he didn't want to return to his miserable status quo.

And if he played his cards right, he wouldn't have to.

The photographers jostled in front of them, clamoring to get Beefcake to look at the camera. He caught Libby's eye as the barrage of flashes continued, and he knew that today, everything would change. He drank her in. With her jet-black hair pulled into a high ponytail and those sparkling amber eyes, the thought that had spiraled around and around in his mind over the last week solidified.

He didn't want to give her up, and he sure as hell wouldn't share her.

That's why he had to win this donkey race. He spied Doug and his burro Ace across the square.

Get ready to have your arse handed to you and your bloody ass.

Just like he'd told Libby the night when he held her and kissed away her salty tears, he didn't lose.

And he wouldn't be earning an *L* today.

Victory would be his.

He could taste it. And then he'd never have to think about Zen Dougie again.

Screw the benchmark screw.

"Miss Lamb," a reporter called. "Is there a reason you and

Mr. Cress chose to run the Ass-in-Nine race in honor of Denver's first responders?"

Raz raised an eyebrow at his burro racing beauty, curious about how she would answer that one.

Mischief glinted in Libby's gaze. "Mr. Cress and I appreciate their hard work. We're thrilled to show them our support."

"I agree," he chimed. "It's amazing what first responders encounter," he added, making Libby blush. He knew what she was thinking. Those encounters they had to deal with included arresting barefoot women and professional athletes for lewd behavior. Harrowing work, for sure, but he wasn't about to refresh the media's memory on that wild incident.

"Miss Lamb, tell us about your relationship with the Lion?" another inquired.

She stared at the reporter, her cheeks growing rosier by the second. "My relationship?"

"Yes, with Mr. Cress, as his Pun-chi yoga coach."

Libby looked him over, her eyes devouring his body. "Erasmus is an excellent student. Extremely compliant."

"Am I now?" he tossed back.

"You went above and beyond what I asked of you this morning," she purred.

And now it was his turn to have his cheeks heat up. He'd spent the better part of the early morning hours between her thighs, making her pant and moan with his mouth. If compliance meant tasting Libby Lamb before dawn, he was on board.

Nonchalantly, he brushed at the corner of his mouth. "That I did. I'm always up for the challenge of going above and beyond." He shifted his stance. *Dammit!* Thanks to the image of Libby's naked body spread out on the bed like a dirty breakfast buffet, his blood supply had headed south.

Bloody hell, he'd be especially challenged if he had to run nine miles with a giant hard-on.

"One last question. That's what we've got time for," Briggs said, staring at his phone and frowning.

"I've got one for Erasmus Cress."

Raz nodded to the reporter.

"Are you concerned that your *pseudo-training* with Miss Lamb will leave you unprepared to face the Irish Snake?"

There's always a knob.

Raz narrowed his gaze, hardening his expression. "No," he bit back. There was no need to say any more than that. This bloke was fishing, trying to provoke him. But he wasn't about to fall for it.

"There are reports you aren't spending as much time in the gym," the man continued, glancing over at Augie, but the stone-faced trainer didn't bite either. "And Silas Scott posted on social media," the reporter continued.

Ah, that's what must have soured Briggs' expression.

"And what wise words did the Snake share today?" he replied, sarcasm coating his response.

"He said that you should think about changing your name from the Lion to the Donkey—or the Jackass. His words, sir, not mine," the knob reporter added.

Bloody prick.

Raz stared the guy down. "It doesn't matter what they call me. My name could be Erasmus Cress, the Pussycat, and I'd still crush Silas Scott." Raz amplified his air of confidence. He could play the part of the badass boxer flawlessly, but that didn't stop the tiny voices from clawing their way back into his head.

Was the reporter right? Was he throwing it away? Was he disrespecting Mere's memory by altering his training?

Stop.

"That's your reply?" the reporter asked. "You believe you'll beat Silas Scott?"

"Without a doubt," he answered, ignoring the twist in his gut.

"That's it," Briggs announced. "Mr. Cress and Miss Lamb have a race to run."

Raz stared across the square and met Zen Dougie's gaze. "No, no, Briggsy, I've got a race to *win*."

"Sorry, our champ's got a race to win. And with that, thank you for coming out. Any questions regarding the upcoming championship fight can be directed to my associates. And a word of caution. If you're new to this part of the country, the Rocky Mountain oysters aren't from the ocean," the agent added as the media dispersed.

"How are you holding up, Briggsy? Keeping your distance from the food tents?" he asked, doing everything he could to maintain a breezy attitude—anything to get the reporter's words out of his mind. He couldn't let one question throw him off. He'd be ready. There wouldn't be a repeat of what happened a year after Mere's passing. There would be no panic attacks, no trembling hands, no gasping for breath on the bathroom floor. Thanks to Libby, he'd be as solid as an ox. He'd fulfill his promise to Mere. He could do it. He could be the best. He could have it all.

Briggs directed a few of his aides to speak with the different media outlets, then slid his mobile into his pocket. "I'm fine—a little smarter and a little wiser when it comes to my choice of lunch in Rickety Rock, that's for sure," the man offered, then threw a furtive glance at Libby. "Just so you know, that matter you sent my way has been taken care of."

"And?" Raz asked, keeping his voice low.

"And the offer was accepted."

"I appreciate your help, Briggs."

"What matter?" Libby asked. He looked over and found her watching them closely. But before she could ask another question, Plum lunged forward as a trio of butterflies flitted through the square.

"Whoa," she called, reining in the donkey. "What is up with the butterflies? I've seen more than twenty butterflies flit by in the last hour."

"Easy, now," he said, patting the Jennie's side. "You can chase the butterflies after the race." The donkeys were loaded with thirty-three pounds of mining equipment for the burro race. Plum's pack shifted from side to side as she whinnied and whined. While the old girl loved to chase insects, she never complained. Something had her keyed up. There was an odd energy about the day. Beefcake must have sensed it as well. He got in on the action, stomping his hoof and tossing his head. Raz followed his burro's line of sight and found what had set off his donkey. But it wasn't anything related to a vortex or the pull of the moon.

Dougie and his burro Ace had positioned themselves by the starting line. Ace craned his neck, looking at Beefcake just as Doug mimicked the movement to get a glimpse of Libby.

Enjoy the view while you can, boyo.

The wanker had tied crystals to his donkey's pack. But he'd need more than the psychic energy from a bunch of rocks to win today. Raz checked his watch. They had ten minutes until race time. He scratched behind Beefcake's ears. "Don't worry, you big blooming arse. We've got this."

"I'm going to find Luanne," Aug said. "Have you got this in hand?"

"I always have it in hand."

"Erasmus?" the man said, then threw a furtive look Libby's way.

"Yeah?"

"Remember what you're fighting for."

That was a bloody odd thing to say.

He understood what he was up against. Silas Scott would be a formidable opponent, and he needed to be ready to face him. And he would be—with Libby in his corner.

"Augie, Dad, the animals are acting crazy. I saw two donkeys rearing up on their hind legs, and look," Sebastian remarked, pointing to the sky. A flock of birds glided in on the breeze, swooped down, then circled above the square before breaking off in every direction. "They've been doing that all day."

"Interesting stuff, Sebastian. You be good now, lad, and help your father stay on track," Aug said, clapping the boy on the shoulder.

"I will, sir," the lad replied.

Raz cocked his head to the side, sizing up his trainer. Aug had known him for more than half of his life, and the man never shied away from speaking plainly. He couldn't make heads or tails of this cryptic language.

Aug said goodbye to Libby, then faded into the crowd as Maud and Bob waved.

"You're getting a taste of what happens in Rickety Rock when the vortex strengthens, and there's a full moon coming," Bob said as the pair surveyed the birds, making another loop above the square.

"Anything can happen under these conditions," Maud added. "But win or lose, Bob and I wanted to thank you."

"Thank us?" Libby repeated. "We should be thanking you. You both were kind enough to share Plum and Beefcake with us, and you showed us the burro racing ropes."

"That's much appreciated, Libby, but like my brother always says, the donkeys know. And they knew you'd do right by them," Maud countered.

"And the extra publicity has helped the town by leaps and bounds. We've never had this many folks sign up for the Ass-in-

Nine. Not to mention, the money you raised for the donkey rescue will allow us to build another barn," Bob crooned when a rollicking British accent cut through the air.

"What's this? Did I hear that my grandson is actually an upstanding member of this community? There must be pigs flying all over town along with these nutty birds."

"Granny, you made it," he exclaimed as the woman made her way toward him with Madelyn at her side. Her arthritis usually left her hobbling with a slight limp, but she walked smoothly across the square today.

"We arrived just now. Madelyn's driver is taking our things to the cottage on the Victorian's property."

"You certainly look prepared," Madelyn remarked, her red scarf flowing in the breeze as she assessed the donkeys. "And it appears Rickety Rock agrees with you."

"This donkey is Plum, and this donkey is Beefcake," Sebastian chimed, introducing his great grandmother and Madelyn to the burros.

"Donkeys are marvelous creatures. I had one growing up," Madelyn tossed out.

"You had donkeys growing up?" Sebastian asked as he took in the posh woman.

Good question! That nanny matchmaker was one hell of an enigma.

"I've lived an interesting life," the woman said with a coy twist of her lips. "Now, Finola, dear, I see two of my former clients. I'll leave you here with your family. I'm sure you'll be in good hands," the woman purred, waving toward the street where Rowen and Mitch and their families had pulled up.

He returned his attention to his grandmother. "Are you feeling all right? How's your hip?"

"Yeah, Gran, you're walking fast," Sebastian added.

"You've been keeping up with the yoga moves, haven't you?" Libby asked, embracing his grandmother.

"That I have. They've done wonders for me, and Madelyn and I have been walking every day. There might be something to this fresh air."

"And who is this lovely creature?"

Raz turned to find the question came from Wobbly Bob. The man had removed his cowboy hat and smoothed his white tangle of beard as he gazed upon none other than Granny Fin. The man might as well have had hearts in his eyes.

What the bloody hell was this?

"I'm Finola Cress, Erasmus's grandmother."

"Folks around here call me Wobbly Bob, but you can call me Robert or Robbie. That's what my Annie used to call me, but I've been a widower for twenty-six years now," the man sputtered, looking downright lovestruck.

Ew!

Robbie?

And was that Wobbly Bob's weird way of saying he was on the market? That he was bearded, single, and ready to mingle?

He chanced a look at Libby. She caught his eye and flashed him, *aren't they cute* eyes to which he flashed back, *bloody hell, no, they aren't!*

"You couldn't be Erasmus's grandmother—his sister, sure, but not his grandmother," Bob gushed.

Wobbly Bob was laying it on thick.

Maybe there was something to this crazy energy vortex scrambling brains.

"Take a breath, Raz," Libby said softly, watching him as she pressed her lips together, suppressing a grin.

At least someone thought this was entertaining.

"I'll take a breath when Wobbly Bob stops making moves on my granny," he mumbled.

"Granny, I've learned how to care for Beefcake and Plum," Sebastian began, and bless the lad for interrupting Bob, or *Robbie* that is. "I brush them every day and clean their stalls. They'll be here for my donkey birthday party. Libby says we can put hats on them," Sebastian reported, pride written on his face.

"Aren't they lovely creatures?" Granny Fin replied, patting Beefcake on the nose. "They look like the pictures you mailed to me in the post, Sebastian. And speaking of birthdays, let me look at you, lad. I think you've grown since I last laid eyes on you."

"And I'm stronger. I've been training with Dad and Libby. Check out my jab-cross." Sebastian widened his stance and knocked out the quick combination of punches.

Raz nodded to his boy. "He's a natural, Granny."

"Is he now?" his grandmother answered with a curious glint in her eyes.

"Five minutes. Racers and burros, please make your way to the starting line," Maud called.

Bob offered his arm to Granny Fin. "It would be an honor to escort you to the seating area. We have chairs and tables set up near where the race starts and ends. You'll get to see all the action by my side, miss."

"All the action? Aren't you a proper gent? I'd be delighted," his grandmother answered, rosy-cheeked.

Bloody hell. He'd never seen the woman blush like a schoolgirl.

"Good luck," his granny said, then turned to the lad. "And Sebastian, why don't you join us? You can tell me more about your donkeys."

"All right, Granny. I just need to do something first." Sebastian hugged Beefcake, then nuzzled Plum. "I love you, donkeys. Run fast," the boy instructed. He expected the boy to hurry along with Granny Fin and Robbie, the white-bearded suitor. But he didn't. Sebastian turned to Libby and wrapped his arms around her waist. "I love you, Mibby. I hope you win."

Love?

Libby pressed her hand to her heart. "I love you, too, so very, very much."

Raz caught his grandmother out of the corner of his eye. The woman glanced up like she was checking for rain, but there wasn't a cloud in the sky. Her lips moved, and he would have sworn she mouthed the words, *I kept my promise, Meredith.*

What was she talking about?

What promise had she made to Mere?

This psychic vortex business was doing a number on this town.

Emotion thickened in his throat at the thought of his wife, but he didn't have a second to ponder his grandmother's curious behavior. Sebastian was there, wrapping his arms around his waist like he'd done with Libby. "Good luck, Dad. Don't trip over a rock," the boy added, squeezing hard.

Raz exhaled a shaky breath. "You tell Libby you love her, and you hope she wins, and then you tell me not to trip over a rock?" He'd tried to inject a measure of playfulness into his reply. Still, between Granny Fin talking to Mere and Sebastian telling Libby he loved her, not to mention the like cures like benchmark hanging in the balance, suddenly, his life went topsy-turvy.

Sebastian waved him down. "We're both fighters, Dad, so we've got to look tough. Especially with the knobby wanker Dougie looking at Mibby like she's a pile of hot dogs. I don't like that bloke, but I would like a hot dog."

Raz scanned the starting line, and yep, Sebastian hit the nail on the head with that observation. The knobby wanker had his sights set on Libby. "Shifty one, isn't he?"

"You've got to beat him, Dad," Sebastian whispered conspiratorially.

"Consider it done."

"And, Dad?"

"Yeah?"

"I do love you...a lot. And I like seeing you every day. Can this be the way it is forever?"

Raz looked up and found Libby busy chatting with his grandmother and Wobbly Bob.

This race wasn't only a make-or-break situation for himself and Libby. Sebastian's heart was on the line as well.

He mustered a grin. "I'll see what I can do. And go easy on the hot dogs, mate."

"Come along, Sebastian," Granny Fin called. "It's time to get a spot to watch the race."

"I see my friends. They're already there," the boy chimed.

Raz inspected the area they'd roped off for the spectators. Yep, the whole crew had arrived. His entire bloody prick chat group was there with their fiancées and kids in tow. Even Landon had made it—albeit incognito, as always, with a ball cap pulled low.

A bell rang out, cutting through the hum of conversation and the twang of the band. "Three minutes until we start," Maud called.

"This is it," Libby said, her eyes glistening with tears. "We better head over."

"Are you okay?" he asked as they led the donkeys to the starting line.

"Sebastian means everything to me, and there's so much riding on this race with the whole benchmark situation. I wish I could fast-forward to the finish line," she replied, twisting Plum's lead in her hands.

"I know how much you care about Sebastian. I see it every

day. And I told you, I don't lose," he replied, needing more than ever for those words to be true when that damn Zen Dougie started waving like a maniac.

"Libby, there's room for you and Plum up here. Hurry, it's almost race time," the man called from the front of the pack.

Libby looked from the Zen douche and back to him. "I'm sure Doug means there's room for both of us."

"I'm sure he does," Raz muttered, knowing that the opposite was true as he and Beefcake followed behind, weaving through the mass of racers and burros. There was space for Libby and Plum to settle in on Dougie and Ace's right while he plodded through to make a spot for himself on Dougie's left—something Beefcake didn't like one little bit. Without Plum by his side, the donkey bristled, stomping and huffing.

Nobody got between Beefcake and Plum.

"Beautiful afternoon for a race," Doug commented. "I added amethyst crystals to Ace's pack to harness positive energy and good luck. But I really don't need it. Burro racing is in my blood."

"Yep," Libby replied politely.

Doug sized him up, then set his sights on Libby. "The offer is still open to get together after the race. I leave for Tibet the day after tomorrow, and I'd hate to not act on our connection."

Their connection?

There was no bloody connection.

"The universe brought us to Rickety Rock. You can feel it, can't you, Libby? The energy is calling out to us. I'd love to take you to my special vortex viewing spot."

Special vortex viewing spot?

What a heap of bullshit.

"Let's see how the race goes," Libby answered.

Raz tightened his grip on Beefcake's lead as the dueling male donkeys traded ominous brays and Plum set her sights on a pair of birds, frolicking in the air. The Jennie seemed oblivious to Ace and Beefcake's antics as they jockeyed for her attention.

Beefcake sidestepped, giving Ace a good shove.

Nice one!

Ace, in turn, opened his giant donkey mouth, groaned in protest, then snapped at Beefcake before craning his neck and rubbing against Plum.

The wanker donkey!

Watching this ass move in on his Plum proved to be too much for Beefcake. Beefcake lunged at Ace, sinking his teeth into the donkey's neck. Ace clinked and clattered as his array of purple crystals jostled like a beaded curtain. The beasts went back and forth, kicking up dust as the rabble-rousing animals engaged in donkey combat.

"Get your donkey under control," Doug bit out, straining to rein in Ace.

"Your donkey could use some bloody manners. Look at him, rubbing on Plum. She's not his. Beefcake had to defend her honor," he hissed back.

Doug huffed. "She could be his. He's donkey enough for her."

Raz leaned in. "Could not. She's Beefcake's girl."

"Plum is her own donkey," Libby chided as the male burros continued to clash, biting and snapping like two backstreet brawlers.

The men pulled their donkeys apart as Maud stood on a platform with a megaphone in one hand and a bell in the other.

"Welcome to Rickety Rock's Ass-in-Nine Pack Burro Race. Our competitors and their burros honor Colorado mining tradition by completing the nine-mile Crooked Mine Loop. There will only be one racing team crowned the winner. Runners and burros, this is it," Maud instructed.

Raz glanced over his shoulder. There had to be thirty teams, possibly more. But Doug and Ace appeared to be his main competition.

"We finish this on the trail," he said under his breath to Zen Dougie.

"The trail," the man echoed.

Raz barely had a second to meet Libby's gaze. Wide-eyed, she stared at him. This was it—the moment that would decide what happened next for them.

The universe was about to cast its verdict.

Libby would be his, or she wouldn't.

"Three, two, one! Go, Ass-in-Nine!" Maud called, ringing the bell over her head.

In a blur of dust and hooves and pounding feet, a sea of runners yelled *hup-hup*, and they were off.

TWENTY-FIVE

ERASMUS

"LET'S DO THIS!" Raz clicked his tongue and signaled for Beefcake to, literally and figuratively, haul ass.

He could hear the cheers, but he'd learned to turn off the external noise and draw his power inward, thanks to practicing Pun-chi yoga. Right off the line, he and Zen Dougie were the front-runners, with Libby not far behind. He could hear her encouraging Plum as one mile became two, then four, then six. Neck and neck, he and Doug rocketed down the trail, neither letting up.

A battle of wills played out between them, with Libby as the ultimate prize.

Good old Dougie might not have a clue about the benchmark experiment, but his interest in Libby was undeniable.

"You might want to pace yourself, this being your first Ass-in-Nine," Doug bit out between breaths as they passed the marker for mile seven.

There were only two miles to go, but these last two miles were the most harrowing and contained the rockiest terrain and a creek crossing. It was safe to say, barreling through this segment of the Crooked Mine Loop wasn't for the faint of heart.

Raz smirked. He had plenty of juice left in his tank, and Zen Dougie's trash talk was the stuff of little old ladies. "Remember who won the last race," he tossed back.

"I'm just saying, the last two miles are the toughest."

"Maybe for you, but not for me and Beefcake."

Beefcake whinnied a triumphant sound. Like their human counterparts, the burros hadn't let up. Anytime the trail narrowed, the Jacks nipped at each other, grunting and carrying on in their alpha donkey dialogue.

"What's your donkey's deal anyway? Why's he such an ass? Pun intended," Raz pressed, looking to get under the man's skin. If he riled up his rival, there was a good chance the man would allow his emotions to drain his energy reserves. It was a trick that worked wonders in the ring.

"Ace likes Plum. That's all there is to it. Donkeys are territorial. He wants her for himself."

"Well, she's Beefcake's companion. Ace can't have her," Raz replied, and unfortunately, he found his emotions taking hold.

"Are you sure about that?" Doug bit out as they navigated a rocky incline. "Plum's been with him all summer, and she still let Ace nuzzle up against her."

Raz clicked his tongue, dialing up the pace, moving from rock to rock. "That doesn't mean she likes him."

"That doesn't mean she doesn't *not* like him. She could like them both," Doug replied through tight breaths.

What a bloody bonkers observation.

"No, she's being cordial to Ace. It's her nature to be kind."

Dougie huffed. "Donkeys aren't cordial."

"How do you know?" Raz squawked.

"My family runs a donkey rescue. I know," Doug replied with the maturity of a five-year-old.

Dammit! In his quest to agitate the Zen prat, he'd gotten himself running hot.

And speaking of hot, a cluster of butterflies zoomed past them, riding the warm mountain breeze. He looked over his shoulder, praying that Plum wouldn't lose her donkey mind over the insects. The butterflies flitted into the grasses, and he resumed pecking away at Doug. "I figured you were too busy teaching yoga to rich old birds in Aspen to worry about shoveling donkey shit."

Doug bobbed from a large stone to the dirt trail, avoiding another group of butterflies.

The damn things were everywhere.

"Maybe I do spend a lot of time in Aspen," Doug conceded. "But I still know more than you do when it comes to donkeys and what makes them happy."

"Ace couldn't make Plum happy if his donkey life depended on it," Raz growled. "There's one donkey for her, and it's Beefcake."

"We'll see about that," Doug shot back, batting a butterfly out of the way.

Seriously, where the hell did these insects come from?

Raz peered over his shoulder. Libby and Plum had fallen back and were trailing by a good hundred yards or so.

"What the hell is that?" Zen Dougie called.

Raz whipped his head forward, then blinked. Moving like a giant looming organism, a bevy of butterflies came together. It was like something out of an Armageddon movie. And it was coming their way.

"It's a butterfly tornado," he called, sharing a panicked look with Doug.

The tiny-winged creatures moved together like they'd been sent to usher in the end of days. They covered the limbs of trees and rested on the wildflowers populating the grasses along the trail.

There was no way the butterfly-obsessed Plum could miss this.

He'd barely had a second to take it in when the mass of flying insects moved off the trail.

Thank God! Hopefully, they'd stay away from the path and out of Plum's line of sight.

He started to cluck his tongue, ready to kick it into high gear when Beefcake and Ace hit the brakes. Stumbling forward, the donkeys came to a dead halt in the middle of the trail.

Raz waved away one of the lingering winged insects and stared at his burro. "What are you doing, Beefcake? We're nearly at the creek. It's time to blow past these butterflies and button-up this race."

"Ace," Doug called. "*Hup-hup*! Let's go!"

But the beasts didn't budge. They stared at the ground at a brown rock.

"What is that?" Raz asked, narrowing his gaze, then jumped when the strange stone hopped.

"It's a toad!" Doug shrieked.

Raz stared at the warty thing, then tugged on Beefcake's lead. "Come on, mate. It's a toad. We'll go around."

But the animals were mesmerized. They barely moved a muscle when the toad opened his mouth and captured a butterfly.

Talk about grabbing lunch.

Raz cringed. "Go on and move it, Doug," he said, delegating.

"No way." Doug shot back. "If I move the toad off the trail, you'll take off and pass me."

Raz stared at the tiny warty roadblock. "Well, I'm not touching it."

"I don't want to touch it either," Doug answered, recoiling at the sight of the creature.

Somebody had to do something.

Raz peered down the trail as a jolt of anxiety tore through his chest. Libby was gaining on them, and four other pack burro teams weren't far behind her.

Zen Dougie might not be his only real competition.

And what the hell did that mean for their benchmark arrangement?

"We do it together. You hold half, and I'll get the other half," Raz suggested as the jolt of anxiety took hold. He had to win. Everything hinged on him earning the blue ribbon.

"Toads are pretty gross. It's bumpy and bulgy-eyed. You don't think it'll give us warts or a rash?" Doug asked.

This wanker.

"How would I bloody know? I didn't grow up here. There aren't toads populating the streets of London."

"Get out of the way!" Libby hollered.

And bloody hell, the butterfly tornado had returned, and Plum had zeroed in on it.

But it wasn't the only hazard heading straight for them.

"Rockslide!" Libby cried.

Rockslide?

"There's no time to waste. We've got to relocate this toad now!" he called.

Dougie picked up one side as he took the other. "We'll toss it off the trail on three. One, two—"

Ace and Beefcake roared a chorus of angry shrieking hee-haws, stifling the countdown.

"You want to save the toad?" Raz asked his beast.

And bloody hell, both Ace and Beefcake nodded.

"We're running with this toad," Raz announced, precious seconds ticking away.

"Move over!" Libby cried as a torrent of butterflies and smattering of pebbles bombarded the trail. She and Plum raced down the side on the path, trampling wildflowers as they flew past the toad pit stop and rocketed toward the creek crossing.

"We have to go!" Raz called as a few larger rocks rumbled past their feet. He glanced behind them and didn't see any giant boulders tumbling toward them—but he wasn't about to stick around. Not just that, with Libby in the lead, he wasn't in first place, and then there was the whole matter of stopping the Jennie from her wild butterfly chase.

With the men in the center holding an agitated amphibian and the burros on each side, they set off down the trail like a jackass amphibian escort service. With the toad in tow, Beefcake and Ace picked up the pace. Side by side with leads in one hand and a toad in the other, the men ran in sync, their feet hitting the ground in unison as bits of rock rolled down the trail. Thankfully, they'd hit a decent incline, and whatever rocks decided to tumble their way couldn't follow them as they made the ascent.

With Libby in his sights and half a toad in his hand, a question turned over in his head.

How was he going to win? He hadn't factored in toads and an apocalyptic-level butterfly invasion. And he'd never entertained the thought of Libby taking first place.

They hit the creek, moving steadily. "Let's drop the toad off on the other side. They like water, right?" he asked.

"I think so."

"Are you good with that, you giant ass?" he asked Beefcake. "We can't run the rest of the race holding an amphibian."

The animal whinnied. Was that a yes? He didn't know. But there was no way he'd have a snowball's chance in hell of catching up to Libby engaged in this kumbaya toad rescue with Zen Dougie.

They came to a stop, then gently set the toad onto the creek bank.

He and Doug looked on as the toad hopped over to another toad.

"Maybe he needed a lift to see his buddy," Doug commented as their toad climbed onto the back of the other toad.

"Blimey, they're screwing! Did we just facilitate a toad booty call?"

For a beat, the men said nothing, observing nature.

"We probably shouldn't watch. It feels a bit intrusive," Doug commented.

"He's a real go-getter of a toad. I'll give him that," Raz said, shaking his head as the toad went to town. He met Doug's eye, and the men broke out into laughter.

"This vortex makes creatures a little crazy," Doug added when the sound of hooves pounding grew louder as the other burro racing teams neared the other side of the creek.

Shit!

What the hell was he doing, getting an eyeful of toad porn? He had to catch up to Libby and make sure she and Plum were safe.

Doug's gaze flicked from the sex-crazed toads to the trail.

The bloke put it together as well.

Before you could say *spontaneous toad sex*, the men clucked their tongues and called out a series of *hup-hups*.

Sprinting, they hit the final stretch of the loop. Raz lengthened his stride, striving to pull ahead, but Doug matched his pace. The pair made the final turn, and the mountain greenery thinned out as they drew closer to town, and he caught sight of Libby and Plum. He couldn't see any renegade butterfly tornados in their path, and the pair didn't appear out of control. He nearly breathed a sigh of relief when a devastating realization hit.

There was no way he could catch up—no way he'd earn the blue ribbon. All he could do now was beat Doug and Ace.

He glanced at the man, who he didn't detest quite as much as he had before the bloody race started. But that didn't mean he wanted the bloke getting together with Libby.

This was it—the final push.

The crowd roared. Spectators rang bells and blew into noisemakers as the lady racers crossed the finish line, capturing first place. And crikey, he was proud as hell of Libby and Plum, but he couldn't start cheering yet. No, he and Beefcake couldn't let up. Doug and Ace were right there, running like their lives depended on it. The donkeys' hooves hit the path in unison, mimicking their human's matching strides. They were like synchronized swimmers—but the slightly terrifying donkey racing version. They sailed past the finish line as another devastating reality took hold.

He and Doug had tied for second place.

What did that mean for the bloody benchmark? He wanted to punch himself in the mouth for suggesting it.

"Whoa, easy, Beefcake," he called as the animal slowed down, still in step with Ace.

"Dad, Mibby won!" Sebastian called from across the square where the boy stood next to Plum and Libby.

As Maud pinned a blue ribbon to the donkey's bridle, their friends waved to him from the periphery of photographers and press surrounding the winner and her burro.

"We've never had a tie before," Wobbly Bob said, excitement dancing in his eyes. "Head over to Maud. We want to get a picture of the three of you."

Raz nodded to his friends and Granny Fin, standing off to the side, then worked his way through the mass of photographers. Like how they'd ponied up at the starting line, Doug and

Ace flanked Libby and Plum on one side as he and Beefcake stood on the other.

Libby leaned in toward him, pink-cheeked from exertion. "I can't believe Plum and I won."

"I can. You're a force to be reckoned with," he said, staring into her eyes. Jesus, he'd had a feeling that everything would change after today, but he hadn't expected this outcome. It was as if his only shot at happiness was slipping through his fingers— like the universe decided to throw another wrench into the workings of his life. He'd stopped running, but his heart still beat like he was sprinting down the side of the mountain.

"I think that glut of butterflies should get the real credit for our win," she said as a flock of butterflies flitted away in his belly.

He couldn't let this wave of emotion overtake him.

Get a grip.

"One of the reporters mentioned that the butterflies migrate through here this time of year," Libby added. "And sorry for screaming about a rockslide. It wasn't much more than some gravel and small stones coming loose, but it freaked me out."

"It's all right. I'm glad you're okay. And I'm proud of you, plum. I am," he said, doing everything he could to keep his voice steady.

"It's a silly race," she said, not meeting his gaze.

"It's not silly. It's your victory."

"My victory," she repeated like it was coming together in her head. "Why did you stop running, Raz? What were you and Doug doing in the middle of the trail?"

He sighed. "Rescuing a toad."

Her eyebrows shot up. "A toad?"

"Yeah, it was in the middle of the trail, and the donkeys were fascinated with it. They wouldn't move until we picked it up."

"Where is it now?"

"We dropped him off at his girlfriend's place on the other side of the creek."

He'd been thwarted by a horny toad.

She looked him over. "Did you bump your head during the toad rescue?"

"No," he said, gazing into her eyes, getting bloody misty like a preteen mooning over the heartthrob Landon Paige. "I know it sounds bizarre, but that's what happened."

She glanced over her shoulder at Doug. "What happens now, Raz?"

He wished he knew.

"I don't know," he answered, heartsick. He'd started this day so sure of how it would end. With his second-place tie with Zen Dougie, he couldn't even begin to decipher what the universe was trying to tell him.

"Hey, Libby?" Doug called.

"Yes?"

"I'd love to take you to the lookout on Rickety Rock Mountain. We could grab a bottle of wine and watch the sunset," the man offered. And as much as he wanted to throttle the guy, he couldn't blame him for wanting to spend time with Libby.

"That sounds...nice," she replied, glancing between him and the golden-haired yogi.

"Look this way, please," a photographer called, interrupting the awkward moment. "We need one more shot for the Pack Burro Racing Association."

Raz stared blankly into the camera as his thoughts raced. He should spill his guts to her now—tell her he needed her, tell her that when they were together, he forgot about the pain that weighed him down. Forget the universe and his stupid winner-gets-the-girl ultimatum. His stomach twisted into knots.

"Got it, thank you," the photographer said with a nod as the press migrated toward the finish line to get shots of the other racers.

"Hey, Sebastian, tell Libby and your dad to look at me and say cheese," Oscar chimed, holding up his Polaroid camera. "This can be the picture that goes in the frame I'm making you for your birthday," the boy added.

"Dad, pick me up," Sebastian called, grinning from ear to ear.

He scooped up his son with one arm, barely holding it together. What did his second-place finish mean for his son?

"Isn't it great that Mibby and Plum won?" Sebastian asked.

He stared at the nanny, smiling at her friends as Charlotte snapped photos of his raven-haired beauty. "Yeah, it is, son."

"Too bad you tied with that plonker, Dougie," Sebastian added, lowering his voice.

Raz shot a glance at his counterpart in toad rescue. "Doug's actually not that bad of a bloke."

"You sure?" Sebastian asked, eyeing the man.

"Yeah, he and I saved a toad together."

Sebastian frowned. "But he likes Mibby. He looks at her the same way Phoebe looks at hot dogs and cookies."

Raz tried to smile. "It's hard not to like Mibby," he answered, taking in the woman. That lovely light shimmered around her, sparkling like diamonds in a sea of blue-violet.

"Smile!" Oscar instructed, but he couldn't comply. He couldn't look away from Libby.

"Did you get it, Oscar?" Sebastian asked, wiggling out of his embrace, then skipped over to his friends. Phoebe joined the boys, and the trio stared at the photo, waiting for it to develop, when a few donkey rescue volunteers came up to them. The people congratulated them, then took Plum, Beefcake, and Ace's leads and led the donkeys to an enclosed area of the square. Brimming with fresh hay, cut-up vegetables, and water, the helpers removed the packs from the animals' backs, then allowed them to indulge in a donkey feast. Beefcake saddled up on one side of Plum, getting his fill of carrots, as Ace moved in on Plum's other side, starting in on the hay.

"What do you say, Libby?" Doug asked. "I'd love to spend some time with you before I leave for Tibet."

Libby looked between the second-place finishers. "Can you give me a second, Doug? I need to chat with Raz."

The man nodded. "My car's parked on the street across from the diner. I'll be there if you decide to take me up on the offer. Good race, Raz," Doug said, extending his hand.

Raz shook it. "Yeah, same to you, mate," he answered, and he meant it.

What was going on with him? Was it the energy of the vortex messing with his mind?

Doug set off for his car, and Libby gestured for them to walk. "I'm not sure what I should do, Raz," she said, twisting the green beads of her bracelet.

He stared at her wrist. "I didn't even notice you had that on."

She stopped next to the Rocky Mountain oyster food tent and gazed at the delicate green orbs. "This bracelet was a gift from my brothers. Green is supposed to bring luck. I wore it the day I had the fake interview with the Derricks, and then, well, you know what happened next."

Yeah, his life got turned upside down thanks to a vibrator-wielding crazy lady who'd stolen his heart with the bang of her gong.

He couldn't let her leave with Doug.

"I don't think—" he began as she started talking.

"I think I should go with Doug."

LIBBY'S WORDS hit like a punch to the gut.

"You want to go with Doug?" he repeated.

She held his gaze. "We didn't plan for what would happen if I won the race."

He glanced away, wanting to punch himself in his big fat gob. "That was the cocky beefcake in me. I should have known that if anyone could beat me, it would be you."

She toyed with the beads. "When I passed you and Doug on the trail, I started thinking about how we got here and how this started—how we started."

"Lopsided chi and your missing O, courtesy of yours truly," he offered, his heart breaking into pieces inside his chest.

She smiled up at him. "And don't forget sixteen vibrators."

He reached down to touch her face but pulled back. "I could never forget, plum."

He couldn't. She'd woven herself into the tapestry of his soul.

She swallowed, and he observed the muscles in her throat constrict. "We've both been clear about how we view relationships. And it's just sex. And not even real sex—benchmark sex."

"Just sex," he repeated. A few months ago, he wouldn't have thought twice about sleeping with a woman. But he'd experienced a shift these last several weeks, and what was once disposable now felt indispensable.

"Then we'd know if the like cures like experiment worked. We should want to know, don't you think?" she asked.

No, for the love of all that's good and holy, hell no! Forget knowing and stay with me.

"Yeah, yeah, of course," he muttered instead.

Lie. Lie. Lie.

"I don't even know if anything will happen with Doug. He might not be interested in me like that. He may want to talk about yoga," she replied, but he knew better.

"Believe me, the guy is into you. Who wouldn't be? You're..."

The best thing that's happened to Sebastian and me in years, and I don't think we can survive without you. I don't want to survive without you.

"I'm what?" she asked, the question hanging in the air as her eyes shined with a hopeful expectancy.

"You're a good person who deserves to know if her O is back," he said, the words tasting like dirt.

"What does this mean for us?" she asked, confusion lacing the question. "I won't lie. I wanted you to win, Raz. And..."

"And?" he repeated.

"And when you tell me you want me, it makes my chi go topsy-turvy in the best way. But what you're saying isn't the forever kind of want, right? Like, I'm yours until you go back to England...until after the fight."

Was that true?

Is that why he hadn't been more explicit? Did he only need her now with the fight on the horizon? Was he that bloody selfish of a prick?

"I...I don't know," he sputtered, grappling with his demons.

It would have been easier if she had a gong to bang in his face or a vibrator to toss at his head. But there wasn't an ounce of judgment in her amber eyes, not a sliver of contempt or a flash of anger.

"I'll see you back at the house. If Sebastian asks where I went..." she trailed off.

"I'll tell him you're on a walk to pick those flowers you like," he supplied.

"Okay," she whispered as a wretched stretch of silence engulfed them. After what could have been a bloody eternity or two seconds, she nodded and headed toward the street.

He watched her until she disappeared, then ran his hands down his face.

What had he done?

"You look like shit, man."

Raz looked up to find Landon.

"I feel like I've been run over by a Mack truck." He stared at the man. The guy looked different. "Where have you been, mate? I've barely seen you this summer."

Landon's expression hardened. "Busy."

"Busy hiding from your fans," he tossed out.

"I know you guys like to give me crap about being recognized in public. But I'm a pretty big deal in a lot of places," the man replied like worldwide popularity was a bad thing.

"Sorry, mate, I'm all over the board. We know you're bloody successful. Rowen and Mitch checked out your thousands of fan groups. And I'm sorry for coming off like a real prat. I'm losing it here."

"Over Libby?" Landon asked.

He nodded as an idea took hold. "You write love songs, don't you?"

Landon cocked his head to the side. "I'm not writing you a love song, dude."

"No, I don't want you to write a song for me. I need help with the romantic stuff. I don't want Libby to be with anyone else, but she left to..."

"Hang with the benchmark guy?"

Raz's jaw dropped. "How do you know about that?"

"I saw the other donkey racer guy staring at Libby, then the two of you walked away to talk. And it looked pretty intense."

Raz narrowed his gaze. "That doesn't explain how you know about the benchmark."

"Libby told her friends about it, and—"

Raz didn't need him to go on. "And Mitch and Rowen told you? It's like a sewing circle."

"I'm surprised you're down with it. I could see the way you were looking at Libby the night she became your nanny."

Was he that easy to read?

"What are you going to do about Libby?" Landon pressed.

Libby.

"I don't know," he answered as a fresh surge of anxiety coursed through him. "This is my doing. I suggested this bloke as the benchmark guy. And just now, when you saw us talking, I couldn't tell her that I needed her, but I do. I don't want to be without her. Mate, this isn't me. I haven't been the hearts and roses type since..."

Since Meredith died.

Landon's features softened. "You want to get the girl?"

"Yes."

"We've got to accentuate the positives." The former teen dream pursed his lips. "What does she like about you, specifically?"

Raz ran his hands through his hair, thinking. "She likes my cock, of course."

Landon glared at him. "For Christ's sake, Raz!"

"Sorry, I'm not thinking straight. I'm not myself. This town has a bloody vortex that scrambles people's brains and makes wildlife extra wild. I saw a butterfly tornado on the trail."

Landon looked at him like he was the sort of bloke who got lost crossing the street.

"Concentrate, Raz. What makes her heart sing? And do not say your cock."

Raz paced along the side of the food tent. It was like he couldn't put together one blooming cohesive thought. The image of Libby and Doug together made him want to lose his lunch.

Focus.

"She loves yoga and Sebastian, and then there's this blue-violet color. It's our thing."

"A color is your thing?" Landon pressed.

"Yes, I know it sounds weird, but it is."

"Get her something that color," Landon offered.

Like a car? Dammit! Her Lamborghini is already that color.

"What about flowers?" Landon tossed out.

This teen dream was a bloody genius.

"We've got wildflowers that grow near the barn that match the shade exactly."

"There you go. Pick the flowers, find the girl, ditch the benchmark dude, then sweep her off her feet. That's how it works in songs. But nothing is guaranteed in real life," the man said, glancing away.

Something was up with Landon. He'd gotten moody, or maybe that was the broody quality his fans adored. But he didn't have time to dwell on the guy—not with precious minutes ticking away.

"It's got to be more than flowers. I need to make a statement."

He stopped pacing and spied Sebastian and his friends, pumping their legs as they swung back and forth on a row of swings the organizers had brought in for the kids' activities. "That's it," he whispered.

"What's it, Raz?" Landon asked, following his line of sight.

"It just came to me. I know what I need to do." He glanced around the square and spotted Briggs about to enter the Rocky Mountain oyster tent. "Briggs, are you mad? Get away from those bull testicles! I need your help, mate."

His agent startled and blushed like a schoolgirl. "I wasn't going to get any of those bull testicles. But they smell amazing, and Mitch explained how they are a delicacy, and when in Rome, as the saying goes," the man blathered, but Raz waved him off. He didn't have time to talk testicles.

He slipped his phone from his pocket and hammered out a message. "Briggsy, I'm texting you exactly what I need you to do. It'll seem a little insane, but you have to make it happen in the next twenty minutes."

The agent's mobile pinged. Briggs stared at the screen and gasped. "Now? You need me to arrange this in twenty minutes?"

"Yeah, fifteen would be better, but it can be done, right? You're the best sports agent out there. You make things happen. And you've got your people here."

At the compliment, Briggs puffed up, then deflated. "Is this a good idea so close to the fight, champ? Where are Libby and Aug? I can't imagine they'd be on board with this."

"I'm doing this for Libby. I care about her, Briggsy."

"Do you?" Penny asked as she and their entire crew, along with Augie and Luanne, joined them.

He nodded to Penny, then surveyed the group. "I need to talk to all of you about Libby. Landon's brought it to my attention that you'll know what I mean when I say that she's with the benchmark guy."

"What?" Charlotte exclaimed, sharing a look with Mitch.

"You know about the whole chi and O debacle, right?"

Penny crossed her arms. "Yes, she's our best friend."

"There's more. Something she might not have mentioned." He took a breath. "I got a little full of myself and told her that if I won the race, it was the universe telling us that we were meant to be together."

"You pulled the universe into this?" Penny chided, sharing a look of horror with Charlotte.

He flinched. "Yeah, I did."

"And then you came in second place," Rowen added, shaking his head.

"And that blond guy with the donkey moved in. He's the benchmark, isn't he? Libby didn't tell us exactly who he was or if she'd picked him," Penny mused.

"But he was giving her googly eyes when they lined up for the race," Charlotte replied.

"Yeah, and now she's with him. I messed up. I shouldn't have let her go, but I know what I have to do."

"What do you have to do?" Augie asked. "And what's a benchmark guy?"

"It's..." he trailed off, not sure how to break it to Augie. Besides Sebastian and his granny, Aug was the only person here who'd known Mere.

"Can I give him the rundown?" Penny asked.

Raz looked from Rowen to Mitch. "The ladies know everything about each other?"

"Yep, get used to it," Mitch deadpanned.

"Okay, Penny, tell Augie because my brain feels like it's gone to mush," he said.

"Libby lost her ability to have an O, thanks to Raz," the woman began.

"I was a wanker, and I messed up her energy," he confessed.

"Yeah, all right," Aug answered in a tone that was more like *what the hell* than an actual *all right*.

"Throughout their time together," Penny continued, "Raz and Libby have been engaging in activities to find her O. The last step in the process was to make sure she could have an O with someone else. Raz and Libby decided there would be a final benchmark guy to see if she'd gotten her O back completely."

"But I don't want that—not anymore," he added, trying to read his trainer.

"Blimey, Erasmus!" Augie answered, scratching his head.

Raz stared into the donkey pen and caught Plum and Beefcake standing side by side, nuzzling each other. "I have to be the donkey, Aug."

"What?" the group questioned in unison.

"You feeling okay, Erasmus?" Augie asked.

Raz gestured to the animals. "The donkey knows."

"What does the donkey know, Dad?" Sebastian asked, skipping over with his friends and Granny Fin in tow.

"The donkey knows what's important," he replied.

"Like Beefcake knowing he loves Plum?" Sebastian offered.

The kid had cut right to the heart of it.

"Yeah, just like that, son."

Sebastian looked around. "Where's Mibby?"

"I want to talk to you about Mibby," he began, his stomach doing somersaults. "I'd like to do something for her, something big because I...because she..."

"Because she won the Ass-in-Nine?" the lad supplied.

"Something like that," he rasped.

"I get it, Dad," the boy replied. "When I got the highest

marks on my spelling test, Auntie Calliope and Auntie Callista took me to the London Eye, and I got to go way up high and see all of London and eat as much sticky toffee pudding as I wanted."

"Yeah, Sebastian, but Mibby and I might be gone a few days." He checked on Briggs. The agent had his mobile pressed to his ear.

"Will you be back for my donkey birthday party?" the boy asked, his joyful demeanor fading.

"Yes, absolutely," he answered, taking a knee to be at eye level with the boy. "I wouldn't miss it for the world."

"Then I think you should go. If you want to do something for Mibby, you should do it."

"Briggs?" he called.

"It's coming together," the man answered, then turned to continue his hushed conversation.

Raz scanned the group and zeroed in on his trainer. "I know this seems crazy, but I need a little time off, Aug."

"Yeah, I can see that. Try to fit in a visit with a shrink, if you can work it in," the man answered, but there was a thread of Aug's wry humor in the reply.

He chuckled, nodding to his mentor. "It must be the mountain air."

Was it completely ludicrous to do something so extreme, so close to his upcoming fight? Yes, of course, it was. But he'd be even worse off if he didn't. He had to act. Maybe it was the vortex, or perhaps it was what his heart had been trying to tell him since he set eyes on the woman, but he had to do this.

"Gran, do you mind keeping an eye on Sebastian for a few days?"

"We'll be fine, lad. Do what you need to do," she answered.

He exhaled a heavy breath.

Was that it? Were there any other loose ends?

"The donkeys!" he exclaimed. He couldn't leave them here.

Sebastian stepped forward, shoulders back. His son lifted his chin like a kid-sized captain of industry. "I can take care of the donkeys, and I can bring them home. I know the way up the trail."

He had a damned great kid.

"We'll go with Sebastian and lend a helping hand," Mitch added as Oscar and Sebastian high-fived each other.

Raz came to his feet. "Okay, the donkeys are sorted. Now, I need a car. We walked here with the burros."

"Take mine," Landon offered, throwing him the keys. "It's the black Porsche. It's parked down the block."

"Thanks, mate," he replied, then eyed Briggs. "Are we good?"

"Part one is ready," the man added, glancing at one of his assistant's mobiles. "We're working on the destination location. Does it have to be exactly where you described?"

He held his agent's gaze. "To the letter."

"We'll get it done," the man answered, then checked his watch. "And you better get on it. Part one is on its way."

"Got it. Thank you," he answered, then turned to the group. "I couldn't do this without you."

"Are you sure about this?" Augie asked.

"There's no other way, Augie."

There wasn't. He'd be a bloody wreck if he didn't at least try to stop what he'd put into motion.

He ruffled his son's ash brown hair and inhaled a few shallow sips of air. It was as if he were in withdrawal. His limbs shook. His heart hammered in his chest. He left the square, sprinting down the block, and found the Porsche. Throwing himself into the front seat, he pressed the ignition and hit the gas. Flying through downtown Rickety Rock, he formulated a plan.

Step one: Flowers

Step two: Drive to the lookout on Rickety Rock Mountain

Step three: Hand Libby the flowers, throw her over his shoulder and disappear into the sunset

Bollocks! This sounded more like a kidnapping than a romantic gesture.

It didn't matter. He had to get to her and put the kibosh on the final benchmark. He'd work out the rest along the way.

He turned off the road and tore down the drive. Gravel and rock scattered as he pulled up to the Victorian and threw the car into park. His pulse racing, he swung open the car door and lost his footing as he attempted to extricate himself from the sports car. He hit the ground with a thud. Rocks cut into his knees as he crawled a few feet before pushing up and dashing toward the barn.

"Flowers, flowers, flowers," he muttered, ripping the blue-violet larkspurs from the ground. Root and all, he worked furiously. Mud and bits of earth fell to the ground, and dirt stuck to his legs. He reached for another wildflower when a door slammed.

"Why are you digging up the yard?"

He looked over his shoulder and couldn't believe his eyes. "Libby, is that you?"

"Are you okay, Raz?" she asked with a crease to her brow.

He glanced from his dirt-covered hands to his clothing dusted with mud. He must look like he'd gone mental. Then it clicked. She was here—and not with Mr. Benchmark.

"Where's Dougie?" he sputtered.

She glanced down the drive. "On his way to visit his brother in Denver."

Denver?

His heart was ready to beat itself out of his chest. "What happened to the plans you made with him?"

"I changed my mind and asked him to bring me home—back to the Victorian."

It took everything he had in him not to dance around and pump his fist in the air.

"Why are you decimating the larkspurs, Raz?" she asked, concern in her eyes.

Hope and joy washed over him.

"I came to pick some flowers for you. You like these. You like the color. It's our color."

She stared at him. "It is."

He took a step toward her as a blue-violet hue surrounded them. "Why aren't you with Doug?"

He had to ask. He had to hear her say it.

"I don't want to be with Doug," she answered, taking a step toward him. "The benchmark is—"

"Total bullshit," he supplied.

She brushed a tear from her cheek. "Yeah."

He closed the distance between them. "I don't want you with Doug or anyone else."

"You don't?"

"No," he answered, then he caught sight of one of the stone stacks Sebastian had built. "Those rock stacks tell us when we're on the right trail. But I'm here to tell you that every path is the right path for me as long as I walk it with you."

"Do you mean that?" she asked, her gaze swimming with questions.

He handed her the mess of wildflowers. "I want you. I don't know who I am without you, plum. I don't want to go back to the pain. I want to live in this safe space with you and Sebastian —a place where nothing hurts, a place where nothing can touch us. And the donkey knows, plum. He knows, and that's why I can't let you go."

That crease returned to her brow. "I was right there with you until the donkey part."

"Beefcake knows that Plum is meant for him, just like I know you're meant for me. I want you, Libby. I can barely breathe without you."

She smiled up at him with tears in her eyes. "I think this is the part where you kiss me."

He cupped her face in his dirt-speckled hands and stared into her amber eyes. He leaned in, his lips hovering above the corner of her mouth, so ready to lose himself when the hum of a helicopter rumbled through the air.

Good old Briggs got it done.

Libby gasped as the sound intensified. "Why is there a helicopter landing in the front yard?"

He smiled against her lips. "The kiss will have to wait. This, plum, is the part where you trust me."

TWENTY-SEVEN

LIBBY

"PLUM, it's time to wake up. We're here."

Libby sighed and nuzzled into the warmth of Erasmus Cress's embrace. She wasn't ready to open her eyes—not yet. She curled into Raz, and he stroked her cheek. "I had the craziest dream," she murmured, sliding her hand beneath his T-shirt.

"Did you?" he purred.

She loved his morning voice. That sexy British rasp with a touch of gravelly gruffness made every inch of her body hungry for his touch and desperate for his kisses.

She drew lazy circles across his hard abdominal muscles. "I dreamed that I was whisked away on a helicopter, had a delicious dinner waiting for me in Aspen, then strutted my stuff onto a private jet."

"That sounds like some dream. Do you remember anything else?" he asked, pressing a kiss to her temple.

"I do. The jet had a section in the back that turned into a bedroom."

He hummed a satisfying little sound. "Was anyone with you in this bedroom on a private jet?"

She continued making lazy circles, slowly working her way down toward the waistband of his track pants. "There sure was. A man."

"I see," he breathed. "Did anything exciting happen in the bedroom with this dashing specimen of male perfection?"

Someone woke up cocky as hell.

She smiled against the crook of his neck. "Define exciting?"

"Did you join the Mile High Club?" he replied, twisting a lock of her hair between his fingers.

"I already belong," she teased with an indifferent shrug.

"You do?" he asked, that possessive growliness coming through.

"I was born in Denver—the Mile High City. I've been in the Mile High Club since birth."

Her beefcake chuckled, and the spike of his domineering alpha energy dropped a few notches. "I was referring to a different Mile High Club, or maybe it should be renamed Mile High Club O."

Oh, there were Os in this club—the man got that right.

The sweet ache between her thighs was a testament to it.

"It's funny you bring that up," she purred. "In this very dream, I got up to some very naughty things."

"I take it you enjoyed it," he rasped, and his panty-melter of a voice had her ready to shimmy out of her clothes again. But she wasn't done teasing him.

"It was...nice." She couldn't let her boxer get too full of himself. While this man was most certainly the giver of Os, he *owed* her some answers.

"Nice," he echoed with a hint of agitation that made her toes curl.

"Do you want to know what was really amazing about my dream?" she cooed.

"Tell me, plum."

"The jet had bowls of candy—so many different types of candy. And it was all for me."

He tensed, and she could picture the indignation on her beefcake's beautiful face.

"That was the *really amazing* part of your dream?" he grumped. "The bowls of blooming jet candy?"

"I'm not sure if it was the most amazing part, but it was pretty great."

Hello, free candy.

She might be all about fitness ninety-nine percent of the time, but who could turn down private jet candy?

"Come to think of it," he said, shifting his body. He pressed a kiss to her neck, then smiled against her skin. "I had a very similar dream."

"Is that so?"

"You were in it," he continued.

"Was I? And what about the candy? Was it there, too?" she teased.

"It was. In my dream, I lined up Gummy Bears between your breasts, devoured them, and then I devoured you."

Swoon.

And that was just what they did with the Gummy Bears. Things got scorching hot with the licorice.

Her nipples hardened into taut pearls. "Sounds like quite a treat," she replied, playing coy and doing her best not to get too hot and bothered.

He slid his hand into her hair. "I like the idea of dreams becoming a reality."

"Me too," she whispered.

"You're not curious about where we are, Libby Lamb?" he asked, propping up onto his elbow.

She exhaled a wistful breath as her pulse thrummed. She didn't want to open her eyes—not yet. She wanted to remain in this perfect in-between world where it was just the two of them. "I'm more than curious. I don't want this to end." Her teasing tone had disappeared. Whatever this was, wherever they were, she couldn't remember ever being this blissfully happy.

"Open your eyes, plum," he whispered against her lips.

She complied, blinking a few times. But it wasn't hard for her eyes to adjust. It was still dim in the jet's cabin. She slid her gaze to the window and was met with a veil of darkness. Wherever they were in the world, the sun hadn't risen.

"Look at me, Libby," he coaxed.

A ripple of trepidation passed through her as she turned toward the man.

He dusted her lips with butterfly kisses. "It's not going to end, plum."

She pulled back a fraction, stared into his gray eyes, and traced her fingertips down the scruff of his chin. He was a gloriously beautiful man, so much more complex than she'd ever imagined, and she wanted to believe him more than anything. For the first time, she wanted to put her trust in a man.

No, not any man.

This man. Her beefcake of a boxer who happened to be a driven athlete, a devoted father, son, and grandson, and possibly the man who'd protect her heart.

But what had sparked his change of heart? Was it the thought of her with another man, or was he telling the truth? Did he sincerely want her beyond their sixty-day arrangement?

Had the pendulum swung from enjoying a temporary lust to desiring a lasting love?

Love.

He hadn't dropped the L-word, but when she'd peered out the window of the Victorian and saw him rooting around, pulling wildflowers out of the earth like a deranged gardener, her heart had swelled in her chest.

He loved her.

She'd sensed that immediately.

And in those few seconds, clarity had taken over.

It was as if the universe were pointing her toward the future —her future. As if it needed her to see that she had a choice, and that choice was whether she would take the chance to trust her heart with the sexy beefcake of a boxer who could tear up a patch of wildflowers like nobody's business.

She'd never seen Raz so earnest, and when she'd walked out onto the back porch and called out to him, a cataclysmic jolt fired through her. Every chakra in her body recalibrated to balance with the man holding a slew of flowers, scraggly roots and all, and covered in bits of earth and flower petals. The frenzied energy pulsing between them had made her both lightheaded and completely grounded.

Every path is the right path for me as long as I walk it with you.

She could still hear his words echoing in her soul—words that kindled hopefulness in her heart.

"Plum?"

"Yes?"

"We have to get off the jet for *it* to start."

She nodded, then left the warmth of his embrace and sat up. "You've been very vague about the *it*, beefcake. And when I say vague, I mean, you haven't told me anything about what's going on. We'll be back for Sebastian's birthday, won't we? We can't miss it."

He shifted his large frame, coming to sit beside her, then leaned in and kissed her forehead. "Of course, we'll be back."

"What about the arrangements?" she pressed.

"Mitch and Oscar are making the cake and cooking up cheese toasties. My sisters are flying in, and they live to throw parties. They're bloody annoying about it, so we'd only be in the way of Callista and Calliope forking over a ridiculous amount of cash on balloons and whatever else piques their fancy. It's all taken care of, plum, and it gives us three days to ourselves."

"Three days to ourselves in...?" she asked, praying he'd simply spill the beans.

"In paradise—or at least I hope it's paradise," he answered with a slight wince.

Why would he wince?

Her lips parted once, then twice, working to formulate a question. "You've never been wherever we are?" she finally got out.

"No."

"Why did you decide to bring me here?"

"You decided, plum," he answered without answering—the infuriating man.

She pegged him with her gaze. "Raz, that makes no sense."

"It's about to. I promise." He paused, clearly chewing on a thought. "Well, as long as Briggs was able to put my instructions into action," he added, then swiped his cell phone from a compartment on the wall. The screen illuminated his face, and the man grinned like the cat who ate the canary.

"I take it you're pleased?"

"I am." He stood, scooped up her sandals, then slipped them onto her feet. "Your carriage awaits, Cinderella. Well..."

"Well, what?" she shot back.

"Forget the carriage part," he answered, scrolling through text messages. "I believe we're looking for a Jeep."

"A Jeep?" She glanced out the window. "Can you tell me what time it is?"

"It's five a.m.," he answered crisply, pocketing his phone.

"Is this non-carriage mode of transportation taking us to a ball that starts at dawn?"

"Something like that," he answered, slipping on his shoes.

She had no idea where they were or what they'd be doing. Still, there was something deliciously intoxicating about Raz orchestrating a surprise for her.

Here's what she knew. They'd been in the air for hours. They could have spanned the Pacific or the Atlantic in that amount of time. Honestly, they could be anywhere.

"Give me a second to freshen up," she said and headed into the jet's bathroom.

Thankfully, before they'd left the Victorian by helicopter, the pilot had assured them that they had a little time to get in a shower.

Truly a godsend.

After running nine miles on dirt trails alongside a donkey, one picked up a certain earthy aroma. Okay, earthy might be overly generous. She'd smelled terrible—not even Raz's gift of wildflowers could have masked the scent. When she'd inquired about what to wear to the mystery location, Raz had told her to put on something comfortable, then asked her to hand over her cell phone. A strange request, for sure, but he wouldn't take no for an answer, citing the need to make this a full-proof surprise.

And speaking of surprises, after pocketing her cell, the man insisted on packing for them both.

He'd thrown a few things into a bag for himself before entering her room. She'd stood in the hallway, peeking in, her hand pressed to her lips to keep from giggling as he methodically rolled her panties into the shape of little sausages, then placed them in his bag like he was making the undergarment version of pigs in a blanket. Still, it was endearing to observe and a little daunting to allow him to do what she'd told herself she didn't want or need from any man—genuine care and concern. But a bigger issue loomed. Could she trust her heart with him?

She adjusted the straps on her sundress. While they'd gotten up to quite a bit of naughtiness, she'd insisted they dress

before falling asleep. She wasn't sure how this private jet business worked, and the last thing she wanted was the pilot and co-
pilot walking in on her naked and drooling in Raz's arms. Luckily, they hadn't been disturbed. She smoothed the front of her
garment, brushed her teeth, then checked her reflection in the
jet's bathroom mirror. A bubbly excitement took over.

Could she trust Erasmus with her heart?

"Plum?"

"I'm almost ready," she called, rinsing her mouth, then
twisting her hair into a bun. She did one last mirror check,
hardly able to believe that she was the smiling, deliriously
happy woman looking back at her. She pictured Penny and
Charlotte. Is this what it was like for them? Is this how it felt to
be cherished? Was this possible for her? The image of her
father, standing in front of the Victorian, flashed before her
eyes. Gaunt, pathetic, and ready to cash in on his daughter's job
to get an inside look at Raz; the man had let her down every
step of the way since she'd lost her mother. But that wasn't Erasmus, was it. Perhaps, like every other man, she'd put him in the
same category as her father, but he wasn't. He couldn't be,
right?

Breathe, just breathe.

She opened the door and spied Raz at the front of the jet,
chatting with the pilot. The co-pilot nodded to her, then opened
the cabin door. She stopped halfway up the aisle as a fragrant,
invigoratingly dazzling aroma tempted her senses. Slightly
fruity with hints of coconut and something akin to gardenias,
she breathed in the warm air as it wafted inside the plane. This
wasn't the crisp, dry-your-cuticles-out Denver air. No, what
she'd inhaled spoke of a tropical world—a world that must be
miles away from Colorado's Mile High City.

Slowly, absorbing it all, she walked the rest of the way up
the aisle and joined Raz. She and her boxer thanked the pilots

before exiting the jet and heading down the stairs. One step at a time, she surveyed their destination.

A string of lights lining the runway highlighted the dense foliage surrounding the sleepy airfield. Thick, towering palm trees engulfed an unassuming one-story building that sat beside a modest runway, slashing a short distance across the lush land.

She'd never experienced an airport like this.

"Is this someone's home?" she asked.

Raz chuckled. "No, but it's pretty remote, huh?" he answered, looking as surprised as she felt.

"You honestly haven't been here before?"

"I wouldn't lie to you, plum. This is my first time," he replied, giving her hand a gentle squeeze.

She scanned the empty tarmac. The co-pilot had set their bag on the runway, not far from the jet. Raz picked it up and slung it over his shoulder as she continued to study the landscape.

This was not Denver International Airport—or even Aspen's regional airfield. There were no taxis, no buses, no expanses of asphalt lined with rental cars. A chorus of insects and birds greeting the day welcomed them as she tried to piece together where they were. Was this the Caribbean? Penny and Rowen had a place there. Could that be it, or did Raz have his own tropical vacation home? It couldn't be that. He said he'd never visited this place before.

She glanced around. "No customs?"

If they'd left the country, a customs agent would have to be there.

"No need," he answered as a pair of headlights pierced the darkness and headed their way.

An open-air Jeep pulled in next to the darkened building, and a lanky man hopped out. No, it wasn't a man. The outdoor lighting revealed a teenager. Tall and sporting shorts and a T-shirt, he couldn't be more than sixteen or seventeen. The kid stood in front of the vehicle. Lit by the headlights, he started moving in place, bobbing and weaving, throwing punches.

Was he okay?

"I can't believe it. I can't believe it," the teen announced, shadowboxing as he spoke. "The British Beast, Erasmus Cress, is on my island," the kid finished before going back to the Jeep and returning with a pair of boxing gloves.

Libby cocked her head to the side. It was safe to say she wasn't expecting this type of reception.

"Why is there a teenage boy dancing around and shouting your name?"

Raz laughed, glanced at his phone, then waved to the kid. "Are you Milo?"

"Erasmus Cress knows my name," the boy called out, his voice echoing in the fragrant air. I'm your ride to..."

The kid stopped bouncing.

"Wait, my grandma told me I'm not supposed to say anything. But we can take a selfie, right? I've gotta post this online. My friends will never believe it. Oh, and can you sign my gloves?"

She sized up her boxer. "You brought me to a tropical paradise populated with your fans? I must say, this is very on-brand for a beefcake like you."

He laughed, raised their joined hands to his lips, and kissed her knuckles. "From what Briggs texted, it appears this fan seems to be what made this entire endeavor possible."

Her jaw dropped. "Wait a second. You weren't sure if we'd be welcome wherever we are?"

Raz tossed her one of his beefiest of beefcake grins. "Plum, you're with Erasmus Cress. Who wouldn't want me on their island?"

Sweet Buddha's belly, this man.

"It's nice to meet you, Milo. I'm Erasmus, but you can call me Raz."

"Raz!" the teen eked out, swiping a mop of dark curls out of his eyes.

Raz pressed his lips together, clearly biting back laughter. "And this is Libby—"

"Lamb!" the boy howled, causing her to nearly jump into Raz's arms.

What did this kid do every day? Wake up and pound a case of energy drinks followed by a few pounds of raw sugar?

"Did you see the video of the astronauts on the space station reenacting your training session?" Milo asked, wide-eyed.

This kid was a riot—and a starstruck riot to boot.

Now, she was the one suppressing a bout of giggles. "Yes, I'm aware of the viral video."

"That's some serious dedication to training," the young man continued, awe coating his words. "You looked totally insane. You really had Erasmus Cress on his toes."

"Training a boxer can induce strong emotions," she replied to the endearing boy. The kid meant no harm, and he radiated pure joy. A pink aura billowed around him, and the color wrapped him in an atmosphere of abundant friendliness. It was hard not to smile in his vibrant presence—a presence that felt oddly familiar.

"Do you have a pen, Milo? I'm happy to sign your gloves, mate."

"Yeah, I've got one right here," the kid answered and pulled a marker from his pocket.

"How long have you been boxing?" Raz asked, holding the gloves in the beams of the headlights as he autographed the items.

"Just a couple of years. My grandma didn't like it at first, but now that she's seen the way you do things, she's more open to it," the kid answered.

What did that mean?

"Can we take a picture, too?" Milo asked.

"Absolutely," Raz answered, handing the kid his gloves.

"Would you like me to take it?" Libby asked.

"No way! I want you in it, too," Milo chimed, beaming with excitement.

"All right," she said, her cheeks warming from the boy's enthusiasm. She'd never imagined anyone wanting to take a selfie with her.

No, that's not quite true.

Her dream was to help people through yoga. She wanted to acquire a following, but she hadn't expected it to be like this—thanks to Raz.

She and her boxer leaned in toward Milo as he held the gloves in one arm and his phone with the other and snapped a selfie.

Milo threw his cell onto the front seat of the Jeep, then gingerly slid his gloves into a gym bag before glancing up at the skyline. It wasn't quite as dark out now. A thin strand of glittering golden light stretched across the expanse of sky. "We better get going. It'll take us about fifteen minutes," he said, pushing the front seat forward. She and Raz climbed into the back, and Milo took his spot as chauffeur. "We'll take a shortcut and go by my family's farm," the boy added as he started the car and shifted into drive.

Raz settled their bag at his feet, then took her hand.

She waved him in. "Can you tell me where we are now?"

He didn't answer. He simply wrapped his arm around her and relaxed into the seat. Nice for him, but she was still on high alert. She had too many questions percolating. She paid close attention to the scenery as the narrow road, thick green vegetation, and fragrant, humid air gave this island a leisurely, easy vibe. Wherever they were, it was no major tourist destination. The Jeep rumbled along for a good ten minutes when they rounded a bend, and a breathtaking view of the ocean spread out before them, and the flowery aroma that had greeted her at the airport intensified.

"That's my family's plumeria farm," Milo called, pointing to row upon row of petite trees, each with a mushroom-like cascade of blossoms bursting from the branches.

"Plumeria?" she said. "Aren't those the type of flowers used to make Hawaiian leis?"

How did she know that? She'd never been to Hawaii. She must have seen it mentioned on TV or in a book.

Raz pulled her in a little closer. "Yes, they're used for making leis. The text from Briggs mentioned that Milo's family owned an agricultural business on the island."

"We're on one of the Hawaiian Islands?" she asked, her voice barely a whisper.

"We are."

Her heart jumped into her throat as the rows of flowering trees disappeared, and an expanse of shoreline shimmered in the early morning light. It was like something one would see on a postcard...or a television program.

Television.

A lightness took over as a thrumming euphoria expanded in her chest. The energy ebbed and flowed within her, gently, like the soothing rhythm of the sea.

Milo pulled over and cut the engine. "This is where I leave you. There are no roads from here. Follow the path. The rock stacks will let you know you're on the main trail. You can't miss the bungalow. It's bright green, and it's stocked with tons of food. I delivered the groceries myself. And there are a bunch of different flavors of ice cream and everything you could want to make hot fudge sundaes."

Hot fudge sundaes?

Her mother used to make those for her.

"And the other thing?" Raz asked.

The teen flashed a knowing grin. "You can't miss that either. You're expected."

Raz and Milo continued talking about boxing, but she couldn't concentrate on their conversation. As if in a trance, she stared ahead at the water. It glistened a glorious blue-green in the early morning light, matching Sebastian's eyes and the aquamarine stone Ida had given her. The color greeted her like an old friend. But the color wasn't the only familiar sight. She slid her gaze from the water to the shore, and a wave of energy sent a tingle through her body. This wasn't just any beach. A tree spread its limbs into the air near the water's edge—a tree with a rope swing hanging from a knotty limb.

She stared ahead, expecting the mirage to disappear, but it didn't. The swing swayed in the breeze, a testament to its permanency.

She pressed her hand to her heart as gratitude flowed through her veins.

There was no doubt about where Raz had taken her—not anymore.

TWENTY-EIGHT

LIBBY

MOLOKA'I.

Her beefcake had brought her to the Hawaiian Island of Moloka'i—the same place where Shandra had filmed her yoga program years ago.

Raz helped her out of the Jeep, and she stared at the stack of rocks at the entrance to the trail.

"Just like at home, yeah?" he said, following her line of sight. *Home.*

She couldn't speak. She could only nod as he took her hand, scanning the landscape, waiting to wake from this dream.

But it wasn't a dream.

They followed the path, and the leaves of the dense, fragrant shrubs lining the trail brushed against her arm in a hypnotic *swoosh.* She allowed her fingertips to slip across the smooth surface as the dirt trail changed to one of sand.

It was almost too much for her to take in. She surveyed the beach then stilled when a woman came into view—a woman she'd watched over and over again on television.

Shandra.

She observed the graceful yogi, her hair blowing in the

ocean breeze as she moved from posture to posture. With her yoga mat spread out on the sand next to the tree with a weathered rope swing, Shandra raised her arms into the air as she flowed into tree pose.

"Are you okay, plum?"

She shifted her attention from the woman to Erasmus. "How?" It was all she could get out.

He smiled a sweet, boyish grin. "I told Briggs about the show and that we needed to get to the island of Moloka'i and find the tree with a swing. His team scoured the internet and made the arrangements."

She studied his face—a face she once couldn't stand, but now she couldn't imagine life without him. "I can't believe you remembered."

"I remember everything when it comes to you, plum." He released a shaky breath. "After you left with Doug, I didn't know what to do with myself. I wanted to crawl out of my skin. I was asking Landon for advice."

"Landon?"

He shrugged, his cheeks growing pink. "He writes love songs. I figured he'd know more than a knuckle-headed boxer when it came to getting the girl."

Getting the girl.

She loved the sound of that, but it still didn't make sense as to how Raz had made this happen.

"Landon couldn't have suggested coming here. How would he know about this place?" she pressed.

Raz's blush deepened. "He didn't. He suggested the flowers, but the idea of whisking you away to Moloka'i came together when I saw Sebastian on a swing with Phoebe and Oscar. The first thing that came to mind was you telling me about Shandra and the beach with a swing and how it brought you comfort. Then I remembered you saying that your mum used to know when you needed an ice cream sundae. I put it together, and everything inside of me told me I needed to take you here, so I could tell you..." he trailed off.

"What did you want to tell me?" she whispered.

His gray gaze intensified like nothing else existed but her. "I want you to know that you're not Libby Lamb, the little girl sitting in the dark watching a woman do yoga on television—a worried little girl caring for her brothers and waiting for her father to come home. You're Libby Lamb, the creator of Pun-chi yoga, the woman my son adores, and the vibrator-throwing crazy lady who's stolen my heart."

She blinked back tears. "I have?"

"Isn't it obvious?" He cupped her face in his hand. "I love you, plum, and this is where I needed to tell you that. You're not alone in the dark. You are the light, Libby. You're my light and Sebastian's light. You make everything better. You make me better. When I'm with you, my pain disappears. The chains that weigh me down crumble to dust when I see you smile."

She swallowed past the lump in her throat. "Remember when I told you I felt bad for calling you a beefcake?"

"Yeah."

"Now I really feel awful," she said, laughing through tears. "No one has ever done anything like this for me, Raz."

His misty gaze gave way to a cocky glint. "Good."

"Good?" she repeated.

"Good, because I want to be the one who takes care of you. I want to eat ice cream sundaes with you. I don't want to be without you. I need you. I don't want to lose this feeling. And..." his heartfelt expression changed to one awe. "I don't believe it! Libby, look," he said, gesturing toward Shandra.

The woman stood on one leg with the bottom of her other foot pressed against her inner thigh in the tree pose, with one exception. Instead of extending her arms into the air, Shandra knocked out a series of punches.

"She's doing a set of the jab-cross tree combo," Libby said, wide-eyed.

"She's doing your Pun-chi yoga, plum," Raz corrected.

Shandra completed the punches, lowered her leg, then turned and pegged them with her gaze. "Namaste," the woman said, her hands in a prayer position as she bowed.

"Namaste," Libby repeated, frozen in place. "We didn't mean to intrude," she blathered, utterly starstruck. She couldn't count how many times she'd seen the woman look at the camera and speak the word. Still, never in a million years did she think she'd hear the woman say it in real life.

"It's no intrusion. You must be Libby and Erasmus. I'm Shandra."

It really was her!

The woman's rich flowing voice washed over her like a fragrant breeze. Like on television, the yogi wore a flower in her hair, tucked behind her ear. And today, the color of the plumeria adorning her wavy hair was a brilliant blue-violet.

Blue-violet.

"I know who you are. I watched your sunrise yoga program every morning when I was a girl. It changed everything for me. You changed everything for me. I'm a yoga instructor now. I don't know what else to say other than thank you."

"I should thank you," Shandra said, waving them over. "You've made me the coolest grandmother on the island. At least that's what Milo said when Briggs Keaton called the farm. Milo is quite a fan of boxing—a sport I never approved of until he showed me a video of you, Libby."

"A video?" she replied. By now, she should simply accept the inevitable. If astronauts had viewed the viral video, it wasn't quite a stretch to imagine an eighty-year-old yogi on a tucked-away island in the Pacific tuning in.

"You were standing in front of a Victorian house in the mountains, demonstrating a new type of yoga. I couldn't take my eyes off you, dear."

The no-vibrators-included video.

Libby released a relieved sigh. "I thought you might have seen another video."

Shandra raised an eyebrow. "You mean the one where you were throwing *items* at Erasmus?"

Oh boy!

"Yep," she answered, her cheeks heating.

"Don't let that embarrass you, dear. There's nothing wrong with embracing the unorthodox."

"That's one way to put it," she replied, still unable to believe she was conversing with Shandra.

"Some of the most remarkable discoveries are made when two opposing energies come together and create order from chaos. Between boxing and yoga, there's an elegant balance to your Pun-chi flows. I've incorporated a few moves into my morning routine." A wry grin stretched across the yogi's face. "It makes me feel like an eighty-year-old badass."

"Your punches were spot on. I wouldn't want to face you in the ring," Raz added with an approving nod.

Shandra patted his arm. "You're very kind, young man."

It still felt like a dream. Libby surveyed the beach and inhaled the ocean air, her senses feasting on the tropics.

"I can't believe I'm here, on Moloka'i, with you. I was heart-broken when your program went off the air a few years ago. Was that hard when it ended?"

A grin stretched across the yogi's face. "No."

"No?" Libby echoed.

"Our chi, our life-force, is like a river, Libby. Sometimes a log or a large rock blocks the flow. That isn't an obstacle. It's an opportunity."

"An opportunity for what?"

"To grow. Love and loss, pain and pleasure. They exist in tandem. They rely on each other for their own definition and meaning. To disregard one upsets the balance. Make friends with the setbacks. Welcome your wounds. Your chi is grounded in truth. That's why I always signed off by saying love is stronger than any force holding you back. But don't be fooled. It isn't quite as easy to do as it seems."

"How so?" she asked, absorbing Shandra's energy.

The woman gazed at the ocean. "The trick is uncovering what that force holding you back is. It's not always what you think, but it's exactly what it needs to be."

"That's deep," Raz said, blowing out a heavy breath as he shook his head.

"What's really deep is learning how to overcome your fears and acknowledge what truly matters. Sometimes, it's right in front of you," the yogi added with a knowing glint in her eyes.

Libby glanced at Raz and found him gazing at her.

"Enjoy your time on the island," Shandra said, gifting them with a warm grin. "You'll have complete privacy here. This beach is part of my family's land. We're honored to have you, and thank you for the donation, Erasmus."

"Donation?" Libby said, turning to her boxer.

"Yes, quite a hefty donation," Shandra answered. "We don't make much in profits. My family's work on the farm is a labor of love. But we believe in giving back. We mail out a percentage of the leis we make to community centers and senior living facilities across the United States. Our flowers bring people a little piece of the beauty of Moloka'i and allow them to savor the scents of island life."

"I'm pleased to do it. Thank you, Shandra. This means the world to us," Raz said, leaning in to embrace the woman.

"I'm grateful our paths crossed," the yogi replied, then removed the flower from her hair and handed it to Raz. "I'll let you help Libby with this," she added before rolling up her mat and heading down the path toward the farm.

Raz slid the delicate bloom behind her ear. "Now, you're my Hawaiian goddess."

She smiled up at him, so completely in love. "You're a good man, Erasmus Cress."

He waved her off. "I told Briggs to do whatever it took to get us here. He and his team got it done."

She looked him over. "Is that humility coming from the British beefcake?"

He bit back a grin. "Only for you. Now," he said, leaning in, all that modesty draining away. "I know what you've been waiting for. Don't you want to touch it?"

She grinned up at him, swooning over the man. "Of course, I do, but we might want to make sure Shandra is out of earshot."

"Plum?" Raz said, amusement twinkling in his eyes.

"Yes?"

"I was talking about the tree swing." He tipped her chin and pressed a kiss to the corner of her mouth. "But I see where your energy is directed, Miss Wham, Bam Pun-chi Yogi. And I cannot say that I'm disappointed," he continued, taking her hand and leading her toward the swing.

"It's like walking into a dream. The aquamarine water is just how I remembered it." She reached toward the gray, braided rope but stopped before touching it. "I thought about this swing so often as a girl. I'd try to imagine how many storms it had weathered."

"And it's still here, looking bloody sturdy," he said. The sun shined on his face, highlighting his strong cheekbones and casting him in a glow.

The man was more Greek god than mere mortal, and he wanted her.

Exhilaration thrummed through her body as she concentrated on the beefcake who'd given her more than she'd ever dreamed. "Take off your T-shirt," she purred.

Sensing her shift in energy, Raz complied without a word of protest, his features growing solemn, his focus on one thing—and only one thing.

Her.

She took the shirt from him and placed it on the swing's wooden bench.

"Take off your shorts and everything else," she continued, watching the Adonis of a man strip at her command. The rays of early morning sunlight kissed his body. Bathed in a golden glow, his ripped torso and muscled, powerful limbs called out to her. She licked her lips, hungry for this man and his perfect cock, ravenous to feel him between her thighs. She dropped her gaze and greedily drank him in. It was safe to say the man was up for it, rock hard and ready to take her over the edge.

"Sit down on the swing," she directed, her body quivering with desire.

The wooden plank creaked, and the ropes groaned as her beefcake complied.

With his gaze swimming with lust, he gripped the rope and set his sights on her.

"Your turn, plum. I want to see every gorgeous inch of you," he growled, rocking back and forth, his powerful legs flexing with each movement. "And Libby?"

"Yes?"

"Go slowly."

Yes, Mr. Beefcake!

She slid one strap, then the other, off her shoulder. The little summer dress she'd slipped on after Raz welcomed her into the jet-set version of Club O proved to not only be something comfortable for sleeping but a garment quickly shed while looking to get it on in paradise. The light fabric pooled at her feet, and she stepped out of her sandals and shook her hair loose from the makeshift bun. She gripped the elastic band of her panties when Raz shook his head.

"Turn around while you take those off."

Leave it to her boxer to take back control. What used to make her want to bang a gong like a madwoman now got her wet with anticipation. When the competitive alpha set his sights on her, every inch of her body craved his touch.

And you bet your bottom dollar she obeyed. Bending forward, she slid her panties past her ass, down her thighs, then kicked them off. She looked over her shoulder. "Was that to your liking, beefcake?"

"Get that perfect arse over here," the beast demanded, clearly pleased with her performance.

Libby exhaled a tight breath. If she were equipped with an arousal meter, the sucker would have blown through the roof.

Slowly, she walked toward him. The warm sand tickled her toes as she stood before him, naked, nipples hard and goose bumps prickling her skin.

"Libby Lamb in paradise is a sight to see," he said, carnal need coating his words.

Swoon central!

His growly tone owned her, body and soul.

She gripped the weathered ropes, then lifted one leg to sit on his lap but stopped midway. "Do you think it's strong enough to hold us?"

"There's one way to find out." Raz palmed the globes of her ass and lifted her onto his lap.

She giggled as the swing rocked back and forth and side to side. She straddled the man, then wrapped her arms around his neck, anchoring herself to him. But she didn't have anything to worry about. Raz widened his legs, gaining control of the movement.

"I've got you, plum."

"You do. You have me."

He did.

"This trip will change everything, love," he whispered, then trailed his fingertips between her breasts, down the length of her abdomen, and stroked her tight bundle of nerves, kindling the heat between her thighs. "Everything," he breathed against her lips.

She closed her eyes, surrendering to the man, lost in a sea of sensations. He worked her in slow circles with the pad of his thumb before sliding a finger inside her.

"Libby, you're mine," he moaned against her lips. She rode his hand, her muscles tensing. Instinctively, she arched back and reached for the rope. She writhed above him, rolling her hips, taking, and taking, and taking, pleasure building as he gathered her hair into his hand. He twisted her locks around his fist, holding her close. He captured her mouth. His kiss demanded all of her. His alpha energy owned her body.

She was his.

"Please, I need you inside me," she pleaded.

He guided her down, and she welcomed his beautiful, weeping cock. She clenched around him, wanting all of him, desperate for the sweet slide of their bodies moving together. Raz inhaled a sharp breath, grinding into her as he pumped his hips. A sheen of sweat glistened on their skin as the balmy air bathed them in the island scents of the ocean and fragrant flowers. They moved together, becoming one with nature. They were the water, the air, the twist of rope, and the slap and slide of skin meeting skin.

Pleasure built like a gathering storm. His cock stretched her and caressed her. Her skin tingled, and her mind emptied of all rational thought as Raz set a pace that left her moaning his name and begging for more, pleading for him to go harder and faster.

They were live wires, sparking hot, ready to ignite.

Yes, yes, yes!

The waves crashed against the shore as her orgasm took hold, and she dissolved into the light, into the sun, into an electric bliss. Everything and nothing existed as she scattered into a million pieces only Erasmus Cress could put back together.

"I'm there. I'm with you," he rasped against her neck, kissing and sucking the soft skin below her earlobe. He met his release, holding her close, the force of the man filling her as he cried out.

She clung to him, coming down from the heavens.

"That was..." she rasped, barely able to speak.

"That was us, plum. That was love. It was the yab and the yum—the balance we've both been searching for, the physical merging with the metaphysical, the energy of every chakra in my body flowing in perfect harmony with yours."

Wow, he sounded like...like her! She pulled back and stared at the man.

"I was going to say, really damned good, but I like your description better," she answered, twisting the hair at the nape of his neck.

"How about this for a description," he said, flashing that cocky grin she'd come to love. "Prepare to be hot, sweaty, and wet. We're not leaving this stretch of beach for the next three days. It's noisy yoga time all the time. We're going to survive on hot fudge sundaes. And when we're not sleeping, I plan on yabbing the yum right out of you. How does that sound, Miss Wham, Bam, God, I love you, Libby Lamb?"

It sounded like the beginning of forever.

"I love you, you beautifully infuriating beefcake," she whispered, but just as the words passed her lips, a chill ran down her spine.

What was that?

She loved Erasmus Cress. She did. Her heart was all in, but the little voice in the back of her mind whispered its warning.

Don't trust a man with your heart.

It was an overreaction—a defensive gesture she no longer needed, right?

Thanks to her father, her past was littered with broken promises, but everything was about to change.

Raz had spoken those exact words.

She ignored the whispers and concentrated on Raz's warm embrace. She leaned in, a breath away from kissing the man she loved. "Beefcake?" she said, the word floating in the warm air.

"Yes?" he purred as his self-assured smile bloomed into a boyish grin, and she cast her worries away.

She rocked her hips, reveling in the glow of her boxer. "Let's see what you've got, Erasmus Cress. I'm ready for all the *yab* you can *yum*."

RAZ GAZED out the jet's window, his mind and his body at peace. A blanket of puffy gray clouds obscured his view of the ground below, but it didn't bother him in the least. He wasn't concerned with the houses and trees below. He had everything he needed thirty thousand feet in the air. And what was the precious cargo that had him completely enthralled?

His love.

His light.

His Libby.

He was a man in love.

If he'd had it his way and could stop time, they'd remain in this perfect purgatory, soaring through the air.

The clouds broke apart momentarily, and the rocky earth peeked through the sea of gray.

They were close to the Aspen Airport. It wouldn't be long now. His pulse kicked up as a thread of anxiety wove its way around his heart. He inhaled slowly, then released the breath.

This isn't the end.

He wasn't about to lose anything. He and Libby might have

left Colorado as two people, but they were returning as one—a couple in love.

What they had wasn't a temporary respite.

He had to keep reminding himself that this was real. He loved Libby Lamb. They'd opened their hearts to each other on a white sandy beach, and now she was his. Their love was real—as real as the sun in the sky and the ocean that had gifted them with a peaceful soundtrack for the last three days. The tide would come in, and it would go out, but Libby's magic remained constant. Her spirit kept his demons at bay like a barrier of protection.

"I think Sebastian will adore this, don't you, Raz?" Libby commented, then reached into the bowl of Gummy Bears and popped one into her mouth.

He reclined in his chair and gazed at the woman who had stolen his heart. Sitting across from him, she twisted a lock of her dark hair as she focused on the items spread across the jet's table.

"This sketch of the island reminds me of the sketches Sebastian does in his book. I saw it, and I knew it would be a perfect birthday gift for him. It's not quite what he wished for when he shared his birthday intention with me."

"You never mentioned Sebastian made a wish."

"He made a couple. He wants to keep the donkeys, and he also wants..."

"Let me guess," he said. "He wants to keep you, his Mibby."

She twisted her jade bracelet. "Yes, something like that. He shared it with me on the trail. And he wants you to be happy. That was the first intention he set the day he arrived in Denver."

He bit back a grin, keeping his features neutral. Sebastian's first intention had come true in spades. He'd found happiness and love. Still, he wasn't ready to reveal what else he had up his sleeve regarding that second intention. But if all went to plan today, they'd be celebrating more than Sebastian's birthday.

She set the image on the table and studied the other trinkets. "Can we talk about the gift situation?" she asked, switching gears.

He leaned forward, assessing the lot. "I'm not sure if you bought enough stuff," he teased.

She waved him off. "Penny, Char, and H will love the jewelry," she said, moving on from the Mibby topic. "These shell bracelets are gorgeous, and we've got bags of coffee for the guys, and then we've got shirts for my brothers. The scarves are for Madelyn, your grandmother, Maud, and Luanne, and do you think your sisters will like the lava bead necklaces? It's so nice of them to fly in early to help with Sebastian with the fight five days away."

Five days.

A prickly sensation worked its way down his spine.

He knew the fight was only days away. Of course, he did. But he hadn't let his mind go there. With the Ass-in-Nine and the Moloka'i getaway, he'd blocked it out.

He inhaled and exhaled another slow breath. He would be fine. He had Libby by his side. This twist of anxiety was simply pre-fight jitters.

He forced a grin and surveyed the table. "My sisters will love them. Everyone will love their gift."

"And don't forget these," she said, popping out of her seat and retrieving two enormous leis from a pile of colorful flowers from Shandra's family's plumeria farm.

He needed her to slow down. He needed the world to slow down so he could savor these last minutes of having her to himself. It wasn't that he didn't miss Sebastian. He did. But the lad was in good hands. Between his granny and his sisters and their friends, as long as Phoebe Gale didn't challenge the kid to a hot dog eating contest, the boy would be fine. No, more than fine. He'd never seen Sebastian so happy. Colorado and one raven-haired woman had done a number on the Cress men.

"Come here, plum," he said, feasting his eyes on her.

She held up the lei, appraising the size, and padded over to him. "I think it will fit over Beefcake's head. He does have an enormous head, though. Must be a trait with beefcakes."

Now, he couldn't stop himself from smiling. In a flowing sundress with a white plumeria tucked behind her ear, even standing in the middle of a jet, she looked the part of an island goddess. The apples of her cheeks and the tops of her shoulders held a touch of pink, sun-kissed from days spent on the beach; their limbs tangled together as the crash of waves mingled with their moans of pleasure.

She set the lei on the table and eyed him warily. "You're not thinking about leis, are you?"

"Oh, I'm thinking about leis," he replied, gathering her onto his lap.

She straddled him and gave him a wicked grin. "I believe you're envisioning a very different type of *lei*."

Damn right he was.

"How do you do it?" he asked, touching the flower in her hair.

"Do what?"

"Look right through me and see everything?"

She wrapped her arms around his neck and rolled her hips. "I don't need to see anything to figure out what you're thinking. I feel it, beefcake."

He ran his hands down her back, and Libby hummed her satisfaction. She dipped her head, pressing a kiss to his lips.

"Thank you, beefcake," she whispered.

"Already thanking me, pre-orgasm? Then again, I am bloody

amazing at making you tremble and bringing on the Os. It is only proper to show your gratitude."

She kissed his cheek and smiled against his stubbled skin. "I'm thanking you for these last three days."

He closed his eyes, inhaling her sweet scent. "No, plum, I'm the one who should be thanking you. I don't know what I'd do without you."

She sighed and sat back, her amber eyes awash with love.

Bloody hell, he was a lucky man—lucky Briggs had pulled off the Moloka'i getaway and even luckier that, when he'd professed his love, she'd accepted it, welcomed it. They'd hidden away, basking in ecstasy and the giddiness of having nothing to do but each other. With Libby in his arms, his worries evaporated. Her energy washed away his pain and wrapped him in a blue-violet blanket of love. His petite yoga pro shielded him from the heartache of his past.

"We'll have to come back to Moloka'i and bring Sebastian with us. He'd love the farmers' market with the Hawaiian vendors and so much food. I've never seen so many tropical fruits. I couldn't even identify half of the produce. I'm glad we decided to put on clothes and check it out."

"You certainly didn't hold back," he teased, glancing over her shoulder at the gifts she'd purchased.

She scoffed, mock-outrage written on her face. "We couldn't return empty-handed. And don't think I didn't notice you sneaking off."

Shit.

He couldn't let her know what he'd gotten up to.

"I didn't sneak off. You ran into Shandra, and the two of you started talking yoga. It gave me time to wander."

He wasn't exactly lying.

"You came back with that look on your face," she said, watching him closely.

"What look?"

"The very-pleased-with-yourself beefcake smirk."

"This one?" he asked, curling his lips.

She sighed, dreamy-eyed. "Yes, it seems to have quite an effect on me now."

"The desire to bang your gong is gone?" He leaned in, ready to let the beefcake in him kiss her into oblivion, but she pressed her fingertips to his lips, thwarting his efforts.

"You never mentioned where you went," she said or maybe accused. That glint in her eyes was downright formidable.

Good thing the British Beast could match that challenging air.

"I was a six-five guy in a little Hawaiian market. I'm not sure anyone could lose sight of me, plum."

"So, you're not going to tell me what you were up to?"

He would—just not yet.

A sparkle had caught his eye in one of the shops across from the open-air market. As if the glittery trinket had called out to him, he'd wandered into the quaint shop to investigate. Minutes later, he'd walked out with a small wooden box.

"I was listening to my chi, love. That's all. I was a man on a Hawaiian island going with the flow, one with the universe."

He widened his beefcake grin.

When in doubt, mix in a bit of yoga-speak.

"Is that so?" she pressed, raising an eyebrow.

"Yep, and you would have known if I'd gotten into trouble, like, for example, chucking vibrators in the middle of a tropical flea market. Had I done that, that news would have made it to outer space by now."

She shook her head. "You've made your point. But..."

"What, plum?"

"I'm not sure what we'll do the day Sebastian learns that I wasn't throwing mini torpedoes at you."

That night did seem like it happened eons ago. And look how far they'd come.

"By then, plum, there will have been so many viral videos that ours will be lost in the web of sexual deviancy," he answered, cupping her face in his hand. For the first time in a long time, he liked thinking about what was to come.

And honestly, screw social media!

He'd only checked his accounts a handful of times while they were away. And yes, he and Libby had garnered some of the internet's spotlight thanks to Milo's post. Last he looked, the kid had gotten over a million likes. But he didn't mind that kind of publicity. The young man was genuinely excited about boxing. And if it brought a bit of attention to the island or his family's business, nothing would make him happier. When they did venture into town, the people of Moloka'i had been nothing less than discrete and hospitable, allowing them to explore the area without interruption. For that, he was abundantly grateful.

But that bubble of privacy was about to pop.

With the big fight less than a week away, they'd be walking into a media circus once they returned to Denver.

"You have a point," she conceded, but worry still lingered in her gaze.

"I promise, if there's anything you need to know, I'll tell you," he answered, glancing at the zipped pocket on the hoodie draped on the seat next to him.

"You're promising me the truth?" she asked. Her teasing tone had vanished, and he knew why. She had a rocky track record when it came to men making her promises.

He kissed her, capturing her mouth tenderly, in a slow, soulful exchange. "I promise that I love you. I love you so much, I can't see straight. I won't let you down, plum."

Like your bloody father—but he kept that thought to himself.

"I love you, too," she answered when a chime rang out.

"And...that's my cell. We can get back to the lei business after I see who's texting," she added and climbed off his lap to get the device.

"Who is it? Sebastian again?"

She stared at the mobile's screen and grinned. "It's your sisters."

"How'd they get your number?"

"Oh, I don't know?" she answered, her lightness returning. "Possibly from your grandmother, or any of my friends, or Sebastian, or Madelyn, or Augie, or Luanne. Maybe Maud or Wobbly Bob? Shall I go on?"

"Smart-ass," he murmured.

"And I might have suggested my brothers reach out to them."

"Your brothers?"

"My brothers are big into volunteering. They build medical clinics while studying to be doctors, and your sisters were doing volunteer work, teaching English. I figured they had similar interests."

He growled. "I'm fine with them being friends. Just let them know Calliope and Callista aren't allowed to date until they're thirty-five."

"You're thirty-two!" she shot back.

"I know," he answered, stewing.

"Oh, stop, you big protective beefcake! They're grown women," she cooed, pressing a kiss to his cheek, then showed him her phone. "Callista sent a pic. She and Calliope decorated the barn. With the rain, they made the call to set up inside."

"Is that a donkey luau?" he asked, then looked closer. "And is that Wobbly Bob in the background with my granny Fin?"

"You mean Robbie," she answered with a twinkle in her eyes. "And Finola's got a pretty wide grin on her face."

He stewed some more. "What's my granny got in common with a donkey rescue cowboy?"

"What's a Zen yoga teacher got in common with a first-rate beefcake?" she tossed back.

He sighed. "Point taken."

Libby scrolled through the message. "Your sisters say that Sebastian got the idea to make his donkey birthday a donkey luau when your grandmother told him you'd taken me to Hawaii. And it appears that we'll be feasting on pineapple grilled cheese sandwiches."

He cringed. "That's a thing?"

"With Mitch and Oscar cooking, I'm sure it'll be an amazing thing. They want to know when we'll be there. We're landing soon, aren't we?"

He reached for his mobile, checked the flight plan, then glanced out the window, now spattered with raindrops. He spied the majestic stretch of the Rocky Mountains through the haze of dark clouds when another chime, this time coming from the jet, pinged, signaling the aircraft's descent.

"There's your answer, plum," he said, then scrolled through his texts. "And Briggs is picking us up. He'll probably want to talk PR, so prepare yourself for a boring drive back to Rickety Rock."

He'd tried to infuse humor into his words, but anxiety panged in his chest. It was starting up again—the countdown until another big fight. He tried to ignore the feeling. He'd be ready. There would be no bloody panic attacks bringing him to his knees this time.

"Help me pack everything up," Libby said, springing into action. "I'll text your sisters back and let them know we won't be long. It's what, thirty minutes from the airport in Aspen to Rickety Rock?"

"Yeah, that's right."

She hammered out a reply, then pressed her mobile to her chest. "I'm so excited to see Sebastian and celebrate his birthday."

"It's a good day to celebrate," he answered, warmth replacing the anxiety rippling in his chest. He glanced at his hoodie's pocket again, then put it on before helping Libby pack up the bits and bobs.

They fastened their seat belts and settled in for the landing. With Libby on his right and, hopefully, the key to their future in his left pocket, he peered out the window.

The terrain was so different from that of England. But Rickety Rock, with its engaging characters and interesting local cuisine, wasn't all that different from the peculiar little villages scattered around the UK.

This place could be home—one of his homes.

He'd keep the flats in London. They didn't have to be tied to one continent. It wasn't such a stretch to imagine making a life here. Sebastian was happy. Augie lived here, and there were his bloody prick chat mates. Rowen, Mitch, and Landon truly were a bunch of wankers, but they were his wankers. A fizzy euphoria buzzed through him. He wrapped his arm around Libby's shoulders, anchoring himself to her and taking solace in her presence.

"Even in the rain, the view never gets old," she remarked, resting her head on his shoulder.

The jet touched down and taxied toward the terminal. They were back. The tropical respite was over. His emotions were all over the board, but he breathed easier with her in his arms.

He could do this. He could be a champion, a father, and a loving partner.

They gathered their things, thanked the pilots, and ventured into the rain. Libby's shopping had added to the load, and he hoisted the bags over his shoulders while she accepted an umbrella from the co-pilot. They didn't have far to go. No self-respecting Londoner would pop open a brolly for such a short stint in the rain, but he wasn't just a Londoner anymore. Part-time Coloradan had a nice ring to it, too.

He glanced at the parking lot and didn't see Briggs. "Let's get out of the rain and wait inside the terminal. I'll text Briggs and see how long it'll be until he arrives," he said as an airport employee held the door to the terminal open for them.

The regional airport had a decent number of travelers milling around. He looked for a few seats and spied a pair by the large windows in the front. "We can wait there," he said, gesturing with his chin. "We'll see Briggs when he pulls up." He glanced from side to side. He could feel the eyes following them, watching their every move. Then came the whispers. It went with the job, but when two men and a woman held up their phones, filming them, he sensed something was up.

That's Erasmus Cress!

I can't believe he's here, too. What are the chances?

Do you think they did this on purpose?

I bet somebody will want to buy this footage.

"Raz, what are those people talking about?" Libby asked, threading her arm with his.

"It's posh Aspen. They probably saw another professional athlete or an actor coming in on a jet," he answered. Still, he couldn't shake the ominous feeling as more people glanced their way.

And he's with Libby Lamb. I wonder if she's going to throw anything at him.

"Ignore them, plum," he said, squeezing her hand.

"Libby Lamb can throw whatever she wants at me," came a man's voice with a gritty Irish accent.

Bloody hell.

Libby stopped dead in her tracks. "Raz, that's..."

A muscle ticked in his jaw. "Yeah, plum, I know."

Ice and fire prickled in his veins as he stared down the unwelcome visitor, and one singular fact had become abundantly clear.

This was an ambush.

THIRTY

ERASMUS

"WHAT IS SILAS SCOTT DOING HERE?" Libby asked, disbelief coating her words.

"I'm not sure, but I'll handle it, plum." He surveyed the bustling lobby, then peered out the window. Briggs was still nowhere in sight, and bloody Silas Scott and his band of morons had planted themselves in front of the exit.

This was no coincidence.

There was no way to avoid them, and he wasn't about to turn tail and scurry off.

The Snake wanted to confront him, but he had to keep himself in check. He couldn't let the boxer turned wannabe internet provocateur provoke him.

The Snake's entourage moved in. A gaggle of scantily clad women and four men dressed like faux thugs tittered toward them, mobiles out, damn near salivating as they filmed the encounter.

Time for cocky beefcake mode.

If these idiots wanted a show, he'd give them one.

Didn't they know who they were dealing with?

This wasn't his first time going toe to toe with an adversary.

He'd won belts—plural. He'd been beating the piss out of a different version of Silas Scott years before this prick stepped into the ring.

That is, until Mere died, and then his life went to shit.

Focus.

He stared down his opponent. Twenty-four years old with a smirk on his lips and a chip on his shoulder and layered in so many gaudy gold chains it was amazing the kid could lift his head, Silas Scott sauntered toward them, clinking and jingling like a tea cart rolling over gravel.

"I see they let you out of Ireland. And you brought a pack of snakes with you," he added, gesturing toward Silas's crew. "You could be St. Patrick. I must say, I'm bloody glad you're here."

"Are you?" Silas tossed back.

Raz set their bags on the ground. "Yeah, we could use someone to carry our luggage."

Silas scoffed, looking him up and down, then set his sights on Libby. "Well, hello, darling," the man purred, his voice as greasy as his slicked-back blond hair. "Look what we have here. The *former* heavyweight champion and his *spiritual coach.*"

A muscle ticked in Raz's jaw.

He shouldn't take the bait, but this wanker was asking for it.

"Step back, plum. It appears Silas has forgotten his manners," he said under his breath as he took a step toward the man who was begging to get his arse handed to him.

"No, I won't," Libby stammered. "And don't do anything, Raz. They're recording this. This isn't some chance meeting. They must have known we'd be here."

"Smart one, isn't she?" Silas cooed. His green snake eyes glittered with mischief. "We caught wind that you were returning from Hawaii today and wanted to welcome you back. How nice to take a break from training so close to the biggest fight of the century." Silas's tongue darted past his lips like a bloody salamander as he eyed Libby. "I might fancy taking you on a posh island getaway, too, Libby Lamb. That is after I beat the Lion, or is it the Donkey? That's your thing now, yeah? You do her and then go out and give it to the donkeys?" Silas paused, giving his moron squad time to hoot and whoop it up. "Wait, wait, you're a geezer," he continued. "You probably need a nap before you can get it up for the livestock."

"Good one, Snake," one of his idiots called.

Raz didn't move a muscle. He knew this game. Trash talk was part of the show. With a hardened expression, he held back his fury. He could hear Aug in his ear.

Don't let it get to you. Save it for the ring, Erasmus.

But an icy trickle of unease, drip, drip, dripped into his psyche.

A shiver passed through him.

Was the Snake more prepared than he was?

"I'll make you a promise, Lion," Silas bit out.

Raz narrowed his gaze.

Stay cool.

"Will you now?" he cooed, playing the game.

"I feel for you, mate," Silas mused in a smarmy singsong tone. "I'll let you get a few hits in during the fight. That is, if you actually make it to the ring."

"I'll be there, Silas," he replied, his voice taking on a predatory tone.

Silas laughed. "After you cry a few tears for your dead wife, yeah? That's what happened last time, isn't it? Couldn't get her out of your head, could ya? What was her name again? Mallory, Marjorie?"

"Her name was Meredith," he spat as his stony facade chipped away.

Crack, crack, crack.

He locked in on Silas's slippery smirk. His heart hammered,

and the ice in his veins turned to fire, incinerating his last shreds of self-control.

But it wasn't anger lighting him up.

It was fear.

Fear of losing the fight.

Fear of failing Meredith.

"*Erasmus, Raz.*"

He could hear Libby calling his name, but her voice was barely a murmur, hardly a blip in the red haze enveloping the room. Blood pounded in his ears. Adrenaline spiked as he balled his hands into fists. "You say another word about my wife, and you will bloody regret it."

Silas lifted his chin defiantly. "I wonder, was Meredith as good in the sack as Libby Lamb?"

Crack.

The final fracture to his arrogant armor left his cocksure mask in a pile of dust on the ground. A ragged rush of palpable pain, raw and festering, flooded his system.

How dare this weasel of a man speak of Meredith or Libby.

He reared back, fists at the ready, prepared to deliver pain and send the Snake to the ground with a swift jab square to his smug face. But the slimy bastard dodged the punch. Skirting his fists, Silas sidestepped his advance. For a fraction of a second, the men's eyes locked, and Raz recognized that glint in Silas's eyes. It was the hunger to win and conquer and leave no man standing—an unabashed desire to succeed at all costs that had once burned white-hot in him.

Did he still have that drive, or had it died with Mere?

Confusion clouded his mind, and in that flicker of hesitation, the Snake landed a quick shot to his kidney. Raz doubled over, working to regain his balance, when Silas executed an uppercut and popped him clean in his left eye.

He should have bloody known the man would fight dirty.

But he wasn't thinking straight. He wasn't thinking at all. A fight-or-flight reaction had taken hold, and alarm bells blared in his head as the world went topsy-turvy.

Do not succumb to a panic attack—not bloody here.

He stumbled back. Electric agony thrummed in his belly as his eye throbbed. Acute and razor-sharp, he leaned into the pain, praying it would ground him. He sucked in a gulp of air and steadied himself, prepared to hurl his body at his rival when Libby threw herself into his line of sight. Standing between the fighters, she raised her hands defensively.

"Erasmus, stop, please!"

He blinked, watching as tears trailed down her cheeks.

"Briggs is here," she rasped, gasping like she was the one out of breath from brawling. "Our ride is here. It's Sebastian's birthday. We need to get to him, to your son," she pleaded.

Punch-drunk, he scanned the lobby. Where was the healing blue-violet aura? Where was the peace and harmony? Where was his bloody balance? Had it all been a mirage? Had he been fooling himself?

He couldn't meet Libby's gaze, but he nodded. An eerie silence consumed the terminal. No one said a word as bystanders held out their mobiles, and Silas Scott puffed up like a peacock and crossed his arms.

The victor—for now.

The bloke had gotten exactly what he'd come for. He'd walked right into the Snake's trap and served up this viral video on a gold platter like a bloody chump.

But no, that's not all the bastard had gotten.

Along with a video sure to skew the odds of the fight, the Snake had delivered something far worse than the pain of a bruised kidney, a black eye, or the sting of another embarrassing video.

The same sickening sensation that left him a heap on the bathroom floor before his last fight returned.

And it had a name.

Doubt.

Five letters.

One syllable.

And it seeped into every cell in his body.

"Have fun at the party. Who needs training when you can wear party hats and play Pin the Tail on the Donkey? That's got to be Erasmus's favorite." Silas clucked as his crew barked out the happy birthday song, clowning and laughing at his expense.

Libby gathered their bags and took his hand. "Let's go, please."

"Call me, Libby Lamb," Silas crooned. "I'll make some time for you to tickle my chakras. And then you can see what it's like to be with a real winner."

"Ignore him," she whispered, tightening her grip on him as she dragged him through the sliding glass doors and ushered him into a large SUV.

"What was that, Erasmus?" Briggs asked, glancing over his shoulder from the front seat. The man had turned as white as a ghost.

Dammit! He could see the ticker, numbers flashing, counting the video views wherever the hell Silas's minions had posted the footage of their skirmish. It would make sense that Briggs would keep track of the Snake's posts.

He shook his head, unable to respond. His thoughts rattled through his brain, knocking into the memories he'd pushed away.

Mere's cold, lifeless body.

Her muted, dead aquamarine eyes.

The sheet draped over her, and Sebastian crying out for his mum.

Breathe, just breathe.

"How do you know what happened?" Libby asked Briggs as the man shifted the SUV into drive.

"I saw it. The world saw it. The whole thing was livestreamed," his agent answered, holding up his mobile.

Just like he thought, another viral video.

And remarkably, that was the least of his worries.

A tiff on social media was one thing.

Losing in the ring with a billion people watching would wreck him, would ruin him. A loss would be the ultimate insult to Mere's memory.

He swallowed past the lump in his throat. He was so bloody sure he was on the right path—so confident that his time with Libby doing Pun-chi yoga was time well spent. He'd convinced himself that with her by his side, he couldn't lose.

He was wrong.

He loved her—he did—but he had to get back to doing what made him a champion.

He cradled his head in his hands, then pressed the swollen skin below his left eye. Stars flashed against his closed eyelid as shooting pain tormented his face. But he didn't move his hand, didn't let up the pressure. He needed to feel it, needed to allow the pain to consume him and bury his failure beneath a mountain of anguish. Only the searing pain could stop the clawing doubt from taking over his mind.

Briggs and Libby spoke in hushed tones, but he zoned them out.

Concentrate on the pain.

He slowed his breathing, glaring at his shoelaces when Libby touched his arm.

"Raz, let me see your face."

"I'm fine, plum."

"Let me take a look. We need to know if we should bring you to a hospital."

"What do you think I do for a living? Ride around on donkeys and meet the day with a sunrise yoga flow? I'm a fighter. What happened was nothing."

Lies, lies, lies.

If it was nothing, he wouldn't be a breath away from shaking like a leaf. He needed his mask, needed to become the beefcake to allow arrogance to disguise his anxiety.

But there was more.

He'd broken the first rule of boxing.

Don't let your opponent get under your skin.

He lifted his chin, forgoing staring at the laces on his trainers. "I don't need to go to the hospital, plum."

Libby met his gaze, worry written on her face as she assessed his eye. "Raz, are you sure? It's already got a blueish tinge to it."

She was trying to help. Of course, she was. She loved him. And he loved her. He wanted to let her in, but it was too dark inside his heart, too raw, too exposed. His only defense was to put up his guard.

"That's what happens to boxers. I'm going to get hit and bloodied up, and if you can't take it..." He couldn't finish the sentence.

"I'm on your side, Raz. I'm only concerned."

She was. He could see the tenderness in her expression. But isn't that what got him here? Thinking she was the answer.

"I have to do everything in my power to beat Silas Scott."

"I understand."

"Do you, Libby?" he barked.

"Champ?" Briggs called from the front.

"Yeah?" he said, grateful for his agent's interruption.

"We're here. I thought you might want a minute to get yourself together."

He stared out the window as a steady stream of rain pummeled the ground, the angry drops assaulting the roof of the SUV as Briggs turned onto the drive leading to the Victorian. He hadn't realized how much time had passed.

He ran his hands through his hair and blew out an audible breath. Agitation prickled beneath his skin, begging him to move, to sweat, to pound the heavy bag until his knuckles bled and he couldn't raise his hands.

"I'm good, Briggs."

His agent nodded with a dubious bend to his placating smile.

What he wanted was to stop feeling, to stop fighting the battles in his head. He had to focus on doing whatever he had to do to leave Silas Scott a bloody pulp, lying on the ground, pleading for the round to end. What he needed was that gleaming, glittery belt around his waist and the ref raising his hand into the air in victory.

"How about I get a bag of frozen peas and you can ice your eye before we head back to the barn?"

"No, please, plum. Let's get this over w—" He stopped himself. "Let's go," he said, amending his words. He could feel Libby's eyes on him, but he had to talk to Aug. The fight was in five days. Every minute not training was a minute lost. That was the ugly truth.

"I'll be in shortly. I have a few calls to make," Briggs said, eyes locked on his mobile.

Damage control to tamp down the fallout from the video, no doubt.

More bloody damage control.

He could feel Libby surveying him from head to toe.

"Your eye doesn't look too bad. How's your side?"

"Plum, I'm fine," he spat. He couldn't help it. He didn't mean to be cruel. He took a breath, forcing himself to modulate his tone. "He didn't get me that hard, plum. He threw those punches to show me he could."

"We were ambushed. Silas planned to catch you off guard, Raz. He said those awful things on purpose."

What she didn't understand was that her explanation didn't make it any easier.

Moving like his legs were made of lead, he grabbed their bags and exited the car, barely registering the rain. He helped Libby out and observed the SUVs parked along the gravel drive. Everyone was here, and then it hit him.

There was a damn good chance they'd seen the video.

"Are you ready to go in?" Libby asked, trepidation coating her words as the scent of Mitch's grilled toasties mingled with the clean scent of rain as music and voices floated from the barn.

"Yeah, sure," he replied, manufacturing what he hoped was a pleasant demeanor. But it didn't work on Libby. If anyone could sense he was out of sorts, it was her.

"I love you. We'll be okay," she whispered with such conviction it nearly cracked his heart in two.

He nodded, but there was no *we* when it came to his mental game.

And as of this moment, his mental and physical game was utter horse shit.

Pull yourself together.

They entered the barn. The earthy scent of hay usually lifted his spirits, but not today. He took in the space. Sebastian, Phoebe, and Oscar were preoccupied with Plum and Beefcake, feeding the animals cut-up apples while the adults huddled together, staring at their mobiles.

Another jolt of clawing doubt entered his bloodstream.

He'd called it. The video was out there for all to view.

He stiffened, shame weaving itself in with the sour doubt weighing like a stone in his belly.

His sisters caught sight of him first as he nodded to Granny Fin and the rest of the group.

Calliope and Callista plastered on smiles, pocketed their phones, and headed over.

"Raz, are you okay?" Callista whispered as she hugged him, then glanced over her shoulder at Sebastian.

"The lad doesn't know about the video, does he?"

"Of course not. The kids have no idea," Calliope answered through a hug. "Our mobiles send us an alert when you pop up in the news. We figured it was another Hawaii sighting."

He sucked in a sharp breath. "So, everyone's seen it? Augie's seen it?"

"Yes, and—" Calliope began, but he cut her off.

"And we're not talking about it," he said, his voice a husky rasp.

His sisters exchanged a worried look.

Concerned marred Calliope's face. "Are you okay, Erasmus?"

"What did I say about us not talking about it? It's a party. We should put on a happy face," he added, glancing at Sebastian, still busy on the other side of the barn.

Calliope turned to Libby. The women looked at each other as if they weren't sure what to do.

He didn't have a clue either.

"Callista and I are happy to meet you in real life," his sister said, falling back on pleasantries.

"Me too. Thanks for helping out with Sebastian while we were..." Libby trailed off, tossing him another wary look.

It was as if the Snake's stunt had tainted everything that had happened in Moloka'i.

It wasn't supposed to be like this.

He'd planned out in his head. They'd arrive at the party, and he'd surreptitiously slide the wooden box in with Sebastian's gifts. When they gathered to open presents, the boy would have plucked it from the pile. When he opened it, that would have been the cue, the moment he'd drop to his knee and give his son, and himself, the best gift they could ask for—a life with Libby.

"Dad, Mibby, you're back!" Sebastian cried, all smiles. "Look at the decorations. I helped Auntie Calliope and Auntie Callista. And look at Plum and Beefcake, and look at what Oscar gave me," the boy prattled, excitedly jabbering a mile a minute as he plucked a rectangular box from a table loaded with presents and cake. He removed the lid and held up a framed photo. "Oscar made the frame at camp, and he took the picture. It's you and me and Mibby and the donkeys after Mibby won the Ass-in-Nine."

He stared at the image in his son's hands. Bloody hell, if only he could go back to that time when everything in life was so clear.

But it wasn't clear. His attention had shifted.

He'd lost sight of what he had to do.

He wanted Libby so badly he'd forgotten that the entire reason for coming to Denver was to train with Augie to win—to beat the Snake and claim the heavyweight champion title.

With the cover of Sebastian by his side, their friends gathered around them. He could see it in their faces. Everyone wanted to ask about what happened, but no one said a word. With Sebastian beaming like he'd won the birthday lottery, the adults ignored the elephant in the room, welcoming them back and peppering them with questions about Moloka'i. He stood there like a giant oak weathering the storm when Aug caught his eye. The man had stood a few steps back as a flicker of disappointment registered on his trainer's face.

"Can we sing Happy Birthday to Sebastian, so we can eat the cake?" Phoebe asked, eyeing the sugary confection on the table next to the gifts.

"My dad and I made a chocolate cake with donkey ears," Oscar chimed.

"Can we, Dad?" Sebastian asked, hopping around.

"Yeah, absolutely," he said, scarcely there. It took every ounce of energy to muster the ghost of a grin. As much as he wanted to celebrate, he couldn't stop replaying the moment Silas landed his first punch.

Like a zombie, he sang along with the group. He stood by as Libby gave the lad the sketch of Moloka'i, then helped Sebastian put the leis on Plum and Beefcake. He made small talk with his granny, Bob, and Maud. Rowen, Mitch, and Landon had gone on about how the group should go on a tropical holiday together. He nodded, and he even chimed in once or twice, but none of it seemed real, or perhaps it seemed too real. He'd catch a glimpse of Libby, and his heart would jump into his throat. He barely knew up from down. When he finally had a second alone, Aug's voice cut through the buzz of sounds.

"Silas faked left, then went in on the right. We've watched the tapes. That's his go-to."

"Yeah, I know. I've been playing it out in my head."

Aug crossed his arms. "You should eat the rest of your cake, mate. You've been holding that plate for an hour."

He checked his watch. How had an hour passed?

He surveyed the barn and spied Libby standing with Penny, Charlotte, and Harper while his sisters and his granny chatted at a card table with Luanne, Bob, and Maud.

He couldn't even look at Granny Fin.

"We have to go, Aug," he said, his voice a scrape of a sound.

"I know what you're thinking, lad. You've got to stop that

right now," Aug murmured, taking his toothpick from between his lips and slipping it into his pocket.

"I should be in the gym—your gym in Denver with no distractions, sleeping on the cot in the back, eating and breathing the basics. Doing exactly what made me a champion."

"Dad!" Sebastian called, running up to him. The boy held a blindfold and a paper donkey tail in his hands. "Do you want to play Pin the Tail on the Donkey with us?"

Pin the Tail on the Donkey.

At the mention of the game, Silas's sneering, smug face flashed before his eyes.

He kneeled. "I'm sorry, Sebastian. You see, Aug and I need to go."

Confusion marred his son's expression. "Where do you have to go with Augie?"

Every pair of eyes in the barn bore into him. He could feel their disappointment, but the weight of judgment didn't hold a candle to the crushing doubt closing in on him from all sides.

"I need to leave to train with Aug. You know how important this fight is, right, mate? It's less than a week away. You understand that your mum would want me to win, so I need to make sure I do everything I can."

"Do you want to do the Chicken Dance before you go? We did it at camp. It's loads of fun," the boy offered, trying to brighten his spirits.

His son so desperately wanted him to be happy. And he would be—after he won.

He kept his emotions in check. "No, Sebastian, I'm sorry, lad. I can't."

"Yeah, all right," the boy said, putting on a brave face. "But you haven't opened your present yet. The one I have for you. I wrapped it myself."

"It's not my birthday, Sebastian."

The lad's smile returned. "I know, but I made it for you, and I finished it at camp while you and Mibby were gone."

It would have been easier if the boy had cried or thrown a fit. His kindness was like a knife twisting in his heart. He'd be the father Sebastian deserved—the man Mere sacrificed for him to be—after the fight.

After the fight.

"How about you save it for me? You could give it to me as a present for winning. We can do the Chicken Dance, too," he said, the words tasting more like defeat than victory.

"But you might want the present now because—" the boy began, but he cut him off. He could take it.

"I promise, Sebastian, I'll open it right after I win. I need to go, but believe me when I tell you, I promise I'll never have to leave another one of your parties early again. This is a special situation."

Sebastian smiled up at him with those aquamarine eyes, Meredith's eyes, welling with adoration. "Dad, don't feel bad. I'm happy you made it to my donkey party. Remember, last year you couldn't come to my birthday, and the year before that, you were training, too."

He nodded, emotion thickening in his throat. He'd do better. He would, right?

"I appreciate your understanding, lad." He stood, hating himself, but not knowing what else to do.

"Take Mum with you," the boy said, reaching into his pocket and removing the watch. "And Libby's special gemstone, too. You can rub it before bed when you think about a time when you were truly happy," he added, placing the items onto his palm.

How much more could he take?

"Thank you." Willing his hand not to shake, he unzipped his pocket, slid the items inside, then felt the box. He looked up and caught Libby's eye. The heartbreak in her gaze was another twist of the knife in his heart.

This isn't what he wanted. But it was what he had to do.

He turned to go, but Sebastian tugged on his hoodie's sleeve.

"Isn't Mibby going with you? She's your trainer, too. And don't you need Beefcake? He's your running buddy."

What was he supposed to say?

"I'll get that sorted. Join your friends and your aunties. It looks like they're ready to play," he said instead of answering.

"Are you sure you know what you're doing?" Aug asked.

"Yeah," he answered, then peered at Libby. Her friends had encircled her and delivered a round of eye daggers his way.

"I'm going to talk to Luanne, then I'll meet you at my car," Augie said, sliding the toothpick back in place.

Raz steadied himself. After he won, he'd fix everything. He'd do better. He'd be better.

"Libby, can I speak with you for a minute—outside?"

For what felt like the millionth time, all eyes were on him as he gestured toward the path. The rain had let up some, but it was still coming down in a slight drizzle. The green of the mountain looked brighter, like the earth was ready to burst at the seams, or maybe that was him, coming apart.

She stopped a few paces from the barn then turned on her heel, amber eyes blazing. "I hope you're not about to make me a promise."

Twist.

It would be a miracle if he had any heart left.

"You heard that?" he said, staring at the ground as the "Chicken Dance" song drifted from the barn.

"Why are you doing this, Raz?"

Her words tore at his soul.

"You were there, plum. You saw me swing and miss."

"That wasn't you, Raz. That wasn't the controlled, targeted

energy I feel when we train together. You let your emotions get the better of you. I sensed it. Your aura went red. It was like you ignored your chi and—"

"It's not my chi or my energy or a bloody aura," he interrupted, ready to break. "I have five days. Five bloody days!" He held her hands. "It'll be like I promised you in Moloka'i. I love you. I want to be with you."

"But after you win," she supplied.

"You know why I have to do this."

"Actually, I don't know that, Raz. And while I'm furious with you, I'm more upset with myself."

"For what?"

She looked him dead in the eyes. "For believing you. What happens if you lose?"

Twist.

"What do you mean?" he asked, flicking his gaze away.

"What happens if you lose, Erasmus?" she asked, holding her ground. "Will you pack up and go back to London?"

His thoughts spiraled. Meredith, Silas, Libby, Sebastian. Their faces came at him as the walls of doubt caved in.

"I don't know. I can't let myself go there."

"What about your fight is my fight?" she bit out.

It killed him to hear her say those words.

"This isn't your fight, plum. It's mine."

She shook her head. "What happens to us if you lose? I'm not an idiot, Raz. I get that you don't want me to come with you to train. So, what happens if it all goes south? Will you blame me and Pun-chi yoga?"

"Libby, plum, this fight is everything. Once I win, it'll be us —you, me, and Sebastian. We'll be happy," he said, taking a step closer when his foot bumped something.

Not something.

One of Sebastian's rock stacks. The stack that signaled the right path now sat scattered on the ground.

She pulled her hands from his grasp and stared at the stones. "You sound like my father."

"I'm not your father."

"Are you sure?"

"Plum, I promise—"

"Please," she whispered, shaking her head. "Don't say it. Don't promise me anything—not if we both know you don't mean it."

He had to make her see that he'd come through for her.

"How about this? I love you, Libby Lamb."

Tears welled in her eyes. "My dad would say that, too. 'I love you, sweetie. Things will be different after I win. Happiness is just around the corner for us.'"

"I don't have a choice," he confessed.

She pegged him with those amber eyes that saw everything. "You do, and you've already made it."

THIRTY-ONE

A GENTLE BREEZE blew through the park as Libby blinked back tears. She gazed at her cell phone's screen, then pressed play for the tenth, no, it had to be at least the eleventh time.

"Hi, Mibby! Hi, Dad! Hi, Augie! It's me, Sebastian. I know you're busy training, but I had to send you this," the boy announced as the video message played on her phone. She hit pause and drank him in, missing him like she'd misplaced a piece of her soul. Sebastian had his mother's aquamarine eyes, but in every other aspect, from his strong jaw to the air of confidence in his stance, he was Raz.

She hit play.

"Aunt Calliope is recording this. We're at an amusement park in Denver, and there's a swing carousel that goes super-fast —almost as fast as Plum and Beefcake, I reckon. You fly through the air like a bird or one of those maniac butterflies we have in Rickety Rock. I was scared to ride it at first, but now, I'm a right pro."

Libby swiped a tear from her cheek. Sebastian wasn't lacking in beefcake confidence either.

"Granny Fin's friend, that nice lady with the red scarf, was impressed. She came out of nowhere, walked right by me, and said, my goodness, you're brave." Sebastian puffed up. But Libby deflated. Of course, Madelyn Malone would sail into the picture. She must have been assessing the state of her nanny match, which at this point, must look utterly dismal.

They say that time heals all wounds. But how many times could a heart break? How many cracks and fractures could it endure? When did the healing center of the body break down into a heap of jagged shards?

She inhaled, then exhaled a shaky breath. She wasn't in complete collapse yet, but sweet Buddha's belly, after the last four days, she was damn close.

"Here's the trick," the boy continued, holding up his sketchbook. "Look right here." He tapped the illustration. "That's the bloke who helps you sit on the swing part and makes sure you're buckled in. He says you've got to keep your balance, hold on tight, and don't tip over." Sebastian handed the pad to one of his aunts. "Now, watch while I do it. Keep recording, Auntie Calliope."

He ran to the ride, his long legs pumping as he snagged the last chair. He settled himself, then held on to the chains connected to an ornately carved rainbow-covered dome. The ride lit up, shading the boy in a kaleidoscope of colors as a jaunty carnival tune blared. The swings revolved, going round and round and faster and faster, opening outward. Sebastian, the little daredevil, leaned over and waved each time he passed.

She smiled, unable to help herself. But it was premature. What would happen in a few seconds would add another piece of her heart to the pile of shards.

The music stopped, and the ride slowed, winding down, the swings drawing in like an umbrella closing as smiling passengers returned to the ground. Sebastian hopped off and barreled toward the camera, laughing as he wobbled, gradually regaining his bearings.

"It's a banger of a ride!" he exclaimed, then his features softened. "But I miss you all. I wish I could be with you, and I can't wait to see you on the day of the fight. Go, Lion! Go, Lamb! Bye, Augie, and namaste," Sebastian chimed, tucking his pad under his arm to bow in prayer position.

And then it was over. She stared at the screen, at her favorite seven-year-old caught mid-bow.

"Oh, Libbs, are you watching that again?"

Libby glanced over her shoulder and found Harper coming toward her. She'd texted the girls, letting them know she'd be at the park, and within seconds, they'd said they'd be on their way over. She'd forwarded the video to H after Calliope had sent it a couple of days ago. She needed someone to see it, someone to share in the moment.

It tore her up inside to think that Raz wasn't that person.

Had he even watched the video? He'd been cc'd on the email, but she had no idea if he'd seen it.

She hadn't heard anything from the man since they'd parted.

She sighed, mustering a grin for her friend. "I'm killing time before I have to head over to the rec center. That's why I suggested we meet here. My old landlord—"

"Smash Cakes?" H interrupted.

"It's Hash Pants."

"That can't be his real name," Harper mused. "Actually, it could be. I once had a piano student named Shishka Bobby."

Libby cocked her head to the side. "You mean shish kebab, like the food?"

"No, *Shishka Bobby*. Interesting family."

"I bet."

"So, what does Smash Cakes want?" Harper asked, plunking down on the bench.

"He texted that his great aunt wanted to meet at the rec center. She found something of mine in the apartment and wants to give it to me in person."

"Any idea what it is?" H asked.

"None at all."

Harper nodded, and for the space of a breath, the woman looked like she had the weight of the world on her shoulders.

What was on H's mind?

There was a good reason she didn't know. She'd been so engulfed with life in Rickety Rock over the last several weeks, she'd barely checked in with her friend. "How are you, H? I'm sorry I haven't asked in ages. Anything exciting on the piano teacher front?"

H glanced away. "I've got a conference in Las Vegas next week."

"And your grandmother? How is she?"

Harper's momentary flash of vulnerability dissolved, and the snarky glint returned to her expression. "You're stalling, Libbs. I'm here for you." H glanced over her shoulder. "And by the way, Penny and Char just pulled up. They should be here any minute." Her friend toyed with the hem of her miniskirt. "Before our *besties living their best lives and rocking diamonds that cost as much as a two-bedroom condo in Crystal Creek* arrive, tell me, after everything that happened in Rickety Rock, are you sure you want to be here? You've been dealing with some heavy stuff, and I know this place reminds you of your mom. It's a lot, even for our resident yoga queen."

Libby drank in the outdoor space.

Harper wasn't wrong.

Her mother had taken a class at the community center across from the playground. She'd babysat Anders and Alec here, keeping one eye on the boys while glancing into the building to try to catch a glimpse of her mother through the windows that lined the exercise studios.

But they weren't all heavy memories.

She'd played at this park with Charlotte, Penny, and Harper. They'd each take a swing and pretend they were flying through air back when they were just a pack of pig-tailed schoolgirls.

"I'm okay, H. I am."

But was she?

She sat back and looked on as a pair of children pumped their legs, sailing through the air on the swing set. The creak and whine of metal rubbing against metal as the children swung back and forth hung in the air above the chatter of boys and girls playing tag and venturing across the monkey bars. She twisted the jade beads on her bracelet and pictured the day she'd met Sebastian and brought him here—to this park, her park. He was a shy kid clutching a sketchbook, and now...

Now, she didn't know if she'd be a part of his life anymore.

She closed her eyes and focused on the scent of lilacs in the air.

"Hey, Libbs, hey, H," Penny said, sitting down next to her as Char sidled up next to Harper. "I was happy to see you texted about meeting up. I've been worried about you. Is everything working out with the Gale Gaming apartment?"

Libby opened her eyes, grateful to be with her girls. "Yes, Penn, thank you."

When she'd returned to Denver, she'd had nowhere to go. And even though she was certain Raz wouldn't be at his mega-mansion in the Crystal Hills neighborhood, she couldn't return to the place where they'd made love for the first time, where the like cures like experiment started, and where her world had been turned upside down by one hell of a handsome slice of beefcake. When she'd texted the girls, asking for hotel recs, Penny mentioned there was an apartment in the Gale Gaming office building. She'd said that the entire place would be empty for the annual weekly summer shut down and that she'd be welcomed to stay there.

It was as if the universe had known exactly what she needed.

Sure, she could have tucked herself away in a hotel. She wasn't penniless anymore. Thanks to the generous nanny salary, her healthy checking account could have covered the cost to stay at any of Denver's glitziest of boutique hotels, but the empty apartment inside an equally empty building offered ensured solitude.

"I know you want to be alone. I get it. But I wish you would have agreed to stay with one of us, Libbs," Char said. "I still can't get over what happened with Erasmus. But don't count him out yet, honey. You never know with these guys."

Char meant well, but Raz had made his choice, and her heart couldn't endure another broken promise. She'd structured her life precisely so she wouldn't have to feel that ache.

But nothing seemed simple or cut and dry anymore.

Could Raz surprise her and come to terms with the fact that he was going down a dangerous path? She understood that he harbored guilt and even blamed himself for Meredith's death. But how much winning would be enough for him to make up for his self-assigned sins? Could he change, or was he like her dad, chasing some pipe dream that everything would magically be okay after that next elusive victory?

She ignored the heaviness in her chest. "The apartment is exactly what I need. But don't get me wrong. I'm grateful you guys offered to let me stay with you, but I needed some time alone, and I had to stay hidden away. Raz and I agreed not to say anything to Sebastian yet. He thinks I'm training with his dad, and I didn't want Phoebe or Oscar to mention something to him if they noticed me at one of your places. And H..."

"No need to explain, Libbs," Harper said, waving her off. "If I had the choice of squatting in the luxurious Gale Gaming bachelor pad or living *la vida geriatric* with my grandma Presley, I'd opt for the bach pad any old day."

Libby playfully bumped H's shoulder, shaking her head as a genuine smile graced her lips.

Leave it to Harper to lighten the mood.

But her burst of happiness was short-lived.

The mention of her temporary lodgings only reminded her of what led her there.

After she and Raz had spoken in the rain outside the barn, and her heart had disintegrated in her chest, the man looked like the world had chewed him up and spit him out. But he still left with Augie. She'd watched him go, staring at the taillights as they disappeared down the drive. Feeling like she'd been run over by a Mack truck, she'd gone back into the barn and spoke to Sebastian, telling him she also had to leave to help his father. Despite it being a lie, the idea that Sebastian believed she and Raz were training together provided a sliver of comfort.

Or was she simply ignoring the inevitable—that it was over? And that Raz, like her father, couldn't see what was right in front of him.

She couldn't wrap her head around it. Her mind felt like a psychic bowl of metaphysical mush.

The last few days had passed in a blur, or perhaps a daze of disorientation was a better descriptor, and her poor chi had been put through the emotional energy grinder.

It seemed unreal to believe that Raz had whisked her away to Moloka'i only a week ago. They'd made love and professed their feelings, sweaty limbs tangled together as they embraced beside the ocean. With salt in the air and the rope swing swaying, she'd opened her heart and given herself to the man she loved.

Yes, loved.

She still loved her beefcake.

Lying in his arms, listening to the water, she'd pictured their forever life.

A life with Sebastian and their friends.

A life where Anders and Alec would visit, and they'd dwell in a cocoon of Pun-chi yoga bliss with donkeys grazing in the yard. On the sandy beach with the ocean stretched before them, everything had made sense. A beautiful symmetry had taken hold.

Little did she know that the balance had hinged on an unsteady precipice. It teetered on a rocky foundation like what she'd experienced after her mother passed, and her father's broken promises had stacked up, one on top of the other.

Her happily ever after with Raz was contingent on him beating the Irish Snake.

His rules, not hers.

And there was no guarantee that if he won, he'd finally find peace.

That wasn't love. It was torture.

"Have you spoken to Raz?" Harper asked, pulling her from her thoughts.

Libby stared ahead, her vision going blurry. "No, he made it clear that his priority was to win and that he didn't want me to get in the way of his training."

Did it hurt to hear him say that?

Yes, like nothing she'd ever known.

"I'm not sure it'll make you feel any better, Libbs," Charlotte began with a crease to her brow, "but no one has heard from him. Oscar and I got together with Callista, Calliope, and Sebastian yesterday and took the boys to the zoo. The girls told me that, as far as they knew, Raz was either at Augie's place in Denver or sleeping on a cot in the gym. He hasn't returned any of their calls or texts either."

"And Rowen says that he's not responding to their group chat," Penny added.

Harper blew out an audible breath. "He's gone dark."

H was right—and not only when it came to shunning communication.

Even separated, she could still feel him and sense his energy like she could with her friends, her brothers, and even Sebastian. When she pictured Raz, he wasn't surrounded by the blue-violet aura. Conflicted and laden with anguish, his light had dimmed to a murky, desolate gray—just like her light had. They'd become the black-and-white versions of themselves, barely surviving, their chi as balanced as a stormy sea.

"It's what he thinks he has to do to honor the memory of Sebastian's mom," she explained, but she couldn't believe that Meredith would want this for the man she'd loved.

At night, when she was helping Sebastian prepare for bed, she'd gaze at Meredith's picture in the pocket watch to get a feel for her.

And she had.

There was no malice in the woman's eyes, only love and kindness. She couldn't imagine Meredith wanting Raz to harbor such pain.

But he'd chosen to embrace the darkness and bask in agony.

She'd had sensed the shift in the man the moment Silas had evaded his punch.

Near palpable doubt had flooded the man's psyche, his aura instantly blackening. But it wasn't only doubt in his abilities as a boxer. The seething emotion had caused him to question their connection—their love. She'd felt it like a prick to her heart.

It really sucked to be highly intuitive some days.

"That's some heavy stuff," Penny replied.

"That episode at the airport really threw him for a loop," Charlotte offered.

"And Silas Scott is a real asshat—like a topnotch sleazeball. No wonder they call him the Snake," Harper growled.

"Believe me," Libby said, hating to hear the defeat in her tone. "I'd love to give Silas Scott a swift kick to the chakras, but it wasn't Silas Scott that made this happen. Sure, the fight at the airport messed with Raz's head, but cutting everyone off in a quest to win is his choice. Just like it was my dad's choice to keep moving the goalposts, keep making and breaking promises."

"What happens if Raz wins the fight?" Charlotte asked.

"I keep asking myself the same question. He wants to honor his wife's memory. I understand that. I do. But will winning this fight be enough? Will he decide he needs to fight someone else even if he wins? Will he ever win enough to fill the hole inside of him?"

There it was.

The crux of it all.

Penny leaned forward. "What are you going to do, Libbs?"

"I don't know. That's why I've been hiding out in your fiancé's building," she answered through a sad little chuckle when her cell pinged an incoming text, and the breath caught in her throat.

Char gasped. "Is it Raz?"

Libby checked her phone, heart pounding. "No, it's Hash Pants, my old landlord. Remember him? He's the guy who sublet his great aunt's apartment to me."

"I call him Smash Cakes," Harper chimed. "And he's set up a meeting with our Libbs and his aunt Ida."

"It's probably nothing," Libby countered. "Ida found something in the apartment that the movers didn't put into storage, and she wants to give it to me in person at the rec center."

"Picking this rec center is sort of strange, don't you think? Of all the places in Denver to meet, she chooses a place close to your heart," Penny mused.

It was a little odd, come to think of it. This rec center was a good twenty minutes from her old place. But hadn't she seen Ida here? Hadn't she caught a glimpse of a woman resembling Ida entering the building?

"Do you want us to come with you?" Char asked, snapping her back.

Libby stood and pocketed her cell. "I'm good. I'll be okay on my own. With my luck, she probably found a forgotten vibrator."

"Or ten," Harper teased. "You are the queen when it comes to battery-operated boyfriends. Even people floating around in outer space know it," H finished, gifting her with a grin, but there was concern in her sassy friend's eyes.

Penny rested her arms across the back of the bench and eyed Charlotte. "We'll hang out here and reminisce about the time Char forgot she was wearing a skirt, hung upside down from the monkey bars, then flashed half of the boys in our fifth-grade class."

"That wasn't me," Charlotte shot back, her red hair whipping over her shoulder as she gawked at Penny. "That was Harper."

"Oh, no, that was you, Char," Harper corrected. "Wait, no, I think it was you, Penn."

Penny's jaw dropped. "Oh my gosh, it was me, wasn't it?"

Libby drank in her girls, and her battered heart took comfort in their presence. "I love you guys."

"We love you, too, Libbs," the girls replied as the foursome embraced.

"Now, go get your ten vibrators," Harper directed. "We'll be here to help you carry the load."

They would. They always would.

Libby gave her friends one last look, then headed toward the rec center, listening to the girls go back and forth over the case of the fifth-grade flashing, so grateful to have these women in her life. But as the sounds of the playground and her besties' chatter faded away, a strange sense of déjà vu set in.

She came around a gentle bend and spied a stack of rocks and her heart ached. "How is this the right path?" she whispered to herself as a black blur flashed in her peripheral vision.

A crow glided through the air, sailing past her before landing on a nearby tree limb. She kept an eye on the bird. The winged creature appeared to be watching her, as well. The bird flew from perch to perch as she moved down the trail.

"Just don't crap on me, buddy," she cautioned, and now she'd clearly entered the conversing-with-animals portion of her heartbreak. But this bird had a familiarity to it. Yes, it was your typical black crow, yet the bird vibed with her.

"Catch you later, bird, namaste," she said as the rec center's entrance came into sight. But before she'd left the trail, a jingling sound caught her attention. She'd barely blinked when an arm shot out from the center of a bush—an arm adorned with several bracelets.

The nature lover's back was to her as the bush dweller twisted her way out of the leafy foliage.

It was a woman.

"I talk to that crow, too, Libby Lamb," the mysterious foliage frolicker chimed.

Libby gasped and pressed her hand to her chest at the sound of a woman's voice.

Who was this?

And how did the covert shrub bandit know her name?

THIRTY-TWO

LIBBY

"LIBBY, IT'S IDA."

Libby caught her breath as a jolt of adrenaline hit her system. "Sorry, Ida, I didn't see you there, chilling in the bushes."

Ida dusted several leaves from her green tunic and plucked a small twig from her white, flowing hair. "I was meditating with a butterfly."

"Good, great, yeah, butterflies have terrific energy. And you do find them outside in bushes," she blathered, her pounding heart beginning to slow.

Ida raised her hand, and a butterfly landed on her palm like she was Snow White, albeit the crystal-wearing, leaf-covered, yogi sage version. "They do. They teach us that we're capable of great transformation."

Libby watched the brightly colored insect open and close its wings a few times before flittering down the trail. She and Ida stood together, silently looking on as the butterfly disappeared, and a crow—that same crow—settled itself in the branches of a birch tree not far from them.

Ida inspected the bird. "I suspect you know what crows symbolize."

Libby eyed the creature, that again, seemed to be watching her. "Many yogis and mystics will tell you crows symbolize the past, present, and future."

Ida nodded. "Notice how its feathers change in the light. A crow's plumage is iridescent. They reflect the colors of their environment. See how this one has taken on a blue-violet hue."

Blue and violet.

She and Raz had once shared those shades.

How she longed to feel his lips on hers. She could almost taste the colors, juicy and sweet, as she disappeared into their auras.

Stop.

She pushed the thoughts aside and concentrated on the bird. "A crow pooped on me after you gave me the aquamarine stone," she said, not exactly sure why she'd shared that nugget of information.

Or perhaps there was a reason.

She studied the bird.

It felt like this crow was the same crow that soiled her yoga wrap.

She was totally getting that vibe from the winged creature.

It couldn't be, could it?

She was no crow expert, but there had to be thousands, if not millions, of the birds circling the city.

Ida pointed to the creature, still hanging out on a branch nearby. "You took a shit on her? My goodness," the woman added, then burst into a rolling belly laugh.

Was Ida okay? There was communing with nature, and then there was losing your damn mind.

"Were you doing anything else in that bush besides meditating, Ida?"

Like psychedelics or popping pot gummies by the handful?

The woman was Hash Pants's great aunt. There was no telling what a dude with that nickname could get his hands on.

"I was, actually. I was thinking of you, Libby," she answered, rosy-cheeked from laughter.

"Because you have something for me? That's what your nephew said when he texted."

Ida's features grew solemn as the yogi looked her up and down, then touched a strand of her dark hair. "It's uncanny to see you in the light after all this time," the woman said, the lines around her eyes deepening.

What was uncanny?

Libby froze as Ida and the crow zeroed in on her as if they were memorizing her every freckle and each strand of her raven-colored hair.

She understood a yogi's contemplative nature. She was a yogi herself. This encounter, however, tapped into a part of her, a part deep within her psyche.

Could Ida and this bird see into her soul?

It certainly seemed like it.

"Come with me," Ida said as the crow took off and landed on the ground near one of the rec center's large floor-to-ceiling windows. "What I have for you is in my bag back in the studio."

She followed a step behind Ida, observing the community center's entryway. "Do you teach classes here?"

"Yes, I've been gone for a while, but I'm starting up again."

Libby nodded, taking in the space as warmth radiated through her body. She hadn't entered the building since her mother passed. And in over a decade, very little had changed. A gumball machine stood half-empty near the door. The boys used to love that thing and beg their mother for quarters. She smiled, recalling how they used to guess which color they'd receive when they opened the metal lid. The circular check-in desk with three pendant lights hadn't moved from the center of the lobby, and the pale green walls were just as she recalled.

"Still the same, huh?" Ida commented, glancing over her shoulder, the crystals around her neck clinking as they walked down the hall.

How would Ida know the last time she'd been here?

"Yes, I haven't been inside this rec center in a long time."

"And I hear you've been in my neck of the woods," the woman continued, but she didn't look over her shoulder this time.

Libby followed her into a small yoga studio. "I'm not sure I understand."

"Rickety Rock," the yogi answered, pinning her with her gaze.

Libby's jaw dropped. "You're from Rickety Rock?"

A smile stretched across the woman's face. "Born and raised. My siblings and I were the first triplets in town."

"Triplets!" Now she saw the resemblance. "You're—"

"Ida Askew."

"Your Bob and Maud's sister?" she said, amazement coating her words.

"I sure am."

"That's quite a coincidence," Libby answered, shaking her head. "Not only did I sublet your apartment. I also spent most of the summer in your hometown. It's a lovely place. I spent quite a bit of time with your siblings. They provided us with donkeys and helped train us for the Ass-in-Nine."

"I heard Doug took a shine to you," Ida tossed out with a twist to her lips.

How did she know that?

Libby glanced away. "Doug is..."

"Not for you," Ida supplied, lifting an eyebrow. "You see, Dougie came to Denver to visit me and Henry Peter. He had some extra time before he left for the yoga retreat because a young lady named Libby Lamb had canceled on him."

Sweet Buddha's belly!

"Henry Peter?" Libby repeated, then put it together. "Wait, Hash Pants is Doug's brother, and his name is Henry Peter?"

Ida looked at her as if she'd sprouted rutabagas out of her ears. "Yes, you didn't think Hash Pants was his real name, did you?"

She shrugged.

Ida released another rolling belly laugh. "We're a little weird in Rickety Rock, but not weird enough to name a baby Hash Pants."

"My friend Harper will be so disappointed," she mused. "Wow, I can't get over all the coincidences."

Ida's expression grew serious. "It's not a coincidence that you and I have connected, Libby, or should I say reconnected."

"It's not?" she asked, not following.

"A swallowtail butterfly in Tibet told me it was time to return. That was the instant the ripple of the intention had begun to play out."

Libby mustered a smile. There was a lot to unpack with that statement.

"A butterfly told you to come back to Colorado?" she pressed, needing a little clarification.

"A butterfly told me it was time to return to you. It was time for our paths to cross again."

There she was with the *again* business.

"Why would our paths need to cross?"

Ida went to her bag and removed a small box with *for Libby* written in her mother's hand.

Libby swallowed past the emotion in her throat. She hadn't seen the box in years. "Where did you get that?"

"It was in my apartment. It had fallen off the top shelf in the closet and was wedged against the back wall." Ida reached out and stroked her cheek. The woman's touch was soothing, like a tactile lullaby. "Libby, you are so very much like her."

"Like who?" Libby rasped, but she didn't have to ask. She knew the answer.

"Your lovely mother, Aurora."

Libby took a step back and studied the studio as that sense of déjà vu unearthed a cascade of memories. Her gaze bounced from Ida to the view out the large windows. She stared at the playground and could picture the twelve-year-old version of herself standing among the children. "You were the teacher—the instructor who taught the stretching class for women going through chemotherapy."

"Yes, that was me."

She inhaled a shaky breath. "Did you know I was living in your apartment?"

Ida gifted her with a warm grin. "I didn't know it was you until I returned and spoke with my nephew. I'd had minimal contact with the outside world during my time in Tibet. When the taxi dropped me off, it was dark, but I should have recognized your energy, your rage. I brushed off the feeling. Whoever you were, I figured you were angry at being booted from your apartment. I gave you the stone because I felt awful for you."

Something wasn't adding up.

"How would you have recognized my rage?"

"When your mother started coming to class, she was a ball of anger. Rage had taken hold of her and disrupted her chi. That aura was something else, I tell you. But of course, she would be furious. She didn't want to leave you, your brothers, and your father. Our stretching class was much more than touching your toes. She and I connected on a spiritual level. I saw a light in your mother, an intuitive quality I believe you share with her."

"Yes," Libby answered, blown away by the revelation. "My

mom had a sixth sense about things, and we could both read auras."

"I helped her craft an intention so she could depart this world peacefully, knowing that you, your brothers, and your father would be okay—that you could carry on," Ida explained. "I gave her an aquamarine stone to dispel her rage and allow healing to take hold."

It made sense.

Her mother's aura had changed after she started attending the classes. Not that her mother had ever been cross or cruel. That wasn't her way. But the hopeless vibrations had stopped once she'd started coming here.

She'd never put together that the instructor had given her mother that gift.

And then she felt a pull, an energy.

The box.

She removed the lid, and there it was. The blue-green stone she recalled seeing her mother slip into her pocket. The stone her mother had removed from the box and pressed into her hand minutes before she'd taken her last breath. The stone she'd clutched as she promised her mother she'd watch out for the twins.

She ran her finger across its smooth surface. "After my mom passed, I never took a second to process the loss. I turned my attention to my brothers and my dad. I can't believe I'd forgotten about the stone."

"It didn't forget about you," Ida said gently, then gestured for them to sit on two yoga mats spread on the ground.

She sat cross-legged, grateful to ground herself. She'd never felt like this.

Lost but found.

Anxious yet at peace.

"When I arrived back in Denver, and my nephew told me

your name, I knew this was your mother intervening. This was her energy and her intention transforming into action. You might have felt alone after your mother died, but you weren't. The ripples of Aurora's intention have always been with you. That intense energy of a mother's love cannot go unchecked."

Libby nodded, unable to speak.

"Your mother's energy is infused in your aura. I'm sure you've sensed it."

"It's blue-violet," she answered, but Ida frowned.

"No, dear, it's indigo. There's quite a difference."

"Indigo," Libby whispered. It had never dawned on her to see the colors as one.

"While blue denotes contentment and peacefulness and violet shows us power, indigo takes elements from both colors to create something new. Indigo is the shade of those who seek truth, who aspire to enlighten others and guide others. Your psychic glow is your truth. Indigo is the color of deep devotion— devotion to loved ones and to their life's work. Your mother and I used these qualities to craft her intention."

"Do you remember the intention?" Libby asked.

Ida closed her eyes and exhaled an even breath. "Aurora wanted her family to embrace love, care for each other, and follow their hearts. She wanted you all to picture your family's happy times and hold them in your heart."

Picture a time when you were truly happy. Hold that feeling in your chest, close to your heart.

"Wow," she said, wonder coating the word. "My mother never told me this was her intention."

"Had she told you about this solemn wish, it might have colored your view of yourself. She understood that there was a path, and it was yours alone to discover."

Libby brushed a tear from her cheek.

"And then," Ida continued, "when Maud called and told

me a Libby Lamb was part of the group renting the old Victorian on the hill, I understood why that butterfly told me it was time to come home. Since that day, I've been keeping tabs on you."

"From Maud and Bob? I thought I sensed a connection to them. It must have been you."

"Yes, Maud and Bob had quite a bit to say about you and Erasmus. But I must say, I learned a lot from the internet. It's come a long way in ten years."

"It has," Libby replied through a teary chuckle.

"I noticed that the aquamarine stone didn't do much to contain your rage the evening we met," Ida added, but there was mischief twinkling in her eyes.

Libby stroked her thumb across the stone. "I took what you said to mean that I should practice some rage yoga."

Ida flashed a wry grin. "Well, my dear, you succeeded. I must have watched those astronauts reenacting that video of you throwing the *objects* at Erasmus Cress a hundred times."

"That night set quite a bit into motion," she said, glancing out the window.

"I know, dear. You love him, don't you?"

She met Ida's gaze. "Erasmus?"

"And the little boy, too."

"Sebastian." She smiled. "Yes, I love them, but it's complicated."

Ida nodded. "When Maud told me you and Erasmus were participating in the Ass-in-Nine, I knew that had to be the ripples of your mother's intention guiding you on your path. Did Bob tell you that the donkeys know?"

"He did."

"Animals are intuitive," Ida continued. "They bond with their caregivers, and that bond lasts. It can also bring humans together. I hear you won the race."

"I did thanks to a butterfly-chasing Jennie named Plum. But my path is a little unclear at the moment," Libby confessed.

"I see. And how are your brothers?"

"They're doing well. They're studying to be doctors."

"And your father?"

Libby's heart sank.

"My dad...he's..."

Ida's brow wrinkled. "Your mother was most worried about him and how he'd handle her passing."

"He didn't handle it well. He still doesn't handle it well. I sensed him falling apart even when she was still alive. That's why I promised my mom I'd look out for the boys."

"Your mother didn't want the responsibility to fall on your shoulders, but we both saw your aura, Libby. We both sensed a well of strength that flowed within you. It's in your nature to step up. But don't count your father out yet. Perhaps the ripples of your mother's intention haven't yet reached him. He loved her deeply. He hated that they didn't learn of her condition earlier—that he didn't pick up on something ailing her. They had a strong connection. He was devoted to her, but she wasn't sure what he'd do with that force, that powerful drive, once she was gone."

"Erasmus is like that, too. His wife, Sebastian's mother, passed away suddenly, and he blames himself. I thought he'd moved past it. I thought that what we have, or had, would have helped him."

"This is where transformation plays a part in healing," Ida replied. "You cannot know love without accepting loss. You can't heap on a serving of love to smother the pain. It might delay, but it will return. You can only know them together. When you limit one, you restrict the other. It's the quintessential balance. The yin and yang."

Libby nodded as Shandra's words echoed in her mind.

Love is stronger than any force holding you back.

The trick is uncovering what that force holding you back truly is.

It's not always what you think, but it's exactly what it needs to be.

She stared into Ida's eyes as an epiphany took hold.

"I can only move forward with an open heart. A heart that's willing to take risks. A heart that's willing to break. Only then will I know love, the kind of love that endures through a lifetime."

Ida's eyes shined with emotion. She looked out the window at the crow. The bird was still there. "See, Aurora, she understands. She got your message."

Libby closed her eyes, pressed her hands to her heart, feeling her mother's embrace as the indigo energy wrapped her in a blanket of love. They sat quietly for what could have been thirty seconds or thirty minutes when a knock at the door pulled them from the trance.

"Is this the class for women going through chemo?" a lady asked, her head wrapped in a pink scarf.

"It is. Go ahead and get yourself a mat. We've got a few more participants coming. The class will start shortly," Ida directed warmly.

Libby came to her feet and pocketed her mother's stone as the woman did a double take. "You're the Pun-chi yoga lady, right?"

"Yes, I guess I am," she answered, taken aback.

The word had really gotten out. Those viral videos were no joke.

"Will we get to do that in this class, too?" the woman asked, directing the question to Ida. "I tried it at home in front of the mirror and felt like a beast," she finished, tossing out a few jabs.

"I'm sure we can have Libby join us very soon, but she has to be going. She's meeting two visitors."

"I am?" Libby asked.

"Yes, and that reminds me. I almost forgot. I found something else of yours," Ida said, turning to dig in her yoga bag. "I believe this belongs to you. I found it near the box," the woman finished, holding up a giant indigo-colored vibrator.

"Yeah, that's mine," she said, feeling her cheeks heat.

Of all the days not to have her tote with her!

The woman in the headscarf chuckled. "I saw you in that video, too. I hadn't laughed so hard in ages. And let me tell you," she continued, "I can use every delightful distraction I can get. I even told my husband he better be on his best behavior, or I might pull a Libby Lamb."

Libby held up the sex toy and chuckled. "They are remarkably easy to throw. But try not to do it in public. You can get arrested for it."

More women entered the room, and Ida circulated between them.

Libby started for the door, not wanting to delay the start of class when Ida called to her.

"There should be two women waiting for you outside the center. I told them to meet you here," Ida rattled off before engaging a trio of ladies.

Who in the world would be waiting for her?

There was no time to ask.

As discreetly as one could, she tucked the vibrator under her arm and walked down the hall. A lightness had taken hold. An almost giddy grace bubbled in her chest. She startled. Oops, that giddy grace was the vibrator. She must have turned it on. She giggled as she left the community center, vibrator in hand, when she spied two women—two young women she recognized.

"Hi, Libby, do you remember us?" a tall blonde asked. She stood next to a petite brunette.

Libby's jaw dropped. Of course, she remembered them! Her once loopy libido couldn't have forgotten their sexed-up ladies' room conversation. She'd nearly combusted from pent-up sexual frustration.

"You're Cleo and Laney from the bathroom, right?"

"That's us," Laney answered brightly.

She glanced between the women, still not sure what the heck they were doing there. "It's nice to run into you again. Can I help you with something?"

"Oh, Libby," Laney gushed. "You don't mind if we call you Libby, do you?"

"It's my name, so, yeah, Libby works."

"And look what she's holding, Laney," Cleo cooed, staring at the vibrator like it was a newborn baby.

"This," she said, waving it in the air as she felt her cheeks heat. "I left it at my old apartment, and the current tenant returned it. I don't usually stroll around with sex toys."

Lie! The world knew she did.

"Sometimes, I do. I used to," she stammered.

Stop talking. She should cram the vibrator into her pie whole.

Cue the embarrassment. But these women seemed downright excited to see her traipsing out of a building with a giant plastic cock in hand.

"We wanted to speak with you since that day we met in the bathroom," Cleo explained, tucking a lock of blond hair behind her ear when Harper called to her.

"Who are your friends, Libbs?"

Libby surveyed the trail as her besties headed her way.

"This is Cleo and Laney. We met in the ladies' room right before I went in for that fake VC appointment with the Tri-Derricks."

"If anyone is going to make friends in the toilet, it's our Libbs," Harper said to Penny and Charlotte, who nodded to the women.

"Libbs, why are you holding a vibrator?" Char asked under her breath.

"It's a long story."

"Actually, it's the perfect transition," Laney chimed.

"Yes, we have a business proposal for you, Libby," Cleo continued.

"You guys aren't with those Derricks, are you? Because I know they're full of crap," she said, eyeing the women.

"Oh, no, we are not affiliated with them," Cleo answered, waving her off.

"Hell no! We were renting space in the building, but when we learned one of the Derrick's dads owned it, we moved our VC office to a different location," Laney explained.

"You run a venture capitalist firm?" Libby asked.

"Yes, but we're not predatory venture capitalists or like the douchebags pretending to be a VC to meet women. We got into this line of work because we want to support women in business," Cleo replied.

Laney reached into her tote, produced a business card, and handed it over. "We're C.L. Investments."

"C.L.," Penny exclaimed. "Libby, emails came in from them when I was holding your phone."

That's right!

"I thought it was my dad, trying to get information about Raz. I deleted them without even opening them."

"Yeah, that was us, reaching out. We only had your email and home address," Laney replied, reaching back into her bag. She removed a sheet of paper that looked as if it had seen better days.

Libby stared at the familiar page. "That's my business plan. Well, parts of it."

"Yeah, one of the Derricks tore it up after you tore into them. Bravo, by the way! Those creeps deserved it," Cleo added.

"And you taped it back together?" Libby asked. The sheet was just as much tape as it was paper.

"We did. Here's the rundown," Laney began. "We got a great vibe from you when we met in the bathroom."

"Okay," Libby answered cautiously.

"Then we saw you tell off the Derricks."

"Like I said, girl, that was fierce," Cleo chimed.

"And after that," Laney went on, "we saw you in the vibrator incident with Erasmus Cress. You know, the video that went viral?"

"Oh, she knows," Harper answered.

Cleo nodded. "That, Libby, was epically empowering stuff. Women don't need to hide the fact that they enjoy sex toys."

Libby's eyes widened as she shared a look with her besties. And from the shock on their faces, they weren't expecting to hear what Cleo just tossed out either.

"Strong women own their sexuality. They can even take those battery-operated beauties and let a man have it," Laney added.

"That's when we got the idea for the Libby Liberator vibrator," Cleo dropped.

And...what?

"A vibrator with my name on it? We are talking about vibrators, right? Sex toys?"

This might be the wackiest convo she'd ever had.

"Yes, that's where Cleo and I made our fortune. We started out as engineers. We're the creators of the Rainbow Screamer."

"Oh, my God, that vibrator changed my life," H gushed as Penny and Charlotte nodded.

"That little hitch vibration is pure poetry," Penny swooned.

"And that's why we want to work with you, Libby," Cleo continued. "We figured we'd make one last-ditch effort to meet with you. We showed up at the address on your business plan yesterday and met Ida. She told us you'd be here today."

"Let me get this straight. You want to finance a venture to make vibrators with me?"

"Yes, you'd be at the helm of connecting sexuality, spirituality, and hopefully, Pun-chi yoga."

"You know about Pun-chi yoga?" she asked, then recalled a random stranger had just asked her about it.

"Have you been under a rock, girl?" Cleo teased.

Libby shared another look with her friends. "I've been under a rickety rock."

"People are buzzing about it since that last viral video," Cleo began. "My family got together a few weeks ago. Everyone from my grandmother to my five-year-old niece and nephew wants to start doing it. People saw your demo and loved it. I asked about it at my gym, and they told me members are asking about it there, too. This idea is hot."

"You've got buzz, Libby. Every viral video of you and Erasmus Cress has hundreds of millions of views," Laney added. "You could be a brand. You could be the face of female empowerment."

"Libby, this is amazing!" Penny breathed, awe coating her words.

"Do you have a contract with Erasmus Cress?"

Raz.

What would he think of this?

Actually, she knew the answer.

He'd be happy for her. He wanted good things for her.

He loved her, but he was lost, battling his demons. And as much as she wanted to erase his pain, she couldn't. She could offer support. She could be there when he needed her, but he had to let her in.

She took stock of her situation.

This opportunity with Cleo and Laney could give her the financial security to help her brothers and support herself.

It was everything she'd ever wanted.

No, it was almost everything.

"I am under contract with Erasmus Cress."

"And when does it expire?" Laney pressed.

Two days.

Her sixty days would be up in two days—the day of Raz's big fight.

For a matter of hours, she was still bound to him.

"It expires the day after tomorrow."

"We're absolutely onboard if you want to continue to collaborate with him," Cleo replied. "It's not a game-changer for us. We still want to work with you. Do you mind if I ask a personal question?"

"The world seems to know a lot about me, but, of course, ask away."

"Are you and Erasmus Cress together?"

That was the million-dollar question.

"I don't know exactly what we are."

It was the truth.

Cleo nodded. "What do you say, Libby? We believe in you. This is your moment. You can make an impact and improve people's lives, men and women alike."

"But mostly women with a super-charged Liberator Libby vibrator," Harper chimed.

It seemed like a dream.

She glanced between her friends when the blur of black returned, and the crow landed next to a smattering of wildflowers—indigo-colored blooms. They were the same type of wildflowers Raz had picked for her the day they'd left for Moloka'i.

A peacefulness set in as she drank in the color, and she focused on the bird.

Could that have also been the crow that crapped on Derrick Dawson?

She had so many questions.

Was that her mom?

Or was that bird, that crow, the harbinger of the past, present, and future, simply reacting to the energy created when Ida had helped her mother craft a heartfelt intention?

As if the crow had read her mind, it stilled, then spread its wings, and flew away, disappearing beyond the towering birch trees.

She'd gotten the message loud and clear.

It was time to spread her wings, follow her dreams, and trust in the power of her mother's intention.

This was her path.

Would she walk it with Erasmus Cress?

She didn't know. What she did understand was that whichever way he went, whatever road he followed, it had to be his choice. Her path had led her here, and with an open heart, a heart ready to take risks and even break, she knew what she had to do.

"I just need a second," she said, pulling her cell from her pocket. She opened her texts and tapped the icon to write a new message.

To:
She typed three letters: *D, A, D.*
Message:
Can we meet up? I'd like to talk.
Send.

This was moving forward. This was trusting in her mother's love—and maybe, just maybe, her path would cross with Sebastian and Raz's again.

Picture a time when you were truly happy. Hold that feeling inside your chest, close to your heart.

She inhaled deeply, then exhaled a cleansing breath as a memory unfolded like a butterfly climbing out of its cocoon. It was a replay of the moment she banged her gong like a wild woman outside the boxing gym.

That was the moment when everything had changed.

The moment triggered by her mother's cherished wish.

It was time to live the life her mother wanted for her.

She visualized the night it all started. She could see Raz's face, stricken with disbelief, and then she recalled the first words out of his mouth—those silly words that spoke to her heart.

She turned to Cleo and Laney and bit back a grin. "What do you think of naming my vibrator the Wham, Bam, Thank You, Libby Lamb?"

THIRTY-THREE

ERASMUS

RAZ STARED AT THE ROAD. His eyes were open, but he didn't see anything. Trees, buildings, and street signs passed in a blur of color. Every once in a while, a bus would pass with his image plastered across the side and the words *Pay-Per-View Main Event* blasted in bold letters. Nothing registered. Nothing made him look twice. The city had adorned flags with boxing gloves to the light posts lining the major Denver boulevards. The Mile-High City had set its sights on professional boxing, and the clock was ticking.

He usually fed off the energy.

Not this time.

He'd been holed up in the gym, eating, sleeping, and breathing his sport, doing anything and everything to dull the pain and distract himself from the soul-sucking doubt.

Aug stopped at a light as a local sports talk radio program played in the background. The voices melded together, droning like a sea of jabbering gobbledygook. Every so often, he heard his name, then Silas's, then more chatter. He leaned his head back and stared at the roof of Augie's SUV. He was barely there, a ghost, an echo, a man intent on one thing and one thing alone.

Victory.

It was the day before the big fight, and despite wanting to pound the bag, Aug had insisted he take it easy. He shifted in his seat, nervous energy coursing through him like he had ants in his pants. But that energy would soon come to serve him well.

Tonight, the cameras would roll, recording live the much-anticipated weigh-in. He and the Snake would growl and hiss and parade around the stage, hamming it up for the cameras before stepping on the scale to record their official weights.

The intensity would be set to pure alpha.

The air, electric.

Two animals sizing each other up, itching to tear the other apart in the ring.

And why was the press in near hysterics?

Three words: another viral video.

It would be the first time he and Silas would meet face-to-face since the incident at the airport.

The entire world had gawked and gaped, watching as he swung and missed, and the Snake dodged and hit.

Twice.

That was the last time he'd looked at his bloody mobile. He'd turned it off. No silent mode. No vibration. Off. Gone. Dead. Do not disturb.

His heart had been put through the wringer.

His confidence, slaughtered.

He hadn't spoken a word to Aug on the drive from Rickety Rock to Denver. They'd pulled up to the gym, and fifteen minutes later, he'd wrapped his hands, gloved up, and had started swinging. It was the only way to put meaning to his pain. The only solution to his agony and the only path forward.

Path.

He recalled the path leading from the barn to the Victorian, darkened from the rainfall, then pictured Libby's face as he tried to explain why he had to leave. When his foot hit the rock stack, the crack of the stones mimicked the cracks in his heart as he stood there, staring into her eyes. Their last words to each other returned to him every night in his dreams.

No, his nightmares.

I don't have a choice.

You do, and you've already made it.

There wasn't another way—at least, not one that he could see.

Between the crippling doubt and the visceral clawing pain, all he had left was the fight.

Truth be told, he didn't care what the media had to say about the matchup. He wasn't fighting for them. He'd done a decent job shutting it out, but he'd heard snatches of conversation between Augie and Briggs.

Unprecedented excitement.

Highest Pay-Per-View preorders ever recorded.

The fight of the century.

Let them concern themselves with that piece of the puzzle.

He'd gone into boxer zombie mode.

All that mattered was strapping on gloves and fighting like the devil.

He'd pounded the heavy bag until his knuckles bled. He'd knocked out hundreds of combinations and sparred with multiple partners. He didn't need rest. He barely required fuel.

When he was in the grind, slick with sweat, limbs trembling, and breaths coming fast, it masked the ache. Like a machine, he'd gone numb. It was as if his head had overridden his heart, turning off the emotions to do what had to be done.

And that was to win.

Beat Silas Scott and send the Snake back to Ireland, a bloody bruised loser.

He pulled the hood of the same hoodie he'd been wearing

since he'd left Rickety Rock over his head and felt the jostle of the items in his pocket.

Libby's aquamarine stone, the timepiece with Mere's picture, and the small wooden box.

He could have grabbed another hoodie. God knows he had a dozen of them hanging on hooks in Aug's gym. But he kept going back to this one—like a child reaching for a cherished teddy bear.

It was his one indulgence, the one item he'd permitted to bring him a sliver of comfort.

He'd craved the life he, Libby, and Sebastian had built in Rickety Rock. Every cell in his body begged to be back with them, doing Pun-chi yoga on the porch, running the trails with donkeys, tucking Sebastian into bed, then having Libby to himself. He missed her scent, missed wrapping her silky raven-colored locks around his fingers, missed cracking open his eyes each morning to find her beside him. He'd stare at her, bloody awestruck, so in love, and so at peace. If he were any other man, he would have taken that beauty, that perfect purgatory, and never left.

But he wasn't just any man.

He was a fighter.

A fighter with much to prove.

A fighter who could not lose.

He was a fighter who owed a massive debt that required payment in blood and sweat.

"Erasmus, there's a file on the back seat. It's from Briggsy. He dropped it off last night. You need to sign off on it," Aug said, keeping his gaze trained on the road.

"Can't you do it, Aug? I don't care about the PR bullshit."

Aug released an audible breath. "I can't do this for you. This requires your specific attention."

"Fine," he huffed, twisting his large frame and plucking the manila folder from the seat. He opened it and read the line.

PR release regarding termination of partnership between Erasmus Cress and Libby Lamb.

The muscles in his chest tightened as a heaviness set in. He skimmed the paragraph.

After a successful partnership training for the Heavyweight Championship fight, spiritual coach and Pun-chi yoga creator Libby Lamb and the Heavyweight Champion, Erasmus Cress, have chosen to part ways and pursue individual projects. Erasmus Cress and the entire sports management team wish Miss Lamb well.

The heaviness felt more like a lead weight.

He read what was left, then glanced at Aug.

"It's dated for tomorrow."

"Yeah."

"That's the same day as the fight."

"Good to know you can still read a bloody calendar," Aug answered tightly, toothpick in place between his lips.

"It says I'm the champion. I haven't won yet."

"Isn't that what you want, boyo?" Augie tossed back, more bloody sour than usual.

"What's got you twisted up?" he bit back.

"I've been stuck with your beastly ass, night and day," Aug complained.

The man had him there. Even he could concede it was no picnic training twenty-four seven. He reread the press release, finding it hard to believe sixty days were almost up.

"Her brothers' schooling is paid for?" he asked.

"Briggs said he released the final payment yesterday."

Raz stared at the page. "So that's it?"

"You're supposed to initial it, then give it to Briggs."

A muscle ticked in his jaw. "I don't have a bloody pen on me. I'll do it later," he barked, folding the sheet into a tiny square and stuffing it into his pocket with the other items.

Would that be it?

He'd fight Silas.

There would be a winner and a loser.

And then what?

He'd promised Libby that after he'd won, they could go back to the way they were. But she'd done what she'd always been able to do. She'd looked through him with those amber eyes, looked right to his very core, and had seen the truth.

Would one win be enough?

He wanted to believe that it would, but when he pictured Libby's face, he'd felt the truth—a truth he couldn't quite acknowledge. All he knew how to do for Meredith was to fight and win. He couldn't see a path forward that didn't include fighting. He didn't know anything different.

Train. Fight. Win. And do it for Mere.

Do it because she believed in him. Do it because she'd made him a champion. She'd been his greatest supporter. She devoted herself to him and started a charity in their name.

And he let her die.

He crossed his arms, his emotional armor in place. "Where are we going, Aug?"

The man didn't answer.

"It's the day before a fight. I have a ritual. You know that. I have fish and chips and then—"

"And then you and Meredith take a walk, and you buy her flowers from some vendor. I know your ritual. I know you've done it in cities across the globe. I know because I was there. I know because, for your last fight, you tried to do it by yourself, and that didn't serve you well. We both know that."

"That was because the last fight was in London and—" his voice gave out.

"And it was your hometown," Aug interrupted. "And it was the exact place where you and Mere got fish and chips, and then you walked to the bench where you sat with her after your first date. I know, Erasmus."

Raz pursed his lips. "It's my ritual. It's what I do."

"Not this time, mate. We're starting a new ritual."

"Says who?" he barked, sounding more like the sullen four-teen-year-old Aug had reluctantly agreed to train.

"Says me, your bloody trainer!"

Raz shifted in his seat as a sickening sensation made his stomach flip-flop.

There it was. The fear and the doubt churning in his belly.

"No, Aug, I need to do it just like I did before. Like I did when I was racking up belts and titles and—"

"And you had your wife. And then it was you, your wife, and your boy. That's not your life, Erasmus," Aug belted, color rising to his cheeks.

Raz didn't answer. He couldn't.

"We're doing something different this time," Aug said, speaking slowly, his tone resolute as he cooled down.

"And what's that?"

"Reminding you who you bloody are, lad."

There's a no-answer answer.

"That really helps, Aug," he grumped.

"Shut your bloody gob, Erasmus. We're close."

"What about the weigh-in? We can't miss that?"

"We'll leave from where I'm taking you. You'll be on time. What do you want? Exact times? If you haven't noticed, I've been busy. Do you think I've had a moment to memorize the tube timetables for the Piccadilly line?" his trainer ranted.

"Look at those knickers in a twist! Why the hell would you need to memorize the London tube timetables? We're in Colorado?" he shot back.

"I'm making a point, Erasmus! Training your arse doesn't give me time to do much else."

"Fine, we go where you want to go, Aug," he answered, sitting back and focusing on the scenery.

They'd left the swanky Crystal Creek neighborhood, sailed past the city's skyscrapers, and ventured into a grittier, more eclectic part of Denver. One- and two-story buildings with funky cafes, little boutiques, and small art galleries lined the street. And bloody hell, there was something familiar about it.

Aug turned the corner and headed toward a large building. Taking up nearly a block, people milled around the courtyard. Teens and young men and women blanketed a basketball court fenced in adjacent to the building. And then he saw the sign.

Helping Hands Shelter and Community Center.

"I know this place. Mitch Elliott is friends with the people who run it."

"The Dagby's," Aug supplied.

He stared at his trainer. How would Aug know that?

"Yeah, Mitch named his first food truck after Louise Dagby."

"Louise and Ralph Dagby run the shelter," Aug added. He parked the car, grabbed a plastic bag from the center console, and got out.

"What are we doing here, Aug?" he asked, exiting the vehicle. "Am I signing autographs?"

"Take this," Aug said, handing him...a tiny net?

"What do you want me to do with it?" he asked, pulling at the elastic rim.

"It's a hairnet. You put it on your head."

"You okay, Aug? Are you off your rocker, mate?" he asked, stretching the thing out in his hands.

"I'm peachy keen. Come on," the man said, starting for the door.

They entered the center's vestibule, and Aug waved him to follow as the man set off down a hallway.

"Have you been here before?" he asked.

"Yep," Aug shot back. "This is the part of the center for kids and teens."

Raz was ready to ask another question when they passed a room, and he recognized a man huddled around a laptop with a trio of teenagers.

"Rowen?" he uttered.

"Excuse me, Augie, do you have a second?" a man asked, walking toward them.

"Give me a minute, Raz," Aug said, then met the man further down the hall.

Raz stood in the doorway, and Rowen came over.

"What are you doing here?" he asked, not expecting to see the nerd.

"Teaching a class on coding. My company is shut down for the week to give the employees time off. How are you, man? We've tried to get ahold of you."

"I've been training hard. I unplugged from everything."

Rowen nodded. "Are you ready for the fight? Mitch, Landon, and I plan on heading out soon for the weigh-in."

Raz released a slow exhale. "I'm as ready as I can be." He shifted his stance and ran his hands through his hair, wanting to ask about Libby.

"She's doing all right, Raz," Rowen said, reading his mind.

"She is?" he rasped. "You've seen her?"

"She's staying at the apartment in the Gale Gaming build-ing. She's been laying low because of your arrangement."

Because they'd agreed not to say anything to Sebastian.

Ice trickled down his spine.

"I'm not sure if I should tell you this," Rowen began, "but Penny and the girls saw her yesterday."

"And?" Raz asked, perking up, eager for any morsel of information.

"And Penny says she got offered a great business opportunity, and she even contacted her dad. They're getting together tomorrow. Penny says that's a pretty big deal for Libby."

Jesus!

"Yeah, it's huge. So, she's okay?" he asked, working to keep the emotion from his voice.

"Penny used the words balanced and peaceful to describe her. But she's taking a page and decided to unplug until after the fight." Rowen shifted his stance. "Is it over between the two of you?"

It hurt like hell to hear those words uttered out loud.

"I don't know what we are. But I want her to be okay. I want her to be happy," he rattled off, saying all the right things.

"Is that all you want?" Rowen asked when Phoebe zoomed over to her uncle and skidded to a stop.

"Hey, Raz!" Phoebe beamed, donning a hot dog headband.

"Hey, Phoebe."

"Say hi to Sebastian for me and tell him to save me some apples," the child directed.

"Okay?" Raz answered, not sure what to make of Phoebe's request when the girl tugged on Rowen's sleeve.

"Uncle Row, how do you spell *bureau?*"

"Why do you need to spell that? We're teaching the kids to code."

Phoebe adjusted her headband. "I was taking a break and showing them how to hack into sites. I need to spell bureau for the Federal Bureau of—"

Rowen's eyes nearly popped out of their sockets. "Raz, I've got to take care of this before Federal agents come for my niece," the man sputtered before sprinting to a computer terminal. "See you at the weigh-in."

"You ready?" Aug called from down the hall.

"Did you know Rowen Gale volunteered here?"

"Yeah."

"Libby's staying at an apartment in his building."

"Is she?" Aug replied nonchalantly.

"He says she's doing well, but she's turned off her phone and decided to unplug."

Bloody hell, he sounded like an idiot.

"I know a bloke who's done the same thing," Aug threw back, raising an eyebrow.

Touché.

He couldn't blame Libby for wanting to shut out the hype, especially after he shut her out. He pressed his hand against his pocket and felt the tiny box, his heart pounding. God, he missed her. He wanted to know more, wanted to congratulate her on her business deal. He wanted....

He caught himself.

He wanted...

He wanted...

He wanted...

It was all about him.

"Raz, I believe you know Louise Dagby," his trainer said as the woman who opened Helping Hands with her husband met them in the hallway.

"It's good to see you, Erasmus. Thank you for putting us in contact with the charities in the UK for the Mr. Cheesy Forever program. I'm not sure if I ever got to thank you in person for that. It's been a whirlwind of activity here at Helping Hands."

"Is that true, Erasmus?" Aug questioned with a curious look in his eyes.

Raz waved the woman off. "I'm glad I could help. I didn't do much besides connect Mitch with a few charitable organizations in London."

"Isn't that ironic," Aug said, sharing a look with Louise.

Raz glanced between the pair. "How is it ironic?"

"Come with me," Louise said, gesturing for them to walk with her down the hall.

He followed behind Aug and Louise when another familiar voice floated through the air. No, more like several familiar voices. They walked through an atrium, and he glanced over to find his sisters, his granny, and Madelyn Malone chatting with a tall older man.

His jaw dropped. What was this? A family reunion?

"What are they doing here?"

"Your grandmother and Madelyn are showing your sisters around," Louise answered.

"I don't mean to be rude, Louise, but what would my sisters want to see here?"

His sisters glared at him. Yep, he was still in the doghouse over Sebastian's birthday and for being MIA these past few days. They also adored Libby. He flashed them the international big brother eyes for *what the bloody hell is going on?* But they didn't give him anything—not a smile, not a scowl, nothing.

There was another strike against their wanker brother.

He'd sort it out after he won.

He continued, following a step behind Aug and Louise, when he encountered another familiar sound. Luckily, this noise wasn't a bunch of women who wanted to kick his arse all the way back to East London. It was the pop and thud of padded gloves meeting a stuffed bag. It was the flick of a jump rope, tapping the ground. It was the rumble of heated breaths and the slide of trainers gripping the floor.

"This is what your sisters got to see today," Augie said, stopping in front of a set of doors. He pointed to a large plaque and framed photograph on the wall.

Raz took it in and froze, dumbstruck, hardly able to believe his eyes. "Is this what I think it is?"

HELPING Hands Boxing Gym

> *A gift from the Cress Family Foundation.*

Next to the plaque hung a photograph. He knew this picture. Years ago, the same photo had run in every major paper in the UK.

"That's..." he said, his heart ready to beat its way out of his chest.

"That's you, Meredith, and Sebastian, when he was a tiny thing," Aug supplied.

He nodded, staring at the image like if he looked at it hard enough, he might be able to go back in time. Of course, he knew the photo. He hadn't thought about this day in a long, long time. Just looking at it made him smile, and the image cracked open a part of his heart he'd walled off.

The part that held the happy memories of his time with Mere.

"That was the first Cress Family Foundation project. We donated funds to build a facility to house a preschool and after-school program for older kids in East London," he reminisced. He drank in the image of his wife, smiling at the ribbon-cutting ceremony. He had Sebastian in his arms, and the boy held a paper butterfly, and the lad wouldn't let it out of his sight. They'd had to slip it from his chubby little hand after he'd fallen asleep. The tension in his body released as he recalled gazing down at his sleeping baby and the abundant gratitude he'd felt in that moment. "I helped Sebastian make the little craft—the butterfly." He shifted his attention back to Meredith. He'd been so proud of her. She'd put her heart and soul into charity work.

"When did you do this? How did you do this?" he pressed.

"Madelyn Malone introduced your grandmother and me to Ralph and Louise Dagby. Your granny Fin believed the organization was a good match with the Cress Family Foundation."

"Is that what she was doing while we were in Rickety Rock?" Raz whispered, more to himself than anyone else.

"Finola believes it's what Meredith would want," Aug added.

"It is," Raz whispered, his gaze growing glassy when the door swung open.

"Dad, you're here!"

Sebastian?

He must be here with Granny Finola and his sisters. He looked the boy over. The kid had on a hairnet.

What was the deal with hairnets here?

"Hey," he said, taking a knee to be at his son's level. "I've missed you." His heart felt ready to explode.

"It's a good picture, yeah?" the lad said, looking up at the photo. "Is Mibby with you? I bet she'd like that I'm holding a butterfly in that picture. You know she and Plum love butterflies."

How would he explain Libby's absence?

He cleared his throat. "Yeah, I think she'd loved the picture."

"Where is she?" Sebastian asked, looking over his shoulder.

"She's not here. It's just your dad, for now, lad," Aug supplied in his, *there it is, take it or leave it,* Aug way.

"Well," Sebastian said, then sighed like he was gearing up to take on the world. "We're on fruit duty, right, Louise?"

Fruit duty?

"You certainly are," the woman answered.

"Did Augie give you the hairnet?" Sebastian asked.

"I've got it right here," he answered, holding it up.

"They're almost ready for snacks," Sebastian explained, but he didn't have the first clue what the boy was talking about.

"Who's almost ready?"

His son took his hand and led him into the gym as Louise gestured to the space.

"The Cress Family Foundation purchased every piece of equipment. They'll be installing a ring in a few weeks," Louise explained as they entered the massive room. "Thanks to your family's donation, we'll offer classes and run an after-school boxing program."

He surveyed the gym. Heavy bags and speed bags dotted the training area. Plenty of lockers lined the walls. A state-of-the-art weight-lifting area with shiny new equipment sat across from a cleared area with yoga mats on the ground. It was packed with boys and girls, working in groups of two and three. He couldn't have designed it better himself.

"This is a proper boxing gym," he said, awe coating his words. "Granny Fin did this?"

"I helped a bit," Aug added when a lanky boy waved to them.

"Hey, Aug! I'm hitting in small circles like you said to do. Can you check my form?"

"Do you mind, Erasmus?" Aug asked, watching him closely.

"He'll be fine. He's with me," Sebastian answered, taking his hand.

His son guided him toward a sink next to a table laden with fruit and cutting boards. "This is the snack station. First, we wash our hands," Sebastian announced as they lathered up. He grabbed a paper towel, then scanned the gym. "Isn't this place great? Granny Fin said Mum used to help places like this. She liked helping kids."

"She did," Raz answered, his voice thick with emotion.

"I think it's a banger of a thing to do. I want to help people, too," the boy mused, then glanced at the table. "We better get to it. Like Aug would say, no lollygagging. There's work to be done. Put on your hairnet, Dad. You've got plums."

"Plums?"

Just hearing the word made him ache to have Libby with them.

"I'm cutting up the apples, and you can cut the plums. We're making fruit salad for the kids to have as a snack after they're done in the gym." Sebastian leaned in. "Some kids don't get many snacks at home. Louise said it's important we cut up the fruit for them. It's called helping the community," Sebastian finished, taking a plastic child-safe knife and slicing an apple in halves, then quarters before adding the fruit to the bowl.

He had one amazing kid.

He fitted the net on his head, stared at the plum, missing his plum more than ever. He picked up the knife, pitted the fruit, and cut it into wedges. They worked quietly for a good fifteen minutes before he spoke. "You're a lot like your mum, Sebastian."

His son focused on the work. "You don't have to talk about her. I know it makes you sad."

That comment cut like a thousand slashes.

"It used to," he admitted, emotion building in his chest. "But seeing this place and knowing that it was your mum who started the charity that makes this possible doesn't make me sad. It makes me remember that we had lots more happy times than sad times."

"Happy times like when you and Mum would push me on the swing in the garden?"

He held his son's blue-green gaze. "Just like that."

Sebastian grinned up at him. "I'm glad you're here."

He blinked back tears. "Me too."

"Sebastian!"

Raz pulled himself together, then turned to find Oscar Elliott running toward them.

"Will you teach me some Pun-chi yoga moves?" Oscar asked, then observed the six-foot-five man-baby beast of a Cress, ready to burst out into tears. "Oh, hi, Sebastian's dad! Can Sebastian help me? My dad said I could hang out with him while he was working with a student."

"Can I, Dad? Can I?" Sebastian chimed.

"Yeah, I'll take care of the fruit. Let's see those Pun-chi yoga skills," he added, his voice thick with emotion.

"Louise wants us to put the cut-up fruit in the bowl. She said one of the volunteers will come and get it." Sebastian tore off his hairnet, dropped it into a trash can, and ran alongside Oscar to the open area.

"That hairnet suits you," his granny said, sauntering over and taking a seat at the table as Aug and Madelyn joined her.

"I see the arthritis is better, Granny," he commented, sensing that something was up. This sage trifecta had set their sights on him.

These three were surely in cahoots.

"Yoga and a roll in the hay can do wonders," his granny Fin dropped like an atom bomb.

"Roll in the, what? Wait, you and Wobbly Bob?" he shrieked, trying not to picture it and...bloody hell! There it was...granny sex. He shook his head, hoping the motion would dislodge the image.

Finola Cress beamed. "It's Robert, or Robbie when we're—"

"I get it," he interrupted, swallowing back bile. "You and Robert are an item." He stared at the fruit, needing something else to concentrate on. He shifted in his seat and tugged at his hairnet.

Blooming lunch lady hairnet!

No man should have to wear a hairnet while listening to his granny go on about knocking boots with the local donkey rescuer.

"Just don't let the twins see me in this hair thing. Knowing them, they'll snap a picture and never let me live it down."

"Done and done, Raz-a-ma-taz!" Callista cooed as Calliope snapped a shot on her mobile.

He hung his head. His family would be the death of him. Between his heart jumping into his throat, talking about Mere with his son, and Granny's revelation, his head might explode.

"Auntie Calliope! Auntie Callista!" Sebastian called, waving over his aunts.

"We'll be back for more hairnet shots," Callista warned as the twins joined the boys.

He removed his hairnet, staring at the balled-up material. "I understand why you brought me here, Aug."

"Do you?"

Raz blew out a tight breath.

How could he make them understand?

"I'm training for Mere. And I'm going to win for her. And to beat Silas Scott, I've got to be the best. That's why I had to..."

"Break Libby's heart?" Granny Fin supplied.

The woman did have a knack for cutting to the chase.

"Yes," he answered, unable to lie.

"Your problem isn't skill, Erasmus," Aug said, looking him dead in the eyes. "Even if you hadn't trained a lick these past few months, you'd be better than the Snake, and I'm not just saying that. I'd tell you if you weren't. I've always been honest with you, lad. You're a fighter. The best I've ever seen, but you forgot what you were fighting for. You forgot what it means to win."

He forgot what it meant to win. What the hell did that mean?

"Do you think Mere wanted you to win?" Aug pressed.

"She didn't like watching me get hit."

"And you decided that meant you had to win at all costs," Augie challenged, then leaned in, his expression softening. "Remember who you were when you met her. You weren't adding belts and titles to your name when she fell in love with you. Meredith didn't keep coming back to the gym because you were a great teenage boxing champion."

Raz rubbed his temples, his head spinning.

So much for a relaxing pre-weigh-in ritual.

"We miss her, too, dear," Granny Fin said, emotion coating her words. "And I need to tell you something. Something it's time for you to hear." She paused as if to gather herself. And that meant something. Finola Cress was a pillar of steel, but whatever she had to say touched her deeply. "Before she slipped away, Mere asked me to watch over you and Sebastian, and after I agreed, I made a promise to her."

He steadied himself, hating that he hadn't been there when his wife had taken her last breath. "What did you promise her?" he asked, his voice a scrape of a sound.

"I promised I'd step in and help if you needed help."

He dragged his hands down the scruff on his jawline. "You did. You and the twins cared for Sebastian. You swooped in, and you did what I couldn't do."

She shook her head. "It was no burden to care for your son, Erasmus. The promise I made to Mere was more than that.

Meredith knew you could be as stubborn as a mule. She had a feeling you'd blame yourself for her illness, and she didn't want that. She wanted you and Sebastian to love and to be loved. She didn't want your heart to harden. Meredith would never have wanted you to grow apart from your boy. I let you mourn. I gave you time, but when I saw you drifting away, really drifting into a dark, dark place, that's when I asked Madelyn for help."

"Sorry you couldn't fix me," he said, nodding to the matchmaker, trying to keep it light, but it was no use. He couldn't hide the shake in his voice.

"That's where you're wrong," Madelyn answered, watching him closely. "I don't fix anyone. I'm only a facilitator. I'm the starting point. You decide who you are at the end of the sixty-day trial period. And we're not there yet. You've got one day to go."

One day.

One day to figure out how to honor Mere and show Libby that he loved her. How could he do that when choosing one meant negating the other?

"Let me ask you this, lad," Aug said. "How many times does lightning have to strike twice in your life? I was there for the first strike. I saw your face the minute Meredith entered the gym. And I was there when those two bolts of lightning struck in Rickety Rock. Not to mention, I saw your face the minute Libby banged that gong outside the gym weeks ago and started throwing..." He paused, then tossed a nervous glance at Granny Fin and Madelyn.

"Vibrators, Augie! You can say the word," Granny lamented. "We old birds quite enjoy them." She shared a look with Madelyn. "With a prude like Aug, I reckon we should send Luanne a Rainbow Screamer," she added under her breath.

Madelyn whipped out her mobile. "Done," the woman answered with a mischievous smirk.

And there it was—more senior sex talk.

"Are ya done, Gran?" Raz asked, cradling his head in his hands.

His granny mimicked zipping her lips.

Augie's cheeks had bloomed crimson, but the man composed himself. "All I'm saying is, everyone sees it. You love Libby, and she loves you. And she loves Sebastian."

Aug wasn't wrong.

He loved Libby.

He truly did.

And Libby was crazy about Sebastian—and vice versa.

But what Libby, his granny, Madelyn, and Aug didn't understand was that he didn't know what came next if he lost.

"What are you fighting for?" Aug asked, his voice a low rasp.

The answer was simple.

"The belt and the title."

That was it.

Cut and dry.

Plain and simple.

But saying it out loud left a hollow space in his chest.

Aug's mobile pinged, and he peered at the screen. "Briggs is here. Time's up. We need to go."

"Another weigh-in," his granny said, gifting him with a smile but concern brewed in her eyes.

The doors opened, and Briggs entered the room, scanned the space, then made a beeline their way. Sebastian caught sight of the man, waved goodbye to Oscar, and joined the agent.

"It's time," Briggs said. "I'll follow behind you and Augie, and we've got cars coming in the next twenty minutes to collect Finola, Madelyn, Callista, Calliope, and Sebastian," he added with a nod to his granny and the nanny matchmaker.

"Can I ride with you and Aug, Dad? I have something for

you," Sebastian said, then procured a rather large box from beneath the table. The thing was nearly half as big as he was.

"Yeah, I think that would be grand," Augie answered.

Raz nodded. "Absolutely, son, I'd really like that."

And he meant it.

He usually spent the time before the weigh-in alone. Even when Mere was still with them, he chose to do this part of the pre-fight song and dance on his own. Aug was close by backstage, Briggs too, but no one entered his dressing room. He used the time to psych himself up and put on the mask to play the role of the cocky boxer and become...the beefcake.

Beefcake.

He took in his son, and the boy beamed.

Maybe Aug was right. Perhaps it was time for some new rituals.

With his granny and Madelyn promising to finish up with the fruit, he and Sebastian left the gym, walking side by side. As they passed through the doors, he took another look at the framed photo, and a sense of calm washed over him. It was like Meredith was there. Like her light and love had returned. He'd focused so much on the pain of losing her that he hadn't allowed himself the comfort and joy of her memory.

In a daze, he climbed into the back of Aug's SUV with his son.

"Here, Dad," Sebastian said, passing him the large box as Augie started the car, and they made their way toward the event center.

He shook the box gently. "Sounds a bit clunky."

"I made it for you."

"Did you now?" he answered. He lifted the lid and stared at the circle. And it wasn't just any circle.

"It's a stool. It was my camp project," Sebastian announced.

"I cut and sanded the wood, then I put the legs on it, using real nails, and then I painted it. Take it out and look."

Raz complied, studying his son's gift.

There were names painted on the seat.

Many names.

Aug, Luanne, Briggs, his bloody prick chat group friends and their fiancées and children, Granny Fin, Callista, Calliope, Madelyn, Harper, Maud, Bob, Plum, and Beefcake.

In the center, Sebastian had painted two donkeys with a boxing glove between them. He added Meredith, Mibby, Sebastian, and Erasmus in white paint over the red glove.

"Granny Fin showed me pictures from when you were starting out in boxing," Sebastian began. "You had two stools in your corner, one for Aug and one for Mum. But now, you've got everyone, right there, on one stool. I added the donkeys because they love you, too."

He ran his fingertips over the names. "This might be the most thoughtful gift anyone's ever given me, lad. Thank you."

"Turn it over. I painted a rock stack on the backside the same color you and Mibby like. The color that's everywhere when we're together."

He stared at his son. "You've seen it?"

"Yeah, it's a little shimmer in the air. Don't you see it, too?"

The breath caught in his throat. "I do. I did."

"Take a look," Sebastian nudged.

Raz did as the boy asked and studied the backside of the circle.

"They're indigo-colored stones. That's the color. I had to mix purple and blue to make it. My art teacher at camp said that when two colors come together, they can make something new and beautiful."

"That they do," he said softly. He stared at the painted rocks —rocks whose purpose was to illuminate the right path.

"Do you like it?" Sebastian asked.

His heart melted in his chest. "I love it, son. It's perfect."

"We're here, lads," Aug said, pulling up at the event center.

Raz looked out the window as a woman wearing a headset with a clipboard in her hands walked up to the vehicle and opened the back door.

"Mr. Cress, your dressing room is this way."

"Briggs and I will find your room and knock when it's time," Aug said, trading places with the valet as Briggs pulled up behind them.

"Can I stay with you, Dad?"

He ruffled the boy's ash brown hair. "I need someone to carry my new corner stool, right?"

"Righto!" the boy chimed as they followed the production assistant into the building.

She led them down a back hallway. Workers carrying lighting equipment shuttled past them. "That's the ring," she said, pointing as the hallway opened, and they could see into the massive space below.

"How many people can fit in there?" Sebastian asked.

"Eighteen thousand and seven," she answered, gifting the boy with a grin.

"That's a huge number!" Sebastian exclaimed. "Eighteen thousand and seven people are going to watch you fight, Dad."

"More like eighteen thousand and seven and hundreds of millions more on Pay-Per-View," the staffer replied.

"Gosh, my friend Phoebe once said she was so hungry she wanted to eat a hundred million hot dogs. But I don't think she could do that, at least not in one day. Now, if she had two, I bet she could," the boy mused.

Raz chuckled, but goose bumps peppered his skin. This was his make-or-break fight, and the pressure had set in.

"The weigh-in will take place on the temporary stage," the

woman continued, pointing it out. "Silas Scott will weigh in first, and then it'll be your turn."

"Look at the lights. There are so many," Sebastian chimed, awe coating his observation.

Hundreds, possibly thousands of lights, pointed toward a stage lined with Union Jack flags for him and the green, white, and orange Irish flags for Silas.

"And look at the cameras," Sebastian said, eyes as wide as saucers.

The woman glanced at her watch. "We're starting a bit earlier. You've got fifteen minutes until we'll need you on stage."

Fifteen minutes.

The clock was ticking.

"Here's your room," the woman said, opening a door. "Silas Scott and his entourage are on the other side of the building. There's a phone on the table. Let us know if you need anything."

He thanked the event staffer, and they entered the swanky room. Sebastian set the stool on the ground, then ran to the table where several pairs of trunks were fanned out across the top.

"Why so many colors for your boxing shorts?" the lad asked, running his fingertips across the collection of trunks.

"I decide which color I want to wear the day of the weigh-in."

From reds to golds to blues and black, the trunks shimmered under the lights. He took in the array of hues, then turned to his son. "Why don't you pick."

"Me?" he whispered, awestruck.

"Yeah, have a go."

Sebastian zeroed in on a pair. "That's easy! The bluish-purple indigo trunks. You can match the rock stack. Then you know you're on the right path to victory."

Victory.

The word floated in the air, triggering Aug's question.

What are you fighting for?

He chewed on the question, running on autopilot as he changed his clothes, slipping on the indigo trunks. He'd never worn this color before. He'd stuck to bold reds, but that didn't suit him now. Checking his appearance in the mirror, he stared at his reflection.

Who was the British Beast?

Who was the Lion?

A sharp knock on the door pulled him from the questions swirling around in his head. "It's time," Aug called.

"Will Mibby be here? She's one of your trainers, too. I hope she didn't get lost," Sebastian said, worry creasing his brow.

Mibby.

He should have been ready for this question.

"She's not coming, lad, not for the weigh-in."

He could see the wheels turning in his son's head.

"Did you make her mad? Did you act like a..." Sebastian asked, then tapped his foot two times.

"Is that Phoebe's foot tap trick?"

"Yeah, but when Phoebe taps twice, it means *butthole*," the boy explained, whispering the naughty word. "But when I tapped, I meant *beefcake*."

"You know about Libby calling me beefcake?"

"Phoebe showed me a training video where Libby was throwing mini-torpedoes at you. And then the astronauts did the same training."

Viral bloody videos.

But he couldn't deny that the kid had boiled it down to its very essence. "Yeah, I was a pretty big..." He tapped his foot twice. "And I hurt her feelings."

He braced himself, waiting for the boy to cry or yell, but he didn't. He nodded, taking on Granny Finola's sage quality.

"Don't worry, Dad," Sebastian replied as a smile spread across his lips. "I made an intention and put my energy into keeping Mibby and the donkeys with us."

"It might not be that easy to do," he bit out, hating having to even utter the words.

"I'm already one for one on my first intention," the boy proclaimed, puffing up.

"And what was that one about?"

"I wanted us to be happy and spend time together."

How did he get such an amazing kid?

Emotion welled in his chest.

"Mibby says the universe is mysterious," Sebastian continued. "And you never know exactly what will happen, but it will always be what's supposed to happen." The boy scratched his head. "She talks like that a lot, and I'm not sure what it means, but it makes me feel like everything will be okay."

He patted his son's shoulder. "She's good at that."

"Champ, we need to move," Briggs called from the hall.

"I'll carry the stool," Sebastian chimed, the little helper.

Raz steadied himself. This was it. This was how it started. He opened the door as the murmur of pounding music drifted down the hall.

"You ready, boyo?" Aug asked, looking him over. "I see you've chosen a different color than usual."

Sebastian lifted his chin. "I chose indigo, Aug."

"Did you, lad?" the man said, and Raz could hear the hint of approval in his trainer's reply.

Briggs came to his side as the music got louder. "Silas is already on the stage. He made weight. Your family and friends are in the crowd. They're close to the stage. You'll be able to see them when you get out there. Stick to the script. Give them a little snarl. You know the drill, champ."

"Is *she* here?" he asked, lowering his voice.

Briggs shook his head. "No, I thought that had ended. I took you leaving Rickety Rock with Aug to mean the partnership had run its course. I gave Aug the press release for you to sign."

"I haven't gotten to that," he mumbled, his emotions on a bloody roller coaster.

He let out a heavy breath. Perhaps it was for the best. He could focus solely on bringing his A game and worry about making amends after the fight. But his thoughts weren't on laying into Silas Scott or which combinations could knock the Snake into next week. His mind drifted to thoughts of two remarkable women and lightning striking twice two times.

"This is where we leave you, Raz," Aug said as they approached the ramp leading to the stage.

Another person with a headset waved him forward. "They're about to announce you, Mr. Cress," she said as an event staffer escorted Briggs, Aug, and his son to their seats.

Alone, he closed his eyes and jogged in place. This is the moment he'd work himself up and become the beast, the roaring lion. He'd pound his chest and gnash his teeth, getting into character, but it felt wrong. He wasn't the Lion anymore. He patted the items in his pocket, then reached inside and removed the stone and pocket watch—his past and his present. But what did the future hold?

The music stopped, and the announcer nodded to him.

"The British Beast, the London Lion, Erasmus Cress!"

The music blasted, and the vibrations thrummed through the floor. He jogged onto the stage. Light coming at him from every angle. He knew this song and dance, but this weigh-in was different. He shook off the ominous feeling.

Just go with it. You know what they want.

He unzipped his hoodie, allowing the cameras to capture his ripped, muscled torso. He stood, basking in the glow, allowing the media to consume him.

"How ya doing, Erasmus? How's the eye?" Silas cooed, his Irish lilt syrupy sweet.

Raz ignored the man and focused on his friends and family, but his heart ached for the two people who weren't there. The two women who'd made him a better man.

How many times does lightning have to strike twice?

"Step onto the scale, please," the announcer instructed.

The refs and judges sat at a table, recording the information.

"Gentlemen," the announcer boomed, inviting the men to the center of the stage.

Nose to nose, the boxers stared each other down. This is the part where he'd usually go full-on beefcake. With adrenaline pumping, he'd slap a twisted smirk to his lips. He'd taunt his opponent, letting loose with the trash talk and playing the part of the beefcake. Instead, he closed his eyes.

Picture a time when you were truly happy. Hold the feeling inside your chest, close to your heart.

A lightness expanded inside him as his chi evened out. Like a key unlocking a door, his chakras came into alignment. With a cosmic click, a wave of images and warmth washed over him. He saw Mere's face on their wedding day. He could feel the tears on his cheeks when he held his son for the first time. And then he was in Denver, standing on the sidewalk the night Rowen had dragged him and the other guys to help move Penny's things into his place. That's where he'd first seen the raven-haired Libby Lamb. The memory lingered as the sound of the ocean and the gentle lullaby of Moloka'i came back to him. Pure joy radiated through his body, recalling the feeling of holding Libby in his arms.

I love you. I love you. I love you.

He could hear her as if she were whispering in his ear.

"It'll be a pleasure beating you, Lion, or do you go by Donkey now?" Silas hissed.

Raz opened his eyes. He softened his gaze and read the Snake's aura. He could see it plain as day—gray and black with a little puce mixed in. He grimaced. "Mate, your spiritual vibe is a cosmic dumpster bin. Blimey, you should get yourself some crystals to clear that psychic blockage."

Panic flashed in Silas's eyes. The nervous fighter turned to the cameras, his shoulders slumping a fraction, but Raz saw it. He'd rattled the Snake.

"Erasmus Cress literally trained to fight me by doing yoga and running around the hills with donkeys. What do you have to say about that, donkey lover?" Silas quipped like an angry old man yelling at kids to keep it down.

Unbothered, Raz nodded. "The donkey knows, Silas."

Wobbly Bob might be banging his granny—and he was absolutely *not* okay with that—but he had to hand it to the guy. The man knew what he was talking about.

The donkey knows.

He got it. He finally got it.

The donkey knows what matters.

Confusion marred Silas's expression. "What does the donkey know? I'm trying to make fun of you, mate!"

"I know, but you gave me quite a compliment," he answered. He took in the sprawling event center complex, the flags, the media circus, and the gleaming ring, then took a few steps away from Silas, removing his hoodie. He inhaled a deep breath and busted out a handstand.

"What the hell are you doing?" the Snake bit out.

He was doing what he had to do.

He lifted one hand and balanced on the other like Libby had done in the police chief's office to shut him the hell up.

In that slip of time, with every muscle engaged, he understood where he'd veered off the path.

He'd hidden behind his guilt.

He'd wallowed in the pain.

He'd distanced himself from his son—the closest, most tangible link to Meredith.

That selfish shell of a man ready to win at any cost wasn't the man Mere loved. It wasn't the man he was meant to be, and thanks to Libby's slightly psychotic intervention, she'd banged her gong, threw vibrators, and gave him the spiritual wake-up call he so desperately needed. Her wham, bam, Libby Lamb love had brought him back from the brink, had transformed his relationship with his son, and now gave him a new lease on life.

Like a ballerina on steroids, he pressed his outstretched hand onto the stage, gracefully lowered his legs, and stood. He put on his hoodie, then pressed his hands into a prayer position and bowed. "Namaste, Silas Scott," he said like a blooming Zen master. He crossed the stage and descended the stairs, heading for his friends and family, determination coursing through his veins.

"Where the hell are you going?" Silas screamed like a sullen teenager. "Are you coming back? Will you be here for the fight?"

He shrugged, striding away, a man on a mission.

None of the event staff seemed to know what to do. Cameramen scattered, breaking away from the pack to follow him off the stage. He ignored the gaggle of men and women lugging recording equipment and went to his trainer. "I know what it means to win, Aug." He surveyed the group, then glanced past the lights where a pair of doors opened into a lobby. "I need everyone to come with me," he said, listening as Silas threw a temper tantrum. He exited the arena, shaking his head. Silas Scott was worse than Calliope and Callista fighting over a...a Landon Paige T-shirt. Wait, how had he not remembered that?

Landon's bloody handsome face printed on a T-shirt!

No matter.

He'd give the heartthrob shit later. Now, his Zen-master mind focused on one objective.

Get the girl.

But how did he prove that he got it, that the fight wasn't what mattered the most?

He stared out the windows, watching traffic as a bus thundered by with a banner splashed across its side.

He read the nine words printed in bold indigo.

Those who can, do. Those who volunteer, do more.

It was as if Mere had sent the message—as if she were guiding him.

"Well, look at that," he uttered, warmth blooming in his chest.

The clap of posh loafers meeting the tiled floor echoed through the lobby.

"Champ, Raz, how about we return to the weigh-in?" Briggs suggested, huffing and puffing and probably shitting his pants.

Raz watched the bus turn the corner. "You sent the final payment for Libby's brothers' schooling, right?"

Briggs sucked in an audible breath. "Yes, of course."

"Do you know about the program they're in?"

"Yeah, sure, I know quite a bit," the man got out, gasping for air. "They take study-abroad courses at uni in Ecuador and work as volunteers building clinics in rural areas."

He nodded. "And you're familiar with my family's foundation?"

"Yeah, champ, I took care of the legal side of donating to Helping Hands."

"I'm going to need you to do a little more of that kind of work," he said, nodding to himself.

"Erasmus," Briggs got out, sounding more like himself. "This is highly unusual."

"And when Briggs says highly unusual," Calliope chimed, joining the pair.

"He means bloody bonkers. What are you doing? Are you off your rocker?" Callista finished as the sound of a stampede of footsteps signified the arrival of his friends and family.

He turned to find his kin, and Aug, and Madelyn, Rowen, Mitch, and Landon, the Colorado friends who'd become like family. "I'm doing what I should have done all along," he answered and removed the wooden box from his pocket.

"Is there something in there for Libby?" Sebastian asked.

He took a knee, coming eye to eye with his son. "Yes, what's in here is for Libby, but I need you to understand something, lad. I love Libby. I want to be with her. I want her to be a part of our family, but that doesn't mean I'll ever stop loving your mum. You don't have to worry about us forgetting about her."

All eyes were on them when the air around Sebastian shimmered like it used to when he was a baby in his mother's arms.

"Why would I worry? I love Mum and Libby, too. We can do that because we have the hearts of fighters. We've got big hearts, and there's always room for more love. See these names on the stool. They're in our hearts. They always will be," Sebastian answered, wise beyond his years.

This kid!

The bystanders gave a collective sigh, and he glanced at his wanker chat group, which he should think about renaming.

Mitch dabbed at his eyes. "I'm not crying. It's an eyelash."

Landon peered at the chef, biting back a grin. "Dude, you're crying."

"I'm crying. Fine! What do you need from us, Raz?" the hothead barked.

What did he need?

"It has to be big. I screwed up, and I need to let Libby know that she can count on me."

"Agreed! You were a major wanker," Callista chided.

"Remember, Raz," Calliope cautioned. "If you go big, you might go viral."

Viral.

But he could do better than viral.

Viral with a purpose.

A plan solidified in his mind—a plan worthy of Libby.

"Do we know where she'll be tomorrow?"

"She's meeting her dad," Rowen replied. "But she's totally off the grid. Penny says her phone is off."

Raz nodded, thinking of the saying on the bus. That was the answer.

"Do you know where and when she's meeting her father?"

"A petting zoo. They're meeting at two."

Raz came to his feet and paced as he worked out the logistics in his head. Libby mentioned her family used to visit a petting zoo in Denver when her mom was still with them. It had to be that one.

Briggs cleared his throat. "Champ, you've got a fight tomorrow night."

"I can't think about that now, Briggsy," he said, patting the man's shoulder. "I've got an idea. But for this to work, I'll need everyone to pitch in. We'll need to work every connection we've got."

"Hello, beefcake!" Mitch bellowed. "Your famous connected friends are standing right here."

"Brilliant! And music," Raz added.

"Like for the Chicken Dance, Dad? We didn't get to do it at my party."

"That might work, lad. Does anyone have a connection in the music world?" he asked, sizing up the group.

Landon huffed. "Raz, dude?"

"Right, right! And could you also sign a couple of T-shirts for my sisters?"

"Erasmus!" Callista and Calliope shrieked in unison, turning as red as a pair of tomatoes.

"What? I remembered you fighting over a Landon Paige T-shirt after I'd gone all Zen."

"I can do both," Landon answered, a blush kissing his heart-throb cheeks. No wonder the chicks went crazy for him. He shook his head. "Enough of bloody that! Aug?" he said, turning to his trainer, the man who'd been like a father to him since he was a lanky fourteen-year-old with a chip on his shoulder. "Are you okay with me doing something a little crazy? Maybe a lot crazy?"

"I'm always on your side, lad."

"That makes the two of us," his granny added when a pair of policemen, one tall and one short, sauntered over.

"Mr. Cress, do you remember us?"

Raz's jaw dropped. Bloody hell! It was the cops who arrested them the night Libby's deranged chi made her attack him with vibrators. "Yeah, George and Joey, right? What are you chaps doing here?"

"Keeping the peace before the fight and wrangling the media," Joey answered, gesturing with his chin toward where they'd kept the cameramen at bay.

"We don't mean to be rude, but are you talking about Libby Lamb?"

"Yeah, I am. I love her." He grinned. Bloody hell, he liked saying that out loud.

"We had a feeling you two would end up together," Joey replied, sharing a look with George.

"We're not together yet. I screwed up, but I'm going to get her back." He scanned the group. "For the record, that's my intention. I'm putting it to the universe. It's not me acting like a cocky..." he glanced at Sebastian and tapped his foot twice.

"Beefcake!" the boy exclaimed.

"I wish that's what Phoebe meant when she tapped at me," Rowen muttered.

"If you need any help from the city's cops, we're here for you. The whole department appreciates you competing in the Ass-in-nine for us. Honestly, none of us wanted to do it."

Excellent! It was never bad to have local law enforcement on your side!

It was coming together.

The light shining in through the windows shimmered a perfect shade of indigo.

Their color.

Their strength.

This was his path—a path lined with Meredith's blessing.

"What do we do now, Dad?"

He turned to Rowen. "Libby's off the grid, right? The only thing she's doing tomorrow is meeting up with her dad?"

"As far as I know," Rowen answered.

This is it. Everything had led him to this point.

Wham, Bam, lookout, Libby Lamb, the beefcake's coming!

Excitement laced with pure adrenaline coursed through his veins.

He surveyed his friends and family. "Alert the International Space Station, and let's get out a press release, Briggsy."

"And what should it say, champ?"

He grinned and held his son's gaze. "Erasmus Cress will be fighting tomorrow—fighting for the woman he loves."

THIRTY-FIVE

LIBBY

LIBBY STROLLED DOWN the path as four little girls zoomed past her, their pigtails swishing from side to side as they skipped along. The girls couldn't be much older than five or six, and their little voices popped and fizzed as they giggled and tittered, headed toward a pen of black and white goats. A little redhead, a blonde, and the third girl with chestnut-brown curls stopped at the gate, waiting for their friend, a curious child with raven-colored locks, who'd stopped shy of the pen to watch a butterfly flit across the path.

"I can't wait to pet the goats," the little blond girl exclaimed.

"Me too," called the redhead.

"Me too," echoed the girl with jet-black hair, waving goodbye to the butterfly to catch up to her friends.

The child with chestnut curls huffed. "My feet hurt, and the goat better not eat my sock again. Stupid hungry goat!"

Libby chuckled. That's what she and her girls must have looked like years ago when they'd come here to visit the Denver Petting Zoo. She gave the little girls one last look before continuing down the path toward a quieter section. The back half of the petting zoo included a small pasture and served as the home for rescued ponies, mules, and donkeys. Unlike the goats, sheep, and chickens, where children were encouraged to wander inside the pens and interact with the animals, these larger residents were for observation only. A few towering oaks provided a leafy blanket of shade over their secluded patch of land, and the animals milled around in the sun-dappled light.

She rested her elbows on the fence and watched a pair of donkeys nuzzle one another. Plum and Beefcake had the same ritual before they'd settled in next to each other at night as the insects and frogs peppered the mountain air with their calls.

How could so much life have been packed into the last sixty days?

If someone had told her that the last several weeks had been a dream, she would have been hard-pressed to disagree. And, truth be told, the last forty-eight hours hadn't let up either.

She'd met with Ida.

She'd agreed to partner with Cleo and Laney.

And she'd texted her father and asked him to meet her here. He'd responded immediately, the dots rippling across her screen seconds after she'd hit send. He'd answered with one word.

Yes.

He didn't usually respond so quickly—or at all. But at that moment, when she'd felt her mother's presence so acutely, she'd listened to a voice whispered on the wind, and she'd taken a chance.

She was done shielding her heart.

Well, that wasn't completely true.

The one thing she couldn't do was immerse herself into the whirlwind of Raz's championship fight—not because she wanted him to lose or even win, but because he'd decided to walk the path alone.

His choice.

She wasn't surprised when Briggs messaged her, letting her

know she didn't need to attend the weigh-in. He'd added that her brothers' tuition had been paid in full and that he was waiting for word from Raz on how their arrangement would proceed.

Arrangement.

She could read between the lines and decipher the sports agent's polite way of conveying that it was over between herself and Raz.

It wasn't what she wanted. But like yin and yang, love and loss balanced each other. She would love again. She just needed to get through this day. Tomorrow would come, and whether Raz won or lost, she would go on with an open heart—and a lot of work to do.

Cleo and Laney had a million ideas, and she was ready to dive in. But she had one stipulation. They'd begin the work after Raz's fight.

Upon reading Briggs' message, she'd decided to give herself a twenty-four-hour respite.

It wasn't a sign of weakness to unplug. It was strength—the strength of giving herself time to meditate and reflect. She'd turned off her phone. She didn't need to hear about the media storm covering the fight. It would come, and it would go, and the universe would decide what happened next.

Did she miss Raz with every fiber of her being?

Yes, and Sebastian, too.

But a serene peacefulness came with knowing she could overcome any loss. She could risk her heart understanding that, while it could ache, it wouldn't break. And she wasn't about to allow fear to hold her back.

With or without Erasmus Cress by her side, she believed in love.

And this new embrace of love started with talking to her father, not as the man who'd let her down, but as the man who'd never made it out of the darkness of grief, longing, and loss.

"You didn't think I'd show, did you, sweetie?"

She looked over her shoulder as Connolly Lamb headed her way. Bright-eyed with a spring to his step, the man carried a satchel and looked better than he had in years. The dark circles under his eyes and the gray tinge to his skin from spending his nights drinking and betting on sports gave way to a healthy glow.

"I'm glad you made it, Dad. It's good to see you."

He stood next to her and leaned against the fence. "This was always your favorite part of the petting zoo when you were little."

She cocked her head to the side. "I thought I liked the goats."

"That was Alec and Anders," he replied with a sentimental bend to his words. "You and your mother liked it here, with the ponies and donkeys. Or maybe you two needed a break from the Lamb boys."

She chuckled. "You're probably right. They could be a handful."

"But you never were, Libby. You were always so strong, so centered. I owe you an apology. I owe you many, many apologies."

While the man had spewed a litany of empty promises and hollow apologies in the past, his words rang true today.

How did she know?

She felt it.

"Thank you, Dad. It means everything to hear you say that."

He had a lovely white aura, a light and healing color. The heaviness that had weighed him down in a murky hue had let up. He was a different man. What she couldn't figure out was what had spurred the transformation. She swallowed past the lump in her throat, needing to get the words out. "I know how much you loved Mom. Her death was hard on you, and I understand now that you didn't have anyone to catch you when you fell."

Tears welled in his eyes. "Can I give you a hug?"

She nodded and allowed her father to fold her into his embrace.

There's magic in stripping off the armor and extending grace—a lovely symmetry that settles in the soul.

He pulled back and patted her cheek. "I wanted to do right by you and the boys, but I got lost somewhere along the way. One day of wrong turns became one year and then a decade. I'm doing better, but I'm not going to make you any promises other than to tell you that I'm making better choices, and through my actions, I'll prove to you and to the boys that I can be the father you deserve."

"That means the world to me," she answered, blinking back tears.

The man exhaled a slow breath, gathering himself. "I thought about reaching out to you before I left, but I wasn't sure if I should."

What did that mean?

"Where are you going?"

He cocked his head to the side. "You don't know? I figured he'd tell you with me leaving today."

"I don't know what you're talking about, Dad."

"Erasmus's sports agency offered me a job."

Was that what Raz was doing when he told her father someone would be calling?

"What kind of job?" she pressed.

"They're opening a location in Kansas City, and they need a facilities manager. I had to agree to stop drinking and attend Gamblers Anonymous. That's what I've been doing these past weeks. I was in a bad place when I showed up in Rickety Rock. I'm not proud of what I did. Erasmus told me that someone would contact me. A man named Briggs Keaton called the next day and offered me a deal. It's good pay, real good pay, and it would be a fresh start in a new city, but not so far from you."

"And you leave today?" she asked, totally and completely floored.

"In twenty minutes," he confirmed. "A taxi is picking me up from here."

Twenty minutes.

"Why didn't you tell me you were moving?" she sputtered as they started toward the entrance.

"I didn't want to burden you or your brothers, and Erasmus made it clear that I wasn't to contact you."

"What did he say to you?" she pressed. She wanted to be furious with him for keeping something like this from her. Still, she couldn't help but see her father's transformation.

"He didn't want me to upset you. But I figured you reaching out to me meant that you wanted to see me. Erasmus cares deeply for you, honey. I think he'd do anything for you."

How she wished that was true.

She shook her head, absolutely gobsmacked. "I still can't believe he didn't mention this to me. I don't even know what to say."

"You can say what I said," he replied, a grin pulling at the corners of his mouth.

"And what's that?" she asked, concentrating on the path as they strolled by the black and white goats.

"Thank you," the man replied humbly. "Erasmus is giving me a chance to start over and get back to being the kind of man your mother married. A man who works hard and loves his kids. Denver holds too many ghosts and too many old haunts that could lead me back to betting on sports and drinking away the winnings. I need a clean start. I don't think it's a stretch to say that Erasmus Cress is saving my life. Do you think you'll be talking to him anytime soon?"

A knot formed in her belly as they passed through the gate. "I'm not sure if I'm going to see him again. We had a falling out."

"If an old dog like me can change, I'm sure there's hope for two people who love each other as much as you and Erasmus do," he added with a knowing glint in his eyes as if he knew something she didn't.

She studied her father's expression. "How do you know that I love Erasmus Cress?"

"You're your mother's daughter, Libby. You radiate love. You always have. I can hear the affection in your voice when you say his name. Don't write him off yet," her father added as a taxi pulled up.

A strange vibration passed between them.

Something else was going on with her dad, but she shook it off.

"Let me know when you get to Kansas City," she said, giving him another hug. "We can plan a time for me to visit."

"I'd like that. And Libby?"

"Yes."

"I might be seeing you a little sooner than later," he added and pressed a kiss to her cheek before getting into the taxi.

That was an odd thing to say.

Her emotions seesawed between being grateful that her father had a real chance to turn his life around and hardly being able to believe that she had Raz to thank for it.

She sank onto a bench next to the petting zoo's entrance and watched the yellow taxi disappear down the road. She removed her mother's aquamarine stone from her pocket. Brushing her thumb over the smooth surface, a word came to mind.

Transformation.

Could Raz change? Was her father on to something? Could there be a path forward for her and that beefcake of a man?

A crow swooped in and perched on the back of the bench.

She glanced at the bird. "Namaste, crow, you keep popping up, don't you?"

The crow didn't reply, most likely because it was just a crow —or was it?

She sat back and pictured her mother, remembering how they used to cozy up on the couch and talk for hours.

"I think Dad's going to be okay. No, I know it. I saw it in his aura. His energy is...transformed."

She glanced at the crow, currently focused on the aquamarine stone glinting in the light. She sighed, understanding Ida's fondness for chilling out with butterflies. She quite liked hanging with this crow.

"Can you believe that Raz got Dad a job, and he never mentioned it?" she continued, gabbing away with the bird. "What does that mean? I know Raz is a good man, and I know he loves me. He does."

She observed the crow, still listening or whatever crows do when they remain motionless.

It hadn't flown away. That had to mean something.

"Should I call him? I can thank him. Maybe I should yell at him for keeping this from me, then thank him. I can't do anything," she said, frustration taking over.

The crow didn't answer, but it seemed oddly interested.

"He's got the fight tonight. His make-or-break must-win moment." She rubbed her temples and peered at the bird. "What do you think, Mom? Maybe I should text the girls and ask about him. Rowen, Landon, and Mitch were supposed to go to the weigh-in yesterday. Or I could message his sisters, but that might be weird. What do you think I should do?"

The crow lunged forward, then snapped the stone into its beak.

She shot up and scowled at the bird. "Hey, Mom, I get that was your stone, but come on? What are you going to do with it now that you're a crow?"

"Miss, are you having an altercation with a bird?"

Libby gasped at the sight of two police officers, one male and one female, walking toward her.

When did they get here?

"There's no altercation here. I'm talking to the crow, but the crow isn't talking back, obviously. As you can see, it has my stone."

"The bird stole something from you?" the policewoman asked.

"Yes, well, sort of. The stone belonged to my mom years ago. You see, I'm speaking to the crow now because the bird might be channeling the spirit of my mother."

The officers shared a cagey look—not that dissimilar from the way the officers had looked at her the night her rage yoga session had taken a turn toward the psychotic.

If she didn't stop talking, she'd earn herself a one-way ticket to a padded cell.

"You believe your mother is the bird?" the male officer pressed.

How was she supposed to answer that honestly?

Libby gestured to the crow with a flat stone in its beak, who seemed quite enthralled with the human hubbub. "I know this bird isn't my actual mother. My mom passed away when I was younger. But there's a chance the bird is acting on her energy, and therefore, I'm chatting with a version of my mother's energy —her essence, her psychic ripple."

"Psychic ripple?" the male officer repeated with a crinkle to his brow.

Libby chewed her lip. "It's not illegal to talk to birds, is it?"

"What's your name, ma'am?" the woman asked.

This was not good.

"Libby Lamb."

The cops shared another ominous look.

"This is her," the male officer said as the woman nodded.

This encounter just went from not good to downright bananas.

"What do you mean, *this is her?*" she blathered, her pulse hammering.

"You've got a charge for lewd behavior. We need to bring you in. We heard you'd be here," the male officer explained.

Libby's stomach dropped. "That charge was dropped, thanks to the donkeys."

The female cop raised an eyebrow. "A donkey told you the charges were dropped, ma'am?"

Gah!

"No," she shrieked. "The chief of police."

"Are you saying the chief of police is a donkey?" the woman shot back.

Hello, padded cell.

The male officer opened the police cruiser's back door. "Come with us, ma'am. We'll figure this out downtown."

"You're not going to handcuff me, are you?" she asked, staring into the back seat.

"Do we need to handcuff you?" the woman asked, again raising an eyebrow.

What?

Libby didn't answer. She slid her ass in the back of the car faster than you can say holy busted karma. The door slammed, and she stared out the window and raised her hand. "Bye, Mom. It's still pretty uncool that you took the stone, but I guess it was yours," she said flatly. What did it matter now? She could start talking to the seat belt or tell them that a birch tree was her great-great-uncle. These cops already thought she was a few slices short of a loaf.

The bird spread its wings, and with the aquamarine secure in its beak, sailed into the sky as the cruiser merged into traffic. As stealthily as she could, she slipped her phone out of her purse and hit the power button.

And...she only had a one percent charge.

Who do you call with one percent? That would give her ten seconds before the power drained.

Think, think, think.

She'd call Penny, and then Penny could ask Rowen to hack into the police mainframe and erase her charge. That was a thing, right? It happened in the movies. She peered at the officers in the front seat, chatting in hushed voices, but they didn't seem too concerned with her. She tapped Penny's name, and the phone rang once, then twice, then—

"Hi, Libby, it's Phoebe! I've got Penny's phone because she's doing the Chicken Dance."

No, no, no.

"Phoebe, Phoebe," Libby whisper-shouted. "Put Penny or your uncle on the phone."

"What?" the child called as a brass band played in the background.

A brass band? Where the heck were they?

She tried again. "Phoebe, honey, get Penny. I'm in the back of a police car," she whispered, curling her body into the back of the seat to keep the officers from catching wind of what she was doing.

"You're driving a pickle car? Wow! I want Uncle Row to get a hot dog car. They make 'em. I saw one on the internet."

"Not a pickle car. A police car," she murmured, burying her head beneath her arm.

"I can't hear you anymore, so bye, Libby. See you soon in your pickle car," the child sang out before the line went dead and her phone went black.

She moaned. "What am I going to do? What am I going to do?"

"You can get out of the car," the female officer said.

Libby froze. Tucked into a vertical fetal position, she hadn't felt the vehicle stop. "The car's not moving, is it?" she asked, not daring to look at the officers.

"We've stopped, and I hope you don't mind, but we had a little fun with you," the male officer said.

Libby lifted her head and stared out the open car door. "This isn't the police station."

"No, it's not," the female officer answered. "We were asked to bring you here as a favor."

"Why?" she asked, unfolding her body and scooting out of the cruiser.

"That's not for us to say, but be sure to call down to the station and let us know when and where we can start taking Pun-chi yoga classes."

"You know that I'm the Pun-chi yoga lady?" she asked.

"Yes, and we know that you won the Ass-in-Nine race while representing Denver's first responders. Good work! Women get the job done," the female officer said, offering her a fist bump for a little girl power.

"I can't wait to try Pun-chi yoga," the male officer added. "That one-handed handstand you and Erasmus Cress can do is impressive."

"When did you see Erasmus do a one-handed handstand?" she pressed. She figured he'd never try that move.

"Have you been under a rock, lady?"

Why did people keep asking her that?

"So, I'm not under arrest?" she asked, trying to get her bearings.

The officers grinned at her.

"We're friends of George and Joey. Your original arresting officers," the policeman answered.

"That's a quasi-unsettling statement, but yes, I do remember George and Joey from the night I was..."

"Arrested for disturbing the peace and throwing vibrators at Erasmus Cress," the policewoman supplied.

"Am I free to go?" she asked, needing to nip this convo in the bud.

"Yes, ma'am, you sure are free to go, and good luck. We're pulling for you two," the policewoman answered with a wink—*a wink.*

She surveyed the area, taking in the festive atmosphere. There was an event going on with music, tents, and a stage in the center of a park. She looked on as a reporter stood in front of a camera.

"And that's where we are, folks," the reporter chimed. "Erasmus Cress's team says that today he's fighting for love. The question is, will we see him in the ring tonight? The answer? No one seems to know."

No one seems to know?

What did that mean?

She barely had a second to ponder the reporter's baffling words when two men came barreling toward her. "Anders, Alec! What are you doing here? When did you get here?" she cried as joy radiated through her body. The boys were so tall she had to jump to wrap her arms around her giant baby brothers.

"We got into town a few hours ago," Alec answered.

This was unreal!

"Do you know what's going on?" she asked, scanning the crowded park, then caught the twins sharing a knowing look.

From the cops to her brothers, these knowing looks were starting to get on her nerves.

Anders pointed to a banner with CFF printed in bold lettering.

What did CFF stand for?

"It's a fundraising event and a volunteer sign-up," Alec explained.

"That's terrific," she answered, feeling like she'd stepped into an alternative universe. "I'm for both, but I still don't understand why two policemen pretended to arrest me, then brought me here. And what's going on with Raz? I overheard a reporter say he wasn't sure if he would be fighting tonight," she said when the shrill bang of a gong vibrated through the air.

"Sorry, sis, it's Chicken Dance time. They must have got another thousand donations," Alec said to his brother as a marching band marched through the crowd, belting out the freaking "Chicken Dance" song.

All at once, like a bunch of possessed zombies at an outdoor wedding, every single person, except for her, busted out the moves.

Clap, clap, clap, clap.

Flap, flap, flap, flap.

Wiggle, wiggle, wiggle, wiggle.

Libby stared at a giant jumbo television screen fixed above a stage. People floated inside a spacecraft that looked slightly familiar. "Is that a movie?" she asked a woman busting out the *wiggle, wiggle, wiggle* part as weightless astronauts did the Chicken Dance along with the people on Earth.

"No, those are the astronauts on the International Space Station. It's a live feed," the lady replied.

Libby cocked her head to the side. "Oh yeah, that is them," she said, wondering if the crow had slipped her some psychedelics when it took her stone. Maybe she had some crazy crow flu because wherever she was, it was pretty trippy.

"What in Buddha's name is going on?" she bellowed, raising her voice a frenzied octave at the very instant the band stopped.

For what felt like a million years, several hundred pairs of eyes focused on her.

"It's for you, plum."

Her heart leaped into her throat at the sound of that voice— Raz's voice. She turned to find not only Erasmus but her father, too.

Was this happening?

She blinked, expecting to see a padded cell, but the men were still there, smiling at her like it was normal to hang out in a park doing the Chicken Dance to a brass band with astronauts.

She shook her head to clear the cosmic cobwebs. "Dad, I thought you had to get to the airport? Doesn't your job start tomorrow?"

"It does. But Erasmus offered me the use of his jet to get to Kansas City so I could be here."

"What's going on, Dad?" she asked, still not even sure where she was or what the hell was going on.

"Don't be too upset with your father, Libby. He was doing me a favor," Raz said, looking at her like she was the answer to all his prayers.

And sweet swooning Buddha, that earnest boyish grin sent tingles straight to her lady parts, which was super weird with her father two feet away. Still, it wasn't her fault her body wanted to ride Erasmus Cress into the sunset.

Get it together.

She needed answers, and she needed them now.

There were two ways to go about this. One way employed love and light, the other, not so much.

"I don't know if I should punch you or kiss you, Erasmus

Cress. I know what you did for my dad, and I'm grateful. But I was just fake arrested, and I demand answers," she belted, choosing the not-so-much route.

"Will you excuse us, Connolly? I have some things I need to say to your daughter."

"Of course," her father answered as her brothers came to the man's side.

"Walk with me, Libby," Raz said, glancing at a screen with a number that seemed to be ticking up incrementally. "We've got a little time."

"A little time before what?" She looked over her shoulder at her brothers and her father, trying to get a read on this situation, but the men simply smiled at her.

"I haven't been drugged, have I?"

"No," Raz answered.

"We're still in Denver?"

"Yes."

"Am I still mad at you?" she pressed.

Next, she'd be asking if the sky was blue and the grass was green because nothing was adding up.

"Come on," Raz said, taking her hand.

She was too discombobulated to pull away, and truth be told, the warmth of his touch sent another round of tingles through her body.

"Did you get here all right?" he asked gently.

"You sent the police to bring me here?"

"There are a lot of people rooting for us."

"Us?"

"Look around, Libby. What do you see?"

"There are a ridiculous amount of people staring our way."

"Look beyond that," he nudged.

She studied the park. Indigo-colored tents dotted the lawn, and each tent sported a sign. Helping Hands Community

Center, animal rescue shelters, community gardens, after-school activities, senior fitness programs, food banks, Rickety Rock Donkey Rescue, and a myriad of other community organizations and charities were represented. People lined up at tables, chatting and gathering pamphlets.

"Is it a volunteer drive?" she asked.

"Yes, and we're also raising money for charity. Every dollar donated will be matched by the Cress Family Foundation."

"Did you do this?"

"With a lot of help from my family and our friends," he answered with a wide, easy grin.

Who was this alternate beefcake?

"Briggsy might be on the verge of a mental breakdown, but we got him a plate of bull testicles to calm him down," he said, staring at her like she made up the entirety of his universe.

She laughed. She couldn't help it, and she still wasn't a hundred percent sure she hadn't fallen over at the petting zoo, bonked her head, and was now lying in a hospital bed, happily hallucinating.

She zeroed in on indigo-colored flags printed with the words *Cress Family Foundation*, then gestured to the jovial volunteer festival. "Why did you say that this is for me?"

He pulled a piece of paper from his pocket. "I hear you've been dodging the news and social media. You might have missed this."

PRESS RELEASE
Cress Family Foundation Festival and Charity Drive.
Sign up to help your community and donate to local causes.
Heavyweight champion Erasmus Cress will be in attendance.
Find out if he trades in his belt for a ring.

She stared at the page. "Why would you trade a belt for a

ring? And why are you here? Shouldn't you be preparing for the fight? It's scheduled to start in a few hours."

"This is the fight that matters, and it's the fight for your heart, Libby," he said as an earnest expression overtook his beefcake demeanor.

"The fight for my heart," she whispered.

He cupped her face in his hands. "I missed you so much, plum, and yesterday at the weigh-in, I finally figured it out."

She melted into his touch. "What did you figure out?"

"Aug asked me what I was fighting for. I thought I knew the answer to that question, but I didn't. The answer came to me at the weigh-in when I was staring in Silas Scott's eyes."

A shiver ran down her spine. "What answer?"

He released a slow, steady breath. "I'm a fighter, plum. I'll always be a fighter. But now I know what I'm fighting for."

She stared into his gray eyes, breathless.

He took her hands and led her onto the stage, situated in the center of the park. Surrounded by a sea of indigo, she looked past the media crowding around the stage, and found her friends. Penny and Charlotte waved as they stood by Rowen and Mitch, who had Phoebe and Oscar on their shoulders while Landon and Harper looked on. Her dad stood with Madelyn, not far from Finola, Bob, Maud, Luanne, and Ida. Augie tossed her a wink as Alec and Anders joined Callista and Calliope, rounding out the group.

She turned her attention back to her beefcake. "What are you fighting for?" she asked as the crowd melted away and all she could see was Raz.

"I'm fighting for you and for Sebastian. I'm fighting to make this world a better place. That's what Meredith would want. She started the Cress Family Foundation. She wanted to help people live better lives like you want to help people through fitness and yoga."

"Mibby!" Sebastian called, running onto the stage.

She fell to her knees and embraced the boy. "I've missed you."

"I missed you, too. Did you hear the 'Chicken Dance' song?" he asked.

"I did," she said, blinking away tears.

"That was my idea. Dad didn't get to do it at my donkey birthday party, so we're doing it here, with everybody in Denver and my new friends on the International Space Station."

"It's a catchy tune," she answered through a teary chuckle.

"Every time we get a thousand donations, the band plays the song, and we dance. We've done it five times already. We're doing this because of my mum and because of you. Because you both like making people happy and because my dad loves you like Beefcake loves Plum." Sebastian glanced up at his dad. "Have you gotten to the good part?"

"I'm getting there, lad, but you're stealing a bit of my thunder with your thoughtful words," he teased.

"Mibby," Sebastian whispered, waving her in.

"Yes."

"You're lucky my dad doesn't fart like Beefcake."

"I certainly am," she answered, not sure if to laugh or to cry.

"Enough of that," Raz said, taking her hands and helping her to her feet. He turned to his son. "You mind if I keep talking to Libby."

The boy beamed. "Go on, Dad. That's why we're here."

Raz gazed into her eyes. "I owe you an apology, and I want everyone we love and the entire world to hear it. I thought that winning belts and titles was the way to honor Meredith's memory. But that's not what mattered to her. I lost my way. I let pain cloud my mind. When I stood on the stage weighing in for the fight, I realized that I was going at it wrong. I'm a lucky man. Lightning has struck twice two times in my life. First, when I met Mere, and then here, in Colorado, with you."

"What are you saying, Raz?" she asked, her heart swelling in her chest.

He brushed his knuckles down her jawline, caressing her cheek. "I'm saying that I've already won. I don't need to win in the ring to know who I am. I don't need the titles or the belts or the accolades. You were right when you said I had a choice. I do. And I choose you. I choose Sebastian. I choose to fight for love and honor you and Meredith, not with victories in the ring but with action here at home."

"And where is home?" she asked, her voice a scrape of a sound.

"Wherever you are, plum." He sank to his knee. "I'm trading one ring for another," he said, tears in his eyes. He glanced at Sebastian. "Do you have it, mate?"

The boy pulled a small wooden box from his pocket. "Sorry, Dad, I was looking at the crazy crow flying above us in circles."

A crow?

She looked up as the bird made another loop, then dropped something.

"Ouch!" Harper called, rubbing her head. "That bird dropped a rock on me."

"Sorry H, but FYI," she said. "I'm pretty sure that crow is the spiritual bird equivalent of my mom."

Harper stared into the sky. "Next time, aim for Charlotte or Penny, Mrs. Lamb," H grouched, then grimaced. "And so nice to see you. Have fun crowing out up there."

Raz cocked his head to the side. "That's your mum?"

"Her intention, her hope for me to find love. It's a long story," she said, smiling down at him. "But it's a good omen, a blessing."

"With your mum's spirit with us, it's only right that I tell you there's one title I'm aiming for now," he said, holding the little box in his hand.

"And what title is that?" she asked, anticipation fizzing through her bloodstream.

A tear trailed down his cheek. "Husband. Will you marry me, Libby Lamb?"

"Yeah, Mibby, we'd very much like to keep you," Sebastian added, taking a knee next to his dad.

This was more than she'd ever dreamed possible.

But...

As much as she wanted to say yes, there was something she had to do—a leap of faith she needed to take.

She pinned Raz with her gaze. "Are you telling me you're not going to fight Silas Scott tonight? You're giving up boxing?"

He nodded. "I've got the jet on standby, ready to take the three of us to Moloka'i." He looked at Sebastian, then turned to her. "Everything I need is right here," he answered when a shrill voice sliced through the air.

"Erasmus Cress!" shrieked a man with a thick Irish accent. Before she could blink, Silas Scott sprinted onto the stage, his gold chains slapping his chest as he sprinted toward them. "If you think you're walking away from this fight, you're wrong. I've trained to beat you. They say you're the best. I say they're wrong. I need to beat you in the ring to show the world that I'm the best. I'm the best!" the man squawked.

Sweet karma pie! Someone's Irish chi was jacked!

"This is not the time, Silas," Raz said, staring up at the blustering man-baby. Her boxer didn't radiate an ounce of malice or anger. The man held steady.

But that didn't mean that she had to.

A deviously delicious thought crystallized in her mind. She slapped on a million-dollar grin and beamed at the blond buffoon. "Hello, Silas, so nice to see you again. How about a Pun-chi yoga demonstration?"

"What?" The fuming boxer looked ready to explode.

"Plum," Raz cautioned with the sly beefcake ghost of a grin.

"I've got a move that will do wonders for your tiny, tiny chakras. Observe the donkey pose," she said, positioning herself in front of the man, then hinging forward. She lifted one leg and gave a sharp donkey pop of a kick. Like with Derrick the douchebag, her heel made contact.

"Ooh!" the crowd lamented in unison. Even the astronauts on the International Space Station winced.

She glanced over her shoulder as the Snake recoiled. "Ain't karma a bitch?" she mused sweetly as Silas staggered back, holding his Rocky Mountain oysters.

"Mate," Raz said with a shrug. "You're supposed to bob and weave to avoid getting clocked in your naughty bits."

"Any boxer worth his salt knows that," Sebastian called as Silas staggered off the stage.

"Wham, bam, don't mess with Libby Lamb," he said, coming to his feet.

This man was ready to give up boxing for her, prepared to fly off to an island paradise and leave it all behind. But she couldn't let him do that.

She wrapped her arms around his neck. "I need to say something to you, beefcake."

He nodded, love, so much love and adoration swimming in his gaze.

"We've set limits on ourselves, on who we can love, and how we can love," she began. "We're not doing that anymore. We don't have to sacrifice one for another. We're stronger than that because we're stronger together. The three of us—the power of three. This is our balance. This is our love, our light," she said, reaching out and bringing Sebastian into their embrace.

She blinked back tears. "We make our own rules, and I'll agree to marry you on one condition."

"Name it, plum," he said as their indigo aura shimmered around them.

"Your fights are my fights, Erasmus Cress. You're going to fight Silas Scott tonight. You'll go into the ring with my love, with Sebastian's love, with our friends' and families' love, and with Meredith's love. Especially with Meredith's love. Love never leaves us. Once given, that energy is always with us. And no matter the outcome, no matter who comes out on top, when the final bell chimes, you leave that ring a winner. I believe in you. I love you. So, what'll it be?"

This was love. This was not compromising, not limiting, not shielding, and not holding back. This man, her beefcake, was ready to walk away from the ring for her, and she couldn't allow him to do that.

"That's an easy one to answer, plum," he said, their indigo aura intensifying. "I promise to enter and leave that ring the same grateful man I am now." He dropped back to his knee with his son by his side. "Libby Lamb, will you take on these infuriating Cress men and be ours forever and for always?" he asked, then opened the box.

She pressed her hand to her heart as he removed a ring—a beautiful, glinting aquamarine stone with a diamond on each side. Three stones, three lives, three pasts, three presents, and three futures, bound together.

"Yes," she answered, the luckiest vibrator-wielding gal on the planet, as Raz slid the ring onto her finger.

The crowd cheered, clapping and whooping. Raz came to his feet and gathered her into his arms.

"Is this the kissing part?" Sebastian asked.

"Yep, get ready for a lot of that," Phoebe called from Rowen's shoulders.

"Let's get to it," Raz said, his gaze welling with adoration. He cupped her face in his hand and tenderly lifted her chin. Their lips met, and in that kiss, they sealed a promise that didn't need to be spoken. A promise that lived in their hearts. A promise that bound their souls. A promise to always fight for each other.

"Wham, bam, thank you, Libby Lamb," he whispered, and the once infuriating words now brought a smile to her face. "I hear you're about to become a posh brand name. What's next for the soon-to-be Mrs. Cress?"

Her beefcake would get a kick out of her news.

She batted her eyelashes at the man. "About that wham, bam, Libby Lamb business..."

EPILOGUE

LIBBY ARCHED HER BACK, gripping fistfuls of the comforter. "That setting is really good, Raz! Just like that. Just. Like. That. Don't stop!"

He drank in his fiancée, writhing on the bed. With her naked body spread before him, he was most definitely the luckiest bloke on the planet. His fiancée was the trifecta of female empowerment. An entrepreneur, a former nanny, turned soon-to-be stepmum, and the sexiest yoga instructor to execute a ball-busting donkey kick. Libby Lamb might be all about love and light, but don't get on her bad side. She was killing it, metaphorically, of course, and the future couldn't be brighter for him and his raven-haired beauty.

She was in talks with major fitness platforms to roll out Punchi yoga in gyms, community centers, and online. She'd extended offers to Shandra and Ida, collaborating with the women to modify the moves to allow older adults and people with disabilities and chronic health conditions to participate in the new fitness craze. And thanks to their connection with Gale Tech, a fitness app was in the works.

But that wasn't all they'd been up to for the last two weeks.

They added a dimension to the Cress Family Foundation that centered on crafting a Pun-chi yoga curriculum in conjunction with academic tutoring to offer to schools across the state. They were doing this side project as a team, and they already had several school districts interested in the pilot program.

The Lion and the Lamb balanced each other, sustained each other, and loved each other.

And that wasn't all.

He enjoyed another perk of being engaged to the new face of female sexual empowerment.

And what perk was that?

Lead vibrator tester.

Yep, it was a tough job, but someone had to do it.

If he'd heard about this occupation when he was fourteen, he might never have started boxing. In fact, just imagining the work would have kept him locked in his bedroom back in East London, tearing through boxes of tissue, draining tubes of lotion at Mach speed, and freaking the hell out of his granny.

Lucky for bloody everyone, he'd only recently learned about the job, but he'd taken to it with the attention and vigor it deserved as only the reigning Boxing Heavyweight Champion of the World could.

Of course, he beat Silas Scott.

With Libby's love, he'd gone into the ring focused, fresh, and on fire—not because he chose to fight out of guilt, doubt, or a misguided notion.

He was there because he finally understood what he was fighting for.

And so did Libby.

Knowing that she believed in him and trusted that he'd come out of that ring the same steady man he went in had given him the edge. Flying on the high of Libby's love, he could have beaten Superman in three rounds or less.

Yep, the Snake barely made it to the third bell.

After it was over, he'd shaken the man's hand. He'd looked the bloke square in the eyes and wished him well.

That's the thing about love—real love.

Once you let it in, it annihilates the bullshit. There's no need to put on a facade. There's no need to pretend.

Nothing is impossible when you believe in love.

Corny?

Maybe.

But it was the truth.

And here's another truth.

That fight was his last.

And he had zero regrets about it.

Boxing had been good to him. It had given him purpose and made him a bloody fortune. It was how he met Mere, and it's what led him to Libby. But there was a wide world out there, and he happily traded his career in professional boxing to be a devoted father, loving partner, and community volunteer, coaching kids at the Helping Hands community center's boxing gym.

The next phase of his life started now.

And that phase included getting down to business—the deliciously dirty kind—with the woman who held his heart in her hands.

"We should be taking notes...about this setting," Libby got out, gasping for breath as he worked the prototype of the revolutionary hand-held massager, aka, the Wham, Bam, Thank You, Libby Lamb deluxe vibrator—soon to be available in an array of empowering colors.

They were partial to the indigo-colored device.

Not a shocker.

The blooming thing even came with a lovely little waterproof bag.

Talk about convenience.

Actually, he'd take a hard pass on talking about convenience. He had something hard of his own to take care of.

"We can skip the notes on this testing session, plum," he said, giving his cock several hard pumps as he expertly drove her wild with the vibrator.

His fiancée whimpered. "Wham, bam, so many women are about to be thanking Libby Lamb when these come out."

"Now, who's the cocky beefcake?" he purred, desire flooding his system.

"Do you have a problem with cocky beefcakes?" she teased, then bit her bottom lip as she pushed up onto her elbows.

"I think you know the answer to that."

She raised a hand and beckoned him with her index finger. "Get up here and finish the job like the beefcake you are."

Challenge accepted.

And this may be a good time to note. It didn't get any better than banging a yoga instructor. He lifted one of her legs, resting it over his shoulder, then turned his attention to the other. He gripped her inner thigh and pressed it into the bed, opening her like she was the sexiest clam ever to emerge from the ocean. With her long, flexible legs, the woman was a celebration of sensual angles. He lined up his cock at her entrance and slid in slowly as Libby concentrated on his thick shaft.

There was nothing hotter than watching her watch him as he filled her to the hilt.

He adjusted her leg on his shoulder, pressing a kiss to her knee, and rocked his hips. He penetrated her sweet center in long, steady strokes, pleasure building. Her lusty sighs fed a hunger deep within him, and he inhaled a tight breath. He had to hold back. This wasn't an easy thing to do, balls deep inside a woman with an iron core. She tightened around his hard length, moving with him, but he controlled the pace.

He still maintained a pinch of cocky and a dash of alpha arrogance.

He was London's Lion, even if he had been tamed by a lamb.

Libby met his gaze, and pure carnal need flashed in her amber eyes.

It was about to get spicy.

She ran her hands up and down her torso, putting on quite a show as she skimmed her fingertips along her killer curves. Moving further north, she cupped her cleavage, then pinched her pink, pearled nipples. The beast inside him growled as her full breasts bounced from the force of his thrusts.

"You are bloody perfect, plum," he bit out, beads of perspiration trailing down his rock-hard torso. "How do you want it?"

"Just like that," she answered before sliding two fingers into her mouth and giving them a good, hard suck. She trailed her wet fingertips between her breasts, past her navel, to her most sensitive place. She rubbed her sweet bud, watching him pump and grind, their pace growing more frenzied, more heated, and more frantic by the second.

Lust clouded his mind as a coil tightened within him. With the air infused in a vivid indigo hue, he could feel her approaching the precipice, close to the titillating thrill of complete release.

But he wasn't ready for this to end.

Not yet.

"In the mood for something yummy?" he asked, keeping her close and under his control.

The dirtiest grin stretched across her face. "I thought you'd never ask."

They didn't even have to slow down to change positions. There were no hiccups interrupting their heated, grinding energy. His chi was her chi, and they moved as one. That's how bloody great it was to bed a woman who could wrap herself into a pretzel.

He released her legs, and she circled them around his waist. Sliding his hands under her ass, he lifted her into his arms, came to his feet, and... "Where's the chair?" he asked, searching the bedroom. They'd yabbed and yummed the hell out of it a few nights ago.

"I thought it looked better downstairs," she answered without missing a beat as they screwed like they were born to do it. He pressed her back to the door, taking her against the hard surface as he did a quick scan of their new bedroom, littered with boxes and piles of clothing and smatterings of crystals and mini gongs.

That was the other thing.

They'd recently invested in real estate.

They'd traded his rental mansion in Crystal Hills for an estate not far from Mitch and Charlotte's place in Crystal Acres.

Why?

The donkeys!

There was no way Sebastian was living without his burro buddies. Their new Denver home was set on five acres and included a barn and area for the animals to graze.

Did a lifelong Londoner ever expect to have giant heehawing animals roaming around his place of residency?

No, but he couldn't imagine life without them.

And for kicks, they'd picked up the Victorian in Rickety Rock as well.

Why the hell not? Who didn't need a summer place with a psychic vortex?

They loved the quirky town, and his granny was pleased as punch to take up residence in the guest cottage. But it wasn't her adoration of the English-style home that had her trading the London Tube for the Rocky Mountain trails.

Granny Fin had a gentleman caller.

That's right, Finola Cress was getting her freak on with Wobbly Bob, or as she called him, Hot Rob.

Did it bother him?

Surprisingly, not that much.

He planned on rocking Libby's world until his dying breath, and that meant making peace with senior snogging. It wasn't like Libby would ever get to find out if the like cures like remedy ultimately worked. From here on out, he'd be the only person making her eyeballs roll back in her head as she cried out his name in total orgasmic bliss. With that being said, he had to maintain his sexual A game to keep her happy. Be it thirty-two years old or eighty-two, he had to be prepared to fulfill her every desire. And that was a pretty sweet gig.

"Bench...end of the bed," she directed as her sweat-slick breasts brushed against his chest.

He sat and steadied himself on the cushion as he held her close, gripping her hips. Libby tightened her hold around his neck and gazed into his eyes. Making love face-to-face with their heated breaths mingling in the slice of space between them, he captured her mouth in a searing kiss. She tasted like every color of the rainbow. Vivid and intense, they met their release, soaring through a kaleidoscope of hues. In this sacred space, sight, smell, touch, sound, and taste merged into a symphony of sensations. He disappeared into the sun, into her brightness, burning to a crisp in her arms as a euphoric wave of gratitude and love cradled his soul.

He was home. Libby was his safe harbor.

Limbs trembling from exertion, he kept her close. Their chests rose and fell in sync, their bodies unraveling. He played with a lock of her hair, recalling the words she spoke each night at Sebastian's bedside.

Picture a time when you were truly happy. Hold the feeling inside your chest, close to your heart.

A cascade of images flickered through his mind—happiness filling his chest like honey, warm and sweet.

"We should check the time," Libby said, her voice infused with a dreamy lilt. "We've got everyone coming for the barbecue a little after four. Our siblings and Sebastian should be back soon."

His sisters and Libby's brothers had been staying with them, helping with the move, and spending time with Sebastian.

Libby had barely uttered the words when the sound of a door slamming cut through their sex haze.

He checked his watch. "It's a little after four, plum."

"Four!" she exclaimed, bolting upright. "Our friends are going to be here any minute."

"Dad, Mibby, we're back!" Sebastian called from the first floor, followed by the rumble of footsteps.

Libby scrambled off his lap. "We have to get dressed."

"Auntie Calliope and Auntie Callista are going out with Anders and Alec. They told me to find you," the boy announced, his steps getting louder.

"Your brothers are taking out my sisters?" he asked, slipping on a pair of track pants.

She twisted her hair into a messy bun. "They've been going out for the last two weeks."

"With Sebastian as their chaperone!" he countered, annoyance coating his words. He couldn't help it. He'd always be a beast when it came to protecting his sisters.

"Chaperone?" Libby repeated. "They're twenty-one years old. This isn't Victorian England, beefcake. You're in the Wild West," she teased, plucking her bra from the floor.

He grumbled. "Maybe you're right."

"Raz, my brothers and your sisters have so much in common. They volunteer, and they're choosing professions where they help people."

"I get that, plum, but they're my baby sisters."

She patted his cheek. "Erasmus Cress, always the protective lion."

Knock, knock, knock.

They stared at each other.

"Yeah?" he called warily.

"It's me, Dad. Are you in there with Mibby?"

"Yep," he answered, frozen. They could not get caught half-naked.

"Are you getting a book off a high shelf for her?" the lad pressed.

Relief flooded his system.

"Yeah, yes, absolutely! Books, shelves," he blathered.

"Phoebe says you should always ask before you run into a bedroom. You don't want to get in the way of a wrestling match," Sebastian explained as Libby pressed her hand to her lips.

"Score one for Rowen and Penny," he whispered, pulling on a T-shirt.

Libby slipped on a sundress and pointed toward the bathroom. "I need a second. I'll meet you downstairs."

He nodded, then opened the door. "How was your day with your aunts and Mibby's brothers?" he asked, walking with his son toward the staircase.

"They did a lot of this," Sebastian answered and tapped his foot twice.

Screw-ing?

Kiss-ing?

His thoughts spiraled.

Those bloody Lamb boys!

Okay, he really liked the blokes. They were great guys and smart as hell, but, like his fiancée said, he'd always be the protective lion.

"Why are you making a growly face, Dad?" Sebastian asked as they descended the stairs.

"I'm having a think, trying to decipher your taps."

"*Talk-ing*," the boy supplied. "What did you think I tapped?"

He released an audible breath. "We'll talk about it in twenty years."

Ding-dong!

"They're here." Sebastian cried, forgoing the final two steps and leaping onto the marble floor.

"Go ahead and let them in," Libby called as she padded down the steps. "Your dad and I need to check the patio and turn on the grill."

"On it!" Sebastian answered, sprinting toward the front door.

"Why don't you get the wine and the glasses, and I'll grab the appetizers. I just looked at my phone, and Madelyn's coming, too," Libby said, taking his hand as they entered the kitchen.

He tucked a few bottles of wine under his arm and found a box with wineglasses. He sauntered onto the porch, then shook his head. "Plum!"

"Yeah?"

"Your mum crapped on the patio again," he called, turning on the hose to wash away the bird poop as a crow landed on a branch of a tall oak overlooking the sprawling yard. He observed the crow, then nodded to the psychic ripple of his soon-to-be mother-in-law.

Yeah, thanks to Libby, his chakras were aligned, and he was

one hundred percent on board with team metaphysical karma-licious yoga-speak mumbo jumbo.

Libby set the snacks on the table and peered at the bird. "It's not my mother. It's the—"

"Ripples of her love cosmically entering our lives," he answered, drawing her into his embrace.

She tapped the tip of his nose. "That was a very zen-tastic explanation."

He shrugged, playing it off. "I am engaged to the hottest yoga teacher on the planet. Something was bound to rub off."

She gasped, mock outrage written all over her face.

"Fine! I'm a Pun-chi yoga super freak and proud of it." He took her hand in his, admired the ring glinting in the sunlight, then kissed her knuckles. "I love you, plum." He cupped her face in his hand and stared into her eyes.

She pushed onto her tiptoes and smiled against his lips. "I love you, too, beefcake."

He closed his eyes and melted into her kiss. He parted his lips, ready to devour her softness, when Phoebe Gale's voice pierced the air.

"This is very common, Sebastian. You'll see this a lot," the child said, her tone clinical.

"And it can happen at any time," Oscar explained. "You don't get much warning."

"It's kind of gross, but it's a great time to raid the cookie jar. You can get away with anything when they're like this," the little girl continued, lowering her voice.

"Or get a popsicle. Popsicles don't last long at my house," Oscar added.

Libby giggled, lowering herself. "We've got an audience."

He surveyed the pint-sized trio. "Sebastian, take your friends down to the barn to say hello to Beefcake and Plum. You can feed them some carrots."

"We'll come get you when it's time to eat," Libby added as the children sprinted toward the barn.

"Get used to being interrupted," Mitch remarked and set a six-pack of beer on the table.

Charlotte, Penny, Rowen, and Landon filed in after the chef.

"Welcome to casa Cress," he said, opening the wine and pouring the women each a glass.

"Thanks for having us over," Penny replied, taking a seat. "Your new place is terrific, and I've got some news."

"Do you remember when Penny thought up Erasmus Cress, Donkey Boxer?" Rowen asked, cracking a beer.

"I thought you were joking," he answered, handing Libby a glass of wine.

"We had our designers put something together to beta test the idea," Rowen began.

"And the players love it," Penny chimed. "What do you say, Raz?"

He shared a look with Libby. Once upon a time, he'd have nixed anything as ridiculous as Erasmus Cress Donkey Boxer.

But now...

"I love it," he answered, embracing every new opportunity.

Penny clapped. "Perfect. We'll talk business later. Now, tell us how you're doing."

"How are you settling in?" Charlotte added.

"Slowly," Libby answered, then glanced into the house. "Harper's not with you? She said she'd be here."

At the mention of Harper, Landon cracked open a beer and guzzled it down in one giant swig.

"Thirsty, mate?" he asked, taking in the heartthrob's nervous demeanor, but before the man could answer, Madelyn Malone strode onto the patio.

"I hope you don't mind that I let myself in," the woman

crooned, adding a bottle of wine to the table. "A housewarming gift for you. Thank you for inviting me."

"You're always welcome here," Libby replied, embracing the matchmaker.

"You made another match," Mitch said, pouring Madelyn a glass of wine.

The woman took a sip. "The matches make themselves. I'm simply the—"

"Facilitator of fate," everyone but Landon supplied.

Madelyn chuckled. "Indeed, indeed."

"I have to ask," Penny said, sharing a look with Rowen. "You're going to match Harper with Landon, right?"

The nanny matchmaker took another sip of wine and remained tight-lipped.

"Come on, Madelyn. This one is a no-brainer. There are four of us and four of them," Mitch offered, gesturing to the group.

"The situation has...changed," the matchmaker replied with a sly grin.

Raz stared at Landon. The guy looked ready to lose his lunch.

"How so?" Libby asked.

"Remember, I work exclusively with single male caregivers," Madelyn explained.

"And what would you call Landon?" Rowen asked.

The matchmaker smoothed her red scarf. "Not that."

Not that?

"What does that mean?" Libby whispered.

Good question.

He was about to ask for a little clarification when Harper charged onto the porch.

"Sorry I'm late," she got out, breathless. "I wanted to get you a housewarming gift and then got into a fight with a lady at the garden center, but I am the victor," she announced, holding a wilted plant above her head like a trophy. She surveyed the group. "What did I miss?"

Landon glanced at Madelyn, then met Harper's gaze and swallowed hard. "What happened in Vegas didn't stay in Vegas."

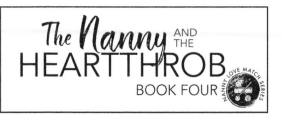

Harper, and that mouth of hers, and Landon, with his dreamy Rockstar eyes, are coming your way in The Nanny and the Heartthrob.

BEEFCAKE BONUS CHAPTER
LOVE SHACK DATE NIGHT DONKEY MANIA

When Raz decides to surprise Libby with a sexy date night, it's safe to say, things do not go as planned. Download the ebook bonus chapter here:

https://BookHip.com/DTGMXJL

The Nanny Love Match Series

A nanny/boss romantic comedy series

Book One: The Nanny and the Nerd

Book Two: The Nanny and the Hothead

Book Three: The Nanny and the Beefcake

Book Four: The Nanny and the Heartthrob

The Farm to Mabel Duet

A brother's best friend romance set in a small-town

Book One: Farm to Mabel

Book Two: Horn of Plenty

The Langley Park Series

A suspenseful, sexy second-chance at love series

Book One: The Road Home

Book Two: The Sound of Home

Book Three: The Beginning of Home

Book Four: The Measure of Home

Book Five: The Story of Home

Box Set (Books 1-5 + Bonus Scene)

The Bergen Brothers Series

A steamy billionaire brothers romantic comedy series

Book One: Man Fast

Book Two: Man Feast

Book Three: Man Find

Bergen Brothers: The Complete Series+Bonus Short Story

Own the Eights Series

A delightfully sexy enemies-to-lovers series

Book One: Own the Eights

Book Two: Own the Eights Gets Married

Book Three: Own the Eights Maybe Baby

Box Set (Books 1-3)

STANDALONES

The Kiss Keeper

A toe-curlingly hot opposites attract romance

Not Your Average Vixen

An enemies-to-lovers super-steamy holiday romance

Sign up for Krista's newsletter to get all the up-to-date Krista Sandor
Romance news!

Learn more at

www.KristaSandor.com

ACKNOWLEDGMENTS

I dedicated this book to Carrie, my alpha reader, and I want to acknowledge her first. The Nanny and the Beefcake is a beast of a book. For reference, it's about the length of three Man Fasts (Bergen Brothers, Book 1). And while I love that about Raz and Libby's story, keeping every aspect of the storyline consistent took a decent amount of work.

Carrie was right there with me during the first read-through. She picked up edits and inconsistencies and made parsing through this beast of a book a true joy. Thank you for putting up with me, Carrie. I'm grateful for your talent and friendship.

It truly takes a village of experts to pull a book together—and help an American author write a growly British boxer.

Nicci, a Book Babes Reader Group member and a posh London gal, answered the call when I asked for help with Raz's bloody colorful language. Let me tell you, Nicci delivered! Thank you for making sure Raz didn't sound like a wanker.

Eric McKinney, with 6:12 Photography, brought us the perfect cover model for the beefcake, Erasmus Cress.

Najla Qamber, with Qamber Designs, created the perfect design for this series.

Marla, Tera, and Amy used their eagle eyes to proofread this beast of a book. Thank you! I'm sure your eyeball will never be the same after editing this beast.

Thank you to the publicity team at Greys PR. These lovely people promoted Beefcake and are an absolute delight to work with.

And last but definitely not least, thank you to my gal in Australia, Alison B. Way back, just after the Nanny and the Nerd was released in July 2021, when I wasn't sure how the nanny books would be received, she was there, cheering me on and filling my heart with joy and confidence.

ABOUT THE AUTHOR

 If there's one thing Krista Sandor knows for sure, it's that romance saved her sanity. After she was diagnosed with Multiple Sclerosis in 2015, her world turned upside down. During those difficult first days, her dear friend sent her a romance novel. That kind gesture provided the escape she needed and ignited her love of the genre. Inspired by strong heroines and happily ever afters, Krista decided to write her own romance series. Today, she is an MS warrior, living life to the fullest. When she's not writing, you can find her running 5Ks with her husband and chasing after their growing boys in Denver, Colorado.

Never miss a release, contest, or author event! Visit Krista's website and sign up to receive her monthly update.

Made in the USA
Las Vegas, NV
30 January 2022

42672078R00360